THE SAINT'S COVENANT

A SEAN WYATT ARCHAEOLOGICAL THRILLER

ERNEST DEMPSEY

PROLOGUE
ENGLAND, 1874

Their world was falling apart. Men who had played God over millions of people, controlling the ebb and flow of their lives like masters of chattel, now faced financial, political, and personal extinction.

Since AD 1600, they had ruled without checks or balances, having been given—or having taken—the authority to do as they saw fit. Now, all of that was being taken from them.

The three men sat in high-back wing chairs, each a throne in its own right, crafted from dark-stained oak and upholstered in aged, cracked leather that bore the imprint of decades of use. The seats were deep and wide, designed for men who lingered over brandy and strategy, their arms resting on curved mahogany armrests with clawed feet gripping the Persian rug beneath. The leather, once a rich oxblood, had faded to a dark umber, its creases and wrinkles whispering of deals and empire-shaping decisions from years gone by. The brass nailhead trim gleamed faintly in the firelight, reflecting the room's flickering glow.

"We all know why we're here," James Wilson led off, plucking the smoldering cigar from his lips. He blew a cloud of smoke into the hazy air and narrowed his eyelids. "The British government is bent on destroying everything we and our forerunners built for the last two centuries."

Wilson was a man of calculated precision, his entire presence exuding the cold efficiency of numbers and ledgers. He was broad-shouldered but not imposing, his frame softened by years spent in the offices of finance rather than the fields of war. His salt-and-pepper hair was neatly combed back, revealing a high forehead and piercing blue eyes sharp with intellect but shadowed by concern. A trim beard, streaked with silver, framed his jawline, giving him the appearance of a statesman rather than a merchant. He wore a dark navy frock coat, tailored to perfection, the fabric stiff with wealth. His waistcoat was embroidered with a subtle gold pattern, a mark of quiet opulence, and a cravat of deep burgundy silk lay knotted at his throat. His fingers, long and tapered, drummed absently against the arm of his chair, a sign of a mind that never truly rested.

"It isn't right!" the man to Wilson's right erupted. "They have no authority!" John Stuart Mill had the lean, angular face of a scholar, but his deep-set gray eyes burned with a quiet defiance. His high cheekbones and thin lips made him look severe but not unkind; his was the face of a man who had spent more time debating ideas than issuing orders. His light brown hair, beginning to thin at the crown, was brushed forward in the style of a man too focused on greater concerns to bother much with vanity. He wore a black woolen suit, slightly worn at the cuffs, as though he cared more for thought than for fashion. His waistcoat was a muted brown, simple and unadorned save for a single gold pocket watch chain, its surface worn smooth from years of absent-minded handling. He sat with a posture that suggested both weariness and resolve, his fingers steepled as he listened, his mind already calculating the consequences of the night's decisions.

A renowned philosopher, he was given to both passion and wisdom, though control over either seemed to wax and wane.

"They do have the right," said Robert Martin, the man nearest the fireplace. "The Crown gave our company its charter. The Crown can take it away."

He had the weathered look of a man accustomed to conflict, though his battles had been fought in the corridors of power rather than on the field. His graying hair was cut short, and deep lines creased his forehead, etched there by decades of manipulating markets and toppling rivals. His dark brown eyes held no warmth, only a cool, analytical detachment; the gaze of a man who had sent thousands to ruin with the stroke of a pen. He wore a charcoal-gray coat, buttoned tight over a dark green waistcoat, the color subdued but rich, like the wealth he controlled. His cravat was black, tied with ruthless precision, and a silver ring on his left hand bore the insignia of the company; a reminder of the power he had once held, and intended to hold again. He sat slightly forward in his chair, his hands clasped, his expression unreadable save for the faintest twitch of a smirk when he spoke.

"You almost sound like you're embracing it like some of the other traitors in our organization." Mill thought he saw his retort spark a flash of ire from Martin's eyes, but the man apparently restrained himself.

"I am not one of them," Martin refuted. "If I were, I would not be here, trying to figure out our next move."

The East India Company had been a dominant force in global events since the establishment of its charter by Queen Elizabeth I in 1600. The EIC operated as a state within a state, though at the height of its power, the company boasted more than 260,000 soldiers, more than double the military numbers of Great Britain. They controlled the seas, trade routes, international commerce, and had gained a foothold in the New World. The company's influence reached all the way to the Far East, and its military might had, until recently, been unchallenged.

All of that had changed in one unpredictable move by the people of India.

They'd grown tired of the way the company ruled the country, how it taxed the citizens, how it plundered the nation of its resources in the name of profit and power. Their embers of iniquity had finally sparked, and when that swelled into the flames of rebellion, the East India Company had been forced to react.

The suppression of the revolution had been swift, brutal, and overwhelming. The men in the room had no way of knowing exactly how many Indians had been killed in the fighting, nor did they care. Their lives had been expendable.

"That kind of talk isn't helpful," Wilson said, tempering the emotions in the room. He glanced around at the space, taking it in for what might be the last time.

It was a room built for secrecy, for dealings that could not withstand the scrutiny of Parliament or the Crown. The chamber was deep below the main structure, carved into the very foundation of London's mercantile empire. It smelled of wealth and power—of old money, fine tobacco, and hints of expensive liquor.

A great fireplace dominated one end of the room, its stone mantel carved with the company's crest—two rampant lions flanking a globe, a silent tribute to an empire built not on kingship but on commerce. The fire within crackled low, casting long, flickering shadows across the chamber's paneled walls. The wood was mahogany, dark and polished to a near-black sheen, the glow of the fire reflecting off its surface like embers on deep water. The walls bore gold-leafed inlay, the pattern of curling vines and laurels meant to evoke Rome—an empire fallen yet remembered and emulated. A warning, perhaps, of what happened to those who failed to adapt.

Above, the ceiling arched with heavy wooden beams, their weight pressing down like the burden of a fading empire. The air hung thick, heavy with the scent of smoldering Havana cigars, the tendrils of smoke curling lazily toward the ceiling, where they mingled with the whispers of power long spoken in that very room. The faint scent of cognac mixed with the tobacco, creating an aroma both intoxicating and oppressive.

The floor was layered in Persian rugs, their intricate patterns woven in blood reds and deep blues, muffling footsteps and lending the room an air of quiet reverence. They were soft beneath the boots of men who had once commanded armies, who had held entire nations under their thumb. Now, they sat in a semicircle of high-back leather chairs, deep and worn, their cracked upholstery a silent witness to decades of clandestine meetings.

A polished walnut table stood at the room's center, its surface reflecting the dim light of an oil lamp that sat beside an open decanter of French brandy. The crystal-cut glass beside it was filled just enough to catch the fire's glow, the amber liquid swirling gently as if the very essence of power rested within. A second decanter, this one of Scotch, stood nearby, its bottle half drained, evidence of the long hours and heavier thoughts that had preceded this moment.

Bookshelves lined one side of the room, their spines gilded with titles in Latin, French, and Sanskrit—records of trade, of conquests, of treaties forged and broken. But one shelf was false, a hidden compartment known only to those who had ruled from behind the company's veil. Within it lay the true ledgers of the empire—the names of men bought and paid for, the nations toppled, the fortunes made on the backs of opium, silk, and stolen gold.

The only sound, aside from the fire's low murmur, was the soft clink of glass as one of the men set his drink down upon a coaster embossed with the company's insignia. The air was thick, not just with smoke, but with the weight of unspoken desperation. These were men who had once commanded the world, who had signed treaties with kings, who had armies at their disposal. Now, they were men grasping for something lost.

The light flickered against their faces, hollowing their features, making them appear almost spectral in the dim glow. Shadows danced across the walls, mimicking the fate of the empire they had built, fading, flickering, but not yet extinguished.

"What do you propose we do?" Mill asked. "The government is taking everything from us unless we agree to their terms and go to work for them. I for one would rather die."

"I'm sure they would be happy to arrange that," Martin chuffed before taking a sip of brandy.

Mill fired him a loathing look but said nothing.

"We have known for a long time that the British government

envied our power, and our positions, on the global stage. This is nothing new. All they needed was an incident to use as an excuse."

"And they generated that themselves," Martin said. "My agents knew about their intentions; the rumblings in Parliament and in secret meetings outside of those alabaster halls."

Martin ran the EIC's intelligence network—a far-reaching agency with fingers in more cookie jars around the world than any government.

"Yes, and yet we did nothing to stop it?" Mill growled.

"We took the necessary precautions to preserve the company and those who remain loyal to it," Wilson corrected. "But the British military is too powerful now. And the government has a monopoly over the trade routes by land and by sea. There is nothing we could do to stop that."

By the time the British Crown moved to seize control of the East India Company, the most valuable portions of its empire had already vanished—at least, on paper. The directors and chief financiers had known for years that this day would come. The Crown had tolerated the company's dominance so long as it remained useful, but with the rebellion of 1857 as a convenient excuse, Parliament had decided it was time to take full control. What they didn't realize was that the company had already ensured its survival.

The most obvious assets—the trading posts, the military forts, the official treasury—had been surrendered without protest. It was a grand sacrifice; a gesture of compliance that allowed the company's adversaries to believe they had truly won. But these losses were little more than a calculated deception. The true wealth of the East India Company, the power that had allowed it to dictate the course of entire nations, had been secured well before the ink dried on the Government of India Act.

Under James Wilson's careful direction, vast sums of company capital had been funneled into European banks beyond the reach of the British Treasury. Swiss accounts, private French banking houses, and Prussian financial institutions had received steady inflows of gold and promissory notes over the past decade, ensuring that when the time came, the company's financial reserves could not be frozen or confiscated. These funds were carefully hidden behind layers of private trusts and family partnerships, making it all but impossible to trace them back to their original source.

Beyond banking, the company had quietly expanded its influence into industries that would outlast its own colonial rule. Investments in steel production, arms manufacturing, and railway construction had been made under subsidiary names, allowing the company to embed itself in the very infrastructure of Britain's expanding empire. The transition from colonial rule to industrial dominance had already begun, and no act of Parliament could reverse it.

The company's fleet, once the backbone of its global trade network, had not been left to the mercy of the Crown either. Over the past several years, key merchant vessels had been quietly reregistered under foreign ownership. Some flew French or Dutch flags, while others had been sold—on paper—to private interests that were, in reality, little more than company-controlled fronts. These ships continued to operate as they always had—transporting tea, spices, opium, and textiles—but now outside the jurisdiction of British authorities.

The most sensitive documents—records of bribes, backroom deals, and debts owed by powerful men—had also been removed from company holdings and secured in private archives across Europe. These ledgers contained leverage worth far more than gold: insurance policies against any attempt by the British government to turn its victory into a true reckoning. The names within these pages were not merely merchants and bankers, but politicians, generals, and noblemen—men who had benefitted from the company's reach and now found themselves bound to its survival.

Even intelligence operations, once officially part of the company's administrative network, had been preserved under a new guise, save for the rogues who'd feared the government's reach. The agents who had once gathered information under the authority of the East India Company now operated as "independent consultants," feeding information not to a corporate office but to private clients—clients who, unbeknownst to the Crown, were still the same men who had steered the company from its inception.

In the end, the British government had claimed victory over a corpse. The East India Company, as a legal entity, was dead. But its purpose, its wealth, its influence, those had merely been transferred, repackaged, and concealed in the very industries and institutions that Britain relied upon. What had once been a colonial trading empire had now become something far more insidious: a shadow empire, woven into the very fabric of global finance, industry, and warfare.

They had lost their name. But nothing else.

"So, we secured most of our assets," Mill said. "What now? What are we supposed to do? Hide in the basement for the rest of our lives?"

"We've broken no laws," Wilson answered. "Not that they know of. We have no reason to hide. We can go about our lives, operating as we always have. The only thing we no longer control is a large military. But we still have a portion of that at our disposal, just not in the public eye."

"In some ways, we have more power than before," Martin added. "Now that the government believes they have total control, and have swept us under the rug, we can manipulate things from the inside to the company's benefit."

"I suppose you're right," Mill surrendered. But he didn't look happy about it. The other two thought they knew why. They saw clearly that the man enjoyed the prestige the EIC gave him. It was a vain metric that Mill held onto too closely. He liked being viewed as someone of influence and power. Perhaps he even enjoyed being feared. They were traits contrary to his philosophical background, but everyone had a vice. His was akin to fame. "So, what do we do now?"

Wilson looked around the room again, trying not to let it get to him. Sooner or later the government would learn about it after they seized the building, which would be any day now.

He hadn't built an empire on nostalgia. This place was just walls and floors and ceilings. Those could be constructed anywhere, and they would be. Soon, Wilson would oversee the construction of a new seat of the company's power, far from the reaches of the British government's greedy arm.

"We continue to build our wealth, and our scope of influence," Wilson answered. "Nothing changes in that regard. We've already allocated all we need. From the shadows, we will be able to change policy in governments around the world and shape the future for those who follow in our footsteps. The East India Company is not going anywhere, my friends. It will continue to thrive until we find a way to emerge from the darkness and take our rightful place in full view of the world."

1

PARIS, PRESENT DAY

Henri couldn't believe his eyes. For most of his adult life, he had been chasing whispers. References hidden in footnotes, secondhand accounts buried in archives no one bothered to examine, fleeting mentions of something that, by all academic reasoning, should not exist. He had read and reread trial transcripts, pored over church records, sifted through countless medieval correspondences, all in search of a single, impossible truth.

A truth that now lay before him, written in fading ink on parchment so brittle he barely dared to breathe.

The Bibliothèque nationale de France held many secrets. Some were hidden behind locked doors, buried in ancient volumes that had not been touched in centuries. Others lurked in plain sight, obscured only by the weight of time and neglect. Henri Devereux had spent years within these walls, but tonight felt different.

The archives were housed in a wing of the library that most visitors never saw—a section reserved for scholars, historians, and researchers who had been granted the necessary permissions to handle delicate, irreplaceable manuscripts. The air was thick with the scent of parchment and ink, a mixture of history and dust that clung to the skin and settled in the throat.

He sat at a long wooden table, the grain polished smooth by generations of restless hands. The chair beneath him was old and stiff, the leather cracked from time and use. It creaked softly whenever he shifted, a sound swallowed by the cavernous stillness of the room.

A single green-shade desk lamp illuminated his workspace, casting a pool of light over the open manuscript before him. Beyond that, the shadows deepened, stretching toward the towering bookshelves that lined the chamber. The shelves were packed tight with leather-bound tomes, their spines faded and peeling, their titles etched in gold that had dulled with age. Some of these books had been untouched for centuries, waiting for hands that might never come.

The room was silent, but it was not the silence of emptiness. It was a living stillness, filled with the faintest sounds that only those who listened carefully would hear—the soft rustle of paper as distant researchers turned fragile pages, the occasional scrape of a chair leg against the wooden floor, the muffled cough of someone lost in thought.

Farther back, in the dim recesses of the archive, the sound of a librarian's cart wheels gliding over stone echoed briefly before vanishing.

Henri exhaled, rubbing his fingers against his temples. The weight of the manuscript in front of him was heavier than its physical form. This wasn't just a text—it was a gateway to something greater. The words it contained had survived centuries of war, fire, and time, waiting for someone to recognize their significance.

His workspace was organized but cluttered, a reflection of his own mind. A notebook lay open beside him filled with careful transcriptions and hastily scribbled translations. His pen rested on the paper, a thin line of ink marking where he had paused midthought. A ceramic cup of half-drunk espresso sat nearby, long since gone cold, its bitter scent mixing with the aged aroma of the books around him.

Somewhere in the distance, a clock chimed the hour.

Henri glanced at his watch—nearly closing time for the archives.

He hadn't noticed the time slipping away, but that was often the case in this place. The archives seemed to exist in a realm separate from the rest of the world, a space where daylight and nightfall lost meaning. Time was measured not in hours but in pages turned, in discoveries made, in questions answered or left unresolved.

He leaned back in his chair, stretching his fingers before resting them on the table next to the manuscript once more.

The silence pressed in around him, but it wasn't an oppressive thing. It was the silence of knowledge waiting to be uncovered, of history holding its breath, of voices long gone still whispering from ink and parchment.

This moment had been a long time coming.

And now, at last, he had found it.

He forced himself to remain still, to not move too suddenly, as if the sheer weight of the moment might cause the fragile document to disintegrate beneath his fingers. He adjusted his glasses, leaning closer to the dim, yellow light of the desk lamp. His pulse quickened.

It was real.

His fingers hovered over the script, hesitant to touch the centuries-old manuscript before him. It was a collection of ecclesiastical records—Benedictine monastic correspondence dating from the mid-fifteenth century, pulled from the depths of the Bibliothèque nationale de France's ecclesiastical archives. He had only requested the documents on a whim, hoping to find a passing mention of Joan of Arc, some overlooked fragment that might point him in the right direction.

But this... this was more than he had ever hoped for.

His eyes scanned the text, piecing together the meaning behind the archaic script. The passage, penned in 1451, was written by a Benedictine scribe named Antón d'Argentan, a monk stationed at the Abbey of Jumièges—one of Normandy's oldest monasteries.

It was an account of a conversation, a record that should have been meaningless, just another monk's quiet observations. But buried within the text was something far more profound.

"It was said that before she fell into the hands of the unholy tribunal, she gave her most trusted man a task. He was to return it to the place where it was first given to her, so that it may only be found when the time is right."

Henri's breath caught.

This wasn't just a reference to Joan of Arc. This was something much more.

His mind raced to decipher the puzzle. "Before she fell into the hands of the unholy tribunal"—that meant before her capture in Compiègne in 1430. "Her most trusted man"—a knight? A noble? One of her commanders? And "return it to the place where it was first given to her"—the missing piece.

What was it?

Henri knew. At least, he thought he did. The hypothesis was the basis for his life's work.

For years, there had been speculation that Joan's ring—the small, unadorned band she always wore, engraved with the names *Jesus* and *Maria*—had held significance beyond mere sentiment. The English had confiscated it after her capture, and it had been lost to history. Or so the world believed.

But what if that was a lie?

What if Joan had never actually been wearing the real ring when she was taken? What if the ring the English took from her was a fake? If she'd known what troubles lay ahead, she would have taken precautions to protect such a powerful talisman.

His pulse hammered in his ears.

If this passage was to be believed, Joan hadn't simply hidden the ring—she had entrusted it to someone, someone who had then returned it to where she first received it.

And where was that?

The consensus had always been that Joan's ring had come from her family in Domrémy, but no concrete records had ever confirmed its origin. Some believed it had been a gift from her parents; others thought it had been bestowed upon her by a priest, or perhaps a noble benefactor. If she had ordered it to be returned to that place, then finding that location meant finding the ring.

Henri pressed his hands against the table, steadying himself. He had to know more.

He forced himself to refocus on the document, searching for anything else Antón d'Argentan might have recorded. There wasn't much—the passage was brief, a small detail buried in an otherwise unremarkable ledger—but he had learned, over years of research, that the smallest details were often the most important.

And then he saw it.

A single line, written in a hurried scrawl at the bottom of the page, almost as if it had been added as an afterthought.

"The words were kept, so that she would not be forgotten."

Henri sucked in a sharp breath. This wasn't just about the ring. This was about the journal.

For centuries, historians had debated whether Joan had ever written anything in her own hand. Her trial records had been preserved, but those were dictated under duress. Her personal letters had been written by scribes. But a journal? That would change everything.

And this passage suggested that it had existed.

Somehow, Joan's words had been preserved, kept by those who had remained loyal to her even after her execution. Henri had no doubt that if the journal still existed, it held the final clue to where the ring had been taken.

The implications sent a rush of heat through him, his skin prickling with excitement.

This was the kind of discovery that defined careers. That rewrote history. But for him, it was a culmination of all his hard work finally paying off.

He let out a slow breath, willing himself to stay calm. He needed to be methodical about this. He needed to confirm his findings, verify the document's authenticity—though he already knew in his gut that this was real.

And more than that—he needed to figure out what came next.

Because if Joan's ring had survived, if the journal still existed somewhere in the world, then he had just stumbled upon one of the greatest lost treasures of medieval history.

And he was the only one who knew it.

Henri exhaled slowly, forcing his hands to remain steady as he reached for his notebook. The leather cover was soft and worn, its pages filled with years of meticulous research, scattered theories, and half-finished translations. This moment—this discovery—was the culmination of everything he had been chasing.

He uncapped his pen with his thumb and started writing, the nib scratching softly against the page as he transcribed the most crucial passages from the manuscript.

Joan of Arc had given her words to a trusted man before her capture.

The writings—possibly a journal—were hidden away to be found when the time was right.

Her ring was returned to the place where she first received it.

Henri paused, tapping the end of his pen against the table, thinking.

The implications were staggering. If Joan's ring had never been captured by the English, then the one that had surfaced in later years —the one auctioned off to collectors—had been a fake, a deception. The real ring was still out there. But where?

He turned the page in his notebook and began making connections between locations and names:

"Antón d'Argentan (Benedictine scribe) mentions an unnamed 'most trusted man.'"

"Possibly one of her generals? Gilles de Rais? Jean de Metz? La Hire?"

"Abbey of Jumièges connection—why there?"

"What does 'first given to her' mean?"

His handwriting quickened, his excitement overtaking his need for clarity. He knew that once he left the library, he would retype everything properly, organize it into something structured. But for now, he needed to get the details down before they slipped from his mind.

Henri pulled out his phone and snapped several quick photos of the manuscript, adjusting the angle to capture the faded ink without the glare of the desk lamp washing it out. The thought of a librarian scolding him for photographing restricted texts barely crossed his mind. He was too close to something monumental. He could seek formal permission later.

Satisfied, he lowered the phone to his lap and glanced around the room. That was when he felt it.

A shift. A presence.

It was nothing tangible—just the prickling sensation at the base of his neck, the sudden awareness of the quiet pressing in around him. The silence had changed. It was no longer simply the comforting hush of the archives, filled with the occasional rustling of pages and distant footsteps. Now it felt... heavier.

Henri turned his head slightly, keeping his movements slow, controlled.

The reading room beyond his small pool of lamplight was cloaked in shadows, the high bookshelves standing like silent sentinels in the dim glow of overhead fixtures. From where he sat, he could see a few other researchers, each hunched over their own work, oblivious to him. A man near the far wall was flipping through a thick tome, while an older woman was scribbling notes beside a stack of books.

Nothing seemed out of place. And yet...

Henri's gaze shifted toward the archway leading to the deeper stacks. That was where he had heard it; a noise, faint but distinct. The soft shuffle of movement, like the quiet adjustment of a coat or the shifting of weight from one foot to another.

Someone was there. Or had been.

The sensation of being watched clawed at the edges of his awareness. He turned his attention back to his desk, forcing himself to remain calm. He was letting his imagination get the better of him. He had been buried in research for hours, his mind hyperfocused, his nerves raw from the intensity of what he had found.

Henri's eyes flicked to the fluorescent light hanging above the shelves to his left. He could have sworn that a moment ago, it had been steady. Now it flickered, buzzing softly, casting brief, erratic shadows against the towering rows of books.

He clenched his jaw, resisting the urge to glance over his shoulder again. But questions filled his mind. Who would be watching him? He was just a historian investigating a legend no one believed in—no one but him.

He closed his notebook, sliding it into his leather satchel alongside his phone. He adjusted the manuscript carefully, ensuring that it looked undisturbed, exactly as it had before he arrived. Then he placed his hands flat on the desk, exhaling through his nose.

The rational part of his mind told him that no one had reason to be watching him. He was just another historian poring over forgotten records. Nothing about his research should have drawn attention.

But the other part of him—the one that had spent years uncovering suppressed truths, chasing down relics the world had long forgotten—knew better.

Something told him he was no longer alone.

And for the first time since arriving at the archives that evening, he felt fear snaking through his veins. Henri tried to focus on the manuscript in front of him, but his mind wouldn't let go of the feeling—the creeping awareness that something wasn't right. He told himself he was overreacting, that the long hours and dim lighting were playing tricks on him.

Then he saw the man.

At first, it was nothing. Just a passing glance as Henri's gaze swept the room, the same way he had done countless times that evening. But when his eyes landed on a figure in one of the far aisles, something tightened in his chest.

The man had been standing in the same place for too long—not reading, not flipping through pages, just... lingering.

He was tall, broad-shouldered but not bulky, his frame lean beneath a well-fitted charcoal-gray coat. His hair was dark, neatly combed back, and even from a distance, Henri could tell there was a sharpness to him—a stillness that didn't match the absent-minded energy of a scholar lost in his work. He held a book open in one hand, but his eyes weren't moving across the page.

The guy was watching Henri.

Henri's stomach tightened.

The man's gaze flicked back to his book the moment their eyes met, but it was too late. Henri had seen the way his head had turned —just slightly, just enough to keep him in his peripheral vision.

This wasn't normal.

Henri swallowed, gripping the edge of his notebook inside his satchel. He shifted in his chair, pretending to adjust his papers, using the movement as an excuse to glance toward the aisle again.

The man hadn't moved. He was still standing there, still holding the same book, still too aware of Henri's presence.

A chill crawled up Henri's spine.

He looked away, forcing himself to breathe evenly. This was a public archive. It wasn't as if someone could simply walk up and—

He shook the thought from his mind. He was being ridiculous.

Still, his instincts told him something was wrong. And Henri had learned long ago to trust his instincts.

He told himself to act natural, to stay calm. But his mind was elsewhere, his pulse a steady drum in his ears. He waited a few moments before allowing himself another glance toward the aisle.

The man was gone.

Henri's throat tightened. He scanned the room, forcing his gaze to remain casual. The other researchers were still there—an elderly woman flipping through a massive volume near the reference desk, a student scribbling frantically into a notebook, an older man hunched over a pile of Latin texts. But the watcher had vanished.

Had he left?

Henri's gut told him no. Part of him wanted to go speak to one of the other people in the building, maybe even strike up a conversation that would have to continue beyond the walls of the archives, somewhere safe like a bar or a café, where there were plenty of witnesses.

"Stop it," he breathed to himself. "You are just a historian. No one even knows what you're working on."

He rubbed the sides of his nose with his thumb and index finger, using the motion as cover, letting his eyes flick toward the entrance of the reading room, then toward the deeper stacks.

There. A glimpse of movement between the towering shelves.

Henri's heart hammered against his ribs. The man had moved—closer. He was no longer pretending to read. Now, he was in the next row of bookshelves, just beyond the lamplight.

Henri straightened, suddenly hyperaware of his surroundings. A second shadow flickered along the far wall—another figure moving through the shelves.

Henri's stomach dropped. One was bad enough. But two?

That was a message. It was time to go.

He moved methodically, not rushing, not giving any sign that he had noticed the men. If they were watching for a reaction, he wouldn't give them one.

He slid his chair back carefully, the wooden legs scraping softly against the polished floor. The sound felt too loud in the quiet of the archives, but no one looked up. No one except them.

Henri could feel their eyes.

Keeping his expression neutral, he turned away from his desk and made his way toward the main aisle of bookshelves. The overhead lights flickered again, their dull hum filling the air between each heartbeat. He resisted the urge to glance sideways into the rows, but he sensed movement just beyond his line of sight—a shifting presence among the towering bookshelves.

The quickest way out was past the reference desk and through the main doors leading to the stairwell. He walked at a steady pace, weaving between long wooden tables, each occupied by scholars lost in their work, oblivious to his growing urgency.

The reference desk loomed ahead, its curved mahogany counter cluttered with stacks of books and a solitary lamp casting a dim, golden glow over an open ledger. The librarian on duty—a wiry man with round spectacles perched at the end of his nose—barely glanced up from his notes as Henri passed.

Almost there.

The reading room doors stood just ahead, their frosted glass panes reflecting the warm glow of the chandeliers above. He pushed through them with controlled force, emerging into the dimly lit corridor beyond.

He didn't look back.

The long hallway taunted him, as if its size alone would be his demise. It was lined with more shelves, framed portraits, and small alcoves where busts of French scholars stood in silent observation. His footsteps echoed off the marble floor as he quickened his pace. At the far end, a wrought iron staircase spiraled downward, leading to the lobby and the main exit.

He took the stairs at a steady pace, resisting the urge to rush, though every instinct screamed at him to move faster. As he reached the bottom, the main doors of the library came into view.

Beyond the tall glass panels, Paris stretched out before him—a blur of glowing streetlamps, passing cars, and the faint hum of a city that never truly slept. The doors were heavy; their brass handles cool beneath his fingers. He pushed forward and stepped out onto the sidewalk as the crisp night air filled his lungs.

He'd made it outside. Was he safe yet? Was he ever in any danger? He'd prefer to get out of here now and ask questions later.

2

The night air was crisp, carrying the scent of rain on the wind.

Henri stepped onto the sidewalk and adjusted the strap of his satchel as he fell into the easy rhythm of the city. Paris at night had a different pulse than it did in the day—more subdued, more secretive. The streets around the Bibliothèque nationale de France were quiet at this hour, the usual foot traffic thinning as the city's scholars and bureaucrats retired for the evening.

Above him, the sky was a deep charcoal, heavy with clouds that threatened an overdue autumn shower. The glow of the streetlamps flickered across the damp pavement, casting long, distorted shadows that stretched toward the gutters. Somewhere nearby, the sound of a passing motorbike echoed against the stone façades of the surrounding buildings, followed by the distant chatter of a late-night café.

He exhaled slowly, willing his shoulders to relax.

The train would be the fastest way home. He lived in the 7th Arrondissement, not far from Rue Cler, an elegant neighborhood known for its quiet streets, small bistros, and art galleries tucked between Haussmann-style buildings. It was a far cry from the more touristy areas, offering the kind of anonymity he preferred.

With a final glance over his shoulder, Henri stepped off the curb and crossed the street, making his way toward the nearest Métro station.

Paris was never truly silent. Even in the later hours, the city carried an energy that hummed beneath the surface. As Henri walked, the air was cool, brushing against his skin with the kind of chill that signaled the first real touch of autumn.

The streets were a patchwork of warm lights spilling from shuttered windows and the cooler, sterile glow of streetlamps reflecting off rain-slicked cobblestones. He passed a row of art galleries, their interiors dim but showcasing paintings in the display windows—landscapes, abstracts, a single haunting portrait of a woman's face obscured by shadows.

A small pâtisserie sat at the corner, its metal shutters partially drawn. The scent of butter and sugar still lingered in the air, mixing with the distant bite of cigarette smoke from a passerby. Somewhere behind him, a group of young people laughed, their voices carrying across the boulevard before disappearing into a side street.

Henri kept his pace even. Not hurried, not slow. Just another man making his way home.

The Métro entrance loomed ahead, a wrought iron staircase leading down into the tunnels below the city. A red-and-white Métropolitain sign flickered overhead, casting a weak glow onto the pavement.

Henri descended the steps, the temperature dropping noticeably as he moved underground. The air turned dense, tinged with the metallic scent of damp stone and electricity. The tunnels always smelled faintly of oil and something musty, like old paper left too long in a cellar.

At this hour, the station was mostly empty, save for a few night travelers. A middle-aged man in a worn trench coat stood near a vending machine, fumbling for coins. A young couple sat on a bench, leaning into each other, whispering in hushed voices.

The overhead lights buzzed faintly, illuminating grime-covered tiles and old advertisements peeling at the corners. The distant sound of an approaching train rumbled through the tunnels, a low vibration that grew louder by the second. He glanced at the digital sign overhead—his train would arrive in less than a minute.

A gust of wind rushed through the platform as the train emerged from the tunnel and its headlights cut through the dim station. The brakes screeched as it slowed, the sound high-pitched and grating. Henri stepped forward as the doors slid open, and the stale warmth of the carriage's interior spilled out onto the platform.

Henri stepped into the train car and found an empty seat near the middle. He settled in and adjusted his bag on his lap. The interior was warmer than outside, almost stuffy, the scent of rubber, metal, and faint traces of cologne and sweat mixing into the artificial heat.

The train wasn't crowded, but it wasn't empty either. A few passengers were scattered throughout: a businessman in a navy suit, scrolling through his phone, his face illuminated by the screen's glow; an elderly woman clutching a small shopping bag, her fingers absent-mindedly tracing the strap; a man in his twenties with headphones, his fingers tapping out a rhythm on his knee.

Henri let his gaze drift as the train lurched forward, the movement rhythmic, almost hypnotic. The tunnels blurred past, nothing but blackness punctuated by the occasional flicker of dim overhead lights.

His fingers tightened on his satchel. The unease from earlier hadn't faded.

He glanced toward the doors at the far end of the car. They remained closed, the window revealing nothing but the empty platform they had just left behind.

Henri exhaled and leaned back against the seat. It was just nerves. That's all. He could control it. He was sixty-seven years old. He'd pretty much seen it all at this point.

Still, he couldn't shake the feeling that somewhere in the city, someone else was riding the train that night, heading in the same direction he was.

The train rumbled through the tunnels, its movement steady, the rhythmic clatter of steel against steel filling the quiet space. Henri sat with his hands resting on his satchel, his fingers absently gripping the worn leather. He kept his breathing even, willing himself to relax.

The station names passed in a blur, each stop marked by the brief hiss of doors sliding open, the soft shuffle of passengers boarding or departing, then the familiar lurch as the train resumed its journey.

Henri glanced at his watch. Nine minutes. That was how long it had been since he boarded. Just a few more stops and he'd be home.

The warmth inside the carriage had become stifling, a stark contrast to the crisp air outside. The scent of rubber, metal, and faint traces of perfume clung to the space, mixed with the lingering odor of damp woolen coats and old train upholstery.

A voice crackled over the intercom, announcing the next stop. The man's voice sounded dull, as if he were finishing the end of a long shift and just wanted to get home. Or worse, he was at the beginning of his shift.

Henri shifted his gaze toward the windows and watched as the darkness of the tunnels gave way to the dimly lit platform of his station. The train slowed, the brakes squealing against the rails, and the overhead lights flickered as if hesitating before bringing him to his destination.

The moment the doors slid open, he stepped out and into the muggy, warm air of the station. It carried the lingering scent of damp concrete, machine oil, and the faint metallic tang of rusted tracks. Somewhere deeper in the tunnel, the distant sound of another train approaching reverberated through the station, a deep, mechanical growl that seemed to vibrate in Henri's chest as he stepped onto the platform.

The crowds were thinner at this hour. During the day, the station would have been packed with commuters, tourists, and students pushing their way through the tiled corridors. Now, only a handful of passengers moved about the platform, each absorbed in their own world.

Henri adjusted his satchel and began walking toward the exit signs, his steps measured, deliberate.

A man in a dark jacket stood near one of the support columns, his back to the tiled wall, his face partially obscured by shadow. He wasn't looking at anything in particular—just standing, his posture too still, too relaxed for someone waiting on a train.

Henri's fingers tightened around the strap of his satchel.

He moved past the station benches, where a homeless man sat slumped against the wall, wrapped in layers of tattered clothing, his head resting against his knees. Nearby, a teenager in a leather jacket flicked through his phone, earbuds in, as he bobbed his head faintly to whatever played through them.

Henri reached the stairs leading up toward the exit gates, keeping his movements casual, but his senses heightened. The air grew thicker, the walls lined with more old advertisements peeling at the edges, their colors faded from years of grime and neglect.

The sound of footsteps behind him made his skin prickle.

He slowed slightly, enough to catch the reflection of the platform in a smudged vending machine glass. The man in the dark jacket was moving now—walking at a measured pace, not rushing, not overtly following, but heading in the same direction.

Henri swallowed as his pulse quickened.

He reached the turnstiles and slid his pass through the reader. The machine beeped softly before releasing the barrier. He stepped through and took another quick glance over his shoulder.

The man was still there.

A second set of footsteps echoed nearby, and Henri spotted another figure—a different man, older, wearing a long overcoat—stepping out of a side corridor near the stairwell. He barely spared Henri a glance, but something about him felt wrong.

Was he imagining this? Henri kept moving.

The stairs leading up to the street loomed ahead, the iron railing cool beneath his fingertips as he began to climb. With each step, the temperature shifted, the thick, stagnant air of the underground giving way to the crisp coolness of the Parisian night above.

He resisted the urge to turn around. If he was being followed, he wouldn't confirm that he knew it.

The top of the stairs was just ahead.

When he reached the exit to the subway station, Henri stepped onto the sidewalk. The cool night air washed over him like he'd opened a freezer door after the heavy, muggy confines of the Métro station. He pulled his coat tighter around himself and adjusted the strap of his satchel as he took the first steps toward home.

The 7th Arrondissement had an elegance to it, even at this hour. The streets were wider here, lined with Haussmann-style buildings, their façades bathed in the soft glow of ornate streetlamps. Black wrought iron balconies curled like delicate lace along the upper floors, some adorned with flower boxes, their leaves trembling in the faint autumn breeze. The rhythmic click of his boots against the pavement blended with the muffled hum of distant traffic and the occasional laughter spilling from a café terrace where a handful of late-night patrons lingered over wine and espresso.

Henri kept his pace steady, but his awareness was sharper than usual.

The feeling hadn't left him. The sense of being watched, of someone trailing just outside his line of sight, clung to him like a shadow. He resisted the urge to turn around too often, instead catching glimpses of movement in the reflections of the café windows and glass storefronts.

The sidewalk was dotted with shops and restaurants, some already closed, others preparing to shut for the night. The air was thick with the aroma of fresh bread from a boulangerie, mingling with the faint bitterness of roasted coffee from a nearby café. A brasserie on the corner still had its outdoor heaters running, their orange glow flickering against the polished tables, warming the few remaining diners.

An apothecary sign blinked neon green, casting a faint glow onto the sidewalk, and just beyond it, a bookstore with an old wooden sign sat darkened for the night, its display window filled with antique volumes stacked in uneven towers.

Henri moved past an art gallery, its lights still on and showcasing a single massive canvas in the window; a stark abstract piece of swirling blues and blacks, almost like a storm captured in paint.

He picked up his speed.

He didn't like how exposed he felt here. The wide sidewalks, the open space—if someone was following him, they could see his every move, track him easily.

As he neared his apartment building, he let out a slow breath. It was a beautiful old structure, like so many in this district—cream-colored stone, tall windows with white wooden shutters, an arched entryway leading into a private courtyard beyond. The heavy black door at the entrance bore a polished brass handle, and just above it, a small wrought iron lantern flickered in the breeze.

Henri reached for his keys; his pulse still unsteady. He would feel better once he was inside.

3

Henri turned the key in the lock, and it opened with a click. He stole another quick glance around the street, then, seeing nothing that caused immediate concern, quickly stepped inside the building.

The lobby was quiet but not silent.

Henri moved deeper inside and let the heavy black door close behind him with a soft, deliberate click. The air inside was warmer than the street outside, carrying the faint scent of polished wood, aged stone, and the lingering trace of someone's expensive cologne. It was familiar—reassuring, even—but his unease refused to lift.

The lobby was small but elegant, lined with cream-colored marble floors that gleamed under the golden glow of antique chandeliers. A plush burgundy rug ran from the entrance to the elevator, its fibers flattened by years of quiet footsteps. The walls were adorned with ornate sconces, their light flickering just enough to make the shadows dance.

To his left, a narrow hallway led toward the inner courtyard, its wrought iron gate barely visible through a set of arched glass doors. To his right, a wooden concierge desk sat unoccupied at this hour, though a small brass bell rested atop its polished surface. A row of black leather chairs lined the far wall, empty, their presence more decorative than functional.

Henri's footsteps barely made a sound as he crossed the floor toward the elevator. He pressed the call button, the brass surface cool beneath his fingertip. A few seconds passed before a quiet ding echoed through the space, and the elevator doors slid open with a smooth mechanical hum.

The interior was small, just enough space for four or five people comfortably. The side walls were lined with dark wood paneling, the corners polished to a soft sheen. A mirrored surface stretched across the back, reflecting his tense posture as he stepped inside.

The door closed with a muted thud, sealing him off from the lobby's golden glow.

Henri pressed the button for the fourth floor, and the elevator lurched into motion, ascending with a steady hum. He let out a slow breath and shifted his weight slightly as he glanced at his reflection in the mirrored back wall. His own eyes looked different tonight; sharper, more alert. His fingers curled around the strap of his satchel.

As the elevator rose, a faint creak interrupted the hum of machinery. A tiny sound, but enough to set his nerves on edge. He turned his head slightly, listening, but the noise didn't repeat.

Just the building settling. Probably.

The elevator slowed, which was followed by another ding, and the doors slid open, revealing a dimly lit hallway stretching out before him.

The walls were lined with deep green wainscoting, the upper portion painted a soft, muted cream. The ceiling was high, with simple molding, the kind that gave the building a timeless charm. A long Persian runner stretched the length of the hall, its intricate patterns muted in the soft overhead lighting.

Despite the quiet, the building wasn't completely still.

Somewhere behind one of the closed doors, a television murmured, its dialogue muffled beyond recognition. Farther down the hall, the faint clinking of glass and laughter suggested someone enjoying a late-night drink. The air carried the scent of something floral, perhaps from a reed diffuser placed near one of the doors, mingling with the faint mustiness of old wood.

Henri's flat was near the end of the hall.

He walked with measured steps, his ears tuned to every shift in sound, every flicker of movement at the edges of his vision. As he approached his door, something in his chest tightened.

He reached for his keys, his fingers brushing against cold metal. The sound of something metal banging against a surface echoed from one of the nearby apartments. Startled, Henri nearly dropped his keys.

"Calm down," he told himself. "You're home now. Stop acting crazy."

There was no one else in the corridor, and if there were, he'd easily see them.

Somewhat more confident, he pushed the key into the lock, turned it, and opened the door.

The door closed behind him with a solid click, the familiar sound grounding him for the first time since he had left the archives.

Henri exhaled slowly as he pressed the deadbolt into place then flipped the additional security latch above it. His fingers lingered on the lock for a moment longer than necessary before he finally turned away.

The air inside was warmer than outside, carrying the subtle scent of aged paper, polished wood, and the faintest trace of spiced tea; a reminder of the cup he had abandoned that morning. It was the smell of home, of routine, of a place untouched by the tension that had followed him through the city.

He stepped into the entryway, a small but well-kept space where he hung his keys on a wrought iron hook mounted beside a framed sketch of Notre-Dame Cathedral. A small wooden table stood beneath it, holding a ceramic dish where he often dropped spare coins or his watch when he came home late.

But he wasn't thinking about routine tonight.

He kept moving, checking the locks once more over his shoulder before stepping farther inside.

Henri's apartment was spacious by Parisian standards, with tall windows draped in heavy curtains that let in the city's soft glow. The décor was a blend of old-world charm and practicality—hardwood floors, high ceilings with simple crown molding, and a neutral color palette that leaned toward warm, earthy tones.

To the left, the kitchen opened into a small dining area, where a round wooden table sat beneath a vintage brass light fixture. A bottle of wine and an empty glass from the previous night remained where he had left them. Beyond the dining area, French doors led to a narrow balcony where he sometimes sat with a book and a drink, watching the city move below him.

To the right, the living room held a deep brown leather sofa, a coffee table cluttered with old books and papers, and a well-worn armchair positioned near a stone fireplace. A few pieces of framed artwork lined the walls, mostly black-and-white photographs of historical sites, with one exception: a large oil painting of an eighteenth-century naval battle, its brushstrokes bold, dramatic.

A short hallway extended toward the bathroom and bedroom, but Henri's focus was on the office, the second door along the hall. In case he really had been followed, he wanted to take out a little insurance.

The office was his sanctuary, the one room in the apartment that was entirely his own world. The space was dimly lit, the warm glow of a desk lamp casting long shadows across the walls lined with bookshelves packed with volumes of history, biographies, ancient texts, and meticulously organized research notes.

The desk was large and heavy, an oak antique with deep scratches in its surface, evidence of years of use. Stacks of books were arranged across it in neat but varied piles, dog-eared and annotated in Henri's precise handwriting. A modern laptop sat at the center, flanked by a notepad, an old brass letter opener, and a half-empty glass of scotch from a previous night's work.

To the right of the desk, a small display cabinet housed historical artifacts—a Roman coin, a fragment of medieval pottery, a rusted dagger believed to have been used in the Napoleonic Wars. Above it, an old world map stretched across the wall, marked with colored pins indicating places of interest.

The desk chair was a deep leather executive seat, worn but comfortable, positioned perfectly before the printer-copier sitting on a lower cabinet.

Henri placed his satchel on the desk and unzipped it, retrieving his notebook from inside. He hesitated for a brief moment, running his fingers over the worn leather cover, as if acknowledging the weight of what was inside.

Then he opened it, flipping to the pages he had scribbled in earlier that night.

He didn't want to take any chances.

Moving quickly, he placed the notebook face-down on the scanner bed of the copier, adjusting the pages before pressing the Copy button. The machine hummed to life, the mechanical whirring filling the room as the first page slid out, fresh ink settling on crisp white paper.

Henri leaned back in his chair as his eyes flicked toward the shadows beyond the lamplight.

The copier continued printing. It seemed to take forever, though in reality the job took only a few minutes.

Once the machine stopped, he took the stack of papers and set them on the desk. He pulled the phone from his pocket and found one of his most trusted friends, a history professor at Cambridge University named Evelyn Langley. She was one of the few people in whom Henri had confided regarding his search for the truth about Joan of Arc and her prized ring. Then, he tucked the notebook behind a series of books on the nearest shelf, just in case anyone came around looking for it.

If there was anyone he could trust with his newfound information, it was her.

He quickly typed out a message then attached the photos he'd taken of the manuscript. He hit the Send button and stuffed his phone back into his pocket. Then, he quickly deleted the message, and then deleted it from the deleted messages folder to make double sure no one could see it other than the person on the other end.

Satisfied with that task being done, he set about his second. He pulled an envelope from one of the shelves and a pen from the right side of the desk, then wrote down the name of someone else he knew from the historical community—Tommy Schultz, head of the International Archaeology Agency.

He paused as he stared at the name then looked back through the doorway. If he really was being followed, there'd be no way the letter would get to Schultz. A wild idea popped into his head, and he wrote down a familiar local address and then stuffed the envelope with the copies before sealing it.

Henri pressed his fingers along the sealed envelope, his writing scrawled in swift, choppy strokes like a physician's. It wasn't much, but it was something—a safeguard against the uneasy feeling that had trailed him for the last half hour or so.

He sighed, finally allowing himself the smallest twinge of relief.

A drink. That was what he needed.

He stood from his desk and ran a hand through his gray-and-brown hair before making his way back toward the kitchen.

The wine chiller was built discreetly into the warm wood cabinetry, its glass door fogged slightly from the temperature difference between the inside and the room beyond. He opened it and reached for a 2016 Château Margaux, a bottle he had been saving but that now seemed ready to open.

Taking a crystal wine glass from a nearby cabinet, he retrieved a corkscrew and worked the cork free with a slow, steady pull. The soft pop was oddly satisfying in the quiet of the apartment.

Henri poured a deep ruby-red stream into the glass, watching the liquid swirl before taking his first sip. Velvety. Dark berries. Just a whisper of oak lingering at the edges.

He let the warmth settle before setting the glass down on the counter.

He suddenly remembered he was still wearing his shoes and

decided to go to the bedroom to take them off and get a little more comfortable.

Henri made his way to his bedroom, stepping onto the thick wool rug that softened the otherwise dark hardwood floors. The room had the same minimalist elegance as the rest of the apartment—tall windows framed by heavy cream-colored curtains, a king-size bed with crisp linen sheets, and a low bookshelf lining one wall, a shelf that was filled with more personal reads than his office collection.

A simple antique dresser sat across from the bed, a glass paperweight and a framed black-and-white photograph of his parents resting atop it. The room smelled of fresh linen and the faintest trace of old books, a scent that always made it feel like home.

He sat on the edge of the bed and loosened his leather shoes, then slipped them off before flexing his toes against the rug. His body was exhausted, but his mind was still wired, the worries of the night replaying in his thoughts.

Henri pushed himself up and walked to the master bathroom. It was sleek, with modern marble countertops contrasting with the vintage claw-foot tub, a balance of past and present. A single frosted-glass window let in the cool night air, the faintest scent of rain drifting in from outside.

Henri turned on the tap and let cold water spill into his cupped hands before splashing it onto his face. The chill grounded him, shaking off some of the fatigue pressing at his temples. He reached for a towel and dried his face with slow, measured movements.

Then he heard it. A sound at the door.

Not the faint creak of an old apartment settling. Not the distant echo of another tenant moving about their home.

Something deliberate. The sound of the lock clicking, and a subtle shift of weight on the floor—the noise of someone trying not to be heard.

A slow chill ran down Henri's spine. He froze, the towel still in his hands, every sense suddenly sharpened. Someone was there.

Henri's breath came fast and shallow as he stepped back into the bathroom, his hands already fumbling for his phone. He barely registered the feel of the cool tile beneath his bare feet as he eased the door shut as quietly as possible, his movements deliberate despite the panic clawing at his chest.

The soft click of the lock sliding into place felt like an afterthought; a pathetic barrier against whoever was outside.

His fingers trembled as he tapped the emergency dial on his screen and pressed the phone to his ear. A ring. Another. Then— "Police emergency," a woman said in French.

"Someone just broke into my home. I'm hiding in the bathroom. Please, send help."

"What is your address, sir?"

Henri sucked in a breath, forcing his voice to stay low. "There's—" He swallowed hard, his throat tightening. He couldn't form the words.

A beat. Then, the operator's voice, calm and measured. "Sir, can you confirm your address?"

Henri's pulse pounded against his skull. He knew they could track the call, but figured he better do what she said.

His hands were shaking, but he managed to whisper the street name and building number, and his apartment number. His eyes remained fixed on the door, half expecting it to burst open at any second.

"How many people are inside your home?" the operator asked, her tone steady but firm.

"I—I don't know," he whispered. "I think—" He cut himself off, his stomach twisting violently as the door handle rattled.

He sucked in a sharp breath, backing up until his spine hit the cold marble countertop.

The operator's voice softened, but there was urgency beneath it. "Sir, stay calm. Officers are en route. Are you in a secure location?"

Henri tightened his grip on the phone. "I locked myself in the bathroom."

"Good. Stay where you are. Keep as quiet as possible."

Henri's knuckles turned white around the phone. He wanted to believe the lock would hold. But deep down, he knew better.

The handle jiggled again. Harder this time.

The operator's voice came through the speaker. "Sir, can you tell me if the intruder is armed?"

Henri didn't answer. Because at that moment, the handle stopped moving.

A long silence. Then—

A thunderous crack as the door exploded inward, splintering around the lock. Henri flinched violently, his phone slipping from his fingers and clattering onto the floor. The screen flickered as the call stayed connected, the operator's muffled voice still echoing from the speaker.

He heard the voice of the operator asking if he was okay, but there was nothing he could do now.

A shadow filled the doorway. One of the men from the archives.

Up close, he was even more imposing than before—broad shoulders wrapped in a dark coat, sharp features cut from stone, his eyes cold and unrelenting. But Henri's gaze was drawn to the pistol in his hand, the sleek black suppressor attached to the barrel, making it feel all the more final.

Henri's breath stalled in his lungs. The man took a step forward, his voice low, almost casual.

"What did you find, Professor?"

The world around Henri narrowed to a single, terrifying point—the gun, the silence, the weight of impending death hanging in the air.

He shook his head, his voice cracking as he answered. "Nothing. I found nothing."

"Don't lie to me." The man's accent was unmistakably English.

"I'm not. I go to the archives all the time to study. It's part of my job. I do my research there."

That part wasn't a lie, but it didn't seem the interloper was buying it.

He tensed his finger on the trigger. "Well, if you didn't find anything, then I guess you won't mind us having a look around your apartment."

"Go ahead," Henri bluffed. "You'll see I'm telling the truth."

The man nodded, and he raised his lower lip as if he might believe the historian.

"Don't worry. We'll make sure to check everything."

His trigger finger twitched. The suppressor barrel puffed a short plume of smoke and flame, and the bullet found the wall behind Henri's head after exiting through the back of his skull.

4

AMSTERDAM

The artifact gleamed under the museum lights, its brass surface catching every flicker of the camera flashes.

Tommy Schultz stood beside the glass display case, his expression a careful balance of confidence and humility as he addressed the gathered media. Around him, dignitaries, scholars, and government officials listened intently, some jotting notes, others merely soaking in the moment.

The Allard Pierson Museum had seen its fair share of significant discoveries, but tonight was different. This wasn't just another historical relic—it was a piece of Dutch heritage recovered from the earth, a link to a time when the Netherlands commanded the seas.

Sean Wyatt leaned casually against a nearby column, arms crossed, watching his friend with a mixture of pride and quiet amusement. Tommy was in his element, speaking effortlessly, relaying their journey in securing the artifact. Sean had no desire to be up there with him. Public ceremonies weren't his thing, and even though he did little to conceal his identity from those who might do him harm, he still tried not to draw attention. There were, after all, still plenty of monsters in the world who wanted him and anyone close to him dead.

He preferred the chase anyway, the thrill of discovery, and in this case, the satisfaction of getting the artifact out of the wrong hands before it disappeared into a private collection.

The artifact—a seventeenth-century astrolabe—rested on a deep blue velvet platform within the museum's most secure glass case.

A brass navigational device shaped like a disc with intricate etchings and a rotating arm, it was one of the few surviving astrolabes from the height of the Dutch Golden Age. It had likely belonged to a high-ranking officer within the Dutch East India Company, used to guide ships across vast and treacherous waters.

Until it was lost. Or rather, buried.

Sean and Tommy had been contacted by the Dutch government after local fishermen in Zeeland discovered something unusual while dredging the bottom of an estuary—an old, rotted wooden crate filled with encrusted artifacts, buried under centuries of sediment. Among the rusted tools and ruined bits of iron, the astrolabe had miraculously survived, its brass resisting the decay of time.

It had taken weeks to authenticate and safely transport the piece without interference. Artifacts like these had a tendency to "disappear" before reaching their rightful resting places, swallowed by the antiquities black market, or hoarded by wealthy collectors who would pay millions to own a piece of history.

Thanks to the International Archaeology Agency, that sort of thing didn't happen as often as it had in the past.

Tommy's voice carried over the crowd. "This astrolabe is a testament to the ingenuity and ambition of Dutch explorers," he said. "It was used to chart unknown waters, to bring ships safely across vast distances. It's a piece of history that, until recently, had been forgotten."

Dr. Ingrid van der Meer, head of antiquities at the museum, stepped forward. A striking woman in her early fifties, with sharp features and an air of absolute authority, she had been instrumental in ensuring the astrolabe made it into the museum's hands.

"This is an extraordinary discovery," she said, her voice even and precise. "Artifacts like these do not surface often, and when they do, they are rarely in such excellent condition. The fact that it has been recovered intact is a miracle in itself. We owe a great deal of gratitude to Mr. Schultz and Mr. Wyatt for securing it."

A ripple of applause spread through the room, punctuated by the click and flash of cameras.

Tommy gave a nod, flashing one of his effortless smiles, but Sean could see he was enjoying himself.

A journalist raised a hand. "Dr. van der Meer, can you speak to the importance of this particular astrolabe in the context of Dutch maritime history?"

She nodded. "Navigation was the lifeblood of Dutch trade in the seventeenth century. Instruments like this astrolabe allowed for precise calculations of latitude, crucial for long voyages. What makes this piece unique is the engraved emblem of the VOC, as well as several notations in Old Dutch, which we believe may indicate modifications made by its original owner. That is something we are still researching."

Another journalist spoke up. "Given its significance, are there concerns that other parties might try to claim ownership?"

A tense silence rippled through the room. It was a valid question. Historically significant artifacts often became contested pieces, with rival nations, private collectors, and even descendants of historical figures making legal or political moves to reclaim them.

Dr. van der Meer's expression didn't waver. "The Dutch Ministry of Culture has verified the provenance of this artifact and has confirmed that it is a national treasure under our laws. There will be no disputes."

Sean wasn't so sure about that. He knew firsthand that history didn't belong to the past—it had a way of bleeding into the present, of pulling people into its gravity.

The applause resumed, and Tommy, standing beside Dr. van der Meer, turned slightly, catching Sean's eye. He winked at his longtime friend as another show, Sean supposed, of feeling like he owned the moment.

Sean just shook his head, barely suppressing a smirk. His friend did love doing this sort of thing. Tommy had been an insecure guy in their youth, always the quiet one of the two. He'd been a touch on the husky side as a youth, but over the years had molded his figure into something more akin to a tank—powerful and muscular. While Sean was functionally strong, and extremely fit for his age, Tommy was easily the stronger of the two.

Another question came from the press section.

"Mr. Schultz, Mr. Wyatt—can you share any details about the retrieval process? Was it as straightforward as it sounds?"

Sean almost laughed out loud. Straightforward? Not even close.

Tommy grinned, glancing at Sean before answering. "Well, it wasn't exactly an afternoon stroll through the Dutch countryside," he admitted, sparking a small chuckle from the audience.

"We had to verify that the find was authentic before word spread," he continued, "which, as you can imagine, wasn't easy. These things have a tendency to attract attention. There were some... let's call them 'interested parties' who would have liked to acquire it for themselves."

Interested parties was putting it lightly.

Sean recalled the "buyers" who had shown up at their hotel in Rotterdam—two men in tailored suits, the kind who never spoke directly but whose presence carried an unspoken warning. They had tried to make an offer. A lot of money.

Sean and Tommy had politely declined.

Then, not so politely.

But that wasn't a story for tonight, or one that needed to be shared publicly. Some of the actions taken by the IAA were best kept in the dark.

Dr. van der Meer took over again, shifting the conversation back to the scientific study and preservation of the artifact.

Sean scanned the crowd, as he often did—partially out of boredom and also as an old habit to make sure there were no threats mixed into the audience.

He recognized several dignitaries and historians among the

guests. The minister of culture was here, as were representatives from the Rijksmuseum and a few international collectors. It wasn't surprising.

Artifacts like this had a way of drawing people out of the shadows.

The questions kept coming, and Tommy handled them like a seasoned diplomat. He had a way of turning dry historical facts into engaging stories, weaving in just enough charm to keep even the journalists engaged.

Sean, still standing off to the side, only partially listened, his mind letting Tommy have his moment while he turned his attention elsewhere. He'd heard all this before—heck, he'd lived it. But the media and museum officials were eating it up, hanging on Tommy's every word.

Dr. van der Meer, standing beside him, spoke next. "We believe this artifact will provide a new lens into Dutch maritime history, particularly in the realm of early navigation techniques. We have confirmed that the engravings along the astrolabe's back panel include markings that are not standard issue—custom additions, likely carved by the officer who used it."

A historian near the front, a man in his sixties with graying hair and thick glasses, leaned forward. "Do you believe these modifications could suggest an alternative navigational method? Something unique to the VOC?"

Dr. van der Meer nodded. "Possibly. This is one of the avenues we're currently researching. If we can cross-reference these markings with existing records from VOC ship logs, we may be able to determine which ship it belonged to and even reconstruct part of its route history."

That got a murmur of interest from the academics. A project like that would take years, but the implications were significant.

Sean barely noticed the conversation now. He had spotted a man standing at the back of the room, close to one of the pillars.

There was something off about him, and the way he lingered just beyond the lights so that Sean couldn't get a detailed look at his face. He wasn't like the other guests, wasn't one of the dignitaries, wasn't a journalist, wasn't even a museum staff member. He was simply... watching.

To most people, the guy would have gone unnoticed. He wasn't technically doing anything wrong.

The man wore a dark peacoat, buttoned up despite the warmth of the room, and his posture was too stiff, too controlled. His hair was short, dark, neatly combed, but something about his expression set off alarms in Sean's head.

He wasn't here for the presentation. His body language, general disinterest in the interview, and the secretive way he clung to the shadows were all dead giveaways that he was up to something.

Was he a thief? A hit man? Were there more of them? Sean found more questions than answers, but he intended to get those soon enough.

Sean's muscles tensed, but he forced himself to move casually, pushing off the column he'd been leaning against. He didn't want to make it obvious that he was watching the watcher.

Keeping to the periphery of the crowd, he moved behind the columns along the side of the aisle, stepping carefully between groups of people, keeping his eyes trained on the back of the room.

The man hadn't moved.

If anything, he seemed even more focused now, watching Tommy and Dr. van der Meer with an intensity that wasn't mere academic interest.

Sean reached the final column and stepped out from behind it. He kept his pace normal, his movements unhurried, as if he were simply heading toward the back to stretch his legs or escape the press of bodies in the center of the hall.

But the moment he reached the spot where the man had been standing—he was gone.

Sean's jaw tightened. He scanned the area. Nothing. No sign of a quick exit, no figure disappearing into the corridors beyond the hall.

It was as if he'd vanished into thin air.

A trickle of irritation ran through him. Had he imagined it? No. His gut was never wrong about these things. Almost never.

Something about this night had just shifted—and what worried Sean most was that he didn't know how, or why.

5

A loud pop filled the air.

Gasps rippled through the crowd as heads snapped toward the sound.

Sean's instincts kicked in hard, his muscles tensing, his hand instinctively shifting toward his waist where—on a normal day—he'd be carrying a weapon. But this wasn't a normal day.

Then he saw it.

A bartender stood near the open bar on the right side of the hall, a freshly uncorked bottle of champagne in his trembling hands, foam spilling onto the polished wood of the counter. His face burned red, clearly aware that every set of eyes in the room had turned toward him.

A ripple of nervous laughter spread through the guests as the tension broke. A few people murmured in amusement, some chuckled, and a man near the front clapped a slow, sarcastic applause.

Dr. van der Meer let out a soft chuckle before stepping back toward the microphone. "Well," she said smoothly, "I suppose that's as good a reminder as any that refreshments are now being served at the back of the hall. Please, enjoy some drinks and hors d'oeuvres, and once again, on behalf of the Allard Pierson Museum, we thank you all for being here tonight."

A round of polite applause followed her words as the crowd loosened, the air shifting from formal attentiveness to the buzz of casual conversation. The attendees began dispersing—some making their way toward the refreshment tables, others lingering near the display case for another look at the astrolabe.

Sean, still near the back of the hall, took in the scene. Everything appeared normal.

He cast one last glance at the spot where the mysterious man had been standing earlier. Nothing. No sign of him.

That should have been a relief. It wasn't.

At the front of the hall, Tommy was immediately surrounded. A mix of dignitaries, journalists, and museum board members took turns shaking his hand, offering congratulations, and slipping in casual questions about his and Sean's adventures.

Sean exhaled, running a hand through his hair as he filtered his way forward, sticking to the edges of the room, avoiding direct entanglements where he could.

He didn't mind mingling—to a point—but there was only so much small talk he could handle before he started mentally planning an escape route.

A server in a crisp white jacket passed by with a tray of champagne flutes, and Sean snagged one without breaking stride. Tommy, midconversation, caught Sean's eye and smirked. "Figured you'd run off already."

"Not yet," Sean muttered, sipping his drink. Champagne wasn't usually his thing, but he'd recognized the high-end brand and knew it was a cut above the norm.

A well-dressed woman in her early sixties, a historian from the University of Amsterdam, turned toward him with a smile. "Mr. Wyatt, I must say, I've heard quite a few stories about you."

Sean raised a brow. "All good things, I hope." He cursed himself silently for the cliché dad answer.

She chuckled. "That depends on who's telling them. But let's just say, I heard about Budapest. Quite the intriguing adventure?"

Sean took another sip, masking his reaction. Budapest. That was an interesting choice.

Tommy turned, clearly amused. "Oh, Budapest? Now that's a story."

Sean shot him a look. "Not one for tonight."

The historian smirked. "Shame. I was curious if all the rumors were true."

Sean forced a smile. He didn't need to rehash Budapest—not here, not now. That little operation had involved a monastery break-in, an underground vault, and a group of men who did not take kindly to their prized relic being removed from their possession.

Some stories were better left untold.

As Tommy continued to work the room with his usual ease, Sean found himself answering a few questions from other guests, mostly the kind he was used to by now.

"Is it true you once found a hidden chamber beneath a Roman temple?"

"Do you actually get chased by mercenaries, or is that just the stuff of legend?"

"Did you really parachute out of a moving cargo plane?"

Sean sidestepped most of them with half-truths and a practiced grin, offering just enough information to keep them entertained but not enough to confirm or deny anything outright. Some of the questions were on the outrageous side and had no roots in any kind of truth. Still, he let the people asking them continue to wonder.

And through it all, he kept his senses sharp. He still hadn't shaken the feeling from earlier.

Maybe it was his old friend, paranoia. Maybe he was just wound too tight from the past few weeks of work. But he didn't think so. His eyes flicked across the edges of the room, scanning faces, checking for anything out of place.

Nothing. But that didn't mean nothing was there.

Tommy, meanwhile, was eating up the attention.

A group of journalists had formed around him, tossing questions his way about the retrieval of the astrolabe and whether he and Sean had encountered any opposition securing it.

Tommy grinned. "Let's just say we had to be a little creative in making sure it ended up in the right hands."

One of the journalists, a young woman with sharp eyes and a press badge clipped to her lapel, leaned in. "You're referring to reports that private collectors were also interested?"

Tommy's smile didn't waver. "I think you'll find that's often the case with valuable artifacts. The real challenge is making sure history doesn't end up gathering dust on someone's private shelf unless it goes through the proper channels first."

Sean grinned into his drink. Good answer.

The journalist scribbled something in her notebook. "And what about your next project? Any new recoveries on the horizon?"

Tommy spread his hands. "History's always waiting to be found, isn't it? But no. Right now, our agents are out in the field on various jobs. As for me and my pal over there, nothing on the docket yet."

The journalist wasn't quite finished. "And Mr. Wyatt? Anything you'd like to add?"

Sean lowered his glass. "Nope. But thanks for coming to the event."

Tommy snorted. "He's not much for speeches."

A few more laughs followed, and the questions kept coming, but Sean had already tuned them out because out of the corner of his eye, he had caught movement—a beautiful woman approaching him.

She was younger, in her late thirties, possibly early- to mid-forties. It seemed to get harder to tell the older he got. Either way, she was walking straight toward him.

The woman moved through the crowd with purpose, her posture upright but not rigid, the kind of confidence that came from years spent commanding the attention of lecture halls and symposiums. Her sharp, intelligent eyes were the color of slate, framed by delicately arched brows that gave her an air of quiet scrutiny. Her auburn hair, streaked subtly with lighter strands, was swept back into a loose but deliberate twist, a few strands escaping to soften her angular features. Dressed in a form-fitting black dress, she exuded a refined but practical elegance, the kind that didn't demand attention but commanded respect.

"Mr. Wyatt?" she said. The accent was clearly English, refined but not overly formal, carrying just enough weight to suggest confidence.

Sean turned and faced the woman who had approached him. There was something else in her expression—something measured. Was it a sort of somberness he detected?

She extended a hand. "Dr. Evelyn Langley. We have a mutual acquaintance."

Sean shook her hand, his grip firm but casual. "Do we?" He suddenly felt a little uncomfortable and hoped she wasn't going to flirt. Where was his wife, Adriana, when he needed her? Oh right. Germany, hunting for another stolen work of art from World War II.

The woman nodded, but no smile accompanied the gesture. "Well, we did. Henri Devereux."

Sean recognized the name immediately. He hadn't expected to hear Henri's name tonight—especially not from a British historian in the middle of a Dutch museum gala. What bothered him more was her use of the past tense—knew.

Sean studied her face. "What do you mean, knew?"

"He was a colleague of mine," she admitted. "He consulted with me often on a project he was working on for many years. We corresponded from time to time—occasional research exchanges. But we weren't close. Still, I was one of the few contacts he had in his records. That's why the Paris police called me."

Sean's brow furrowed. "The police?"

Dr. Langley exhaled slowly, shifting her stance slightly, as though hesitating to say too much too quickly.

"Henri is dead," she said.

Sean went still.

She said it plainly, with no sugarcoating, no prelude. Straight to the point.

Sean's instincts flared hard, but he kept his expression neutral. "What happened?"

Dr. Langley took a small step closer, her voice dropping slightly. "The police found him murdered in his flat two nights ago. Shot."

Sean didn't react outwardly, but his pulse picked up. Murdered? Not a break-in gone wrong. Not an accident. But murdered.

"Home invasion?" he asked. "I can't imagine why someone would want to murder Henri. He didn't bother anyone, as far as I know. Honestly, Tommy is the one you should talk to. He and Henri communicated most of the time."

She ignored the second question, reached into her purse, and pulled out a slightly crumpled envelope, holding it out to him. "I was contacted because my name was in his phone records. But when I arrived, they had already processed the scene." She hesitated, then added, "They let me collect some of his personal effects—his watch, a few books, and this."

Sean took the envelope, turning it over.

"Whoever killed him took his phone. I'm sure they've tried to hack it. We'll likely never know if they succeeded. What do you make of this?"

His stomach tightened.

The name on the front read Tommy Wyatt. The combination of Tommy's first name and Sean's last was a clever move by Henri.

"When I saw this," Langley said, "I knew he meant it for the two of you. Probably wrote it this way so it would go unnoticed."

Sean felt a flicker of reluctant admiration. Even in death, Henri had outmaneuvered whoever killed him.

"The killers had ransacked his apartment looking for something," she said, "Likely this letter—but they hadn't touched it."

"Where did you find it?" Sean asked, still turning the envelope over in his hands.

Dr. Langley gave him a curious look. "On Henri's desk. The apartment had been completely turned over—drawers dumped, bookshelves torn apart, even the floorboards lifted in some places. But this envelope was exactly where he had left it, untouched."

Sean met her gaze. "Because the address is meaningless to anyone who doesn't know what they're looking at. A purloined letter."

Dr. Langley raised an eyebrow. "I'm sorry?"

"'The Purloined Letter' by Edgar Allan Poe," he said. "When you hide something in plain sight, people often miss it."

Dr. Langley crossed her arms. "I haven't read it. Would you mind taking a look at the contents? I haven't opened it."

He admired her ethics.

Sean glanced across the room. Tommy was still deep in conversation with a museum board member, but Sean caught the way his eyes flicked toward them every few minutes, as if waiting for an opening to break away.

"Yeah," Sean said. "We will. Just let me get my friend out of the net he's been caught in."

Fortunately, Sean saw Tommy excuse himself from his conversation and head toward them, his usual confident stride unhurried but purposeful.

Dr. Langley turned at the sound of his approach and gave a polite nod. "Mr. Schultz. We've met before."

Tommy smiled, shaking her hand. "Dr. Langley, right? Cambridge symposium on antiquities recovery?"

She nodded. "That's right. I'm impressed. We only spoke briefly, but I remember you were quite passionate about, what was it... 'keeping priceless artifacts out of private safes'?"

Tommy smirked. "Still am." His gaze slid to Sean. "What's going on?"

Sean gave him a look that said they may have just found their next case. He passed the envelope to Tommy. "This is for you."

Tommy scanned it, then frowned. "This isn't my address."

"Nope," Sean said.

Tommy looked back at Langley. "Where did you get this?"

"Henri Devereux left it on his desk," she said, watching his reaction closely.

"Oh, Henri! How is he? I haven't heard from him in a while."

"He's dead," Sean and Evelyn said at the same time.

"Dead?" Tommy's face darkened. "Oh no. What happened?"

Dr. Langley gave a short version of what she'd told Sean, then explained finding the letter on the desk.

Dr. Langley exhaled. "Henri didn't have family. No next of kin. The police don't seem to be treating his murder as anything more than a home invasion. But I don't buy that."

"There is something else," she added. "It may have to do with the contents of that envelope. Just before he was killed, Henri sent me a series of text messages. Pictures he'd taken of a manuscript he discovered in the archives earlier that evening."

Tommy's curiosity spiked, and he looked back down at the envelope. He peeled it open and removed the folded papers tucked inside.

He unfolded the stack of papers, his brow furrowing as he scanned the dense handwritten notes. Some pages were covered in neat, methodical script, while others were messier, the result of hurried writing—Henri's mind clearly moving faster than his pen.

Sean leaned in, reading over Tommy's shoulder. French, Latin, and occasional English annotations filled the pages, along with dates, names, and locations connected by quick underlined notes. It was a web of research, one that had clearly taken years to construct.

Dr. Langley adjusted her posture slightly, her academic curiosity flaring as she examined the documents. "These are from the National Archives in Paris," she murmured, recognizing the faint official stamps on the corner of some pages. "It looks like Henri was compiling information from multiple historical records."

Tommy flipped to another page. "Some of this stuff goes way back."

Sean gestured toward a section of notes marked with thick red ink. "Look at that," he said, pointing to the piece he'd been reading.

Dr. Langley's eyes moved quickly over the words. French medieval texts were second nature to her, and she recognized the references almost immediately.

"The Secret Gospel of Joan of Arc," she said under her breath.

Sean and Tommy both looked at her. She met their gazes.

Tommy flipped through another page, his eyebrows drawn

together. "This all looks like historical research. Mostly French records, some Latin, a few notations in English. But what was he actually working on?"

Tommy turned another page over, skimming the dense handwriting, then stopped when he recognized a name among Henri's notes.

He tapped the page. "Joan of Arc."

Dr. Langley gave a knowing nod. "That's right. Henri consulted with me several times over the years about her history. His research was focused on one specific artifact."

Sean and Tommy waited.

Dr. Langley continued. "He believed he had found new evidence regarding the lost ring of Joan of Arc."

Tommy's brow lifted. "Her ring?"

"The one she was wearing during her trial," Langley confirmed. "It was taken from her and later given to Cardinal Henry Beaufort, one of her English inquisitors. After that, the records are fragmented —some claim it was lost, others say it was hidden away by the Church, and a few argue it resurfaced centuries later before vanishing again."

Tommy frowned, flipping back to an earlier page. "Henri thought he had found something new about it?"

Dr. Langley nodded. "He was convinced that the official history was wrong, that the ring wasn't lost to time but had been deliberately hidden. And that Joan hadn't been wearing the real ring when she was captured. He'd spent years piecing together fragments of medieval documents, private letters, and ecclesiastical records trying to trace it."

Tommy rubbed his chin, glancing at the notes again. "And he actually thought he was close?"

Dr. Langley gestured to her handbag then pulled out her phone. "Before he was killed, Henri sent me several text messages. I didn't think much of them at first, but when I reviewed them after hearing about his murder, I realized they might be his last attempt to get this information out."

She scrolled through her messages then held up the screen.

Sean took the phone first. The image displayed a faded medieval manuscript, handwritten in uneven script—likely copied by a monk or scholar centuries ago. The ink had faded to a dark brown, but the words were still clear enough to read.

At the bottom of the page, Henri had highlighted a passage.

Sean narrowed his eyes. He could read some of the Old French, though parts of it were difficult.

Tommy read over his shoulder. "What's it say? I can only make out some of it."

Dr. Langley translated slowly. "And she did not fear the flames, for in her hand she bore the mark of the Maiden, the gift which no blade nor fire could sever."

Tommy blinked. "That's... vague."

Dr. Langley took the phone back. "It is, but this is only one of the images he sent. There's more."

She swiped to the next picture. This one showed a different part of the manuscript. It had a name scrawled near the margin, written in an older, more elaborate hand.

Jehanne d'Arc.

Tommy pointed. "That's Joan's supposed real name."

"Supposed?" Sean asked.

"Her true name isn't known; other than the fact we know she wasn't from a place called Darc or Tarc."

Dr. Langley nodded. "This manuscript isn't well documented. It was likely part of a private collection before it found a home in the archives in Paris, or perhaps it was considered too obscure to study seriously. But Henri believed it contained a firsthand account of someone close to Joan—possibly one of her commanders or a member of her household."

Sean looked at the phone again, scrolling further. The next image was a rough sketch, faded with time but still identifiable as a ring.

Beneath it, an inscription in Latin: *Virtus Dei per eam.*

Sean's Latin was rusty, but he caught the meaning. "The power of God through her."

Tommy let out a slow breath. "He really was looking for her ring."

Dr. Langley folded her arms. "And now he's dead."

The weight of the statement settled between them.

Henri had been searching for an artifact that, depending on who you asked, was either a priceless relic, a medieval trinket, or something with far greater significance. To many, it was mythical, a piece of folklore.

But someone had killed Henri for whatever he'd discovered.

Sean glanced at Tommy. "We need to take this conversation somewhere private."

Tommy agreed with a nod. "Yeah. Just let me say some goodbyes, and we can head out." He looked to Evelyn. "You have a place in mind?"

"Yes. There's a quiet café nearby. No one will bother us there."

Sean hoped that was the case, but he couldn't shake the feeling that they'd just jumped into a fire.

6

FRENCH COUNTRYSIDE

Victoria was irritated.

She paced the length of the grand drawing room, her heels clicking softly against the polished marble floor, but she wasn't pacing out of nerves. Victoria Sterling did not get nervous. The pacing was measured, deliberate—an outward display of impatience meant to unsettle the man on the other end of the phone.

The earbuds in her ears remained perfectly in place as she adjusted the phone in her manicured hand, tapping the edge of the screen with one perfectly polished nail. She hadn't spoken in twenty seconds, which, for the man waiting for her response, likely felt like an eternity.

She stopped at the floor-to-ceiling window, gazing out over the rolling hills of the French countryside. The sun had set beyond the vineyards, leaving only a lingering twilight glow that bathed the estate's gardens, fountains, and winding stone pathways in soft, fading light.

Then she finally spoke. "Say that again."

Her English accent was crisp and precise, the tone calm—probably too calm for the man on the phone with her.

There was a hesitation before the reply came. Good. He was

nervous. He should be. He and his team weren't the type to make such careless mistakes.

"The professor is dead," the man repeated. "But we didn't recover what he was working on."

Victoria's jaw tightened, but outwardly she remained composed. She had expected a clean operation. "You killed him," she said, voice smooth as silk.

Another pause.

Victoria's fingers brushed absently along the stem of a crystal champagne flute on the side table beside her, though she didn't pick it up. She turned from the window, letting her gaze settle on the lavish room around her.

The walls of the drawing room were lined with gilded paneling, floral motifs curling across the intricate moldings. The ceiling above was adorned with a rococo-style fresco, its painted gods and muses frozen in eternal reverie. Beneath them, in the warm glow of a tiered chandelier, stood a mahogany writing desk, an antique clock resting atop it, ticking softly—an ever-present reminder that time was a currency more valuable than money. She was a woman who understood true value.

She turned back to the conversation. "You searched the apartment," she said, her voice even but edged with something colder now. "And you found nothing?"

A slight hesitation. "He called the police. They arrived quickly. Our search was hurried. We managed to get his phone."

"Have you been able to hack into it yet?"

"Yes."

Victoria closed her eyes briefly. At least they got one thing right.

She inhaled through her nose, smoothing the silk cuff of her champagne-colored blouse, before speaking again.

"What did you find?"

"He sent a series of pictures to a history professor in Cambridge. Looks like pages from one of the books he was studying at the archives."

"What is this professor's name?"

"Evelyn Langley."

"Do you know where she is now?" Victoria didn't alter the tone of her voice at all. She rarely gave into emotions such as hope or fear.

There was no answer at first.

Finally, he surrendered. "No, but we will know if she goes anywhere. And if she doesn't, we know where to find her. It's only a matter of time."

Victoria almost smiled. That was the wrong answer. "Did you try calling her from Henri's phone?"

"No." He quickly added, "Because Henri plainly said in his text not to take any calls or texts from him, and that he would find her if he could."

A dead end. That wasn't good. But at least they had the name of Henri's last contact. Once they found this Langley, Victoria's team could eliminate the loose end.

"So, you say you got the images sent to this professor, but you didn't find anything else?"

"Nothing in the apartment, ma'am." Mercer was respectful. She had to give him that. The man knew his place.

Perhaps she was overthinking this. Maybe the images were all she needed. Her men were thorough. It was one of their strengths.

She took a slow step forward, the fireplace casting flickering gold shadows across her tailored black slacks, then turned her head just enough to glance at the tall antique mirror near the mantel.

She saw herself reflected there; the olive-toned skin still untouched by time, the hazel eyes sharp with calculation, the chestnut hair swept into a sleek, low chignon. She was in control.

"We need to focus on what we have right now and not on what we don't have. Send me the images of the manuscript. I'll analyze them myself and see what I can learn."

"Of course."

"And find this Cambridge historian. Find out what she knows. Then eliminate her. We don't need any loose ends floating around."

"Consider it done."

"Good."

She ended the call without a send-off and set the device down on a small table next to the window.

Beyond the tall arched windows, the French countryside stretched in rolling waves of vineyards, cypress trees, and distant hills, all bathed in the pale silver glow of the moon. A thin mist clung to the earth, curling over the trimmed hedges of the immaculate estate gardens, where stone pathways wound between marble fountains and sculpted topiaries. The distant silhouette of a château-style gatehouse stood at the entrance to the property, its iron gates locked and unmoving. Beyond that, the dark ribbon of a narrow country road vanished into the trees.

Soon, she would reclaim her birthright.

7

AMSTERDAM

S ean faced the door from his seat at the table in the back corner of the café. He always sat in that position—an old habit that he would never let die.

They had left the Allard Pierson Museum without fanfare, slipping away once the conversations had run their course and the interest of the press had shifted elsewhere. There was no urgency in their departure, but Sean had been aware of every set of eyes on them as they moved through the crowd. He had ignored the feeling of being watched before—he wasn't making that mistake again.

Dr. Langley had suggested the café, a quiet place tucked into a side street just off the main canal, away from the tourist-heavy areas. It was a historian's kind of place, filled with bookshelves along the walls, old maps framed above the tables, and the kind of décor that suggested the owners had a deep appreciation for Amsterdam's past.

Sean had chosen their table deliberately—the farthest one in the back, with a clear view of the entrance and most of the room. It wasn't paranoia. It was habit, and habits like that were the reason he was still breathing.

The café had a timeless charm, the kind of place where conversations happened in hushed tones over strong coffee and well-aged spirits.

A long wooden counter stretched along one side of the room, polished smooth by decades of use. Behind it, a barista with gray-streaked hair moved methodically, tamping fresh grounds into a portafilter before locking it into the gleaming espresso machine. The soft hiss of steaming milk filled the air and blended with the clinking of ceramic cups and the occasional scratch of a pen against a notepad.

The place smelled rich and earthy, a mix of brewed coffee, warm spices, and something faintly sweet—perhaps fresh stroopwafels baking in the kitchen. A faint trace of pipe tobacco lingered near the bar, a sign that the older gentleman near the window had been here long enough to leave his mark in the air.

The lighting was subdued, a mixture of hanging pendant lamps and candlelit tables, giving the space a warm, golden glow. A row of tall, narrow windows framed the street outside, where bicycles lined the sidewalk and the occasional passerby cast a shadow against the glass.

Along one wall, a collection of old books and artifacts sat on display—old compasses, nautical charts, and a rusted Dutch East India Company coin sealed in a small glass case. The décor wasn't just for show; it was a nod to Amsterdam's deep maritime history.

The clientele was a mix of locals and travelers, some hunched over laptops or leather-bound journals, others engaged in low, murmured discussions. No one stood out immediately, but Sean had been around long enough to know that just because someone looked harmless didn't mean they were.

A waitress in a black apron approached their table and set down their drinks with a polite nod.

Sean took a slow sip of his black coffee as the bitterness grounded him for a moment before he shifted his attention back to the others.

"I'm sorry about Henri," Tommy said. "He was a good guy, a truly dedicated historian of the sincerest kind."

Evelyn allowed a slow nod. She took a sip of her drink. "Yes, he was as ethical a person as I ever met. I will miss our conversations. We didn't see each other often, but I felt a personal connection to him. In many ways, he was more than a friend. He was a mentor."

A reverent pall fell over the corner for a minute.

The silence was interrupted by another customer entering the café—a young woman in a bright red dress and a black jacket. She walked over to the counter and got in line to place her order.

"So," Sean said, ending the moment of silence, "Henri really was working on locating the lost ring of Joan of Arc?"

"Yes. And as I said before, it was his life's work. Through it all, the disappointments, the ridicule, he continued despite the naysayers. It seems he got closer than someone wanted."

"Any idea who that might be?" Tommy asked.

"No," she shook her head. "I've been asking myself that ever since I got the call. Henri didn't have any enemies."

"Even in the historical community?" Sean pressed. "Anyone who didn't want him finding the truth about the ring?"

"I'm sure there were some," Evelyn said. "But none of them would go to those lengths."

"You might be surprised. Some folks are threatened when the status quo is. They cling to their dogmatic views like a child with their favorite stuffed toy."

"He's right," Tommy agreed. "We shouldn't rule anything out. Heck, it could be a jealous peer who wants the glory for themselves."

"You really think it could be someone from our community?" she asked.

"Anything is possible. And I'm sure the police are checking every possible angle."

"I'm not getting my hopes up. So many of these things go unsolved every year. One like Henri's seems to fit the bill for that."

"Unfortunately," Sean said, "we have a lot of experience with this sort of thing." He quickly thought through the faces of friends and colleagues they'd lost over the years in such a tragic, similar way. It seemed there was no end of people who would go to the most extreme measures to get what they wanted, and hijack the discovery.

The world of history and archaeology was much more dangerous than most would ever believe, no matter how many exaggerated movies they might see.

Tommy removed the contents of the envelope from Henri and spread them across the surface.

The table, once just a place for coffee and quiet conversation, had now become a makeshift war room—a battlefield of aged paper, frantic notes, and centuries-old secrets waiting to be unraveled.

Sean leaned forward, his hands resting on the worn wood as he scanned the chaotic arrangement before him. Evelyn's phone, propped against her coffee cup, displayed the last images Henri had sent; photos of the medieval manuscript he had discovered in the archives.

It was all connected. Somehow. They just had to figure it all out, which was easier said than done.

Tommy exhaled loudly. "All right. We need a system. If we keep staring at this mess, we're just going to confuse ourselves."

Sean nodded, already separating the notes into different piles. "We have two sets of information here. The images Henri sent Evelyn before he died and the notes he left for Tommy. Whatever he discovered, it's hidden somewhere in these."

Evelyn, her brow furrowed in thought, picked up one of Henri's pages. "Henri was methodical. He wouldn't have written down anything unnecessary."

Tommy smirked. "So what? You're saying he left us a perfectly written guidebook to Joan of Arc's secret treasure? Because that would be awesome."

Sean shot him a look. "More like breadcrumbs—and we need to follow them."

He grabbed the first page and studied the text. The script was hurried, uneven, different from Henri's usual clean and structured writing style. That meant one thing—Henri had been rushed when he wrote this. And for a historian who was always deliberate, that said a lot.

Sean's gaze landed on a specific passage heavily underlined in red ink. "Where the light was born, the secret rests."

Evelyn sat up straighter. "That sounds almost identical to the passage in the manuscript." She flicked back to the photo Henri had sent of the ancient text. "Here—'The Maiden's light does not dim, for in the hollow of her beginning, it remains.'"

Tommy frowned. "That's interesting. The maiden is definitely a reference to Joan."

"Right," Sean agreed. "That hollow of her beginning is a tad creepy."

Evelyn glanced between the notes and the image, biting her lip. "Henri wouldn't have focused on this if he didn't believe it was real."

Tommy leaned on the table and rubbed his chin. "All right. So, 'where the light was born'—you think that's supposed to mean Joan of Arc's birthplace?"

Sean considered it then shook his head. "Not sure. It seems more specific than that."

He rifled through another set of Henri's notes then pulled out a page covered in doodles and diagrams. Unlike the others, this page had no historical excerpts or translations—it was purely Henri's own thoughts.

At the top of the page, a single word was scrawled in bold ink: *Domrémy*.

Evelyn inhaled sharply. "Her hometown."

Tommy tapped the page. "So we're on the right track. But that's a whole town. Where exactly are we supposed to be looking?"

Sean flipped through another few pages, looking for anything Henri might have marked. Then he found it. A rough, hand-drawn sketch. Not a map. Not a structure. An object. A circular stone basin.

Sean's heart kicked up a beat. He recognized it instantly. "The baptismal font," he said, and pushed the page toward the others.

Evelyn's breath caught. "The Church of Saint-Rémy."

Tommy sat back and blinked in disbelief. "Are you saying Henri thought something was hidden in the church where she was baptized?"

Sean ran a hand through his messy blond hair. "Think about it. Joan of Arc wasn't just born in Domrémy. She was baptized there. That's the moment she was brought into the faith—the first formal step on the path that made her who she was. If you're looking for 'the hollow of her beginning,' that's it. That's where the light was born."

Evelyn's gaze flicked back to the manuscript image on her phone. The words suddenly made sense.

Tommy pointed at the sketch of the font. "Okay. But why this? Why would someone hide something inside a baptismal font? And that was a long time ago. What are the odds it isn't there?"

Sean grinned. "Pretty sure defying the odds is kind of our thing."

He studied another passage in Henri's notes. His eyes narrowed. "Maybe it's because that was the only place they knew would never be disturbed."

He read aloud another hurried note scribbled by Henri: "A hollow space beneath. Sealed. No record of removal." He looked over at Tommy. "Guess that answers the question."

Evelyn's lips parted slightly. "It's been there for centuries."

Tommy whistled. "That is… actually genius."

Sean sat back and stared at the baptismal font sketch with renewed understanding. "If Henri was right, then we're looking at something that's been hidden inside that church since Joan of Arc's time."

Silence fell over the table.

Sean could feel the weight of the moment, the realization that they had just uncovered something Henri had died for.

Tommy exhaled, breaking the silence. "Well. That was easy."

Sean gave him a flat look. "You call that easy?"

Tommy smirked. "No. I'm trying to be positive."

Evelyn shook her head, but a small, exhilarated smile had formed on her lips. "So we know where to go. The Church of Saint-Rémy in Domrémy."

"We?" Sean asked.

"I'm a part of this now whether you like it or not. And don't try to tell me it's not safe. It's only a matter of time before Henri's killer figures out who else he's spoken to about this. I'm in."

Tommy leaned back in his chair while tapping the table with a rhythm that only came when he was anticipating trouble. "Can't argue with that."

Sean raised an eyebrow. "I don't like it. But I can't tell you what to do. Henri was your friend too." He turned to Tommy. "I guess we're leaving Amsterdam earlier than scheduled."

8

PARIS

The steady hum of voices blended with the rolling echoes of wheeled luggage gliding across polished floors as Sean, Tommy, and Evelyn stepped into the arrivals terminal of Orly Airport. The fluorescent lighting overhead cast a cool, sterile glow over the massive hall, a space constantly in motion, filled with the restless energy of travelers who had just arrived or were eager to depart.

Sean and Tommy had chosen this airport over the larger Charles de Gaulle, primarily because there would be fewer people, and it was easier to get in and out.

The scent of brewed espresso, fresh pastries, and faint traces of jet fuel lingered in the air, a sharp contrast of luxury and industry that defined one of the busiest airports in the world. The towering glass-paneled windows reflected the constant stream of movement—businessmen in sharp suits tapping at their phones, exhausted families wrangling children, groups of tourists clutching their maps and luggage while scanning overhead signs for directions.

A distant announcement crackled over the intercom in both French and English, instructing passengers on a flight to Montreal to proceed to their gate. Near one of the many café stands, a pair of uniformed airline pilots sipped espresso, engaged in quiet conversation while a woman in a dark trench coat rushed past them, heels clicking against the marble floor as she hurried toward a waiting taxi.

Sean took in every detail automatically, not because he expected trouble but because old habits die hard. He never walked into a place like this without scanning the exits, noting security personnel, and getting a sense of who was paying attention to them.

Tommy, on the other hand, was already stretching. "Man, I hate long flights. I could go for some of that famous French cuisine, though."

Sean shook his head while adjusting the strap of his bag over his shoulder. "We're not here for fine dining. Let's find our contact."

"Maybe just a quick croissant?"

Sean rolled his eyes at his friend. "I'm sure our liaison will be taking us somewhere good to eat."

Tommy resigned to the loss, pulled out his phone and began scanning his messages.

"Jean-Marc should be waiting for us near ground transportation," he said.

They moved past a row of glass-walled boutiques where luxury brands displayed their newest collections for bored travelers willing to drop a fortune between flights. A perfume shop exuded the cloying scent of expensive fragrances, mixing with the warm, buttery aroma of a bakery selling fresh pain au chocolat and croissants.

They exited the bustling terminal and walked outside where the air was noticeably cooler. The space was lined with rows of rental car counters, taxi stands, and designated pickup points, everywhere bustling with activity as drivers held signs for arriving passengers and freelancers who had evaded security lured tourists into their private cars.

he transition from the sterile, climate-controlled interior to the crisp, open night was immediate—a stronger scent of jet fuel mixed with damp pavement and the exhaust fumes from dozens of nearby idling vehicles, all of it mingling with the lingering aroma of pastries from the nearby cafés inside. Sean almost asked Tommy if he'd lost his appetite. Sean's eyes locked onto a man near one of the support columns, standing with his hands in the pockets of his wool coat.

Jean-Marc was in his late thirties, his salt-and-pepper hair neatly combed back, and his wire-rimmed glasses perched on the bridge of his nose. He had the academic air of a historian, but the sharpness in his gaze suggested he was no stranger to discretion.

As they approached, Jean-Marc offered a polite nod. "Monsieur Schultz." His French accent was refined—clipped but not heavy.

"Jean-Marc," Tommy greeted, shaking his hand. "Thanks for coming on such short notice."

Jean-Marc turned to Sean and Evelyn, offering them a warm but reserved smile. "I assume you are the friends Tommy mentioned. Pleasure to meet you," he said.

"Good to see you again," Sean said, shaking his hand.

"Always, my friend," the Frenchman said with a smile. The two gave each other a quick hug to go with the handshake, then Sean let go and indicated Evelyn. "This is Dr. Evelyn Langley," he added.

"A pleasure," Jean-Marc said. He shook her hand then motioned toward the exit. "We should get going. My car is in the car park outside."

Sean didn't miss the way Jean-Marc scanned the area before leading them toward the waiting car.

Sean exchanged a glance with Tommy. This historian wasn't just a liaison.

Beyond the drop-off zone, a steady stream of taxis, private cars, and shuttle buses lined up, their headlights cutting through the dim glow of the streetlights. Horns honked intermittently, impatient drivers trying to maneuver through the congestion of travelers loading luggage into trunks and saying hurried goodbyes.

Jean-Marc led them toward the covered pedestrian walkway that stretched toward the airport's multilevel car park. The concrete pathway was lined with sleek metal railings, its floor still damp from an earlier drizzle, reflecting the soft glow of overhead lights.

As they entered the car park, the sounds of the airport faded slightly, replaced by the muffled echo of footsteps and distant car doors slamming shut. The air was cooler here, carrying the faint scent of oil and rubber, the unmistakable mix of metal and asphalt found in every parking garage.

Jean-Marc walked with purpose as he weaved through rows of parked vehicles, his gaze continuously flicking to his surroundings with subtle vigilance. They reached his car—a black Citroën DS7 Crossback, its sleek, polished exterior reflecting the dim overhead lighting.

He unlocked it with a click. "This is me," he said while opening the rear passenger door for the lady. She thanked him and slid inside the perfectly clean interior.

"Did you bring the items we requested?" Tommy asked when her door was closed.

"Of course."

Jean-Marc moved around to the back and opened the trunk. Inside lay a matte-black metal case with a combination. He turned the numbers to the required sequence, then opened the lid. Inside the case, in a black foam cushion, lay a pair of Springfield XD .40-caliber pistols, along with four spare magazines.

"My favorite flavor," Sean said, reaching in to take one of the guns. He ran a quick check over the weapon, ejected the magazine and noted the rounds inside, then pulled the slide to make sure one wasn't in the chamber. It was empty. Sean dry fired the pistol as he always did as a safety precaution then stowed the weapon in a shoulder holster Jean-Marc had provided in the case.

Tommy repeated Sean's process and quickly concealed his weapon before a black sedan drove by. They didn't need people to see them packing, and with the level of surveillance employed by the government, they'd have to be extra careful. The party would be over before it started.

"I know how much you like the Springfields," Jean-Marc said.

"And I know you're partial to SIG Sauer. Both great options. I would have been cool with one of those too."

"Because you're a man of good taste," the Frenchman said with a wink.

He loaded up their belongings in the back, fitting the bags together like in a game of Tetris, then closed the trunk door and got into the front seat.

Sean cast one last glance around the quiet car park then slipped into the passenger seat. He couldn't shake that annoying feeling that they were being watched. Sometimes it felt like that sensation was always around—perhaps an occasionally lingering paranoia left over from his secret government service—though in truth it was only in times such as these, when they were on a mission to uncover something, that he felt it most acutely.

The Citroën hummed as it pulled away from the airport, merging onto the highway that stretched toward the French countryside. The Parisian skyline loomed in the distance; the illuminated structures softened by the early evening haze.

Inside the car, Jean-Marc drove with practiced ease, his hands steady on the wheel. Sean sat in the front passenger seat, while Tommy and Evelyn occupied the back. The interior was quiet, save for the occasional hum of passing traffic and the rhythmic clicking of the turn signal.

Jean-Marc was the first to speak. "I was sorry to hear about Henri." His voice was steady, but Sean felt there was a genuine heaviness to his words. "When Tommy called, I assumed the situation was urgent, but I had no idea how bad it was."

Evelyn, who had been gazing out the window, turned back toward him. "You knew him well?" She tried to switch away from the murder and focus on Henri.

Jean-Marc nodded. "Yes. He and I crossed paths many times over the years. We weren't close, but I respected him. He was an honest historian, a rare breed." He let out a soft breath. "He never let politics or personal gain interfere with the pursuit of truth. That kind of integrity is hard to come by."

Sean watched Jean-Marc carefully. The man wasn't just offering condolences—he was assessing their reactions, reading them the way a trained operative would.

"We appreciate your help," Sean said, drawing the driver's attention. "We needed someone we can trust. You fit that bill."

Jean-Marc's lips pressed into a thin line. He nodded. "You can always count on me, my friend."

During one of Sean's Axis missions, Jean-Marc had been with the French special forces. He'd been a tremendous asset during the mission, and ever since the two had an unspoken bond that those who'd never served would never understand.

Sean shifted slightly, adjusting his seatbelt. "Henri was murdered for what he found. The police won't call it that, but we all know the truth."

Jean-Marc's grip on the wheel tightened slightly, a barely perceptible motion. "Based on where we're going, I'm assuming this has something to do with Joan of Arc. I know Henri was working on something to do with her. What exactly did he find?"

Sean answered first. "We're still figuring that out. We only know the location."

"Well, we think we know," Tommy corrected.

Jean-Marc didn't look convinced, Sean thought, but the Frenchman didn't push. Instead, he focused on the road, maneuvering effortlessly between slower vehicles.

Evelyn pulled out her phone and scrolled through the images Henri had sent her before his death. "He was working on something tied to Joan of Arc's lost ring. His research led him to believe it wasn't destroyed or lost in some forgotten collection—it was hidden. Intentionally."

Jean-Marc raised an eyebrow. "And you agree with this?"

"We do," Sean said. "At the very least, it's plausible. Henri was onto something. And he was murdered hours after making a breakthrough. That's not a coincidence."

Jean-Marc exhaled slowly. "No. It's not."

Tommy leaned forward slightly. "You ever hear anything about the ring? Any legends or whispers?"

Jean-Marc considered the question. "There were always stories, but nothing credible. Some believed it was taken by one of her followers before she was captured. Others said it was hidden after her death to prevent it from falling into the hands of the English. But no one ever found any proof."

Sean glanced at Evelyn. "Seems Henri did."

Evelyn nodded. "And he left us enough to follow his trail."

Jean-Marc's gaze flicked toward the rearview mirror, watching them for a moment before returning his focus to the road. "And that trail leads to Domrémy?"

Tommy smirked. "It's our best guess. And at the very least, it's a place directly tied to Joan."

Jean-Marc's expression didn't change, but Sean noticed something in his posture shifted slightly. "Her birthplace."

Sean nodded. "And specifically, the Church of Saint-Rémy."

Jean-Marc absorbed this, his mind working behind his calm exterior. "If you're right, and Henri was onto something…" He trailed off, exhaling sharply. "It's a good bet whoever killed him is still on the hunt."

Sean watched him carefully. "Yeah, we usually operate under that assumption. Don't think I don't see you checking the mirror every few seconds. I guess you'll let us know if we have a tail."

Jean-Marc didn't answer immediately. Instead, he adjusted the rearview mirror, his expression sharpening. His left hand rested on the wheel, but his right hovered closer to his coat, where Sean had no doubt a weapon was concealed.

"We have a tail," Jean-Marc said evenly.

"Wait. What?" Sean turned around and looked out the back window.

"Dark gray Renault Megane," Jean-Marc said.

Sean found the vehicle several cars back. It followed at a steady distance, keeping two cars between them but maintaining their speed.

Tommy, catching the shift in mood, frowned. "How long?"

Jean-Marc's voice was low, controlled. "Since we left the airport. I noticed them merging onto the highway a few seconds after us."

Tommy tried to be optimistic. "Could be a coincidence."

Jean-Marc's jaw tightened. "Could be. But they're staying back at the same distance as when they left."

Sean shook his head, still looking back. "They're keeping pace, not passing, not falling back."

Tommy muttered under his breath, "Yep. That's not a coincidence."

"What are you going to do?" Evelyn asked, clearly not accustomed to these kinds of scenarios.

Jean-Marc was already adjusting his approach. "We're going to lose them," he said, as if the answer should have been blatantly obvious.

He eased off the gas, letting a few cars slip ahead of them. The Renault followed suit, matching their change in speed, and remaining several cars back.

Jean-Marc's expression darkened. "That's confirmation enough."

Sean flexed his hands. He felt the pistol under his arm calling to him like an old friend who always showed up at just the right time.

Evelyn swallowed but kept her composure. "So what now?"

"Now we lose them."

9

The headlights in the mirror hadn't wavered.

Jean-Marc tightened his grip on the wheel, his jaw clenching as he weaved through the steady flow of Parisian traffic. The gray Renault had been shadowing them since they left the airport, maintaining a careful but deliberate distance, never overtaking, never falling too far back. A hunter tracking its prey.

He exhaled slowly. No room for reckless moves. Not yet.

The thick air inside the car was heavy, making everyone inside feel trapped as if in a box.

Sean sat in the front seat, eyes fixed ahead but keenly aware of the situation. Tommy and Evelyn, in the back, had stopped speaking altogether. There was no need to state the obvious. The danger was real, and it was right behind them.

Jean-Marc flicked his gaze toward the digital clock on the dashboard. Only a few minutes had passed since he had confirmed they had a tail, but it felt far longer.

The streetlights overhead cast long, shifting shadows across the wet pavement as they passed beneath. A low fog clung to the streets, swirling slightly as their tires cut through the damp air. The last remnants of light drizzle dotted the windshield, streaking slightly as the wipers cleared away the moisture.

Spring. The transition between seasons had left Paris damp and cold, the scent of wet stone and exhaust fumes lingering in the air.

Sean watched Jean-Marc inhale, appearing to steady his thoughts. Sean knew he'd been in worse situations—much worse—and had details about a few of them.

Sean's instincts told him one thing: Whoever was in that Renault was patient. They weren't in a hurry. They weren't trying to force a confrontation. They wanted to follow.

Jean-Marc kept his voice low and controlled as he spoke. "We're taking the next exit."

Sean didn't argue. Neither did Tommy nor Evelyn.

The sign for the upcoming off-ramp flashed past—a narrow exit leading off the main highway and into a more urban district. Jean-Marc took it without hesitation, turning onto a wider boulevard lined with Haussmann-style buildings, their pale stone façades glowing softly in the ambient city lights.

The roads were still active but quieter than the highways. Pedestrians walked along the sidewalks, some glancing toward their vehicle as it maneuvered through the intersections. Cafés and brasseries still had life in them, their outdoor seating areas speckled with Parisians enjoying late-night meals and cigarettes.

Sean checked through the rear window again. The Renault was still there. It had taken the exit behind them, just as he suspected. It had made no attempt to hide its pursuit. The driver was either careless or didn't care that they were easy to spot.

Jean-Marc didn't make a sound, didn't change his expression. He simply turned onto a smaller side street, winding through the denser urban core, where the roads narrowed between older buildings and alleyways that disappeared into darkness.

Sean noticed the shift immediately.

Jean-Marc nodded, eyes scanning ahead. "Just a quick test," he said.

Tommy let out a slow breath. "They're not breaking off."

Evelyn glanced out the rear window. The Renault had maintained distance, never gaining, never retreating. They weren't making a move.

The road sloped slightly as they entered a district with taller apartment buildings, their balconies cast in deep shadow. A couple on the sidewalk shared an umbrella, laughing softly as they passed a parked motorbike. The hum of distant sirens wove into the city's soundtrack, a low and constant reminder that there was rarely a dull moment in Paris.

Jean-Marc took another turn. Then another. Each time, the Renault adjusted seamlessly.

It was amateurish at best. At least that's what Sean was tempted to think.

Jean-Marc tapped his fingers once against the wheel. He turned onto a narrow street lined with shuttered bookshops and dimly lit art galleries. The kind of place where the road was just wide enough for two passing cars but with nowhere to pull off easily.

The Renault followed, still patient.

Jean-Marc took a left at the next light. Then a right. Looping back onto another road parallel to the one they'd just driven.

Sean caught it in the mirror—the Renault was now two cars behind.

Tommy shifted in his seat. "We're still not losing them."

"Relax," Jean-Marc said. "We will in a moment."

Jean-Marc navigated the streets of Paris with practiced precision, making another calculated turn down a narrow street lined with shuttered storefronts, iron-lattice balconies, and rows of parked scooters. The Renault remained behind them, a dark specter lingering in the rearview mirror, patient and unshakable.

The hum of the city surrounded them—the faint blare of a distant siren. The glow of streetlights reflected off the rain-slick pavement, streaks of amber and white sliding across the windshield like brushstrokes.

Sean looked back again, his posture relaxed but his muscles coiled beneath the surface, ready. In the back, Tommy and Evelyn remained silent, though Sean could feel the weight of their attention pressing against the tension inside the car.

Sean couldn't help but wonder who they were dealing with.

"We're almost there," Jean-Marc finally spoke, his voice even but laced with what seemed like calculated intent.

Sean wondered where *there* was but didn't ask, trusting the Frenchman to know what he was doing.

Jean-Marc flicked the turn signal and veered onto a wider boulevard. The buildings became taller, more modern, though the charm of old Paris still lingered in the wrought iron railings and stone façades.

Then Sean saw exactly what Jean-Marc was doing.

Several police vehicles sat parked along the street, engines idling, uniformed officers standing near the entrance of a large stone building with the distinct markings of the Paris Police Prefecture. A police station.

Sean exhaled sharply, a mixture of admiration and amusement surfacing as he finally understood Jean-Marc's game.

Clever, he thought.

Jean-Marc pulled up right in front of the police station, guiding the car into a vacant space along the curb. He shifted into park, resting his hands on the steering wheel as if they'd simply stopped for a casual break.

Sean didn't look back immediately. He didn't need to. The Renault was still behind them. But now, it had a problem.

They were parked in front of a fully staffed precinct, in plain view of armed officers standing outside. No way the pursuers would try anything with all these cops around.

Sean finally turned his head, watching as the Renault rolled slowly past them, gliding through the intersection. The darkly tinted windows revealed nothing of its occupants.

Jean-Marc, with a calmness that bordered on mockery, raised a hand and gave them a slow, deliberate wave, the kind of wave reserved for a parent teasing a child or a predator taunting prey.

Sean caught a subtle shift behind the tinted windshield—a movement—slight but unmistakable. Whoever was inside had noticed. He guessed they weren't happy about it.

The car didn't stop. It just continued down the street, vanishing into the depths of Paris.

Sean exhaled slowly. "Well played."

Jean-Marc finally leaned back. "Not my first rodeo," he said with a smirk.

From the back seat, Tommy leaned forward, his head tilting slightly as he peered past Sean, looking toward something across the street. His stomach growled audibly.

A small, warmly lit bakery sat nestled between two other storefronts, its golden light spilling onto the wet sidewalk. A fresh tray of croissants was being placed behind the glass display, the scent of buttery dough and warm sugar somehow reaching across the road.

Tommy sighed dramatically. "I know this probably isn't the time, but that croissant I wanted earlier?"

Sean didn't even look at him. "Let it go."

Jean-Marc chuckled under his breath as he pulled away from the curb, steering them back onto the streets of Paris.

They had lost their tail. But Sean knew that didn't mean they were safe.

Not by a long shot.

10

Mercer watched the side mirror, waiting for his prey to reappear. He sat in the passenger seat of the gray Renault Megane, his fingers lightly drumming against the armrest as he observed the Paris Police Prefecture from a discreet distance.

The street outside was alive with the quiet rhythm of the city—pedestrians lingering near late-night cafés, the occasional whine of a scooter weaving through traffic, the steady hum of idling engines. The scent of damp pavement and lingering tobacco smoke hung in the cool night air, mingling with the distant aroma of fresh bread from a nearby boulangerie.

Mercer barely noticed any of it. His focus was on the car parked outside the police station, and more specifically, the men inside.

His initial interest had been Dr. Evelyn Langley, a historian from Cambridge with a known specialization in medieval artifacts. But she wasn't the problem. She was an academic, not a soldier. The real concern was the men traveling with her—Sean Wyatt and Tommy Schultz.

Mercer had already dug into their backgrounds.

Tommy Schultz had been an easy read—his life was well documented. A well-respected archaeologist and historian, he had founded the International Archaeological Agency after his parents had supposedly perished in a plane crash. A tragic story, one that had fueled his relentless pursuit of lost history.

He wasn't just a scholar—he was a man with resources, connections, and experience.

And then there was Sean Wyatt.

On paper, Wyatt's life was straightforward—an IAA field operative, a skilled investigator, and security and transportation specialist for artifacts.

But Mercer had seen gaps in his record. There was a missing period in Wyatt's history, a section of time between his college years and his official employment with the IAA. That was a red flag.

Mercer had encountered similar gaps before, always in men who had worked in the shadows. Intelligence operatives. Soldiers in black-budget programs. Ghosts who had been trained for things the public would never hear about.

Sean Wyatt had the markings of a man with classified experience. And that meant Mercer had to assume he wasn't just an artifact hunter.

He pressed his lips into a thin line. This was going to be interesting, at the very least.

His thoughts were interrupted by movement in the mirror.

Through the windshield, he watched the dark Citroën pull away from the police station, slipping back into the traffic. Mercer didn't react.

Instead, he pressed the comm in his ear, his voice calm.

"They're moving."

The response came instantly from the second vehicle he'd ordered to follow farther behind, a black Renault Megane, still on the street a few blocks back.

"I see them," the driver said. "Falling in line."

Mercer allowed himself a slow, knowing smile. They thought they had lost him.

The trick had been a clever one. Pulling into a parking spot in front of the police station would certainly deter most people in Mercer's situation. But he'd taken precautions beforehand.

He wasn't one to bet everything on one play. He always had a backup.

His car had been made by Wyatt, but the one following behind had gone unnoticed. It remained out of sight, far enough back to remain unseen by Wyatt or his driver.

Mercer turned to the driver and gave a nod. "Let's move."

A voice crackled to life in response. "Maintaining visual," reported the driver of the black Renault Megane trailing Wyatt's vehicle from a prudent distance.

Mercer's eyes narrowed, tracking the Citroën as it merged into the sparse late-night traffic on the street. He turned to his driver, Levi. "Let's not lose them. Take Boulevard du Palais, then loop around to Quai de l'Horloge. We'll intercept from there."

Levi nodded, smoothly guiding the Renault into motion. The vehicle glided through the wet streets, tires whispering against the slick asphalt. As they navigated the turns, the illuminated façades of Parisian architecture cast fleeting shadows across Mercer's contemplative face.

"Status?" Mercer inquired; his tone clipped.

"They've turned onto Rue d'Arcole, heading toward Quai de la Corse," the second driver relayed.

Mercer processed the information swiftly. "Maintain your distance. We're repositioning to Quai de l'Horloge. We'll parallel their route along the river."

The gray Renault emerged onto Boulevard du Palais, the imposing silhouette of the Palais de Justice looming to their left. Mercer's gaze flicked to the stately structure, a fleeting acknowledgment of its historical gravity, before refocusing on the task at hand.

"They're approaching Pont d'Arcole," the voice in his ear continued.

"Copy. We're on Quai de l'Horloge now," Mercer replied. "We'll shadow them from this side of the Seine." As Levi steered the Renault onto Quai de l'Horloge, the Seine River stretched out to their left, its surface shimmering under the city lights. The reflection of the Hôtel de Ville danced upon the gentle ripples; a picturesque scene lost on Mercer's focused mind.

"They've crossed the bridge and are continuing along Quai de l'Hôtel de Ville," the second driver updated.

Mercer calculated the trajectory. "That way," he said, pointing at the next street up.

The gray Renault maintained a steady pace, the hum of its engine blending with the ambient sounds of the city. Mercer's fingers drummed lightly on his knee, a subconscious manifestation of his strategic mind at work.

"They've made a right onto Rue du Renard," came the next report.

"Interesting choice," Mercer mused.

Levi glanced at Mercer, awaiting instructions.

"Adjust our route. Take the next right, then left after that," Mercer directed.

The Renault responded seamlessly, weaving through the labyrinthine streets with practiced precision. Mercer's earpiece buzzed again.

"They're heading west."

A satisfied smile tugged at Mercer's lips. "Perfect. We'll merge behind you. Keep your position."

"Yes, sir," the second driver acknowledged.

As the gray Renault approached the intersection, the iconic Louvre Museum came into view, its glass pyramid glistening under the ambient glow. The city's heartbeat was palpable, a blend of history and modernity converging in the nocturnal tableau.

Levi expertly merged into the flow of traffic, positioning their vehicle several car lengths behind the other Renault. Mercer's eyes scanned the road ahead.

He tracked the dark Citroën carrying Sean Wyatt and his team as it blended into the steady flow of traffic.

Both vehicles continued to trail at a careful distance. Its driver, a quiet professional from Mercer's team, reported over the comms, "They're maintaining a steady pace, no unusual maneuvers."

The highway's asphalt stretched out beneath a sky obscured by a thin layer of clouds, with the distant city lights fading into the dark expanse of the French countryside. Mercer's mind worked methodically, mapping out the potential route that Sean's crew would follow. For now, his prey were oblivious to the silent pursuit.

As the Citroën moved steadily along the autoroute, the men in the tail vehicles remained silent. There was no need for any chatter now. Mercer didn't want any distractions.

Mercer allowed himself a brief smile. "Good. Let them think they're alone on the road."

He glanced at his own dashboard clock.

The black Citroën continued straight, unbroken by any sudden lane changes or unexpected stops. Mercer's voice, measured and cool, broke the silence over the comms once more. "Stay alert for any sign of acceleration or deviation. If they make a move, be ready to adjust our distance accordingly."

A soft static replied from the black Renault, affirming that everything was proceeding as planned. Mercer's thoughts drifted momentarily to the implications of their pursuit. The obliviousness only heightened his anticipation; soon enough, their path would converge with a destination he had deduced long ago—Domrémy, the birthplace of Joan of Arc, and the location that Henri Devereux's research ominously pointed toward.

As they neared an interchange on the autoroute, Mercer maintained his focus as the driver let the car drift subtly toward the right lane, positioning it in such a way that the black Renault could easily switch lanes if needed. Mercer's own vehicle remained hidden behind the dark silhouette of a ramp, its presence masked by the subtle curves of the road.

"They're still heading west," the other driver said, his voice calm.

Mercer's eyes glinted with quiet determination. The silence in his car was punctuated only by the soft hum of the engine and the occasional murmur from the comms, a reminder that every detail mattered. They were following a predetermined route, and Mercer knew it was only a matter of time before they reached the critical juncture.

Then, as the Citroën continued along the dark highway, Mercer's comms crackled with a new update: "They're approaching the on-ramp for the A86."

Mercer's pulse quickened imperceptibly. The A86 was a well-known route out of Paris, and it would lead them toward the countryside—and eventually to Domrémy.

His mind raced through his next instructions. "Maintain current distance," he ordered. The black Renault's driver acknowledged in a low tone.

Mercer's gaze fixed on straight ahead as the vehicle maintained its steady pace.

His driver didn't need to be told what to do. The man naturally slowed down a little, letting another car pass by in the parallel lane, putting a little more distance between them and their quarry. Staying the same distance back was a dead giveaway of their intentions.

As if on cue, the lead car following their marks did the same thing, slowing down a little to allow the same passing vehicle to get between them and the IAA agents. They would accelerate again at some point, perhaps closing the gap but for now, there was no need.

Mercer and his team had the Americans and their companions right where he wanted them.

11

DOMRÉMY, FRANCE

Sean didn't feel comfortable the entire ride to Domrémy. He'd looked back several times to see if their tail had reappeared, but he never saw the gray Renault. The drive to the small French town seemed to take much longer than it actually did, and every moment felt as if it were pressing down on him with the weight of a sumo wrestler.

Finally, they arrived at the exit to Domrémy, and Jean-Marc guided the vehicle off the highway. The landscape transitioned from the expansive stretches of the French autoroute to the intimate charm of rural northeastern France. The moon cast a pale hue over the countryside, accentuating the gentle undulations of the terrain. Fields of vibrant green, interspersed with patches of wildflowers, stretched out on either side of the narrow road, leading them toward the historic village of Domrémy-la-Pucelle.

Sean checked back through the rear window again, even though he knew Jean-Marc had been looking in the rearview mirror almost every minute of the journey. There was no sign of the gray Renault, and for the first time since they left Paris, he felt his fight-or-flight response ease a little.

Nestled in the heart of the Meuse Valley, Domrémy-la-Pucelle exuded a serene ambiance, its quaintness amplified by the surrounding natural beauty. The village held a profound significance as the birthplace of Joan of Arc, a legacy that permeated every corner of the locale.

As they approached, they were greeted by the Basilica of Bois-Chênu. Perched on a gentle rise overlooking the village, the basilica's impressive architecture exuded a reverence held for the Maid of Orléans. Its spires reached skyward, silhouetted against the dark canvas above, while intricate stone carvings adorned its façade, narrating tales of valor and faith. The basilica, though constructed centuries after Joan's time, had become an integral part of the village's identity, drawing pilgrims and history enthusiasts alike.

Descending from the basilica, the road meandered into the heart of Domrémy-la-Pucelle. Cobblestone streets, polished smooth by time, wound through clusters of traditional stone houses. These dwellings, with their sloping roofs and shuttered windows, bore the marks of generations, each telling its own story of the past. With the windows down, the scent of freshly baked bread wafted from a local boulangerie and mingled with the earthy aroma of the surrounding fields, creating an olfactory tapestry that was both comforting and evocative of a simpler France now long gone.

Tommy's stomach growled again. Everyone in the car was hungry now, and they'd already discussed a place to have a good meal once they had arrived at the inn where they would stay for the night.

Central to the village stood the smaller Church of Saint-Remy, a modest yet venerable structure where Joan of Arc was baptized. Its weathered stone walls and simple bell tower exuded an air of solemnity, grounding the village in its historical roots. Adjacent to the church, a modest stone cottage marked Joan's birthplace. Preserved through the ages, this humble abode offered a tangible connection to the past, its walls silently bearing witness to the early life of the young girl who would alter the course of French, and English, history.

The village square, though small, bustled with a quiet energy. Locals engaged in leisurely conversations, their voices a gentle murmur against the backdrop of rustling leaves and distant birdcalls. A fountain burbled softly at the center, its clear waters reflecting moonlight. Children played nearby, their laughter ringing through the air, a testament to the enduring spirit of the community.

Surrounding Domrémy-la-Pucelle, the landscape unfolded in a patchwork of agricultural fields and dense woodlands. The Domrémy Wood, a small, forested hill to the west, rose gently, its trees whispering secrets of bygone eras. The Meuse River meandered nearby, its waters glistening, provided a lifeline to the flora and fauna that thrived along its banks.

Jean-Marc guided the car onto a narrow cobblestone street shaded by mature trees whose leafy branches formed a gentle canopy overhead. The street was quiet, its tranquility only broken by the soft hum of their vehicle and the distant chirping of birds settling in for the evening. On either side, charming stone cottages and small storefronts stood close together, their rustic façades adorned with climbing ivy and vibrant flower boxes bursting with color.

At the end of this picturesque lane stood the inn, a quaint two-story structure built from aged, honey-colored stone that seemed to glow softly in the moonlight. The roof was pitched steeply, covered in slate tiles weathered by decades of gentle rain and seasonal snow. Wooden shutters painted a faded, pleasant blue flanked each of the inn's windows, some open to allow a refreshing breeze to flow through the rooms within.

Jean-Marc slowed the car as they approached and maneuvered into a gravel parking lot tucked discreetly behind the building. The tires crunched gently over loose stone and came to rest beneath a large, leafy chestnut tree whose canopy stretched across the parking area. Only a handful of other vehicles occupied the lot, emphasizing the intimacy and quiet charm of their accommodations.

From their position in the lot, they could see a small garden extending from the rear of the inn, enclosed by a low stone wall.

Wooden tables and chairs were arranged neatly on a terrace, inviting visitors to enjoy a relaxing evening beneath the string lights that hung gracefully from tree to tree.

Warm lamplight glowed from inside the inn, illuminating an inviting lobby where an antique wooden desk awaited their arrival. The innkeeper, visible briefly through the window, prepared to welcome them, reinforcing the sense of hospitality that enveloped Domrémy.

Jean-Marc switched off the ignition, and the peaceful silence of the countryside returned, settling gently over the travelers as they prepared to step out into the soft night air.

The group climbed out of the car and collected their sparse belongings from the trunk, then followed Jean-Marc to the entrance.

The front of the inn was marked by a heavy wooden door painted the same faded blue as the shutters and framed by weathered stone arches. Iron lanterns hung on either side, casting a soft golden glow onto the threshold, welcoming guests into a small, sheltered porch area paved with uneven stones polished smooth by generations of footsteps. Above the doorway, an antique wooden sign swayed gently, depicting the faded emblem of a knight's shield entwined with ivy. A few pots of vibrant geraniums stood beside the entrance, adding splashes of color and warmth to the charming, rustic façade.

The Frenchman led the way through the entrance and into the foyer beyond.

The moment they stepped inside, a gentle warmth embraced them, enhanced by the soft glow of bronze wall sconces that cast flickering light across the exposed wooden beams above. The scent of aged oak and freshly brewed coffee mingled in the air, blending with a faint trace of lavender from a nearby vase perched on an ornate side table.

The front desk was a sturdy, hand-carved piece of mahogany, polished to a warm sheen, its surface adorned with a brass service bell and a neatly stacked ledger book. Behind it stood the concierge, an older gentleman with kind eyes and a posture that suggested both patience and experience. His vest and crisp white shirt, paired with a well-worn pocket watch chain, fit seamlessly with the inn's rustic yet refined atmosphere.

To the right of the foyer, an inviting breakfast area was set with small round tables, each covered in linen and neatly arranged with porcelain teacups and silverware. A large stone fireplace dominated one corner, its hearth lined with stacked logs and an iron poker, though the embers within had long since cooled from the morning's use. The walls bore paintings of the French countryside, each framed in dark wood, depicting rolling fields, vineyards, and the occasional historic château.

Further in, a cozy lobby space extended beyond the front desk, featuring plush armchairs and a long, tufted settee positioned around a low wooden coffee table stacked with books about the region's history. A grandfather clock ticked softly in the corner, its rhythmic sound blending with the distant murmur of conversation from deeper within the inn.

Jean-Marc walked over to the desk worker and spoke to him about their reservations while the other three looked around the interior.

The man behind the desk pecked away at his computer for a moment, then passed the credit card and identification he'd received back to Jean-Marc. The concierge thanked him with a pleasant smile and then returned to his previous tasks while Jean-Marc returned to the group with the room keys.

"Here you are," he said, handing out the plastic cards. "Seems even a traditional inn such as this has kept up with the times in regard to room security."

"I would have expected a skeleton key," Tommy half joked.

"So," Jean-Marc said, "Dr. Langley has a room for herself, while our rooms are on either side. I hope that is acceptable."

Evelyn nodded, as did Sean and Tommy.

Sean didn't like the idea of her being alone, especially considering the trouble they'd almost found themselves in earlier today. Someone had been following them, and if they somehow found their way here to this village, the danger was still lurking close by.

"Let's get to our rooms and unpack," Sean suggested.

"Yes, and then can we please, please for the love of all that is good, go get some food?" Tommy pleaded.

"Of course, Schultzie," Sean answered with a smile, his tone as if he were talking to a child. "You're a growing boy, after all."

12

"What do you have for me?" the woman's voice said calmly through the earpiece of Mercer's phone.

"We're in Domrémy."

"Interesting. One of the key places where we narrowed our search. Her birthplace." The casual reference to Joan of Arc almost sounded like the woman knew her on a personal level.

"Yes, ma'am. They checked into an inn ten minutes ago."

"Will they go to the church, then?"

"It's getting late. They may wait until the morning."

"Do I need to ask if you were spotted?"

The question came as an insult, but Mercer let it go. "No. We weren't."

He couldn't be absolutely certain that statement was true, but he didn't know it wasn't either. As far as he could tell, Wyatt and his companions hadn't noticed them since the police station in Paris. And they'd not reacted to the other car following them, and they'd not diverted course since trying to lose the tail in the city.

There was no reason to think they'd been made. Or so he told himself.

"You're sure?"

Mercer had expected the follow-up question and prepared himself not to express irritation or defensiveness.

"Yes. I'm sure. We believed, if you recall, that this was one of the places they might visit. Once we knew the direction they were headed, it was simple enough to hang back farther to remain unnoticed."

"Very well. What is your plan now?"

Mercer shifted in the seat of the car, his eyes remaining fixed on the inn at the end of the street. "We will keep an eye on them throughout the night. I doubt they're going anywhere. They must have found something that relates to the church, or perhaps something else here in this village. But my guess is the church."

"As is mine."

"If they try to go anywhere this evening or in the morning, we'll know about it."

"If they found a clue that leads to something in the church, they'll be eager to get to it in the morning. Stay as close as you can without being detected."

If there was one thing Mercer hated, it was being micromanaged. He didn't need his employer—a woman who had spent the majority of her life sunbathing at luxurious resorts on the Mediterranean, living off a massive trust fund—telling him what to do. She was a spoiled brat, but a brat with extensive resources, and power she'd wielded expertly behind the scenes in global politics and finance. For that, Victoria deserved his respect. But that didn't mean she should tell him how to do his job.

"We'll take care of it."

"Good. Let me know when you have something to report."

She ended the call, leaving Mercer there with the device against his ear. He held it there for a moment then lowered it and looked over at his driver. He pressed the button on the radio and spoke.

"Listen up. Our targets are going to be here for the night, from what it looks like. So it's likely they may go eat at one of the local restaurants."

He knew his men were hungry after the long day and a bite to eat before taking their post at the inn would keep them alert. Mercer would send out a couple of the men to grab foot while he and the others stayed in place. It was a waiting game now, and Mercer knew how to play.

13

Sean and Tommy stepped out into the hall, where Jean-Marc waited. He stood in front of Evelyn's door as she changed clothes and cleaned up a bit.

"Still in there, huh?" Tommy asked.

"Yes," Jean-Marc said in a curt tone, as though the answer should have been apparent.

"June takes a long time to get ready for stuff too."

"Where are we going to eat?" Sean asked.

"There's a little place a few blocks from here. It's a traditional French country place. I think you'll like it."

"You're not going to try to get us to eat snails, are you?" Tommy wondered.

Jean-Marc grinned like the devil in a hot tub. "Only you, my friend."

The door to Evelyn's room opened, and she stood at the threshold for a few seconds, effortlessly captivating despite the simplicity of her attire. Her dress was understated—a soft, pale green that echoed the lush countryside they'd traveled through earlier—yet it complemented her perfectly, accentuating the warmth in her eyes and the graceful lines of her figure. Her reddish hair fell softly over her shoulders, framing a face illuminated by a quiet confidence and gentle charm. In that moment, Evelyn's natural elegance made anything more extravagant seem unnecessary.

Jean-Marc gestured for the others to follow as he led the way back to the elevator, whose soft chime announced its arrival. The four of them stepped inside, the warm glow of the overhead light casting long shadows against the polished wood paneling. The descent was smooth and silent, save for the faint mechanical hum of the lift lowering them toward the ground floor.

"Where are we going?" Evelyn asked, curious.

"A local place," Jean-Marc said.

"Apparently, they aren't going to serve us snails," Tommy joked.

She made a sound of disgust at the mere thought of eating the slimy creatures, to which Jean-Marc merely shook his head.

As the doors slid open, they moved through the cozy foyer, past the front desk where the concierge offered a polite nod. The scent of fresh-baked bread and that earlier trace of lavender from a nearby arrangement lingered in the air, a reminder of the inn's quiet charm. The atmosphere was inviting, but their focus was now on the evening ahead.

Pushing through the entrance, they stepped outside into the crisp, night air. A cool breeze drifted through the cobbled street, carrying the scent of earth and distant woodsmoke, hinting at the approaching night.

In the parking lot, the light crunch of gravel beneath their feet filled the quiet space. The world outside was still, save for the occasional distant murmur of voices from the village.

"Are we walking?" Evelyn asked.

"Yes, it isn't far from here," Jean-Marc answered. "This way."

The four of them set off down the narrow street, the cobblestones beneath their steps still holding traces of the day's warmth. The air had the crispness of night, carrying the scent of damp earth and woodsmoke from distant chimneys. The gentle rustling of leaves accompanied their footsteps as a breeze whispered through the trees lining the road.

Sean looked around now and then, taking in the surroundings but also surveying the area for trouble. He hadn't noticed anything suspicious, but that might well mean that if someone were watching them, they were doing a good job of staying out of sight.

Domrémy was settling into the evening. Golden light spilled from windows, illuminating the stone and timber-framed houses that flanked the quiet streets. Many of the homes bore those flower boxes beneath their windows they'd noticed earlier, still vibrant with late-season blooms in shades of deep red, violet, and soft yellow. A few villagers moved about—an elderly man watering potted plants along his stoop, a woman hanging freshly laundered linens on a small wooden rack, and a couple chatting in hushed tones as they strolled in the opposite direction.

The smells tugged at Tommy's stomach, and for a moment he considered suggesting they go there instead of wherever Jean-Marc was taking them. He resisted, though, and decided to trust their guide to take them somewhere that would be more than satisfactory.

As they neared their destination, the village square came into view, centered around a modest stone fountain, its waters shimmering like silvery blades in the moonlight. A few children played nearby, their laughter light and carefree, their shadows dancing in the glow of old-fashioned streetlamps.

The restaurant stood just beyond the square—a charming establishment housed in an old stone building with wooden shutters painted a deep burgundy. Above the entrance, an ornate wrought iron sign hung from a curved bracket, its lettering elegant yet slightly worn from years of exposure to the elements. It swayed gently in the evening breeze, the faint creak of metal blending with the quiet sounds of the village. The door itself was thick, aged wood, its surface darkened with time and use, adorned with black iron hinges and a matching handle, shaped in the style of old French craftsmanship. A small lantern, affixed just beside the frame, cast a soft glow over the entrance, inviting guests into the warmth within.

Small tables and chairs were arranged outside, though only a few were occupied, as most diners had chosen to sit inside where the atmosphere was cozier.

Through the large front windows, the soft amber glow of candles and low-hanging lights illuminated the rustic interior, where tables were neatly set with linen napkins, delicate glassware, and earthenware plates.

As they stepped inside, the welcoming vibe of the restaurant wrapped around them, a comforting feeling that made every person who entered feel like they were home. The scent of simmering sauces and freshly baked bread filled the space, mingling with the quiet hum of conversation. The interior was cozy yet refined, with low wooden beams, soft candlelight, and shelves lined with bottles of wine from the surrounding regions. A waiter in a crisp white apron passed by, carrying a steaming plate of something that smelled richly of butter and herbs.

A young hostess, petite with dark curls pinned neatly behind her head, greeted them with a welcoming smile. She wore a simple black dress and a white apron tied at the waist, embodying the effortless charm of French hospitality.

"Bonsoir, messieurs, madame," she said, her accent soft. "Welcome. Will you be dining inside or on the terrace?"

Jean-Marc offered a polite smile. "Inside, please. In the back, if possible."

"Of course," she said with a nod. She reached for a stack of leather-bound menus from the polished wooden stand near the entrance, then gestured for them to follow.

The restaurant's interior was a blend of rustic charm and understated elegance, a space where history came alive. The walls were made of exposed limestone, their rough texture softened by the glow of wall sconces and flickering candlelight. Overhead, dark wooden beams stretched across the low ceiling, their aged surfaces hinting at centuries of stories whispered within these walls.

The floor was laid with wide terracotta tiles, their surface worn smooth by the passage of time. Along one side of the room, a large stone fireplace dominated the space, its hearth filled with smoldering embers, casting a faint orange glow that flickered across the tables. Above the mantel, a collection of vintage wine bottles and copper pots gleamed in the soft light.

Small vases filled with fresh lavender and rosemary sprigs added a delicate fragrance to the already intoxicating aroma of simmering butter, roasted meats, and fresh-baked treats wafting from the open kitchen in the back.

A long wooden bar, polished to a deep luster, ran along one side of the restaurant, its shelves lined with local wines and aged spirits. A chalkboard menu hung above it, listing the evening's specials in elegant cursive script.

They moved past tables of locals and travelers alike, weaving through the warm glow of candlelit chandeliers, until she led them toward the back of the room where a corner table awaited, offering both privacy and a perfect view of the rustic dining space—and the front door.

The hostess stood by while Jean-Marc and Sean took seats with their backs to the wall, while Tommy and Evelyn sat opposite.

Once they were seated, the hostess handed out the menus and told them their server would be by momentarily. She returned to the stand at the front of the room while the visitors opened the menus and began perusing the offerings.

The menu was a simple yet elegant leather-bound booklet, its cover embossed with the restaurant's name in subtle gold lettering that had slightly faded with time. Inside, the pages were made of thick, cream-colored parchment, the text printed in flowing, hand-scripted French, with smaller English translations beneath each item for visiting travelers.

The starters included classic French fare: French onion soup with melted Gruyère, a delicate pâté de campagne served with toasted baguette slices, and a salad of fresh greens, walnuts, and Roquefort cheese drizzled with honey vinaigrette.

The main courses showcased the best of the region's rustic cuisine. A tender coq au vin, slow-braised in red wine with mushrooms and pearl onions, shared the spotlight with a duck confit, crisp-skinned and rich, served with rosemary-roasted potatoes. For those craving something heartier, there was a bœuf bourguignon, its deep, velvety sauce infused with wine, thyme, and smoky lardons.

Seafood lovers could opt for a trout amandine, fresh from a nearby river, pan-seared with butter and almonds, accompanied by a side of haricots verts. There was also a vegetarian option—a ratatouille of eggplant, zucchini, and tomatoes, slow-cooked in olive oil and herbs.

For more serious vegetarian diners, the menu offered a selection of thoughtfully crafted dishes that highlighted the region's fresh, seasonal produce. A ratatouille, made with slow-cooked eggplant, zucchini, bell peppers, and tomatoes, simmered in fragrant olive oil and Provençal herbs, stood as a hearty centerpiece. Another option was a wild mushroom risotto, its creamy arborio rice infused with earthy truffle oil and topped with shaved Parmesan. For something lighter, a warm goat cheese and walnut salad was drizzled with honey and served alongside a crisp baguette. Each dish was designed to be simple yet deeply flavorful, embracing the essence of French countryside cuisine.

The desserts were elegantly simple: a velvety crème brûlée with a perfectly caramelized top, a light and airy chocolate mousse, and a tarte Tatin, its caramelized apples glistening against a buttery pastry crust.

To accompany the meal, the back page featured an extensive wine list, highlighting local Meuse valley reds and crisp whites from Alsace, carefully selected to pair with the dishes on offer.

Although he wouldn't try to order everything on the menu, Tommy took his time with the descriptions, seeming to carefully consider each item as he imagined his perfect French dinner.

"Everything on this menu is incredible," Jean-Marc said, setting his down on the table in front of him. "You're sure to enjoy whatever you order."

A few seconds later, a waiter in a black vest and matching tie over a white button-up shirt and black slacks appeared around the corner and walked over to the table.

"May I get you something to drink to get started?" he asked in French. The waiter, a man in his early twenties with salt-and-pepper hair and sharp, observant eyes, stood attentively beside the table. His demeanor suggested he had worked here for a few years, moving with the effortless grace of someone who had long perfected the art of hospitality.

Jean-Marc leaned back slightly, scanning the wine list with practiced ease before settling on his choice. "A bottle of Côtes du Rhône," he said smoothly, selecting a medium-bodied red with notes of blackberry, pepper, and earthy spice, an excellent complement to both the heartier dishes and the lighter fare. "And four waters, please."

The waiter gave a small approving nod while jotting down the order. "I will bring out some bread for you in a moment." He slipped away, leaving the warm glow of candlelight flickering across the polished wooden table.

After the four had figured out what they wanted to order, Jean-Marc rested his elbows on the table and folded his hands together near his chin.

"So, what time would you like to visit the church in the morning?"

"As soon as they open," Sean answered without hesitation.

"Fine. What do you need from me?"

"I doubt the people running the place would like us snooping around," Tommy said. "We do tend to make a mess now and then."

"Now and then?" Sean questioned with a raised eyebrow.

"I mean, we don't always do it."

Evelyn allowed a smile to ease across her face, and a muted laugh escaped her lips. "Are you two always like this?"

Sean snorted. "That's a question we get a lot."

"I'm not surprised."

"I'm sure we can work something out to keep prying eyes away from your efforts," Jean-Marc said. "It would help if you would be discreet."

"We'll do what we can," Sean said.

"Yeah, we can do discreet," Tommy added.

The waiter returned with a basket and set it down in the center of the table. Freshly baked French bread rested atop a white napkin.

"Are you ready to order?" the young man asked.

"Yes, I believe so," Jean-Marc answered in French. "You ready?" he asked the others.

They all nodded that they were.

The waiter looked to the lady first.

She flashed a brief smile, and her fingers traced the edge of her menu before she spoke. "I'll have the duck confit with the roasted potatoes, please."

The waiter gave a small nod and jotted it down before turning to Tommy.

"I'll go with the bœuf bourguignon," Tommy said without hesitation. "And if it comes with bread, bring extra."

The young waiter chuckled. "Of course, monsieur."

He then turned to Sean, who set his menu aside and leaned slightly forward. "I'll take the ratatouille," he said. "And a little extra baguette on the side."

The waiter arched a brow. "You also want extra bread?"

Sean smirked. "No thanks. I'm good," he said, casting a sidelong glance at Tommy.

The waiter gave a knowing nod before finally looking to Jean-Marc.

Jean-Marc exhaled through his nose, taking a brief glance at the menu once more, though he already knew what he wanted. "Coq au vin," he said simply.

The waiter scribbled the last order, offered a polite nod, and collected the menus. "I'll bring out your wine shortly." He turned and disappeared toward the kitchen, leaving the four of them to settle in for the evening.

The group talked while they waited for their food, discussing the plans for the morning and how they would have to be careful navigating the church so as not to arouse suspicion. The conclusion they collectively reached was that there was no easy way to do that, and that they would have to play it by ear once they were at the old building.

Twelve minutes—a kind of land speed record for a French kitchen—passed before the waiter returned with the first plates of food. Then the table descended into a hungry din, the kind that seemed to settle over a table when a group of people were truly enjoying their meal.

The four plowed through the food as if they hadn't had anything to eat in days. In truth, they hadn't eaten in a while, and once they finished dessert—one of the best crème brûlées Sean had ever tasted—they felt full and more than a little lethargic.

"That was incredible," Tommy said, taking in a long, deep breath to wash down the dinner.

"Glad you're feeling better," Sean said. "You should sleep like a baby tonight."

"Yeah, that did not suck."

The waiter returned with the bill, and Tommy quickly retrieved his credit card and passed it to the young man before Jean-Marc could do it.

"You're not paying for our food too," Tommy insisted. "You're already going far out of your way to help us."

"Yeah, your money is no good with us, brother," Sean added.

"Thank you," Jean-Marc said with a coy smile.

"Yes, thank you so much," Evelyn offered.

The four collected their things and walked back out of the restaurant, a little slower than when they had come in.

They stepped out into the cool air of night.

"Is there a bar around here where we could get a drink?" Evelyn asked, obviously not satiated by the extraordinarily good wine they'd just consumed.

Jean-Marc was looking across the street at a narrow thoroughfare between a couple of old buildings; a clothing boutique and a cheese shop. He quickly snapped out of his daze and smiled. "Of course. This way. There's one not far from here."

He led them away from the building at a brisk pace. When they'd gone roughly thirty steps, Jean-Marc raised his right arm and pointed at a building up ahead on the other side of the street.

"Just keep walking," he said with a calm smile.

"Okay," Evelyn answered. "Wasn't that the plan?"

"Yes. But we're not going to a bar."

"We're not?" Tommy wondered. Then the realization hit him before Jean-Marc spoke again.

The Frenchman leveled his gaze and met Tommy's. "We've been followed after all."

14

"Followed?" Evelyn asked, a little louder than the three men would have preferred. Fortunately, it didn't seem her voice reached the other side of the street. There was no echo, and a young couple standing outside a café didn't look over at them.

"Two men," Jean-Marc clarified. "One standing in that little alley back there across the street. He wasn't smoking, wasn't doing anything except standing there."

"Maybe he just didn't feel like waiting until he got to a bathroom," Tommy half joked.

"He wasn't doing that either. He was also sticking to the shadows. Wasn't easy to see him."

"You said there were two," Sean said without being so foolish as to look back at the alley, or search the street behind them for the other man.

"The other was in a coffee shop one building over. He's by the window. Stared at us the entire time we were standing outside the restaurant."

Evelyn frowned. "That couldn't have been more than thirty seconds."

"More than enough to be creepy," Sean said.

"Or ill intentioned," Jean-Marc added quickly.

"So where are we going?" Evelyn asked.

"The inn. We can hang out in the bar downstairs for a while, watch the doors for anything suspicious."

"Then what? What if we do see something suspicious?"

"We'll take it from there," Sean said. "But you might want to plan on sleeping in a room with me, just to be safe."

"Oh really?" she scoffed at the idea for obvious reasons.

"We both know I'm married, and fiercely loyal to Adriana," Sean poked back.

"Yes, I know. I was only messing with you."

Sean detected a hint of disappointment in her voice, and wondered for a moment if maybe Jean-Marc should stay in a room with her. He wasn't married, after all. But Sean doubted she would go for it. She'd only just met Jean-Marc that day, and though he'd proved himself so far, that kind of trust needed more than just an afternoon to develop.

They moved in silence, the four of them walking at a measured, natural pace, their steps in sync with the quiet rhythm of the village settling into the evening. The knowledge that they were being watched also walked between them, unspoken but understood.

Jean-Marc led the way, his posture at ease, as though he were simply enjoying the night air. But Sean caught the subtle shifts in his movement, the way he kept them in the middle of the sidewalk, not too close to doorways or alleys, and the way he occasionally flicked his gaze toward reflective surfaces to catch glimpses of what lay behind them. The instincts of a man who had spent years in dangerous places.

Sean matched the pace, keeping his shoulders relaxed, his hands casually tucked into his jacket pockets, as though the biggest concern on his mind was whether the bar they'd intended to visit had decent whiskey. He didn't turn his head, didn't look over his shoulder. He didn't need to. He could feel it. The sensation of being followed, the weight of unseen eyes just beyond his periphery. It wasn't paranoia. He knew the difference.

Tommy walked beside him, maintaining the easygoing demeanor he carried so well, but Sean knew he had already mapped out the streets around them in his mind. How many possible exits. Where the shadows were deep enough to disappear into. Just like old times.

Evelyn was the only one who didn't have a past in fieldwork, but she was smart, and she followed their lead. No nervous glances, no fidgeting, just quiet composure. Sean noticed her clutching the strap of her purse a little tighter than before, but otherwise, she moved with the same deliberate grace she always carried.

The village had gone quiet, the kind of stillness that came when most people had retired indoors for the night. The warm glow of streetlamps flickered against the deepening night. A few shops remained open, their interiors spilling soft light onto the cobbled walkways.

Somewhere in the distance, a dog barked once then fell silent.

Their footsteps echoed faintly, swallowed quickly by the narrow streets.

Jean-Marc took them along the most direct route back to the inn, avoiding any unnecessary turns that might have suggested they were trying to shake someone. They had no interest in a chase. Not yet.

They passed a narrow alley where an old iron lantern hung from a wooden beam overhead, its glass cracked, the light within flickering unsteadily. Sean caught movement in its reflection. Just a faint shift in the background, too deliberate to be natural.

He resisted the instinct to look. Instead, he adjusted his stride slightly, keeping it fluid.

Tommy must have noticed too because he gave the smallest nod; a signal they had used for years. A silent way of saying, "Yeah, I saw it too."

Ahead, the inn came into view, its soft golden light spilling onto the quiet street. It was one of the few buildings still illuminated, its wooden sign swaying gently with the night breeze.

They kept their pace steady, no rush, no urgency.

As they reached the entrance, Jean-Marc placed his hand lightly on the door handle, pausing just long enough to listen. Not to the voices of the patrons inside but for the absence of sound behind them. The kind that meant someone had stopped moving, someone who didn't want to be heard.

Then, without hesitation, he pushed open the door and stepped inside like a man with not a single concern in the world.

Sean followed, then Evelyn, and finally Tommy, who let out a quiet, almost imperceptible exhale as he shut the door behind them.

The inn's interior was alive with conversation, a stark contrast to both the quiet streets outside and how relatively empty the lobby had been earlier. The low, rustic beams overhead seemed to trap the sound, amplifying the murmur of voices, the occasional burst of laughter, and the clinking of glasses against wooden tabletops. The warm glow of candlelight and hanging lanterns bathed the space in a golden hue as they flickered against the aged stone walls.

To the right of the entrance, the bar stretched nearly the entire length of the room, its polished oak counter lined with locals and travelers alike, each nursing drinks in various states of half-finished conversation. The bartender, a broad-shouldered man with rolled-up sleeves and a neatly trimmed beard, worked as efficiently as his appearance suggested as he poured wine and pulled pints from brass taps, his movements quick and practiced.

Behind the bar, shelves stocked with bottles of deep reds, crisp whites, and aged spirits gleamed in the dim light. The scent of spilled beer, oak, and something faintly herbal—perhaps absinthe—hung in the air. A pair of men near the bar spoke in hushed but animated tones, gesturing over their drinks. A woman in a dark dress leaned against the counter, laughing at something the bartender had just said.

Across the room, smaller tables were packed with guests, most engaged in meals that had now turned into long, lingering conversations over drinks. The occasional clatter of cutlery echoed as waiters weaved through the crowded space, balancing trays of wine glasses and plates carrying the last remnants of evening meals. A fire crackled in the stone hearth, adding to the thick, comforting warmth of the inn.

Sean took all of it in without looking like he was taking it in.

The front door was behind them now, but there was another entrance—a side door leading to a narrow alley, one that could be used for deliveries or for slipping in unnoticed. He scanned further, spotting the back hallway where the inn's private rooms were located, and another door that likely led to the kitchen and staff areas.

Jean-Marc had already spotted the same details.

Without a word, he led them to a corner table near the far wall, a position that allowed them a full view of the room and every exit. It was a calculated move—a quiet, unspoken understanding among men who had seen the wrong side of too many seemingly harmless situations.

Evelyn slid into the seat with her back against the wall, her expression carefully neutral, but Sean could see the tension in the way she held herself. Tommy, on the other hand, looked as relaxed as ever, though Sean knew better. His friend had chosen the chair closest to the main dining area, the most open seat, but also the one where he could move the fastest if necessary.

Jean-Marc took the seat directly across from Sean, his back to the wall that ran alongside the side door. He reached for the menu on the table, glancing at it in what looked like casual interest, but Sean knew it was just a cover.

Sean leaned back slightly in his chair, letting his gaze flicker over the room one more time. No sign of the men who had been watching them.

Not yet, anyway.

"So," Jean-Marc said, "here we are. Now what's your plan?"

"We wait," Sean answered. "Maybe they do something stupid and come in here. But I doubt it. The only reason they would do something like that is to intimidate us."

"Intimidate?" Evelyn asked.

"What he means," Tommy took the question, "is that when pros like that come in and show their hand, it means they know we know."

"You think they will do that?" Concern stretched across her face, and deep lines crossed her forehead.

"No way to know for sure," Jean-Marc said. "But now that we know they're here, they must have already guessed where we were headed. Following was just a byproduct. Whatever it is you three are here to find, they want it too."

"So, we just sit here and wait? For how long?"

Sean shrugged. "As long as it takes. I doubt they know which rooms we're in, but this is a small place."

"You think they may try to come to our rooms?"

Sean had considered the question before she asked it. Now every pair of eyes at the table was on him.

He wasn't going to say what he was thinking; that a small inn like this may have an innkeeper whose morals were for sale. It would be an easy thing for those men to bribe whoever was working the front desk for a little information on four of the occupants. At some point, money always meant something. It was just a question of the price.

"I don't think it's a good idea to stay here," he admitted.

"Okay," Jean-Marc said, throwing up his hands as if he couldn't think of another answer. "Do you have any ideas?"

Sean grinned. "Actually, I do. But it requires a little help on your end."

Jean-Marc raised an eyebrow. "Oh?"

"How well do you know this building?"

15

The inn had fallen into the stillness of late night, the once-lively hum of conversation now reduced to the occasional creak of aging floorboards and the distant clink of glassware as the last of the bar patrons finished their drinks. Outside, the streets were deserted, the only movement coming from the occasional flicker of a curtain as some sleepless villager peered out into the darkness.

Steven Mercer pushed open the heavy wooden door, stepping into the dimly lit lobby with his men flanking him. The air inside was thick with the lingering scent of woodsmoke and spiced wine, but beneath it, Mercer could smell something else. The weight of the night. The anticipation of what was coming.

The night manager sat behind the front desk, half distracted as he scribbled something in a ledger. He looked up as Mercer approached, his expression shifting from mild annoyance to wary concern when he took in the size of the men standing behind him.

"Bonsoir," Mercer greeted smoothly, placing a folded stack of euros on the counter. Crisp bills, easy money. "I need some information."

The manager blinked, then straightened his vest. "I—I'm not sure I can—"

One of Mercer's men, a broad-shouldered brute with a shaved head and cold eyes, casually parted his jacket, revealing the sleek grip of a pistol nestled against his side. He didn't say a word. He didn't have to.

The manager's throat bobbed as he swallowed hard, his gaze flicking between the money and the gun. Mercer smiled faintly. "Take the money. Then take a break. Fifteen minutes, maybe twenty. Go outside, breathe some fresh air. When you come back, everything will be just as you left it. I am looking for a couple of Americans. They would have come in here with a woman, and another man, a Frenchman. I need their room numbers."

The manager hesitated only a moment before his greed overpowered his fear. He scooped up the cash, tucked it into his pocket, and reached for a small card from behind the desk. With trembling hands, he scribbled down three room numbers and slid it across the counter. Mercer picked it up, glanced at the numbers, then folded the card into his pocket.

"Take your break," he reminded him.

The manager nodded quickly, grabbed his coat, and slipped out the side door, disappearing into the night.

Mercer turned to his men, his expression unreadable. "Let's go."

The stairs creaked softly under their weight as they ascended to the second floor. Mercer moved with the deliberate confidence of a man who had done this before. His men followed, silent as shadows, their movements disciplined and controlled. At the top of the stairs, Mercer unfolded the card and glanced at the numbers again. Three adjacent rooms. He lifted his head, and his eyes scanned the dimly lit hallway. He signaled with his hand, and his men moved with precision.

Two men split off, taking positions at either end of the corridor to ensure no one slipped past them. Two more took up positions outside to watch the exits.

Mercer stepped forward, pulling on a pair of black leather gloves, smoothing them over his fingers with practiced ease.

"This is clean," he murmured, his voice low and even. "No one leaves breathing."

One of his men, a wiry figure with ice in his veins and a knife strapped to his vest, gave a slow, approving nod. "Understood."

Mercer listened carefully.

Nothing.

The hallway was silent save for the faint groan of wood settling under its own age. No voices. No sounds of movement from inside the rooms.

"Asleep?" one of his men whispered.

Mercer didn't answer right away. His instincts were sharp, honed from years of operations just like this. But something about this felt... off. Too easy.

Mercer retrieved his phone and typed out a single message to the men stationed at the stairwell. "Ready."

There were three rooms for them to check, and Mercer had no way of knowing who was in which. Not that it mattered. He and his men had the element of surprise. Whoever was behind the door would meet a swift end. Then they would move on to the next.

His men drew their weapons, the faint metallic click of suppressors being threaded into place barely audible over the stillness of the inn. One of them reached for the door handle to the first room and turned it slowly.

The door eased open with a whisper, barely disturbing the still air of the darkened room. Mercer stepped aside as one of his men, a wiry figure with a drawn suppressor-fitted pistol, slipped in first, moving like a shadow against the dim light filtering through the window. Another followed, sweeping the space with a practiced efficiency.

No movement. No sounds.

Mercer stepped inside, his gloved fingers brushing against the smooth wooden frame as he entered. The bed was unmade, a single bag still resting near the foot of it. There were signs of occupancy, but the room was empty.

Too empty.

One of the men motioned toward the adjoining door. Another nodded and eased into the second room, another of Mercer's men had already entered the third. The soft scuff of boots against the wooden floor was the only sound as they moved methodically.

Then a voice, a sharp whisper through the earpiece.

"Clear."

The word struck Mercer like a blow.

His jaw tightened as he took another slow step forward and scanned the room again as his mind raced through the implications of what he was seeing.

They were gone. But where?

He exhaled slowly; his frustration concealed beneath a layer of practiced composure. The evidence was all around him—a damp towel hung haphazardly near the washbasin, a chair slightly pulled out from the desk, a faint imprint on the bedsheets where someone had been sitting. They had been here. Recently.

One of his men moved toward the window, parting the heavy curtains just enough to peer down into the street below.

"No movement," he muttered.

Another checked the closet, the bathroom, even beneath the bed, as if Sean Wyatt and his team had somehow folded themselves into the shadows.

Nothing.

Mercer rolled his tongue against the inside of his cheek as his gloved fingers flexed slightly. This wasn't right. This wasn't possible.

They had men at the exits. Watching. Waiting. There had been no sign of anyone slipping out.

His gaze drifted toward the adjoining room, where the rest of his team had come to the same conclusion. Empty.

Sean Wyatt had played him.

He exhaled through his nose, then turned and strode toward the hallway, his boots falling heavier now, his patience wearing thin. As he reached the door, he tapped his earpiece once and spoke in a low, clipped tone.

"Regroup outside. Now."

No arguing. No questions. His men knew better.

The night air was sharp and cool, wrapping around Mercer's frustration like a vice as he stepped into the silent street. His men followed, spilling into the alley and the main road, their movements fast but controlled, weapons hidden beneath their jackets to avoid unnecessary attention.

Mercer let his eyes sweep over the village square, taking in every shadowed alley, every empty street, every window where the dim glow of candlelight still flickered behind drawn curtains.

Nothing.

His men had been stationed at every exit, both inside and out. The manager had given him the room numbers only minutes before they went upstairs. So how did Wyatt and his friends get out?

His second-in-command, the same broad-shouldered enforcer who had flashed his weapon at the night manager, came up beside him.

"They didn't walk out of there," the man said quietly.

Mercer's eyes flicked to him, expression unreadable. "No, they didn't."

Then he turned while looking at the building itself. The inn was old, built in a time when people thought about history, not security. Were there secondary exits, hidden passages, maintenance tunnels? His gaze narrowed. If Wyatt had gotten out, it meant Mercer had overlooked something.

A sharp exhale, then he looked to his men. "Spread out. Search the perimeter. I want eyes on every alley, every back door."

They moved instantly and split into small groups. Some circled behind the inn while checking for missed rear exits; others fanned out into the adjacent streets while scanning for movement.

Mercer himself strode toward the side of the building as his eyes scanned the lower-level windows, the drainage pipes, the locked wooden gates leading to small courtyards. He ran a gloved hand over the rough stone exterior while feeling for anything out of place.

The man wasn't just lucky. He was smart. And that was what irritated Mercer the most.

They had been careful. Precise. There had been no gaps in their surveillance. So either Wyatt had found a way out that Mercer hadn't anticipated...

Or someone had helped them.

That thought lingered as Mercer made his way back toward the main entrance, where his enforcer was waiting.

"Nothing," the man said, irritation threading through his usually detached tone.

Mercer nodded once, and his jaw tensed in thought.

"If they left, it wasn't through the front. And it wasn't through the back." He exhaled while glancing up at the inn's rooftop then back toward the quiet village square. "They had another way out. One we didn't account for."

The others returned, and reported the same thing. No movement. No sign of their targets. For now.

Mercer's expression smoothed; his frustration buried beneath an impassive mask. This wasn't a failure. Not yet.

"They're still here. Somewhere."

16

Jean-Marc shone his phone light into the darkness ahead. The passage was barely wide enough for them to move through in single file. The stale, cool air inside brimmed with the scent of damp earth and old stone, as though no one had set foot in the tunnel for centuries.

"Places like this," Jean-Marc whispered, his voice low to avoid carrying through the walls, "they were built in times of war, rebellion. Smugglers, soldiers, priests—someone had to have a way out."

He'd led the group down to the inn's wine cellar while the staff weren't paying attention, and then found an old metal door with a chain and lock over it. Dispensing the chain's lock was simple enough, and once they'd opened the door, they slipped into the darkness beyond.

Tommy let out a low whistle. "Finding stuff like this never gets old. How did you know this was here?"

The Frenchman replied with a coy smile first. "I didn't. But these things are somewhat common in the older buildings. Could be an abandoned smuggler tunnel," Jean-Marc said, his eyes scanning the rough edges of the stone opening. "Or something older. These kinds of places were sometimes connected to monastic escape routes."

Sean didn't waste time admiring it. They had to move.

Before stepping inside, he reached for the edge of the hidden door and examined its hinges. "We need to close it behind us. If those guys search the rooms, they can't know we were ever here."

Jean-Marc nodded, already looking for the mechanism. He found a small, recessed handle on the inside of the wooden panel. He tested it, then let the door swing back into place with a soft thud.

Darkness swallowed them whole.

Now, the narrow tunnel stretched out before them, winding and undulating every few meters like an underground serpent.

The air inside was stale and cool, filled with the scent of damp earth and old stone, as though no one had set foot in the tunnel for centuries.

Sean took point, leading them forward with careful steps. The stone beneath their feet was uneven, some areas sunken from age, others slick with condensation. The walls, rough and cold to the touch, narrowed in places, forcing them to squeeze through gaps just wide enough for a grown man.

"This thing just keeps going," Tommy muttered from behind Sean.

"Better than the alternative," Sean replied.

Evelyn, just behind Tommy, breathed shallowly, her eyes flicking between the walls and the darkness ahead. Claustrophobic or not, she knew stopping wasn't an option.

Jean-Marc brought up the rear, pausing every few minutes to listen behind them. The hidden passage had sealed shut when they entered, but if somehow the men following them discovered it, they'd have no way of knowing how much time they had.

Sean felt the air begin to shift, the musty, trapped feeling giving way to something fresher. "We're getting close to the end."

Jean-Marc checked his phone's GPS, but it was useless this deep underground. "If I had to guess," he whispered, "we're somewhere under the edge of the village by now."

Minutes passed. Then Sean's boot hit something solid—wood instead of stone.

He stopped. "End of the line," he murmured, shifting his phone light downward. Beneath them was a set of worn wooden steps leading to a narrow wooden door, its iron hinges rusted with age. Dust and cobwebs coated the frame, making it clear that no one had come through here in a long time.

Sean turned and lowered his voice. "Looks like we made it."

Jean-Marc stepped forward, brushed past Tommy and Evelyn, and crouched near the door. He ran a hand over the wood, then placed his ear against it, listening. Silence.

He reached for the iron handle and tested it gently. It didn't budge.

"Locked?" Evelyn asked.

Jean-Marc shook his head. "Maybe. Or it's just warped from age."

Tommy rubbed his temples. "Of course it is. Can't ever just be an easy exit, can it?"

Sean moved past Jean-Marc and examined the door himself. It was sturdy but not impenetrable. The hinges were thick with rust, the wood swollen from years of moisture.

"We've got two options," Sean said. "We break through, which makes noise, or we try to pick the lock—if there even is one."

Jean-Marc pulled a folding knife from his pocket and wedged the tip into the gap between the door and the frame. He jiggled it slightly, then frowned. "It's locked, but it's an old latch. If I can get enough leverage..."

Sean stepped back, giving him space. Jean-Marc worked in silence, using his knife to work the old latch free. A soft metallic click. He paused before testing the handle again. This time, it shifted slightly.

"I think I've got it."

Evelyn exhaled in relief, but Tommy raised a hand. "Before you open that, let's make sure we're not about to step into a room full of sleeping villagers."

Sean knelt beside the door and put his ear to it. No sounds. No movement. Jean-Marc slowly pushed the door open.

The hinges groaned softly, dust shaking loose from the frame as the passageway revealed its final secret.

Beyond the door was a dimly lit underground wine cellar—long rows of wooden casks and stacked bottles lined the walls, their surfaces covered in years of dust and cobwebs. The stone floor was uneven; a few discarded crates stacked near the far end.

Evelyn blinked in surprise. "A wine cellar?"

Jean-Marc stepped through first, sweeping his phone light across the space. "A good one too... Or at least, it used to be."

Tommy smirked. "Shame we can't enjoy it."

Sean, still watching the doorway they'd just come through, motioned for everyone to move inside. "Let's not celebrate just yet."

The four of them stepped into the cellar, moving carefully. The ceiling was low, supported by thick wooden beams, and dust motes swirled in the phone light.

Jean-Marc moved toward the crates stacked near a narrow stone staircase leading upward. He placed a hand against one of the support beams. "This place has been sealed off for years, but someone must own it."

Evelyn looked at the aging bottles lined along the walls, reading faded labels that hinted at vintages long past their prime. "If we're in a private cellar... where's the exit?"

Tommy gestured toward the staircase. "Only one way to find out."

Sean took the lead again, moving toward the stairs with careful steps. At the top, a heavy wooden door barred their path. Unlike the first, this one wasn't locked—but it was stiff, swollen from years of neglect.

Sean pressed his ear against it and listened. Silence.

He tested the handle. The door gave slightly, creaking as he pushed. A faint glow seeped through the widening gap, and a moment later, Sean stepped out into the back of what appeared to be...a small, dusty storage room. Shelves lined the walls, which were filled with old wooden crates and bottles. A small lantern hung from a hook in the corner, its candle long melted away.

Beyond a half-open door, Sean saw a much larger room—an abandoned wine shop. The kind of place that probably hadn't seen much foot traffic in years. Sean turned back and nodded for the others to follow. One by one, they slipped out of the cellar and into the storage room, then closed the hidden door behind them.

Jean-Marc peered past him into the quiet wine shop. "Looks like it hasn't been used in a long time."

Tommy rubbed his hands together. "Think they left a bottle or two for us?"

Sean shot him a look. "Focus."

Jean-Marc checked his watch. "If Mercer's men are still watching the inn, they have no idea we're out. We've bought time, but not much."

Evelyn, still gripping the strap of her bag, exhaled. "Where do we go from here?"

Sean moved to the front door of the shop, and peered out the window.

The village beyond was quiet, the streets empty. A stray cat howled in the darkness from a nearby alley.

"I have a friend with a house in the country about forty-five minutes from here," Jean-Marc said. "I'm sure he and his wife would be okay with us staying the night. They have spare rooms."

Sean considered the idea. "That's safe, but it puts us nearly an hour from the church."

"We regroup, put together a new plan. Lay low for a few days. Those men will think we skipped town."

Sean knew the Frenchman was right. It was the safe play, and they would be extremely difficult to track. He wouldn't say impossible, but pretty close.

The other side of that was it would be the equivalent of throwing in the towel. They'd have to assess when to pick up the investigation again, and the answer to that might be an indefinite postponement, something Sean wasn't keen on in the least.

There was another option. It was riskier, but it would give them the advantage of surprise. They'd need a vehicle since Jean-Marc's was probably still being surveilled. He would deal with that once a decision had been made.

"How far did you say the church is from here?" Sean asked.

The left side of Jean-Marc's lips stretched to the side, as if he could read Sean's mind.

17

Sean and the others crouched behind a thick row of neatly trimmed bushes across the street from the church. The cool, damp air tickled their skin despite the jackets they wore as a shell against the chill.

The church stood silent before them in the moonlight, its stone walls bathed in silver, the towering façade both beautiful and imposing. Stained-glass windows, now dark and lifeless, stretched toward the heavens, hiding whatever secrets lay within.

Sean exhaled slowly, watching, listening. The village remained quiet as it had during their walk from the hidden tunnel's exit to where they now lurked.

No headlights in the distance, no footsteps on the cobbled streets. For now, they were alone.

Beside him, Tommy shifted slightly, then adjusted the strap of his backpack before leaning in. "So, breaking into a church. That's a new one for us."

Sean smirked, glancing up toward the star-speckled sky, then gave a small shrug of apology. "Yeah, we'll definitely owe the big guy an apology."

Jean-Marc, crouched beside Evelyn, gave a small shake of his head. "That's a great sentiment, but we shouldn't waste time. Every second that passes gives those guys a chance to figure out what happened."

Sean knew he was right and nodded. "Right. Let's go."

They darted across the empty street; their footsteps muted against the old stone. In seconds, they were at the church's outer wall, then pressing themselves into the deep shadow along its perimeter.

Evelyn breathed softly, her heart pounding in her chest. "Do we even know if this place has alarms?"

"Doubt it," Tommy whispered. "What would they be protecting? Holy water?"

No one laughed.

Sean scanned the exterior, his trained eyes searching for telltale signs of motion sensors, security cameras, or infrared beams. He found none. He would have brought a Wi-Fi jammer, but they only had so much room in their bags.

"Looks clear on the security system. No wires. No cameras. Could be one when we go in, but we'll just have to risk it."

Jean-Marc knelt beside the main entrance and began running his fingers along the frame of the massive wooden doors. The main doors were a no-go. Heavy, locked, and most likely rigged with an old-fashioned security bar from the inside.

"We need to find another way in," he said. "There should be a side door or back door."

They worked their way around the side of the building, sticking to the shadows, moving quickly and carefully. The basilica was old, its design a mixture of Romanesque and Gothic styles, and Sean knew where to look for weaknesses.

Near the back, a small wooden side door stood beneath a curved stone archway, half hidden by an alcove.

"This looks promising," Tommy whispered.

Jean-Marc ran a gloved hand along the handle, testing it. Locked but not unbreakable. He gave a nod, then pulled a small leather pouch from his pocket.

Sean smirked. "I knew you carried a lockpicking kit."

Jean-Marc didn't look up. "Old habits."

He worked quickly, inserting a thin tension wrench into the keyhole, then a pick, maneuvering with the quiet skill of someone who had done this before. Within seconds, he felt the pins click into place.

A soft turn of the handle. The latch gave way with a muted clunk.

Jean-Marc stepped back, gesturing to Sean. "After you."

Sean exhaled, reached for the door, and pushed it open. A cool breath of air swept out from inside, carrying the scent of aged wood, stone, and the faint lingering aroma of incense. The dark interior stretched before them, silent and untouched.

With a final glance over his shoulder, Sean stepped inside.

As soon as they stepped inside, darkness swallowed them whole.

The heavy wooden door eased shut behind them, sealing them in the vast silence of the church. The air was cooler inside, carrying a stronger scent of burned incense and the musty aroma of the aged structure.

Sean flicked on his flashlight, the beam slicing through the blackness, illuminating the high, arched ceiling above. The light caught on gilded carvings, intricate murals painted along the curved vaults—scenes of Joan of Arc's visions, her battles, her martyrdom.

Evelyn turned on her phone light, sweeping it across the nave. The rows of wooden pews stretched out before them, their polished surfaces reflecting the dim glow of their lights. A grand altar stood at the far end, adorned with ornate gold detailing and towering candles that would have bathed the space in warm light during services.

Stained-glass windows framed the upper walls, their intricate depictions of saints and angels now nothing more than dark panels, lifeless in the absence of daylight.

They all stood silent for a few seconds, every one of them expecting to hear the warning beeps of an alarm just before a klaxon started blaring.

Jean-Marc scanned the aisles. "No sign of alarms," he said, realizing their fear wasn't going to materialize.

"I guess no one wants to steal the holy water," Tommy joked, again to the sound of crickets.

Sean merely shook his head in disdain. "We need to start looking."

"For what?" Jean-Marc asked for clarification.

Sean's flashlight beam swept across the vast interior, illuminating the towering pillars and gilded icons that adorned the basilica. The silence pressed down around them, thick and almost suffocating in the cavernous space.

"We need to find the feet of the maiden," Sean said, turning toward Evelyn, who was still scanning the walls, the glow from her phone light casting eerie shadows along the pews.

"The clue mentioned 'the feet of the Maiden,'" she confirmed in a hushed voice. "That has to mean Joan of Arc. At least that was what we deduced."

Tommy frowned, glancing around. "She really is a big deal in this place. There are statues and paintings of her everywhere. A true hero."

Sean nodded. And that was the problem.

There were at least three different statues of Joan inside the church that he could see from here. One stood near the main altar, another near a side chapel, and a third, smaller one was mounted near the entrance to a recessed alcove.

"Well," Sean muttered, "let's start checking."

They split up, moving quickly but cautiously. The stone floor echoed and amplified their footsteps.

Sean approached the largest statue, which stood prominently near the main altar. Joan of Arc was depicted in full armor, holding a sword, her expression serene yet determined. The base of the statue was engraved with an inscription detailing her visions and her faith.

He knelt down and began running his fingers along the edges of the base, searching for anything unusual; a hidden panel, a loose stone, something that felt out of place.

Nothing.

Tommy came over, rubbing the back of his neck. "Anything?"

"No hidden compartments, no loose stones," Sean murmured. He tapped the statue lightly while feeling the solid marble beneath his fingertips. "If there's something here, it's not obvious."

Meanwhile, Evelyn and Jean-Marc inspected the second statue, located inside a small, candlelit side chapel. This one depicted Joan kneeling in prayer, her hands clasped, her sword at her side. The stone floor beneath it was smooth and undisturbed.

Evelyn pressed her fingers along the base of the statue, searching for gaps or cracks.

Jean-Marc crouched down, using his phone light to check the edges of the stone tiles surrounding the statue's foundation. He ran his hand along one, then paused.

"This one feels... off."

Evelyn looked at him. "Loose?"

Jean-Marc pressed a little harder, but the tile didn't budge. "Not loose. Just... different." He knocked lightly on the stone. The sound was dull, hollow.

Evelyn's pulse quickened.

"There's something under it," Jean-Marc whispered.

Sean and Tommy rejoined them as Jean-Marc pointed at the suspicious floor tile beneath the second statue.

"You think this is it?" Tommy asked.

"If I had to bet," Jean-Marc murmured.

Sean knelt down and ran his hands along the edges of the stone. It was larger than the surrounding tiles, and the surface wasn't quite as worn—as if it had been replaced at some point. He traced the seam with his fingers, looking for a way to lift it. Nothing.

"There has to be a release," Evelyn whispered.

Jean-Marc glanced back at the statue. "If they hid something here, they would have wanted it to be accessed by those who knew what to look for."

Sean studied the statue's base again, then the sculpted folds of Joan's robe. His eyes narrowed. "Maybe it's part of the design."

He reached out and pressed his palm against the hilt of Joan's carved sword.

It shifted slightly.

The others froze.

Sean applied more pressure, gently twisting the hilt. A soft click echoed beneath them.

Jean-Marc immediately pressed his hands to the floor tile, and this time, it moved slightly under his grip. Sean helped him lift it, and with a soft scrape of stone against stone, the tile came loose, revealing a dark cavity beneath.

Evelyn shone her light into the hole.

At first, all she saw was dusty darkness. Then... stone steps descending into the church's foundation.

Tommy leaned over the opening; his voice hushed. "I guess we're going down there."

Sean smirked. "Did you have other plans?"

"Hilarious. I'm just saying... It looks sketchy."

"Which makes it so much different than every cave and tunnel we've ever been in? Like the one we just left a few minutes ago?"

"Fair," Tommy nodded.

Jean-Marc lowered his phone into the opening, its light revealing a narrow, dust-coated staircase leading downward into what looked like a forgotten chamber.

Evelyn swallowed. "Whatever's down there... it's been waiting for a long time."

Sean adjusted his flashlight. "Let's not keep it waiting, then." He turned to Jean-Marc. "Watch the rear. I'll go first."

He pointed his light down into the narrow stairwell and began his descent.

18

"You're certain they didn't come out any of the exits?" Mercer demanded into his radio mic.

"Yes, sir," the man said immediately. "We haven't taken our eyes off the exits the entire time."

Mercer stood next to the dark Citroën parked in the same place it had been for several hours. If Wyatt and his crew left the hotel, they went on foot. But that wasn't possible. Mercer's men had been vigilant in their surveillance of the inn. There was no way they could have slipped past them.

He stared at the vehicle for a few long seconds, the men around him awaiting orders.

It was a tricky situation. Act too rash, and their quarry could slip away permanently.

Mercer's jaw tightened as he lowered the radio mic, his eyes locked on the quiet, unassuming façade of the inn.

Something wasn't adding up.

His men had been stationed at every possible exit, watching for hours. No one had left. That meant one of two things—either Wyatt and his crew were still inside... or they had found a way out that Mercer hadn't accounted for.

He hoped it wasn't the latter.

He turned to his team, his voice calm but edged with frustration.

"Two of you stay here and keep watching the exits. If they're hiding inside, they'll have to come out eventually." He looked at the others. "The rest of you, with me."

With a silent nod, his men fell into step behind him, moving quickly across the dimly lit street.

The inn's front door creaked softly as Mercer pushed inside. The warmth of the interior hit him first—the lingering scent of burned wood from the stone fireplace, the faint aroma of wine and old upholstery. The only other person in the lobby was the night clerk, now back behind the counter, hunched over a book, pretending not to notice them.

Mercer approached, letting his gloved hands rest on the wooden counter. The clerk hesitated, his fingers twitching as he turned a page, pretending to read.

Mercer smiled thinly. "Quiet night?"

The clerk swallowed hard, his eyes darting up briefly before dropping back to the book. "Yes," he answered reluctantly.

"We're going to have a look around. We're trying to find someone, and we suspect they are somewhere here in your inn."

The clerk was too nervous to say no. Mercer's matter-of-fact way of speaking allowed no room for resistance.

Mercer turned to his team. "Start here. Sweep the lobby, check behind everything."

The men fanned out, moving quickly and methodically.

One checked the coat rack near the entrance, nudging aside the hanging garments in case someone had tried to conceal themselves. Another moved toward the lounge area, scanning the dimly lit sitting room, where a few overstuffed armchairs faced a cold, dormant fireplace.

Nothing.

Mercer stalked toward the dining area, where the remnants of earlier meals lingered—half-empty glasses, a few stray plates left for the morning staff to clean. The tables were all empty. Chairs pushed in neatly. No signs of disturbance.

His frustration deepened. If Wyatt and his crew had managed to escape, every second that passed put them farther away.

Two of his men had already disappeared into the kitchen, their boots clicking softly against the tiled floor. Mercer followed.

The kitchen was small, rustic, but well kept. A large wooden island stood in the center, surrounded by hanging pots and pans that reflected the dim glow of the emergency lighting overhead. Shelves lined the walls, stacked with dried goods, bottles of wine, and jars of preserved fruit.

One of the men pulled open a pantry door and peered inside. Another checked the walk-in refrigerator, its metal door creaking as he swung it open. The cold air rushed out, curling into the warm kitchen like a ghost.

Mercer stepped past them, moving toward the service entrance at the back of the kitchen. It was locked from the inside. Not their exit point.

He ran his gloved fingers over the wooden counter while scanning the space with narrowed eyes. If Wyatt had hidden somewhere nearby, there should have been signs—a knocked-over utensil, a chair out of place, something. But there was nothing. It was as if they had vanished into thin air.

One of his men returned from the small staff break room adjacent to the kitchen, shaking his head. "No one back there. A couch, some chairs, that's it."

Mercer turned sharply. He could feel it now—the frustration creeping in, the sense that something was very, very wrong. Wyatt wasn't in the kitchen or the lobby or the first floor.

They moved back toward the main hallway, checking every unlocked door—closets, storage rooms, even an old linen cupboard.

Nothing.

Mercer patience thinned with each passing second. His mind was already working through the possibilities. If they weren't on the main floor, then either they were still upstairs, hiding in some crawlspace or attic Mercer hadn't considered; or they had gotten out—somehow.

His jaw ticked with irritation as he returned to the lobby, and he stared at the wood-paneled walls, the old furniture, the quiet hearth once he got there.

They had checked everywhere reasonable. Except... Mercer's eyes narrowed.

Except places that weren't meant to be checked. Old buildings like this—especially in towns with deep history—had secrets. Smuggler's tunnels, servant passages, forgotten spaces built centuries ago and left to time.

If Wyatt had gotten out without being seen, that meant he hadn't used a normal exit.

Mercer turned to his men. "They're not here."

One of them frowned. "So... we move to the second floor?"

Mercer stared at the floorboards, deep in thought. Then his eyes lifted slowly toward the wooden panels along the walls.

"No," he said, his voice colder now.

Mercer exhaled slowly, forcing his frustration into something more useful—calculated patience. His men waited for direction, shifting uncomfortably in the dim glow of the lobby's wall sconces. He had chased enough men in his life to know when something wasn't adding up.

"They escaped," he muttered under his breath.

"That's not possible."

Mercer ignored him.

His eyes moved across the polished wooden floors, the aged paneling on the walls, the furniture arranged neatly as though no one had disturbed it. Yet something felt off—an unease that itched at the back of his mind.

Wyatt and his people hadn't walked out. His men had eyes on every exit the entire time.

"Sweep the entire main floor," he ordered.

One of the men, a broad-shouldered mercenary in a black tactical jacket, approached Mercer and gestured toward the grand staircase leading up to the guest rooms.

"You want us to check upstairs again?"

Mercer hesitated, calculating.

If Wyatt and the others were hiding in a closet or attic crawl space, they would have to come out eventually. But something about it felt wrong.

Wyatt was too smart for that. Still, Mercer wasn't going to leave any possibilities unchecked.

He gave a curt nod. "Yes, but only the floors and stairs. We can't go barging into every room in the place."

The three-man team moved up the staircase, boots silent against the thick carpet runner.

Mercer turned his attention back to the lobby, pacing near the wood-paneled walls. His fingers lightly brushed along the edges of the furniture, the shelves, the fireplace mantel.

Every instinct told him he was missing something. A subtle clue.

"Sir," a voice called from the other side of the room.

Mercer turned sharply."Yes?"

"I think I know where they went."

Mercer waited for him to continue.

"There's a door down in the wine cellar. It was chained, but the chain is on the floor now. The door was blocking a tunnel, probably an old escape passage."

There was no hesitation. Just a simple order to the rest of the men in the building. "Let's move. We know how they escaped. Two of you stay here and help the others watch the inn."

19

Sean led the way, his flashlight beam cutting through the thick darkness as he carefully descended the ancient stone steps. Each footfall sent small clouds of dust swirling into the stagnant air, and the deeper they went, the colder it became. The narrow walls pressed in around them, their surfaces rough and uneven, shaped not by precise tools but by centuries of damp erosion.

The passageway smelled of earth and decay, the air thick with the scent of damp limestone and rotting timber. Somewhere above them, far beyond the tunnel's unseen exit, the church remained still and undisturbed, unaware of the secrets lying beneath its sacred floors.

The stairs continued downward for nearly twenty feet, leading to a corridor barely wide enough for two people to walk side by side. Sean ran his hand along the wall as he moved forward, his fingers brushing against carved stone reliefs worn almost smooth with age. Faint etchings of crosses, symbols of saints, and archaic script lined the walls—silent echoes of forgotten history.

Behind him, Evelyn and Tommy followed carefully, their footsteps muffled by the thick layer of dust and fallen mortar beneath them. Jean-Marc, ever the cautious one, brought up the rear, pausing every few moments to glance back toward the tunnel's entrance. The darkness behind them felt almost hungry, watching, though he dismissed the thought as an old soldier's instinct acting up.

The group moved in silence, almost fearful to say anything that might give away their presence. Sean didn't believe the men watching them before had figured out where they'd gone after leaving the inn, if they had even come to that conclusion yet. But he knew there was no such thing as being too careful.

They kept pushing forward, and a couple of times Sean found himself wondering how long this tunnel would be, and how long it must have taken to construct all those centuries ago. Sooner than he expected, the passageway opened into a small underground chamber, its arched ceiling supported by massive stone beams, weathered with cracks from centuries of weight pressing down from above. The air was heavier here, filled with the scent of dried wax and burned oil, as if lanterns had once illuminated the place. How long ago was anyone's guess.

Sean swept his flashlight across the chamber, revealing rows of old wooden chests, their lids warped from time, some slightly ajar. Dust coated everything in a fine layer, undisturbed for what must have been decades, if not centuries.

"Wow," Evelyn breathed, breaking the group's silence. "This is... incredible."

She swept her gaze around the room slowly, taking in every detail.

The floor was littered with fragments of broken pottery, discarded parchment too faded to read, and rusted iron brackets that once held torches. Along the far wall, remnants of an old wooden shelf had collapsed, its contents—ancient glass bottles, metal reliquaries, and a few rotting scroll cases—now lay scattered in disarray.

"I wonder how long it has been since someone was in here," Jean-Marc said.

"Centuries," Tommy guessed, judging from the dust, and the lack of evidence that anyone had recently been there. "Possibly all the way back to the time of Joan. That was the point, after all, to keep this place safe and undiscovered until the right people came along."

"And we're the right people?"

Tommy snorted a laugh. "I would hope so. Better than those guys following us."

"Indeed."

Sean took a slow step forward, scanning the space. This chamber held the secrets of one of the most mysterious, legendary artifacts from history. He wondered what the people looked like who had built it, who had tended it, and who had sealed it off from the rest of the world.

Evelyn ran a hand over the edge of a stone pillar, her fingertips collecting the fine layer of dust clinging to it. She could feel the weight of history pressing down here.

Tommy muttered something, his tone just above a whisper.

Sean turned. "What is it?"

His friend nodded toward the ceiling. "This structure... It's older than the basilica."

Sean followed his gaze. The archways above them were different from the stonework of the church. Where the basilica's interior had been a blend of Romanesque and Gothic influences, the underground chamber was more rudimentary, almost crude in design. The chisel marks on the stone weren't from medieval masons but from something older, more primitive.

"This isn't part of the church," Evelyn murmured, glancing at the walls. "This predates it."

Jean-Marc scanned the uneven stone wall as they pressed forward. His flashlight skimmed over symbols and markings, some of them barely legible through layers of dust or from prolonged erosion.

Something felt off about this place. The air was too still, too heavy, as if the passage itself was holding its breath.

As the Frenchman moved alongside the others, his eyes caught on a strange indentation carved into the wall just ahead. It wasn't decorative like the other engravings—it was precise, mechanical, a small recess cut into the rock with a thin, metal lever protruding from it. The iron had aged with time, but it was clear that it had been designed to move.

Jean-Marc reached for it, his fingers curling around the cool metal handle. It gave the faintest resistance; a coating of rust laid down by the passage of time.

Sean turned just as Jean-Marc started to pull.

"No, wait! Don't touch that!"

But it was too late.

The lever jerked downward with a metallic clank, and a deep rumbling echoed from above them.

The walls groaned as dust and small stones trickled from the ceiling. A sharp cracking noise splintered through the air, followed by a sudden, violent collapse of stone and dust.

Sean instinctively lunged forward and grabbed Evelyn's arm as the floor beneath them shuddered. Tommy stumbled sideways, barely managing to keep his footing as the thunderous roar filled the tunnel.

The passageway behind them gave way with a deafening crunch, sending centuries-old rock and debris crashing down, sealing off the entrance completely. A thick cloud of dust billowed outward, forcing Sean and the others to cover their mouths and step back. A cascade of ancient stones and debris collapsed in a rolling mass, slamming into the ground where they had been moments before. A thick cloud of choking dust surged outward, swallowing the tunnel in near-total darkness.

For what seemed an eternity, they stood in total silence.

The collapse sent tiny vibrations through the chamber, loosening more dust and fragments from the ceiling. The sudden stillness that followed was oppressive, as if the very walls had inhaled and were now waiting to exhale.

Jean-Marc coughed, blinking through the haze, his pulse hammering in his ears. "Merde!" he swore in French.

Tommy shot him a glare, waving dust from his face. "What the heck did you just do?"

Jean-Marc looked down at the lever, then back at the collapsed passage. "I don't know. I'm sorry. I thought it might be what we were looking for."

Sean wiped the dust from his forehead. He didn't let the seemingly dire situation hit him too hard. "Well, we weren't planning on going back that way anyway."

Tommy coughed and waved his flashlight toward the collapsed passage. "It's definitely blocked. Good news is if those guys did follow us here, they ain't getting through that mess."

Jean-Marc kicked a loose stone. It tumbled against the wall of rubble now blocking their way back.

Sean clenched his jaw. He turned his flashlight toward the far end of the chamber, scanning for another exit. If the passage behind them was gone, they had no choice but to go forward.

Evelyn sighed while glancing back at the blocked tunnel. "I was really hoping we wouldn't have to say the words 'find another way out.'"

Sean smirked despite the situation. "Wouldn't be an adventure if it was easy. And like I said, we had to figure on another exit from this place. Otherwise we could have run into a different kind of trouble."

She took his meaning and said nothing else about it.

Sean turned toward the shadows beyond the chamber.

"Let's keep moving."

They pressed on, weaving through the relic-strewn chamber, stepping over rotting wooden planks and the remnants of shattered ceramic vessels.

At the far end, a tall iron gate, rusted and covered in grime, stood partially ajar. Beyond it, another passage stretched into darkness, disappearing even deeper underground.

The walls surrounding the iron gate were etched with timeworn reliefs, their once-bold carvings now softened by centuries of dust and decay. Faded images of warriors in battle lined the stone, their forms barely distinguishable, yet unmistakable in their purpose. Armored knights on horseback, their spears raised high, clashed with opposing forces whose banners had long since faded into the stone's uneven surface.

Near the top of the arch, an inscription in Old French curved around the gate's frame, its meaning obscured by erosion. Evelyn traced her fingers over the lettering, mouthing words that had not been spoken aloud in generations.

Below, another panel depicted a woman in shining armor, her stance defiant as she raised a war banner above a battlefield filled with fallen soldiers. Though her face was worn away, the radiance of her presence was still palpable in the craftsmanship.

Farther down, a smaller carving showed a ring resting upon a cushion, framed by two crossed swords. Time had nearly erased it.

"Awesome," Tommy said. "This is definitely the right place. These battles are ones Joan would have fought in, and the symbols certainly match up to the time she was alive."

Sean reached for the ancient gate, everyone's breath catching for a moment as he gave it a light push. It groaned in protest but moved, the rusted hinges complaining after centuries of disuse.

Evelyn swept her light into the tunnel ahead, revealing a long, descending corridor, its walls lined with worn religious carvings—crosses, figures of saints, Latin inscriptions that had faded with time.

"This isn't like any crypt I've ever seen," Sean said.

Tommy nodded. "And we've been in our fair share of those."

If Henri had traced Joan of Arc's lost ring to this very location, then whatever they needed to find was waiting somewhere ahead.

Sean took the lead, stepping through the gate.

The air grew dense as they ventured deeper into the corridor, the cool dampness giving way to an almost metallic scent, like stone and time fused together. The passage had narrowed, the walls pressing closer on either side, their once-carefully carved designs now half erased by centuries of wear. The farther they went, the more Sean became aware of how silent it was—too silent.

His boots scuffed softly against the ground; the dust disturbed only by their presence. The others followed close behind, their flashlight beams cutting narrow paths through the inky darkness, revealing the uneven stonework ahead.

Evelyn's breath hitched as she swept her light across a series of ancient engravings that had been partially chipped away by the passage of time. "Look at this," she murmured, stepping closer.

Sean moved beside her and angled his light over the carvings. The worn relief depicted a series of figures kneeling before a central image of a woman holding a sword. The etchings of halos above the figures' heads suggested that the artist had meant to portray something divinely inspired.

Jean-Marc brushed the dust off the lower portion of the stonework. "Joan."

Evelyn nodded slowly. "It has to be."

Tommy crossed his arms. "It's different from the usual depictions of her, though. There's no armor, no warhorse. Just... reverence."

Sean studied the lower portion of the relief, feeling the uneven ridges where the stone had cracked over time. His instincts told him that this carving wasn't just art—it was a message.

"Someone took the time to preserve this," he said. "Even if it's worn down, the positioning of the figures, the way they're arranged... it means something."

Evelyn took a step back while shining her light along the adjacent wall. More markings, though much fainter, were etched along the base of the passage. The script was Latin, the letters almost unreadable under the thick layers of dust.

Sean knelt beside the inscriptions, wiping his palm across the stone to reveal a single phrase.

Ubi ignis primo probavit fidem.

He narrowed his eyes. His Latin was rusty, but he could still piece together its meaning.

"Where the fire first tested the faithful."

A chill ran down everyone's collective spine.

Jean-Marc frowned. "That could mean a lot of things."

Evelyn leaned in, her mind working through the possibilities. "Fire. Joan of Arc. It could refer to Rouen—where she was burned at the stake. Or... something else."

Sean considered the words carefully. Tested.

That word stood out.

It didn't say 'where fire consumed her' or 'where she was taken by flames.' It specifically said tested.

"This isn't about her execution," Sean said firmly. "This is about something earlier in her life."

Tommy gave him a skeptical look. "What, like a trial?"

Sean ran fingers through his scruffy blond hair, his mind racing. Joan of Arc's life had been filled with tests of faith, trials of fire—both literal and figurative. But this wasn't a broad reference to her suffering. This was specific.

Where had she been tested by fire before her death?

Evelyn's voice was soft but sure. "Poitiers."

Sean looked at her.

"That's where she was questioned by theologians, right?" Tommy asked.

Evelyn nodded. "Yes. Before she was given command of the army, she was summoned to Poitiers to be examined by the Church. They wanted proof that her visions were real, that she was truly sent by God."

Jean-Marc rubbed his chin. "And if she had the ring then... it might have been hidden somewhere connected to that moment in history."

Sean looked back at the relief of Joan on the wall, the kneeling figures carved beneath her feet. If the ring was a source of power, something she held on to as part of her divine calling, then it wouldn't have simply been discarded.

"She was tested there," Sean murmured. "Her faith, her purpose, her mission... It was all put under scrutiny."

Evelyn traced the inscription with her fingertips.

A slow realization settled over them. The answers weren't here—they were waiting somewhere else.

A sudden metallic creak echoed from deeper in the passage, snapping Sean's focus forward.

Jean-Marc's hand instinctively went to his concealed pistol as they all turned toward the noise.

Tommy shone his light along the far end of the corridor, revealing a narrow, arched doorway, its wooden frame warped with time. The door itself was ajar, the hinges rusted and barely holding together.

Sean motioned for them to stay close as he pushed the door open farther.

The room beyond was small, no larger than a monastery cell, with a single stone pedestal at its center. Upon it sat an aged, ornate wooden box, its surface carved with intricate symbols—crosses, fleurs-de-lys, and more markings that had faded with age.

Evelyn sucked in a breath. "What is that?"

The wooden box sat in eerie stillness atop the stone pedestal, its presence both inviting and foreboding. Unlike the scattered debris and forgotten relics littering the chamber, this container bore no signs of decay or exposure to time's relentless passage. The craftsmanship was extraordinary—oak reinforced with iron bands, its corners braced in tarnished brass.

Sean inspected the surface, frowning. The wood should have rotted long ago in the damp air, but instead it felt oddly smooth, as if time had barely touched it.

Evelyn ran a finger along the intricate carvings before brushing her fingertips against the edges of the box. A faint, resinous texture remained on the surface.

"This has been treated," she murmured. "I think it's coated in bitumen or beeswax."

Sean arched a brow. "Medieval waterproofing."

"Essentially." Evelyn nodded. "Monks and scribes used it to seal manuscripts, sometimes even wooden reliquaries. Bitumen would have repelled moisture, while wax would've protected against mold."

Tommy tapped a knuckle against the wood. "Well, it worked."

Even after centuries underground, the box remained intact, its surface darkened but unyielding. The iron bands along the edges had rusted, but they still held firm, reinforcing the intricate lock at its center.

Evelyn tilted her head, studying the circular dial protruding from the lid. "This isn't just a simple latch."

Sean swept his light over the carvings, tracing the delicate Latin inscription on the pedestal beneath it.

Aperi iuste, aut claudetur in aeternum.

Evelyn read it aloud, her voice barely above a whisper. "Open it correctly... or it will be locked forever."

Sean frowned. "That's encouraging."

Jean-Marc gave a dry chuckle. "That means no mistakes."

"Maybe not so encouraging." Sean stepped closer while shining his flashlight over the locking mechanism. It wasn't a simple latch or keyhole—it was a dial with rotating metal rings, each ring engraved with different letters and symbols. The design reminded him of an early combination lock, but far more complex.

Evelyn tilted her head. "I've read about something like this before. Some medieval chests were built with rotating letter combinations—set them correctly, and the mechanism unlocks. Get it wrong... and some were designed to jam permanently."

"Perfect," Tommy muttered. "A six-hundred-year-old booby trap."

Jean-Marc crouched and studied the worn inscriptions on the rings. "This must be the combination."

Evelyn nodded. "The only question is... what's the right sequence?"

Sean swept his light over the carvings on the box, searching for anything that might indicate the correct order. The images told a story—a maiden kneeling before a crown, a ring raised toward the heavens, and a battle with flames consuming a fortress in the distance. It was clear that this box had been created to guard something of immense significance.

Then his eyes caught a barely visible inscription near the bottom edge of the lid, almost obscured by dust. He wiped it clean with his sleeve, revealing the words *Fides, Fortitudo, Ignis.*

Evelyn's breath caught. "Faith. Courage. Fire."

Sean exchanged a glance with Tommy. "That has to be it."

Jean-Marc reached for the first metal ring, hesitating just long enough to ensure no one objected. Then he began rotating the dial, carefully aligning the first set of letters. The faint scrape of metal against metal echoed through the chamber as he turned the rings one by one.

F. I. D. E. S.

The mechanism didn't move. Tommy adjusted the next ring.

F. O. R. T. I. T. U. D. O.

Still nothing.

A single drop of sweat traced a slow path down the side of Sean's face as he watched Evelyn set the final ring.

I. G. N. I. S.

The room held its breath. For a long moment, nothing happened. Then—a soft metallic click.

The tension in the air snapped like a coiled spring being released.

Jean-Marc let out a breath. "Well. That was stressful."

Sean reached for the lid; his hands steady but his pulse still thrumming in his ears. Slowly, he lifted the cover.

Inside, wrapped in decayed silk, was a scroll.

Not a book. Not a full manuscript. But something small, fragile, and centuries old.

Sean set his backpack down and dug out a pair of white gloves.

Jean-Marc and Evelyn gave him a funny look.

"What? You never know."

He slipped on the gloves then carefully touched the weathered scroll and removed it gently from the wrapping, feeling the delicate fibers of the parchment as he unrolled the edge. The ink had faded but not beyond recognition.

Sean unfurled the document with the utmost care, deliberately moving a millimeter at a time to make sure he didn't destroy any of it. He was surprised it had lasted this long in this environment.

Evelyn stepped beside him. She breathed faster now. The words written there sent a fresh jolt of adrenaline through them all.

The scroll was a directive. A written instruction on where something had been moved.

Sean's eyes flicked over the text, and then he read aloud the most critical passage:

"*Ad locum ignis primo temptavit.*"

Jean-Marc's voice was a low murmur. "Poitiers."

The fire had tested her there first.

Evelyn's voice was almost breathless. "This is what Henri died for."

Sean carefully rolled the scroll back up and secured it inside his pack. He glanced toward the doorway and the tunnel stretching beyond.

"We've got what we need," he said. "Now let's find a way out of here."

Sean swept his light slowly across the room's stone walls, the narrow beam catching fragments of soot, age-darkened mortar, and deep gouges carved by time. His pulse hadn't quite settled. The scroll in his pack felt like it vibrated with its own weight, like it wanted to speak again.

But there was no time to dwell on it.

"You're "sure they built in another way out?" Evelyn asked, her voice hushed, reverent.

Sean didn't answer, and instead stepped away from the center of the chamber, eyes scanning for irregularities—edges that didn't match, gaps where none should be. That's when he saw it. Just left of the archway they'd entered through, where the wall looked uneven in the torchlight, a thin vertical seam caught his attention.

He pressed his fingers against the seam. The stone was cool but rough. Solid. Still, something was off about it.

He dropped to one knee, running his hand along the floor at the base of the wall. A slight depression. Almost imperceptible.

"Help me with this," he said.

Evelyn joined him, and together they pressed inward against the false wall. At first, nothing happened—then Sean's hand found a notch beneath a carved fleur-de-lis barely the size of a thumbnail. It clicked under his thumb.

With a low groan of shifting weight, the stone pivoted inward.

A rush of musty, cold air rolled out, brushing their faces with the breath of a place that hadn't been disturbed in centuries.

Beyond the narrow opening, stone steps curved down into the dark.

Sean turned to Evelyn. "Looks like Joan didn't leave through the front door."

She nodded, eyes wide with awe. "This is how she escaped."

"Or how they tried to protect what she left behind," Sean added. Then he the beam of his headlamp.

"Let's find out where this leads."

20

Mercer stepped carefully into the tunnel, his boots crunching against loose gravel and debris as he moved forward. The air was thick with dampness clinging to his skin like a second layer. The stale scent of mold and old stone filled his nostrils, mingling with the underlying trace of something older, something left to rot in the dark for centuries.

His flashlight beam cut through the suffocating blackness, illuminating the passage ahead. The walls, rough-hewn limestone, glistened in places where moisture had collected, forming thin trickles of water that slithered down the rock like veins of ink.

His team followed close behind, their movements precise, disciplined—no wasted effort, no unnecessary noise. They knew the stakes. Sean Wyatt was ahead of them somewhere, and Mercer intended to find him before he slipped away again.

Mercer's thoughts raced as he pressed deeper into the underground tunnel. How had Wyatt known about this passage?

It wasn't something one stumbled upon by chance. This wasn't an ordinary escape route, it was a secret buried in history. That meant someone had led Wyatt to it. Mercer needed to know who.

His grip tightened around his flashlight, irritation bubbling beneath the surface. This game of cat and mouse had gone on long enough.

"Keep your spacing tight," he ordered in a low voice. "Eyes on every shadow. They could have left something behind to slow us down."

He wasn't wrong to worry. Wyatt was resourceful. If they had time, he and his team might have set traps, covered their tracks. Mercer didn't believe in underestimating his quarry. That was how men like him ended up dead.

A few minutes in, Mercer stopped, signaling for his men to hold position. The silence was absolute—the kind of quiet that pressed against the ears, making the absence of sound feel heavier than any noise could.

He swept his flashlight across the dust-covered ground, scanning for footprints.

Nothing.

But that didn't mean Wyatt hadn't passed through.

One of his men—Klein, a wiry, sharp-eyed operator—stepped forward and knelt near the edge of the left passage. He ran his fingers lightly across the stone floor, then exhaled through his nose.

"They went this way," Klein murmured. "It's subtle, but the dust has been disturbed."

Mercer nodded. He trusted Klein's tracking ability.

"Move."

They took the left passage, pressing deeper into the subterranean maze. As they advanced, the corridor widened slightly, revealing hints of forgotten history buried beneath the modern world.

The remnants of worn-out murals were barely visible on the walls, their faded pigments only catching the light when a flashlight beam struck at just the right angle. Ancient iron torch brackets, long rusted, jutted out at uneven intervals, some bent under the weight of time.

Mercer's men moved in silence, methodically sweeping the area with their lights. Every inch of the passage was analyzed, every shift in the air felt. They were trained for this—for the hunt, for the chase.

Something glinted ahead—a discarded object resting against the tunnel wall. Mercer crouched, picking it up.

A boot print smudged the dust nearby.

Wyatt had been here. And he was only minutes ahead.

The deeper they went, the more time felt like an enemy.

Mercer checked his watch. How long had they been underground? Five minutes? Ten? The tunnel warped time in a way that made it hard to gauge. Too much longer, and Wyatt would have too much of a lead.

The floor tilted slightly downward, making their movements feel heavier as they adjusted to the uneven slope. The air became stagnant, thick with the scent of ancient stone and something almost metallic.

One of his men muttered under his breath, scanning the tunnel ahead. "This place is a crypt."

Mercer didn't respond. His focus remained locked forward. He felt the space narrowing again, the walls tightening around them as if the earth itself was trying to squeeze them back.

Then, up ahead—a wooden door. Slightly ajar.

Mercer's pulse quickened. This was it. The way out. He signaled for absolute silence as he approached the exit. Reaching out, he pushed the door open fully. The hinges groaned softly, but the structure held. Beyond it, faint moonlight spilled through the opening. He stood in an old wine shop, and from the looks of it the place had been shuttered years ago.

Mercer stepped out of the opening, and found himself in an old storage room. He didn't take the time to look around, and instead walked through the open door and out into an abandoned wine shop. After a quick survey of the place, he moved to the front door, and peeked through he windows.

His men followed him across the threshold. Once outside, his boots crunching softly against the dew-covered grass. The cool night air brushed against his skin, a stark contrast to the suffocating weight of the tunnel behind him.

He took a slow, sweeping glance around. No one was around. No sign of movement. No sound of footsteps in the distance. Wyatt was gone.

Mercer's jaw tightened. His fingers curled into fists.

"What now, boss?" Santos asked, his voice carrying a faint Iberian lilt—Portuguese, maybe, or Spanish. He adjusted his gloves, his thick fingers flexing like a man who was always ready for violence. He was broad-shouldered and heavyset, but there was no sluggishness in his movements—Santos carried himself like a man who had been in more than a few fights and walked away from all of them.

Mercer didn't answer immediately. He swept his gaze across the clearing, searching for any sign that Wyatt and his crew had left something behind. The damp grass was undisturbed, the dirt too hard packed to show footprints. There was nothing. Not a bent blade of grass, not a discarded scrap of fabric.

They didn't disappear into thin air.

Mercer clenched his jaw, turning over the possibilities in his mind. If Wyatt had skipped town, where would he go? They had cars, but they were parked near the inn, not here. That meant Wyatt and the others were still on foot.

Mercer had spent enough time studying Wyatt and Schultz to understand them. They weren't just adventurers, they were relentless. They wouldn't have come all this way just to turn around and flee.

His eyes narrowed slightly. That left only one option. "They went to the church," Mercer said, his voice certain.

Klein, who had been scanning the edge of the clearing, turned. "How do you know?"

Mercer glanced at him. "Because they're not running. Not without whatever they came here to find."

Santos gave a small, amused grunt. "So, you think they're still there?"

"Absolutely. How far away is that church?"

Klein took out his phone and did a quick search for directions. "Not far. Just on the other side of the village."

"Perfect. We may even get lucky and catch them by surprise."

21

The air thickened as Sean stepped into the passageway and his flashlight cast long, restless shadows across the uneven walls. A fine layer of dust and centuries-old debris coated the narrow floor, the disturbed particles dancing in the stale air as they moved forward.

The tunnel seemed to breathe with them, an ancient corridor forgotten by time, its very existence a whisper of an era long buried beneath stone and memory.

Sean didn't like it.

Not just because it was tight, winding, and steep—but because it had been sealed for a reason. Someone in the past had gone to the effort of making sure this passage was hidden, blocked, lost. And now, here they were, walking into a place not meant to be walked again.

Jean-Marc took point, moving with calculated precision, his sidearm loose in its holster but close enough for an instant draw. Tommy followed, his flashlight beam swaying slightly, eyes flicking across the rough-hewn walls, trying to see the story left behind in the cuts of the stone and the crude carvings etched in places where hands had lingered.

Evelyn was just ahead of Sean, her posture rigid but not from fear. More like an academic curiosity at war with an ever-growing unease.

Sean brought up the rear, his instincts screaming for him to keep checking behind them, making sure nothing else was moving in the dark. The tunnel stretched on, narrow and winding, its walls damp with condensation, giving the rock a glassy sheen that reflected slivers of light.

No one said a word.

Every step they took echoed, bouncing through the confined space, warping slightly as the sound traveled down the unknown lengths ahead. The tunnel curved left, then right, its serpentine nature disorienting, as if whoever built it had wanted to ensure that no one who entered would have an easy time leaving. Sean's fingers tightened around the flashlight, resisting the urge to check his watch. Time was meaningless down here, swallowed by the endless dark.

Something shifted in the air. The dampness still lingered, but now there was something else; a faint, earthy scent, deeper than stone.

"Smell that?" Sean asked, his voice barely above a whisper.

Jean-Marc grunted in confirmation. "Soil. We're getting closer to the surface."

Sean nodded, even though no one could see him. But closer didn't mean safe.

They continued forward, the passage tilting upward more noticeably, forcing them into a slow, steady climb. The incline pressed against their legs, turning the quiet march into something more deliberate, laborious.

Sean's boots scuffed against the dirt, and for a brief moment the noise seemed too loud, like it would carry all the way back to the chamber they had left behind.

They rounded another bend, and suddenly, Jean-Marc stopped abruptly.

Sean froze; pulse steady but ready to react.

"What is it?" Tommy whispered.

Jean-Marc angled his flashlight downward.

Sean stepped up beside him and saw it immediately.

The floor ahead was uneven, the packed dirt giving way to scattered chunks of rock and debris, likely a partial collapse from decades past. The stones looked unstable, some tilting at unnatural angles, ready to shift with any wrong movement.

"We go slow," Jean-Marc murmured.

Sean nodded. "Watch where you step."

Jean-Marc went first, placing his boots carefully, avoiding the most unstable sections. The others followed suit, each movement calculated, each step deliberate, avoiding loose debris that could send a cascade of rubble tumbling farther down the passage. It took them several grueling minutes to cross, but eventually, they were past it.

And then they saw it.

Ahead, the tunnel flattened out, leading to what looked like a reinforced archway, its frame made of thick wooden beams, bound with iron brackets that had rusted with time.

Evelyn's breath hitched slightly. "That looks like an entrance."

"Or an exit," Sean said.

They reached the threshold, and Jean-Marc ran his fingers along the edges, looking for a way to open it. "No obvious handle," he murmured.

Sean inspected the wood. Old. Thick. Treated. Designed to last centuries, which it had.

Evelyn pointed at the base of the frame. "Look—air's moving through there."

Jean-Marc nodded. "There's open space on the other side."

Tommy stepped up, rolling his shoulders. "So how do we get through it?"

Jean-Marc stepped back, then without a word, drove his boot into the center of the wood. The thud echoed through the tunnel, but the door barely budged.

"Again," Sean said.

Jean-Marc planted his feet and delivered a harder, more precise kick—this time, the ancient wood groaned, the metal brackets grinding against the frame.

One more.

Crack!

The impact sent a splintering noise through the corridor as the old beams gave way, snapping near the hinges. The door lurched inward, revealing a darkened space beyond.

They stepped through cautiously, flashlights sweeping the room beyond, revealing rows of wooden racks, stacked high with dust-covered bottles.

Evelyn let out a breathy laugh. "Another wine cellar?"

Sean scanned the space, heart still pounding. "Not just any wine cellar. An old one."

Jean-Marc took a slow step forward, glancing around. "This must be connected to an estate or a monastery."

Sean turned, looking for stairs, an exit, anything that would lead them up.

Tommy tapped one of the racks with a knuckle. "This stuff's probably worth a fortune."

Jean-Marc ignored him, moving toward a set of stone steps at the back of the room. "This way."

They ascended; their steps muted by the thick layer of dust coating the floor. The air grew lighter, fresher with every step, and then....

Jean-Marc pushed against a heavy wooden door, and this time, it swung open easily.

The night embraced them, cool air rushing against their skin as they stepped into the open.

Sean exhaled, scanning the area.

They stood on the outskirts of a small estate, its silhouette barely visible against the moonlit landscape. The vineyard stretched behind them, rows of dormant grapevines reaching toward the horizon.

Sean inhaled deeply, filling his lungs with the cold night air. The difference between the stale, damp confines of the tunnel and the open space of the vineyard was almost overwhelming.

The silence here was different. Not dead, not stagnant—alive. The world had movement again. The whisper of a soft wind rustled through the vines, the distant hoot of an owl, the subtle creak of a wooden beam somewhere behind them.

Tommy stretched his arms and exhaled sharply, his breath a thin cloud in the night air.

"Not the worst place to crawl out of a hole," he muttered.

Sean didn't answer. His eyes scanned the surroundings, cataloging everything. They had emerged near an old vineyard estate, its main structure a modest two-story house, darkened and silent. A small barn stood to the right, its doors slightly ajar, swaying faintly with the wind.

Behind them, the vineyard stretched in neat, endless rows, long abandoned, the grapevines gnarled and twisted like skeletal fingers reaching skyward.

But it was the land beyond the vineyard that captured Sean's focus.

Below, nestled in the heart of the village, stood the church.

From this vantage point, they had a clear, elevated view of Domrémy. The stone streets, the cluster of old houses with their warm golden lights flickering through drawn curtains, the occasional lamp post casting pools of dim light along the pathways.

And then—movement. Sean froze, muscles tensing. Near the church's entrance, dark figures moved, their silhouettes elongated by the streetlights, their pace slow, methodical.

Jean-Marc crouched beside him, his sharp eyes narrowing. "They're searching the perimeter."

Sean nodded, his jaw tightening. Four men.

One of them—a tall, broad-shouldered man with a buzzed head and a thick military-style coat—paused near the old stone steps leading up to the entrance, sweeping his gaze across the street before signaling to the others.

Sean recognized that stance. That level of professional caution.

They weren't just looking. They were hunting.

Jean-Marc motioned toward a low stone wall a few feet away, half collapsed from age and covered in patches of moss. "We need to get lower."

Sean, Evelyn, and Tommy moved quickly, crouching behind the stacked limestone blocks, pressing their backs against the cool stone. The rough surface dug into Sean's jacket, but he didn't adjust. He didn't move at all.

He could hear everything; his own heartbeat, the rhythmic inhales and exhales of his team, the faint shifting of dirt beneath Tommy's boots.

Below, the men continued their search, weaving around the stone foundation of the church, checking windows, doorways, the empty street beyond.

Sean's pulse remained steady, but his mind was already calculating. They had to be careful. One wrong move, one sound too loud, and they'd lose any chance of a clean escape.

Jean-Marc leaned in slightly, voice barely above a breath. "They're thorough. If they don't find anything outside, they're going in."

Sean agreed. And once they were inside, they'd realize no one was there. That's when the real problem begins. This guy wasn't an idiot. If they weren't inside the church, then they would simply widen their search. But Sean knew they would find the secret staircase, and it wouldn't take the men long to catch up.

Evelyn seemed to read his mind, and pressed closer to the wall; her eyes locked on the men below. "We don't have much time."

Sean knew it too. But rushing wasn't an option. So they waited.

Seconds dragged into minutes, stretching time painfully thin. The night air felt colder against Sean's skin. The streetlights seemed brighter than before, illuminating too much, betraying too many shadows.

Then—movement again. The men at the front of the church stopped searching, their focus shifting toward the heavy wooden doors. Sean watched as one of them pulled the handle, testing it.

Locked.

Another motioned toward the guy who Sean believed to be the leader, a man who stood just off to the side, partially hidden in the shadows. Sean recognized the slight tilt of his head—an order.

A moment later, the tallest of the group stepped forward and pressed his shoulder against the wood, pushing hard.

The doors groaned, resisting at first. Then—a dull thud. A low creak. A final push. The doors swung inward, revealing the dark interior beyond. One by one, the men disappeared inside.

Sean let out a slow, measured breath.

They had mere minutes before their pursuers realized the church was empty.

Jean-Marc turned toward him.

Sean didn't hesitate. He turned to the others, keeping his voice low but firm.

"Back to the hotel. Get the car. Get out of here."

No one argued.

Sean moved first, keeping his body low, his steps silent against the damp earth. The others followed in practiced rhythm, their movements quick and controlled. Behind them, the church loomed, its ancient stone walls swallowing Mercer's men into the darkness within. But Sean knew it wouldn't last. Mercer would realize soon enough that their targets were long gone. That meant every second counted.

Jean-Marc led them down the slope, toward the clustered buildings on the outskirts of the village. A small dirt path snaked between them; an old service road likely used by vineyard workers generations ago. The worn cobblestones glistened with moisture, a thin layer of mist rising from the cold ground.

The hotel was on the far side of the village, a ten-minute walk in broad daylight. Tonight, that journey might as well have been a mile of open battlefield.

They stayed close to the crumbling vineyard wall, moving through the cover of overgrown bushes and leaning wooden fences. Shadows stretched long in the dim glow of scattered streetlamps, and every noise—a creaking shutter, a distant voice, the wind rattling old windowpanes—sent a fresh bolt of tension through Sean's spine.

Jean-Marc paused at a corner, peering around the edge of an old stone house. The street ahead was empty, but lanterns from a nearby café still cast pools of golden light onto the cobbled road.

A figure moved inside—a bartender cleaning up for the night, stacking chairs onto tables, wiping down counters. They couldn't risk being seen, not even by a civilian.

Jean-Marc signaled then took them through a narrow alleyway, its walls so tight that Tommy had to turn sideways to squeeze through. The passage smelled of damp stone and old cooking smoke, likely an area where shops dumped scraps from the kitchens.

They emerged onto a small courtyard, just behind an old bakery. The scent of fresh bread still clung to the air, mixing with the crisp bite of the autumn night. Sean kept his breathing steady, scanning their surroundings. The hotel wasn't far now; a few more streets, a few more turns.

Then, just as he stepped forward, a noise snapped through the silence. A rustling movement. A sharp sniff. And then—a low, guttural growl.

Sean's eyes flicked right.

Near the bakery's back entrance, standing rigid beside a stack of wooden crates, was a large black dog. Its ears flattened, its body tense, its dark eyes locked onto them. A guard dog. Sean cursed silently.

Jean-Marc held up a hand, stopping Evelyn and Tommy in their tracks. No sudden movements. The dog lowered its head slightly, its muscles coiling. It didn't bark—not yet—but the low growl in its throat vibrated through the quiet night air.

Sean weighed the options.

They couldn't make a run for it, the dog would bark, alerting anyone nearby. And they couldn't risk a fight—if it attacked, there was no way to keep that silent.

Evelyn's hand moved slowly to her pocket, her fingers closing around something small and wrapped in paper.

Sean glanced at her, and she gave the slightest nod.

Without breaking eye contact with the dog, she knelt down slowly, unwrapped the small bundle, and held out a piece of soft bread. The dog's ears twitched. The growl faded slightly. It sniffed the air, hesitating.

Evelyn placed the bread on the ground, then backed up carefully, never turning her back on the animal. The dog remained still for another second, then cautiously stepped forward, sniffing the food.

Sean didn't wait.

He signaled the others, and they moved—slowly, controlled—slipping through the next alleyway before the dog decided to change its mind. Once they were clear of the courtyard, Tommy exhaled, shaking his head. "That thing looked like it could have eaten my face."

Sean smirked. "Probably could have."

Evelyn dusted off her hands. "Good thing I had something better to offer."

Jean-Marc motioned ahead. "We're close."

They reached the final stretch of road, keeping to the edge of the buildings. Ahead, the hotel stood dark and still, its front entrance barely lit by a flickering streetlamp. And, more importantly, the men following them were nowhere to be seen.

Sean didn't trust it. "Stay sharp," he murmured, leading them across the street.

They entered the parking lot, moving swiftly toward their car. The vehicle sat untouched, the windows reflecting the moonlight.

Jean-Marc reached for the driver's side handle. Suddenly, a distant noise stopped him.

Sean snapped his head around, instincts flaring.

A figure emerged from the hotel's side entrance—one of Mercer's men, yawning as he lit a cigarette. Sean's pulse kicked up.

The man hadn't seen them yet—but if he turned his head even slightly....

"Get in. Now," Sean ordered.

Tommy didn't hesitate. He yanked open the back door and slid inside. Evelyn followed. Jean-Marc climbed into the driver's seat, Sean right behind him. The car doors clicked shut.

The man with the cigarette turned slightly, glancing toward the lot.

Sean held still, barely breathing. For a second nothing happened.

Then the man shrugged, turned back toward the hotel, and disappeared inside.

Jean-Marc didn't wait. He turned the key. The engine rumbled to life—soft but clear in the quiet night.

Sean's heart thumped hard in his chest as Jean-Marc pulled the car into reverse then eased it toward the exit. They were moving. They were clear, for the moment. Then—a flash of headlights in the rearview mirror.

Sean's stomach dropped.

A black Renault. Engine on. Watching them.

It pulled out onto the road, falling in line behind them.

Sean exhaled sharply, jaw tightening. They weren't out yet.

Jean-Marc met his gaze through the mirror.

"What now?"

Sean's answer was immediate. "Now we lose them."

22

Mercer and his men fanned out in the dark. The church loomed around them, its high, arched ceiling disappearing into the shadows, where only the faintest slivers of moonlight bled through the stained-glass windows. The air was cool and still, thick with the scent of old stone, burning wax, and the faint remnants of incense clinging to the air like an echo of past prayers. Their footsteps barely made a sound against the worn flagstone floor, the uneven surfaces smoothed by centuries of worshippers who had knelt, walked, and wept here.

Wooden pews stood in long, orderly rows, their dark oak surfaces polished to a muted sheen. The altar, bathed in dim candlelight, cast long shadows over the carved reliefs that adorned its base. Above it, a towering crucifix hung over the empty nave, the figure of Christ half hidden in the darkness.

Flickering votive candles lined the side walls, their small flames wavering at the sudden intrusion of the men moving through the sacred space.

There was no sign of Wyatt.

The men looked around for a moment, as if their eyes deceived them. Then confusion filled their faces, and one by one they turned to their leader for further orders, or an explanation.

For a moment, his cheeks burned, both from frustration and the twist of the gut that came with being wrong about a critical decision. He felt his men's eyes boring through him as they waited for his next command.

"Check everything," he barked, his tone leaving no doubt who was still in charge. "They're here somewhere."

His second-in-command stared at him with a blank expression for a moment. Mercer could see the doubt in the man's eyes, the unspoken questions dripping from his lips.

Then, after the moment of hesitation, he broke the stare and began checking the rows of pews, looking under and around them for any sign of Wyatt.

Mercer stalked over to the front of the sanctuary and studied the walls, the floor tiles, everything he could. Had he been wrong? Did Wyatt and his companions trick them into coming out here and then skip town? It was starting to feel more and more like that was the case with every second that ticked by.

The men rummaged through the interior, turning over everything that would move. But there was no sign of Wyatt.

Shadows danced erratically along the walls, cast by the flickering glow of scattered votive candles. A thick layer of dust kicked up from neglected corners, swirling in the dim candlelight. Mercer moved through the space with a calculating gaze, his patience wearing thin. Wyatt had been here. He could feel it. Yet the church was small, there was nowhere to hide.

One of the men shoved a wooden chair aside, sending it clattering across the stone floor, but there was nothing beneath it. Another pushed against the altar, testing for any movement or hidden compartments. Still nothing.

A third man ran his hand along the walls, feeling for gaps in the stonework where a concealed door might be. But the walls were solid, ancient. Immovable.

Mercer clenched his jaw. This was wrong. They should have found them by now.

Then—a shift.

It was subtle, barely noticeable, but enough to halt his movement. The stone beneath his boot had given way slightly. Mercer looked down at the tile, and grinned.

There it was. A faint depression beneath his foot, a floor panel that was different from the rest.

"I know where they went," Mercer said.

The rest of the men looked over at him for a second, then moved to where he stood, staring down at the tile.

"Another secret passage?" one of the men asked.

"So it would seem." He noticed that the dust had been disturbed around the tile, and a little debris had settled just outside the seams.

Mercer crouched and ran his fingers over the cool stone beneath his boot. It was subtle, almost imperceptible, but the tile had shifted ever so slightly under his weight. He pressed down again, feeling the faintest give. His expression hardened.

Using the edge of his gloved hand, he brushed away the thin layer of dust gathered in the shallow grooves around the tile's perimeter. Unlike the others, this one had a slight gap along its edge, as if it had been removed before.

Mercer reached for his knife, slipped the blade into the gap, and twisted. Then, with a dull scrape, it shifted.

Mercer pried the slab upward.

A rush of cool air greeted him, carrying the scent of damp earth and stale stone. Below, darkness yawned open, the entrance to a passageway carved deep beneath the church.

A slow, knowing smile curled at the corner of Mercer's lips.

Wyatt hadn't vanished. He had gone down for the second time.

Mercer stood up and looked to the others.

"Klein," he said to the man closest to him. "Take point."

The man nodded and started to step down into the stairwell when a voice through Seven's radio interrupted.

"Sir," Kraus said, his voice urgent. The groan of a car engine filled the background. "We are pursuing the targets now."

Everyone in the church heard the statement, and confusion immediately settled into the room.

"Say again?" Mercer ordered.

"Levi and I are on the road, in pursuit of Wyatt and his team."

"How is that possible?"

There was a pause on the other end, and Mercer knew immediately that Kraus didn't want to say he and the other guy had screwed up.

"We were watching the entrances to the inn, sir. They must have slipped into their car while we were focused on the building."

"Where are they now?"

"Looks like they're heading out of town."

Mercer looked at the rest of his men in the church. "Everyone outside. Now. We have to get back to the inn."

They scrambled, hurrying back to the door. As they spilled outside, Mercer spoke to the man on the radio again. "Did you bring both cars?"

"Working on it," Kraus said. The answer sent a frustrated twinge through Mercer's chest, but he also knew why.

He stepped out of the church and immediately heard the sound of a car engine roaring toward them. The headlights of the Citroën raked across his eyes, momentarily blinding him and his men.

They instinctively drew their weapons, ready to open fire, but the car zoomed past them in a flash, followed closely by the black Renault.

"Hold your fire!" Mercer shouted. "We don't want to hit our men. They have the situation under control for the moment. We need to get back to the other car."

23

Jean-Marc gripped the steering wheel with both hands, his knuckles taut, the veins along the backs of his fingers pronounced from the pressure. The car pitched forward as he pushed the accelerator, the engine roaring in protest before settling into a low, powerful hum. The darkened road stretched ahead, winding and dipping through the countryside, its curves treacherous, its edges unforgiving.

The black Renault behind them stayed locked in pursuit.

Tires hummed against the asphalt, the faintest screech of rubber against the damp road surface echoing through the valley. A fine mist clung to the air, the cool humidity thickening as they passed through the lowest points in the terrain, where old, leaning fences lined fields that disappeared into darkness. The high beams illuminated the dust kicked up from the roadside gravel, swirling in chaotic spirals before dissipating into the night.

The road ahead curved sharply to the left, bending around the rise of a tree-covered slope. Jean-Marc handled the turn with expert ease, the wheels gripping just enough before the car threatened to slide. He adjusted fluidly, working with the momentum rather than against it, allowing the weight of the car to pull into the turn naturally.

The Renault followed suit, the driver handling the curve with equal skill. These guys were no amateurs.

The countryside around them blurred into streaks of shadow and flickering moonlight. To the left, dense woodland pressed in close, ancient trees stretching upward like dark sentinels against the night sky. To the right, the land fell away into rolling farmland, the fields barely visible in the dim glow cast by scattered farmhouses far in the distance.

Another sharp dip in the road sent the car briefly airborne. A half second of weightlessness. The tires slammed back down, sending a jolt through the frame, but Jean-Marc kept steady hands on the wheel, adjusting for the impact before it could throw them off course.

Evelyn braced herself against the overhead handlebar, her posture rigid, knuckles pale from the tension in her grip. The interior of the car felt suffocating, a pressure chamber of motion and silence, filled only with the rhythmic pulse of the revving engine and the hum of the tires racing over the uneven pavement.

They were gaining distance on the Renault, but not enough.

The road ahead straightened, stretching for nearly half a mile after it curved again.

Jean-Marc took the opportunity, pressing harder on the accelerator. The speedometer climbed. The car responded instantly, its smooth acceleration a testament to his precision handling. For a few fleeting moments, the Renault dropped farther behind.

Then the high beams flared in the mirror again. Their pursuers were closing the gap.

The driver behind them wasn't just keeping pace—he was waiting. Watching. Calculating. Jean-Marc adjusted his grip and considered his next move.

The road pitched downward, sloping toward a narrow bridge crossing a shallow ravine. The old stonework looked ancient and unforgiving, its low walls meant more for marking the path than preventing accidents. The mist hanging low over the bridge thickened, swallowing the far end in a haze of white.

He took the incline fast, letting the momentum carry them forward, the car momentarily light on its suspension before slamming back onto even ground.

The Renault followed. It had gained more ground now.

The high beams bounced against the road ahead, throwing erratic shadows along the tree line. The driver was pushing harder, more aggressive now that they were beyond the village outskirts.

Jean-Marc barely spared a glance at the mirror. He didn't need to. He could feel them closing in.

The road veered left, cutting through another dense patch of forest before leading them toward a stone church at the village's edge. The looming structure was just visible beyond the next bend, its weathered walls and Gothic spire bathed in faint silver light.

Jean-Marc's mind worked quickly. These roads weren't built for sudden maneuvers. Any attempt to swerve off course could result in disaster. He had to use the natural layout of the land to his advantage.

The black Renault lurked closer. The driver was waiting for a straightaway—waiting to make a move.

Jean-Marc let them get comfortable. Just before reaching the church, the road narrowed again, pinched between a short stone wall on one side and a steep incline on the other. The road would curve sharply again just past the church entrance, opening up toward the next stretch of countryside.

Jean-Marc waited until the last possible second before making his next move. Instead of braking into the curve, he took it fast.

The tires fought for grip, the entire chassis shifting beneath them, a controlled slide that barely skimmed the edge of the road. The vehicle tilted slightly before Jean-Marc corrected, regaining traction as they shot past the church's towering walls.

For a brief moment, the Renault's headlights vanished from view. Jean-Marc pressed the accelerator again, taking the next incline with ease.

Then the lights reappeared. Still with them. Gaining again.

Jean-Marc's eyes flicked to the mirror one last time before he focused ahead.

Beyond the next bend, open country awaited.

The narrow village streets were far behind now, the glow of streetlights swallowed by the sprawling darkness of the countryside. Their car barreled down the winding road, Jean-Marc pushing the engine harder, demanding more speed from the machine beneath his hands. The tires whined against the damp pavement, gripping just enough to keep them from careening off the edges.

Here, the landscape was different. No buildings. No alleyways. No sudden turns to disappear into. Just the vast openness of the Vosges foothills, where rolling farmland stretched for miles and dense patches of woodland cast long, black shadows in the moonlight. The road was a snake of asphalt, cutting through the valleys and climbing into the hills, narrowing as it weaved between steep embankments and sharp drops.

The Renault stayed on them.

It was relentless, its headlights bouncing as it absorbed every twist, every dip in the road. Whoever was driving it wasn't just good—they were calculated, patient. They weren't desperate. They operated exactly like professionals would in this situation.

Jean-Marc clenched his jaw. He had to lose them before they made their move.

The road dipped suddenly, and the car lurched forward, suspension straining under the shift in terrain. The descent was steep, forcing him to ease off the gas for a fraction of a second to keep control. The Renault did the same, mirroring their every move.

A fine mist clung to the lower ground, a ghostly layer of fog rising from the cool earth and swirling in their wake. The fields beyond the road were barely visible, shadowy patches of farmland divided by occasional wooden fences and the faint outlines of scattered barns.

Then came the turn. It was a brutal, tightening left curve that hugged the side of a steep incline.

Jean-Marc adjusted, tilting into the bend, letting the car's momentum carry them through smoothly. The tires fought for grip, the body of the vehicle shuddering under the tension, but they made it. The Renault did too. Still there. Still waiting.

Then—impact.

A sharp jolt rocked the car as the Renault slammed into their rear quarter-panel; a move often used by police in this kind of scenario. The sudden force jerked the back end sideways, sending the entire vehicle into a wild fishtail. Jean-Marc fought it.

The steering wheel trembled violently in his hands as the tires skidded, shrieking against the pavement. The right-side wheels caught the gravel at the road's edge, kicking up a storm of dust and loose stones. The embankment on that side fell away sharply, a steep drop leading down into darkness.

For a fraction of a second, gravity threatened to claim them. Evelyn sucked in a breath, fingers clawing into the handle above her door.

Jean-Marc reacted out of sheer instinct.

Instead of slamming the brakes, which would have guaranteed a roll, he rode out the slide, letting the weight of the car shift naturally. Then—at exactly the right moment—he jerked the wheel left, countering the spin while slamming the accelerator.

The tires caught the pavement again. The car snapped back into alignment with a final shuddering lurch. They were still on the road. Still alive.

Jean-Marc exhaled; his pulse steady but his mind racing.

The Renault hadn't backed off. That had been a warning.

A second later, the black car surged forward again, closing the gap once more. Jean-Marc gritted his teeth. The road straightened only briefly before curving again, leading them up into the higher elevations of the countryside.

Here, the fields gave way to patches of dense woodland, trees pressing in closer on both sides. The darkness thickened, swallowing the landscape beyond the reach of their headlights.

Jean-Marc's fingers tightened around the wheel. He had to predict their next move.

The Renault was too controlled. Too patient. Whoever was

behind the wheel wasn't going to recklessly attempt another pit maneuver. No, they were setting up something else.

The road dipped again, leading them across another narrow stone bridge, but this one arched over a shallow ravine. Beyond it, the asphalt stretched into a brief straightaway—the perfect opportunity.

Jean-Marc realized the danger a second too late.

The Renault closed in—this time faster. Not for a ramming maneuver. For something worse.

Sean turned in his seat. His posture stiffened.

Jean-Marc caught the shift in the mirror.

Sean was watching something. Something outside the car. Then —moonlight caught the movement.

A dark silhouette leaned out of the Renault's passenger-side window. Jean-Marc didn't need to see what was in his hand to know. The outline of a gun was easy to see beneath the silver glow.

The chase had just escalated.

Gunfire tore through the night; the crack of the shot swallowed almost instantly by the roar of the engines.

Sean barely had time to register it before the rear windshield exploded, sending shards of glass flying past his ear and bouncing off the dashboard. A second round punched through the front windshield, narrowly missing Jean-Marc's head.

"Down!" Sean shouted, already reaching for Evelyn and pulling her lower into the seat. She let out a strangled gasp, her hands gripping the door handle as she ducked her head.

Jean-Marc's hands remained steady on the wheel, though his jaw was locked tight, his focus entirely on the winding road ahead. He didn't flinch, didn't hesitate, even as another round snapped through the air, ricocheting off the trunk.

Sean turned, pistol already drawn, twisting in his seat to face the black Renault chasing them. The car loomed close, headlights burning white-hot, its front grille glistening like the bared teeth of a predator.

The shooter was halfway out of the window now, bracing his arm against the doorframe, lining up another shot. Sean was faster.

He jammed his foot against the base of the door, pushing it open slightly to give himself more room, then raised his pistol and fired two quick shots. The first hit the grille, sending a burst of sparks cascading onto the road. The second slammed into the left headlight, shattering the bulb instantly, leaving only the flickering glow of the other to illuminate the road ahead.

The Renault's driver swerved slightly, struggling to maintain control, and the gunman jerked backward, momentarily ducking into the car for cover.

Sean seized the opportunity. He lined up his sights and squeezed the trigger. The bullet pinged off the hood, narrowly missing the gunman's shoulder.

Jean-Marc suddenly jerked the wheel to the right, yanking them into a hard turn down a narrow side road. The tires screamed in protest, struggling for grip on the loose gravel. Sean's body slammed against the door from the force of the turn, and Evelyn let out a breathless gasp as the car rocked violently.

Trees whizzed by in a blur on either side, their thick canopy blotting out the sky.

The Renault stayed close behind, but it hit the entrance to the forest road too fast, its remaining headlight flaring wildly as the driver struggled to adjust to the quicker turning conditions.

Jean-Marc didn't slow down. His hands remained firm on the wheel as he weaved through the snaking turns, tires spitting up dirt and small rocks as he fought to keep the car from skidding. The scent of scorched rubber filled the cabin, mixing with the lingering stench of gunpowder.

Sean twisted back again, heart pounding. The gunman in the Renault had recovered, already bracing himself against the window frame again.

Sean reacted instantly and fired before the man could take his shot.

The round struck the windshield, spiderwebbing the glass. The shooter ducked down, and before Sean could fire again, the Renault's driver reacted; cutting hard left, ramming the rear quarter panel of their car. The impact sent the Citroën into a fishtail, tires losing traction for a split second.

Sean's stomach lurched. They were going off the road.

Jean-Marc fought the wheel, gritting his teeth as he worked to correct. Instead of jerking it immediately, he let the car slide for an extra half second, then yanked left at just the right moment, punching the gas.

The tires caught the pavement, and the car snapped back into alignment.

Sean barely had time to exhale before another shot ripped through the night, this one punching into the trunk, embedding itself in the metal.

Tommy cursed. "That was too close."

Sean didn't respond. His attention was locked on the shooter, who was reloading.

"We're coming up on a dip," Jean-Marc gritted out. "Hold on."

The road dipped suddenly, and Sean's stomach flipped at the sudden weightlessness. The dense trees fell away, revealing a wide, open valley below stretching out beneath the pale glow of the moon.

For a brief moment, they had a clear road ahead. But the Renault wasn't giving up. It burst from the tree line seconds later, its remaining headlight flickering against the mist rolling in over the fields.

Jean-Marc exhaled sharply. "We need to end this."

Sean agreed. The open space meant they were vulnerable—no sharp turns to use, no blind corners to disappear behind.

The Renault was gaining again.

Sean turned, just in time to see the gunman leaning out the window again. The muzzle flashed again. Rounds struck the trunk again, and one went through the back window and out the windshield.

Tommy braced himself. Jean-Marc made his move.

He cut the wheel hard to the left, then threw them into a drift turn.

The entire car spun sideways, tires kicking up a storm of dust and gravel as they pivoted on the road. Jean-Marc slammed the gas again at the apex of the turn.

The Citroën rocketed forward—straight toward the Renault.

The other driver swerved right—too fast. The Renault whipped one way, then the other as the man behind the wheel tried to correct the vehicle's motion. But it was too late. He'd lost control.

The car's right-side tires bit hard against the asphalt. Then time slowed down. The Renault surged ahead toward the road's shoulder and launched off the ground. The weight of the engine pulled the front end down as the vehicle soared through the night. Its flight was short-lived. It nosedived into the ground beyond a ditch then flipped end over end, twisting in a violent ballet of destruction.

It tossed sideways a few turns as it continued to tumble forward, sending a spray of dirt and debris into the air before it slammed top first into the tree line, leaving the crumpled vehicle standing on its front, the crushed roof leaning pressed against a tree.

Jean-Marc kept driving, only slowing for a few seconds out of the natural human instinct to stare at the crash.

"Good job," Sean said. "That ought to slow them down for a while."

Evelyn sat up and looked back through the rear window, catching a glimpse of the mangled vehicle before it disappeared out of sight behind a hill.

"Should we make sure they're—"

"No," Jean-Marc answered before she could finish. "If they're not dead, they're badly injured. They won't be troubling us again."

"That's only a few of the group following us," Tommy reminded.

"Always a ray of sunshine, Schultzie," Sean joked.

"I'm just saying."

"Where are we going now?" Evelyn asked, trying to be more productive with the conversation.

"She's right," Sean said. "We need to a place to stay for the night. Once this adrenaline wears off, we'll have to get some rest."

"I have a friend," Jean-Marc said. "He has a house in the country.

It's not in Poitiers, but it's not far. I'm sure he would let us stay for the night."

"I don't want to put your friend in danger. Or be an inconvenience."

Jean-Marc smiled. "Oh, this friend doesn't mind danger. As to the inconvenience... I don't think he'll mind."

24

The tires shrieked as Nikolai took a curve at high speed, forcing everyone in the car to lean hard to the right. Mercer gripped the dashboard with one hand, his other curled into a fist against his thigh.

This wasn't how it was supposed to go. Wyatt should be dead. And they should have the artifact, or whatever it was they were meant to find in the village. Instead, Wyatt was ahead—somewhere in the French countryside—slipping farther away by the second.

The countryside blurred past in a mix of moonlit fields and shadowy tree lines. Their gray Renault hurtled forward, its engine roaring as Nikolai pushed the car hard, chasing the taillights that had long since disappeared over the horizon.

Mercer's jaw clenched. He exhaled through his nose, fighting back the heat rising in his chest. There was no room for anger now. No room for failure.

"This road is dangerous at this speed," Nikolai muttered, his thick accent clipped.

Mercer shot him a cold glance. "Then don't crash."

From the back seat, Santos chuckled under his breath. He'd

always been more of an adrenaline junkie. Dangerous situations seemed to feed him to the point others might consider him deranged.

Klein, seated beside him, said nothing, his gaze fixed on the road ahead, hands resting lightly on his thighs, his posture relaxed but ready.

Mercer turned back to the windshield, scanning the road ahead. The Renault's headlights carved twin tunnels of light through the darkness, illuminating rolling hills and tight bends but nothing else.

Mercer grabbed the radio clipped to his vest. "Team Three, status?"

A crackle of static. Then a voice: "No sign of them in the village. They're gone."

Mercer had left the other two men behind in Domrémy for two reasons. One, this wasn't a clown car, and two, there was still the possibility that Wyatt had used their vehicle as a diversion. When the vehicle had zoomed by, Mercer hadn't been able to see how many people were inside. Only the driver. It was possible the guy behind the wheel had left Wyatt and the other two there at the inn, hiding until his men predictably chased after the car.

Mercer spoke into the radio again. "Then get a car. We can rendezvous later."

"Yes, sir."

The Renault's speedometer ticked past 130 kph Nikolai pressed harder on the accelerator. The car hummed with tension, the tires gripping the winding roads with barely enough traction.

Another tight turn—another sharp correction. Nikolai was pushing it to the limit, but Mercer wasn't about to tell him to slow down.

Nikolai yanked the wheel left, and the Renault tilted slightly before its tires gripped the road again, pulling them through the sharp bend. The countryside stretched out ahead in ghostly silver and shadow, the open fields vast and empty, broken only by the occasional darkened farmhouse, skeletal tree line, or crumbling stone wall.

Inside the car, no one spoke. There was no need.

Only the groan of the engine and the hiss of rubber on asphalt filled the air, an ominous soundtrack to the chase. Mercer sat in the passenger seat, eyes scanning the road ahead, jaw tight with calculation. Wyatt was out there, somewhere beyond the next turn, beyond the next ridge. He couldn't run forever. No one could.

Mercer had seen it before. The moment a man realized he wasn't going to escape.

A flicker of memory surfaced—Southeast Asia. Another chase. Another mark who thought he could outrun death. Mercer had been hired to track him down—an ex-intelligence officer who had made the wrong kind of enemies, the kind who didn't just want him dead but wanted a lesson made of him.

The man had been good. He had run, hidden, changed identities. But Mercer had been better.

He had found the target in a rural village, not unlike this one. A nowhere town with nowhere roads. The hunt ended in a cane field; a narrow path lined with thick stalks of sugarcane that swayed like silent witnesses.

Mercer had followed the blood trail—small drops at first, then bigger ones, streaked across the dry earth. The man had been wounded, slowed down. It was always that way. No matter how well they ran, the fear slowed them down.

He had found him curled behind the stalks, breathing hard, hand clamped over his side where the bullet had grazed him. Eyes wide with a desperate, silent plea.

Mercer had crouched beside him, pulled a knife, and said nothing. The man had talked then. They always did.

Mercer never rushed those moments. Fear was a blade just as sharp as any steel. A man would spill his secrets when he knew he wasn't getting out alive—not because he thought it would save him but because the weight of holding on to them suddenly felt like too much.

The memory faded, but the feeling remained. Wyatt wasn't there yet. But he would be.

Mercer tapped the door panel twice, eyes narrowing.

Nikolai pushed the machine harder. He pressed the accelerator, the engine growling deeper as the Renault pushed past 140 kph, cutting through the countryside like a bullet.

The road was long and winding, flanked by rolling hills and stretches of forest that swallowed the moonlight. Shadows moved in the distance—wildlife scattering from the approaching machine.

Still no sign of Wyatt.

That bothered Mercer. His fingers curled against his knee, a slow, controlled movement. Wyatt should be within reach by now. Even if he had taken another road, there weren't many options out here.

Unless he knew something Mercer didn't. Or unless…

Mercer's gaze flicked to the tree line on the left. If Wyatt had gone off-road, they'd never see him. Not unless he made a mistake.

Nikolai took another turn hard, and the Renault's tires skimmed the edge of the asphalt before gripping again. The silence in the car deepened.

Santos shifted slightly in the back seat while rolling his shoulders and watching the road like a wolf watching for movement in the brush. Klein remained still, his hands resting lightly on his thighs, unreadable.

As the car reached the apex of the curve, Nikolai naturally started to accelerate like a race driver, but after a second let his foot off the gas. Up ahead, he saw what appeared to be smoke, or steam piling into the night sky from a forest off to the left.

Mercer saw it too.

"Is that…?" Nikolai said, cutting off his sentence as they drew closer to the crash site.

Mercer clenched his jaw, grinding his teeth. He nodded grimly. "Pull over."

Nikolai didn't question the order. He feathered the brakes and turned the car over to the left-hand shoulder, easing it to a stop with a few feet of clearance in case another car came through that direction.

Mercer flung open his door before Nikolai turned off the engine.

The others got out immediately and followed Mercer off the side of the road and down the steep embankment.

They jumped across the six-foot ditch at the bottom and clambered up the other side to a 125-foot stretch of grass that ran from the bank to the wreckage.

Steam billowed out of the crumpled hood. Some of the interior lights were on, but there was no movement from the inside. The doors hung open on both sides. The wheels were bent at different angles. The windows, from what he could see, were shattered.

Mercer kept up his pace, hurrying toward the vehicle, passing huge chunks of excavated earth where the car must have struck multiple times.

"Fan out," he ordered his men.

The men did as they were told and spread out in a line across the field.

Mercer didn't have to explain why. The command was obvious to the others. They all knew that there was a high likelihood that one or both of the car's occupants had been thrown from the vehicle as it tumbled toward the trees. There was a faint possibility that they could have been thrown clear of the crash, but he didn't hold out any hope for that unlikely scenario.

They pressed forward at a more deliberate pace, each pair of eyes scanning the deep grass for signs of life.

Mercer waded ahead, brushing aside the grass with his boots. He looked carefully down at the ground in front of him, sweeping his gaze from left to right so he wouldn't miss anything.

The search didn't take long before one of the other men shouted.

"Sir? I have something."

Santos stood still, staring down at the ground about thirty feet from Mercer's position. The others moved with their leader, converging around Santos.

On the ground was a sight that would have turned any ordinary human's stomach to the point of vomiting. But these men had seen things this bad, and worse in some cases.

One of the men from the car lay splayed out on the blood-smeared grass. One of his arms had been severed from his body, probably lying on the ground nearby. His face was unrecognizable, crushed under the immense weight of the car that had rolled over onto him on its way to the tree.

Mercer immediately figured he'd been partially ejected from the car as it tumbled through the field, and on one of the flips had been caught under the doorframe.

"Keep searching," he said. "There's nothing we can do for him."

The others lingered for a moment, realization and the gravity of the sight setting in. Then they spread out again and resumed their grim march toward the wreckage.

Something spewed out of the hood and spilled to the ground around the base of the tree, causing the men to momentarily halt out of caution. As far as they could tell, there wasn't a gas leak, and with nothing to ignite it if there was, it seemed there was no danger of an explosion.

Mercer pushed ahead, reaching the car first. He faced the undercarriage of the vehicle, which had come to rest standing on its grill and front bumper, tilted slightly at enough of an angle to keep it in its position. The roof wrapped around the tree trunk also kept it stationary.

The men moved around to either side, Mercer taking the driver's side, prepared for another grisly sight.

He wasn't disappointed.

The driver was pinned against the tree by the roof of the car, crushing him like a tomato. It was one of the bloodiest, most gruesome scenes he'd witnessed, previous one included. The tree bark and windshield were stained with the dark crimson liquid. One of Mercer's men looked away. It was only for a split second, and he quickly realized he needed to remain resolute.

Mercer simply stared at what was left of the driver's body. He took a deep breath and then turned away. He waved his hands out on both sides, ushering the men back to their vehicle.

"What next, boss?" Santos asked in his deep Spanish accent.

"We rendezvous with the other two."

"What about Wyatt and his group?"

Mercer didn't look down at the first body as he tromped by. "We have the tracker you put on their car, right?"

Santos gave a single nod.

"Then we know where they're going."

25

POITIERS, FRANCE

Every pair of eyes in the car were cloaked in fatigue. Jean-Marc had shaken his head more than a couple of times while driving.

The road winding through the countryside northeast of Poitiers narrowed the farther they drove, pressed in on either side by thick hedgerows and overhanging limbs. The headlights swept across the foliage, casting long, twitching shadows that stretched across the lane then retreated like ghosts into the brush. Patches of fog clung low to the earth in the open fields beyond, hovering just above the frost-bitten grass, softening the edges of the landscape like breath on a cold windowpane.

Above, the night sky was vast and unclouded, spattered with stars that pulsed like ancient beacons. A silver sliver of moon hung low on the horizon, rising slowly behind the hills, barely cresting the tops of distant trees. There was a kind of purity to the quiet—a stillness that came only in places where modern life hadn't seeped too deeply into the soil. Out here, it felt like the past had simply curled up and gone to sleep without ever quite letting go.

They drove on, the Citroën's tires humming softly against the worn country lane, the hum interrupted now and again by the crunch of scattered gravel or a low thump where the road dipped. The trees began to part, revealing wide tracts of open pasture stitched together by stone walls and wooden fencing. A narrow stream glinted in the moonlight as they passed a small bridge, the water barely moving beneath the arch, as if frozen in time.

Ahead, twin lanterns glowed at the edge of a wrought iron gate, each affixed to stone columns capped with weathered limestone. Ivy crawled up the stonework, gnarled and thick with age, its leaves dark and leathery under the stars. The gate itself stood partially open, swinging slightly on the breeze as if it had been expecting them.

"Uh, Jean-Marc?" Tommy asked in a groggy voice. "Exactly what kind of place does your friend live in out here?"

The driver offered a tired grin as he glanced back in the rearview mirror. "You'll see."

The gravel drive beyond the gate curled gently uphill through a line of cypress trees, their shapes tall and narrow, swaying slightly in the wind. The farther they climbed, the more the countryside revealed itself in the distance—soft ridgelines silhouetted against the lighter hue of the sky, clusters of trees dark as ink, and the scattered pinpoints of farmhouses flickering faintly on the horizon.

Then the home appeared—at first only a suggestion of light and shadow at the top of the rise. But it wasn't a simple country house as Sean and the others had believed. It was an enormous château.

Sean leaned forward and looked at the Frenchman. "What is it you said your friend does again?"

Jean-Marc's grin widened. "I didn't."

As they drew nearer, the building came into full view, its pale stone walls catching the moonlight and reflecting it with a quiet brilliance. The roof line rose and fell with an old-world elegance, steep and peaked, punctuated by tall chimneys and narrow dormer windows. Vines clung to the lower floors like aging armor, creeping up from planters that flanked the broad front steps.

A circular gravel driveway stretched out before the entrance, ringing a sculpted garden with a low stone fountain at its center. Though the water had been turned off for the season, the basin held a faint glimmer of frost, and the edges of the surrounding flower beds were laced with silver.

The windows glowed with low amber light, not electric, but warm—like candles behind glass. The glow softened the edges of the stone façade and painted the shutters with a soft golden hue. The main entrance was framed by twin columns and an arched wooden door that looked older than the republic itself, its surface worn smooth by generations of hands and weather.

A pair of dormer windows on the second floor cast angled shafts of light out over the gravel drive. Somewhere behind the house, a dog barked once, then went quiet. Beyond the château, the landscape dipped again into another field, where trees lined the far edge and rustled quietly in the wind. Somewhere back there, a barn or outbuilding might be hiding in the darkness, tucked away from sight, waiting like everything else for morning.

The whole place carried a kind of timeless calm—grand without pretense, aged without decay. The château didn't announce itself; it simply existed, rooted into the land like it had grown there. A place forgotten by time, and perfect for disappearing from the world were it not for the size of the place.

Jean-Marc slowed the vehicle to a stop off to the left of the circular driveway and killed the engine.

The engine ticked as it cooled, the only sound in the stillness that followed their arrival. One by one, the doors opened with soft thuds. Sean stepped out first while adjusting the strap of his shoulder bag as the others gathered their belongings from the trunk. The gravel crunched beneath their feet, a dry, delicate sound that seemed to echo louder in the quiet countryside. The scent of damp soil and late-season grass drifted in on the night breeze, mingling with the faint aroma of firewood from a chimney somewhere nearby.

Sean drew in a slow breath, letting the crisp air settle him. It had a faint trace of pine and smoke, and beneath that the earthy smell of old stones and fields. The kind of air that always smelled older than the cities, like it remembered the centuries.

The front door of the château creaked open, spilling warm light onto the gravel like a pool of gold. A figure stepped into the glow.

"Antón," Jean-Marc said with a note of warmth.

The man who emerged from the house was a striking presence—five foot ten, broad-shouldered and lean with the unmistakable build of someone who'd never let himself go soft. He moved with the quiet assurance of someone used to dangerous things, but his smile was genuine as he stepped onto the threshold, arms spreading in welcome.

Antón's skin was deep brown, his face angular and clean shaven, eyes sharp and observant beneath thick brows. His head was shaved close, and a silver hoop glinted in his left ear. He wore a dark navy button-up shirt with the sleeves rolled to his forearms, and tucked neatly into gray wool trousers. A heavy cardigan hung open over the shirt, the thick weave of it hinting at a practical warmth suited for old stone walls and midnight air.

He gave Jean-Marc a firm clasp of the shoulder before turning to the others.

"You must be Sean," he said with a nod, his voice a smooth baritone edged with a faint French accent. "And Tommy."

Sean stepped forward, offering a handshake. Antón's grip was solid. "Appreciate you letting us land here on short notice."

Antón nodded then extended his hand to Tommy. "Any friend of Jean-Marc's is a friend of mine."

Tommy returned the handshake. "Thanks for having us."

Antón turned slightly toward Evelyn, who had slung her satchel over one shoulder and held her coat closed against the breeze.

"And you must be Dr. Langley," he said. "Welcome."

"Thank you," Evelyn said, her breath fogging slightly in the cool air. "You have a beautiful home."

Antón smiled. "It's too big and far too old, but it keeps the weather out. Come in, all of you. The fire's going."

He stepped aside, holding the door as they filed in, the warmth from within curling around them as they crossed the threshold. Inside, the air smelled faintly of woodsmoke, leather, and something rich and comforting—perhaps the last traces of a stew or slow-roasted meat. The entryway was spacious, with flagstone floors worn smooth by years of footsteps and a thick wool runner that led toward the interior.

Heavy oaken beams stretched overhead, their grain darkened by time and polished to a quiet sheen. Light from wall sconces and table lamps cast a warm glow across the plastered walls, where a few framed maps and oil paintings hung without pretense. A coat rack stood to the left, already home to several jackets, and a tall umbrella stand waited beside it.

Antón gestured toward the interior. "Come. We'll get you settled in first, then something to drink if you want it."

They followed him deeper into the château, their footsteps softened by thick rugs and the occasional creak of old wood. The warmth from the fireplace ahead was a welcome relief after the chill of the drive, and it flickered invitingly from a sitting room just off the main corridor.

Antón moved with practiced ease, the kind of host who didn't fuss, didn't fill the silence with unnecessary chatter. But he glanced back now and then, making sure his guests were still close. Sean watched the way he carried himself—relaxed but tuned to his surroundings. The kind of man who could hold a conversation in one breath and throw someone through a window with the next if the situation called for it.

He liked him already.

Antón led them deeper into the château, past corridors lined with soft carpets and oil paintings that had dulled with age. Sconces on the walls glowed gently, casting flickering shadows against aged plaster walls. The house itself seemed to exhale warmth, an enveloping comfort against the chill that lingered outside.

He guided them up a winding staircase, the steps groaning quietly beneath their weight, polished wood smooth and dark from centuries of use. At the landing, Antón gestured down a hallway lined with doors—heavy oak, their handles polished brass. He opened the first, stepping aside to let them peer inside.

The guest rooms were simple yet elegant, each furnished with an antique bed topped by thick quilts and soft, inviting pillows. Rich wooden furniture, likely older than the nation itself, filled each chamber—a heavy wardrobe, an intricately carved nightstand, and plush rugs beneath their feet. Small lamps on bedside tables bathed the rooms in a gentle glow. Through tall windows, moonlight spilled across the floorboards, casting ghostly shapes that seemed to dance silently across the floor.

Antón opened another door at the end of the corridor, revealing a master suite, slightly larger than the others, with a view of the fields stretching away into darkness. The air smelled faintly of cedar and lavender, mingled with the subtle hint of furniture polish—a fragrance that spoke quietly of the attention given to this old place.

Once everyone had claimed their spaces and set down their belongings, Antón led the group back down the hallway, down the staircase again, and deeper into the manor's lower level. They passed a formal dining room, its long table stretching beneath a gleaming chandelier, chairs lined up in perfect symmetry. Beyond this, he led them into a kitchen spacious enough to comfortably serve a small restaurant. Copper pots and pans hung above polished marble countertops. A large stove sat ready and waiting for use, but the room's real centerpiece was a massive oaken table at its center, worn smooth by generations of hands preparing food.

Antón didn't linger. Instead, he led them into an adjoining sitting room—a cozy space dominated by a large stone fireplace, its mantel lined with carved woodwork and softly glowing candles. Shelves packed with books, framed photographs, and a few tasteful sculptures flanked the walls. Plush chairs and a well-worn leather sofa surrounded a low wooden coffee table, creating an inviting circle of warmth and comfort.

Antón crossed to a polished wooden cabinet along the wall, opened it, and carefully selected a dusty bottle of deep-red wine. He held it up momentarily, studying the label with approval, then carefully removed the cork with practiced ease. A gentle pop echoed softly through the room, releasing the sweet, earthy scent of aged grapes and oak.

He produced delicate stemmed glasses from a nearby cupboard, their crystal surfaces catching the light with a sparkling clarity. Antón poured slowly, filling each glass generously, the deep red liquid shimmering invitingly. The fragrance of the wine filled the air, rich with notes of blackberry, spice, and something faintly smoky.

He passed the glasses around, inviting his guests to take seats wherever they felt comfortable. The fire in the hearth crackled quietly, sending flickering shadows dancing gently across the stone walls and the wood-beamed ceiling above.

As the group settled into their seats, tension eased from tired shoulders, replaced by the warmth of good wine, good company, and the comforting embrace of a place untouched by the chaos they had left behind.

"To new friends," Antón said, raising a glass.

The others did the same, and repeated his salutation. After they took a sip and set their glasses back on the table, Antón let out a sigh. "You all look exhausted," he said.

"It's been a furious couple of days," Tommy replied.

"Well, if you've been hanging around this guy," he indicated Jean-Marc, "that doesn't surprise me." He chuckled. "But I won't keep you up long. You can tell me all about it in the morning."

"It's okay," Evelyn said in a weary voice. "It's good to unwind a little. We'll sleep better for it."

Sean leaned back in his chair, turning his glass of wine thoughtfully. "So, how exactly did you two meet?" he asked, glancing between Antón and Jean-Marc.

Antón's mouth curled into an easy smile as he exchanged a knowing look with Jean-Marc. "I guess you could say we share a colorful past."

Jean-Marc chuckled softly, giving a slight nod. "That's one way to put it."

Antón set down his wine glass carefully. "It started about ten years ago. I was running my security consultancy, handling discreet jobs for private collectors, museums, wealthy estates—you know, the kinds of clients who don't want their valuables to vanish overnight. One of my contracts was particularly complicated: a priceless set of Renaissance paintings, stolen from a private estate in Florence. Not only were the paintings extremely valuable, but one had sensitive historical documents hidden inside the frame. The owner was desperate."

Jean-Marc's eyes narrowed slightly as he picked up the story. "The situation had gotten complicated. Interpol was involved, the local police were useless, and intelligence networks suspected the art had ended up in the hands of a black-market dealer who had ties to terrorist groups. My special forces unit was sent to track down the dealer—initially, it was purely about intelligence gathering."

Antón inclined his head in agreement. "Exactly. While Jean-Marc's team was gathering intelligence, my firm was contracted privately to recover the paintings and documents discreetly, without tipping off the authorities and causing a diplomatic mess. Our paths crossed in Madrid, each team initially unaware of the other's presence. You can imagine how tense that was."

Jean-Marc smiled dryly. "We spent the first twenty-four hours suspiciously watching each other, wondering who would make the first wrong move."

Tommy leaned forward, intrigued. "So, who did?"

Antón laughed quietly. "Neither, actually. Jean-Marc tracked me down one evening in a café on the Plaza Mayor. He sat across from me, ordered an espresso, and after a tense couple of minutes, he simply asked if I wanted help getting my client's paintings back without creating an international incident."

Jean-Marc shrugged. "Made sense. We had the intel; Antón had the resources and connections. Working together was the obvious play."

Antón's expression softened at the memory. "Turned out we were a perfect match. My firm handled logistics and cover; Jean-Marc's team executed the tactical recovery. We retrieved the art without a shot fired."

Evelyn leaned forward slightly, clearly fascinated. "That couldn't have been the only time."

Antón shook his head, smiling. "It was just the first. After Jean-Marc left the service, we continued collaborating. He became my primary operative for sensitive assignments. Eventually, business was good enough that I retired early, bought this château, and stepped away from that life."

Jean-Marc raised his glass slightly, a gesture of respect. "And yet here we are again."

Antón laughed, holding his own glass aloft in response. "Some habits die hard, my friend."

Sean smiled, satisfied. "Sounds like we came to the right place."

26

Victoria wasn't happy.

She felt the muscles in her jaw tighten as Mercer's voice delivered yet another disappointing update. Two of his men dead, and Wyatt slipping farther from their grasp. She drew a long, slow breath, steadying the flare of irritation she felt toward Mercer's continued inability to bring this situation under control. She pressed both palms down on the surface of her desk while staring at the screen with Mercer's name on it, the timer showing she'd been on the phone with him for just over a minute.

"So, where are you now?" she demanded, doing her best to keep her voice calm but still carry enough authority to keep Mercer in his place.

"Just outside of the town of Poitiers."

"And you said you know where they are?"

"Yes, ma'am. We tracked them to a property in the countryside."

At least he hadn't screwed that up, she thought.

Poitiers.

The name rang clearly in Victoria's mind, drawing her away from the building anger she felt toward Mercer's continued setbacks. Her pulse quickened slightly at the historical gravity of the place. Poitiers was no ordinary footnote in Joan of Arc's remarkable story—it was a site of critical revelation, a proving ground where Joan's divine purpose was confirmed by an assembly of skeptical religious scholars.

She leaned back in her leather chair, fingers tapping a rhythm against polished mahogany. A heavy silence hung over the phone line, stretching for several seconds. Victoria knew that Mercer knew better than to interrupt her thoughts.

"You're certain they're already at this château in Poitiers?" she finally asked, her tone measured but cold.

"Yes, ma'am," Mercer replied steadily, careful to conceal the tension beneath his professionalism. "We tracked their vehicle. It's parked inside a gated property just outside the city."

Victoria narrowed her eyes. "Who owns the property?"

"Records show a man named Antón Durand. Former private security specialist, ex-military background. Made a lot of money in the private sector. Jean-Marc likely knew him from their shared military days."

She tightened her jaw, displeased by this revelation. Another complication—another unpredictable variable. "What's the status there?"

"We're positioned nearby, close enough to maintain surveillance but not to be detected. But there's an issue. Durand's property has cameras monitoring the main gate, and there's likely additional security scattered throughout the grounds. Given Durand's past and training, we have to assume he's well prepared. And with Wyatt, Schultz, and Durand himself in the mix, we might find ourselves outnumbered if we move prematurely."

Victoria exhaled quietly, allowing herself a brief moment of irritation. Mercer's caution was justified, but time was slipping away rapidly. Every delay brought the financial crisis closer, the market dominoes she'd painstakingly arranged teetering dangerously close to collapse. She could almost hear the clock ticking down toward catastrophe—or triumph.

"Either the ring is in Poitiers, or there is another clue as to its location," Victoria said firmly, as much to herself as to Mercer. "Wyatt and Schultz must have deciphered something we missed from Henri's research—something pointing directly to a specific location. Joan's trial at Poitiers wasn't recorded in great detail. Many believed her answers were divinely inspired, but others hinted that she presented something tangible, a sign or relic that proved her divine sanction."

Mercer listened silently. Victoria continued, working through the puzzle aloud. "If Wyatt knows exactly where to look, he's going to move soon—probably tomorrow. If he gets the ring first, we lose our advantage permanently."

Mercer had come to the same conclusion. He spoke cautiously. "We could assault the château, ma'am. But there's significant risk—security measures, surveillance systems. If we trigger alarms or a firefight, local authorities will respond, and we lose our chance entirely."

"Absolutely not," Victoria replied sharply. "You're right to hesitate. Wyatt and his team could be prepared for something like that, and this Durand complicates things. Keep your men in position and continue watching. If they move, follow discreetly. I'd prefer Wyatt do the work for us and lead you directly to the artifact."

"Understood," Mercer acknowledged immediately.

There was another matter too. A variable she couldn't control. There were multiple sites in Poitiers that could be where Joan either hid the ring or left another clue critical to finding it.

Victoria pinched the bridge of her nose, eyes closed momentarily as Mercer remained silent on the line, intuitively sensing that she was deep in thought. She exhaled softly before speaking again.

"Poitiers was more than a single moment, Mercer. Joan's brief but significant stay there left several historically important sites; all of them potential locations for what Wyatt's after.

"The first obvious possibility is the Palace of the Counts of Poitou," Victoria continued, picturing the building vividly. "Now the Palais de Justice—Joan stood trial there, interrogated by religious authorities who tried desperately to prove her visions fraudulent. It was in those chambers where Joan's legitimacy was tested and accepted. She might have hidden the ring somewhere within the palace itself—beneath its ancient stone floors, within its heavy, time-worn walls, or tucked inside an unnoticed recess behind one of the massive timber beams in the great hall. If Joan believed herself divinely chosen, it's plausible she left behind something there, hidden in plain sight, secured where only those who knew exactly what to seek could discover it."

Mercer remained silent, clearly processing the possibilities. Victoria pressed on, her voice firm and precise.

"Yet Joan was deeply religious," she said, thinking aloud. "Which leads us to the Church of Saint-Hilaire-le-Grand. It was one of Poitiers' holiest sites in Joan's day; a sanctuary where she might have hidden something sacred. Its crypt has existed since the early medieval period, layered with tombs and reliquaries of saints. Joan revered Saint Hilaire, and she might have entrusted the ring or clues about it to the protection of the church itself. There could be hidden compartments within tombs or beneath altar stones—places she felt no one would dare disturb."

She paused again, visualizing each possibility. The urgency made her chest tighten slightly, but she maintained her composure. "There's also the Baptistère Saint-Jean, one of Europe's oldest Christian monuments, predating Joan herself. The building rests upon ancient Roman foundations, and Joan likely visited it during her stay. Historical whispers say she received a private blessing from priests there, prior to her trial. A hidden chamber—an ancient baptismal font—it would have held deep symbolic significance for Joan. If Wyatt discovered a connection there, he might already be planning to search for it."

"Understood," Mercer finally said, absorbing her points. "That's three potential locations. Do you have reason to favor one over the others?"

Victoria considered the question carefully, lips pursed in quiet frustration. "No. And to complicate matters further, there's also the Abbaye de Sainte-Croix, a monastery slightly outside central Poitiers. Joan stayed briefly at a monastery near the city. Sainte-Croix is partially ruined now—isolated enough to make it a secure hiding spot, yet close enough historically to fit the narrative. If Joan or her followers wanted the ring secured away from prying eyes, this monastery would have been ideal. It could contain hidden alcoves beneath the crumbling ruins or tunnels sealed long ago."

Mercer exhaled softly on the other end, frustration subtly coloring his usual composure, she thought. "That's four significant locations, each potentially guarded or difficult to access discreetly."

"Precisely why we need to let Wyatt move first," Victoria reminded him. "We can't risk blindly searching all these locations ourselves, especially now that your resources are limited. Keep surveillance tight on their movements. Once Wyatt reveals the specific location, we'll have our answer. Only then do you act."

Mercer's reply was firm. "Agreed. We'll remain concealed and prepared."

Victoria felt her anxiety lessen slightly at his confidence, yet the pressure of time remained. "Mercer, remember—the markets are poised to collapse within days. Every minute counts. Joan's ring isn't just symbolic. It's the linchpin of our plan. Failure isn't an option."

"Understood," Mercer assured her. "We'll be ready the instant Wyatt makes his move."

Victoria held the phone in thoughtful silence, Mercer's assurance echoing briefly in her mind. But even as she heard his words, another problem gnawed persistently at her thoughts; a troubling uncertainty she could not control. Poitiers wasn't merely one clear historical marker in Joan's narrative; it was a web of historical intersections, each spot potentially holding the key she needed. Wyatt could be pursuing any one of several sites within the city, complicating their strategy.

Victoria drew a slow breath as irritation prickled at her. Four significant locations. Each plausible, each historically justified, each equally capable of harboring Joan's greatest secret. Mercer could never search them all without revealing their hand, risking exposure and potentially disaster.

Frustration welled momentarily, but she quelled it immediately.

She reminded herself of their strategy, a reassuring balm against the uncertainty. Wyatt and Schultz, driven by urgency and their innate curiosity, would do the hard work of narrowing the possibilities. Mercer merely had to watch and wait. Wyatt's own determination would inevitably lead them directly to Joan's secret.

Yet the pressure remained, insistent and unyielding. Once this was over, she'd be able to manipulate the markets as she saw fit, remaining one step ahead of the rest of the world—even the market makers whose immense volume moved prices up and down. Only Joan's ring, with its fabled precognitive powers, could assure her of emerging stronger from the chaos she herself had engineered. Every second mattered; every delay amplified the risk.

She allowed herself one final glance toward the window, the darkness of the grounds outside providing no reassurance.

Victoria's gaze shifted to her darkened reflection in the window glass. The urgency she felt was nearly suffocating. Joan's legacy had remained hidden for centuries, guarded by secrets and uncertainty. Soon, though, the power Joan had wielded would belong to her, and she alone would control the turbulent new world rising from the impending chaos.

Victoria paused, eyes scanning the softly illuminated shelves of books and ancient manuscripts around her. She'd always been fascinated by history, by how the echoes of the past resonated so clearly in the present. And Joan's legacy was proving more powerful than she'd initially anticipated. Over time, she grew to realize there was much more to the young warrior than first met the eye.

"I trust your expertise," Victoria instructed. "Wyatt and Schultz are resourceful, and if they find the ring, they'll move quickly. Let them show their hand. Stay discreet until you're certain of their objective. Once the location of Joan's secret is confirmed, you'll seize the opportunity. At that point, use whatever force necessary to retrieve it."

"Yes, ma'am," Mercer replied firmly. "My men understand what's at stake."

Victoria's voice softened slightly, not in compassion but in steely resolve. "I certainly hope so. The global financial collapse is imminent, Mercer—it's only days away, perhaps less. We've invested everything into controlling the outcome. Without that ring, without the advantage it provides, everything we've built will fall apart."

Mercer's reply came without hesitation. "We'll be ready, ma'am. As soon as Wyatt reveals the location, we'll have the ring."

"Make sure you do," Victoria concluded, her voice cold and final. "We don't get another chance at this."

She ended the call, placing the phone carefully onto the desk. Her gaze drifted to the darkened landscape outside. The estate stretched into shadow, serene beneath the starlit sky—yet within her, a storm brewed.

Victoria knew with absolute certainty that the ring was within reach, close enough to almost feel its power. It was her destiny to possess it. Her ancestors had commanded empires; she would command something even greater—a new global order, reborn from chaos.

Poitiers would be the turning point. It had elevated Joan, and now it would elevate her.

27

The phone only rang three times before Sean heard his favorite voice answer.

"Well, it took you long enough to call me."

He grinned at the sound of his wife's voice.

"You know, phones work both ways," he said coolly.

She giggled. Sean loved it when she did that. Adriana Villa was a strong, beautiful woman, and extremely dangerous to those who called her an enemy. But for Sean, she was always the woman he loved, the deeply passionate, caring human he'd fallen for years before.

"Where are you right now?" she asked.

"A town called Poitiers in France. Know the place?"

"Of course. There's a lot of Joan of Arc history there."

Sean wasn't surprised. She probably knew more about European history than he did. Which made sense since she and her family were from Spain. Even though he'd studied that topic in depth for thousands of hours, she'd been immersed in it since birth.

"Are you looking for something related to her?"

Sean's gaze drifted over the lavishly appointed bedroom as he listened to Adriana's voice on the other end of the line. The room he occupied felt timeless, bathed in an aura of quiet elegance, the sort that whispered wealth without needing to announce it loudly.

The bed itself was a centerpiece of refined luxury. It was king-size, draped in smooth white linens that gleamed softly under the muted glow of antique brass lamps positioned on carved oak nightstands. A plush duvet, embroidered subtly in intricate patterns, lay folded neatly at the foot of the bed, inviting and warm. The mattress beneath Sean was indulgently comfortable, conforming effortlessly to his shape—a stark contrast to the hard bunks or cheap motel mattresses he'd grown accustomed to during countless assignments around the globe.

At the head of the bed stood an imposing headboard, clearly handcrafted by an artisan from another century. Dark walnut panels intricately carved in delicate floral motifs framed a larger central design of twisting ivy vines, their forms interwoven in endless loops—a fitting emblem of the ancient family lineage that Antón so casually represented. The rich wood had been polished to a deep luster, its surface gleaming gently beneath the dimmed lights, adding warmth to the cool serenity of the space.

Along one side of the spacious room, thick velvet drapes in a shade of deep royal blue were drawn partially back from tall, arched windows, revealing glimpses of the star-filled night beyond. Ornately framed paintings, pastoral landscapes and classical scenes from French history, adorned cream-colored walls, enhancing the room's sophisticated charm. Beneath Sean's feet stretched an immense Persian rug woven in deep reds, soft creams, and hints of muted gold, each thread seemingly narrating stories from distant lands and forgotten eras.

Before calling Adriana, Sean had briefly explored the adjoining bathroom, an oasis of equally refined splendor. Marble tiles in cool gray tones spanned the floor and walls, broken only by subtle veins of white and silver. An oversize porcelain claw-foot bathtub dominated the space, complemented by polished nickel fixtures that reflected the glow of soft overhead lighting. Opposite the tub, a spacious glass-walled shower offered a more modern comfort, with multiple showerheads and gleaming faucets promising relaxation and renewal after a day filled with tension and uncertainty.

Returning his attention to the conversation, Sean felt a rare, momentary sense of calm. Despite the risks he knew awaited him, the elegance surrounding him provided an odd comfort, grounding him in this rare moment of peace. He leaned against the headboard.

"Yeah," he answered. "Something to do with Joan's lost ring."

"Interesting. The stories and histories suggest the English took it. Then no one knows for sure what happened after that."

Her knowledge impressed him again.

"Right. Did you ever wonder if that was true?"

"We both know history is full of mysterious artifacts, relics, and objects that purportedly had some kind of power imbued in them. Some of it's real. Some of it's not. Her ring was rumored to hold several different powers. It's hard to separate which one, or ones, could have been real. I considered it briefly, but didn't have the time to dive deeper into the subject."

He knew exactly what she was talking about. They both lived it—the search for truth amid the mishmash of wild theories and far-fetched guesses. Sean recalled one of his favorite shows that had the tag line "The Truth is Out There." That line was the motto the IAA followed, and was a guide stone for every one of his missions. It didn't mean they always found what they hoped, but the truth didn't care about hopes or desires. It simply was. It was objective, uncaring, unmotivated. Understanding that kept any whiff of disappointment at bay. Because the discovery of truth, not merely things, was the real mission.

"So, you think the ring is in Poitiers?" Adriana continued.

"Hard to say. There are a lot of places in this town steeped in Joan's history, spots that were important in her life in different ways. It could be here. Or it could be another clue to the final resting place of the ring."

"Yes, there are many potential locations in that town. Which one do you think you're going to investigate first?"

"Not sure yet. We're going to have to pare that down in the morning." He paused then added, "That's not all. There is a group of men hunting for the ring too. They tried to take us out a couple of times. Well, maybe only once so far. But they were tailing us out of Paris."

"That doesn't sound like anything new for you," she said dryly.

"No. It isn't," he chuckled.

28

Sean awoke slowly, pulled from sleep by the soft glow of morning sunlight gently filtering through the velvet curtains. He blinked several times, focusing his vision on the ornate ceiling overhead decorated with intricate moldings and delicate scrollwork that spoke of generations of wealth and refinement. For a brief moment, he lay perfectly still, allowing the quiet stillness of the château to embrace him—a welcome calm before what would inevitably become another tense, uncertain day.

He rose from the luxurious bed, its warmth reluctantly relinquishing him as he stood. Stretching his arms overhead, he moved to the antique wardrobe that stood regally against the far wall. Opening the heavy oaken doors, he found his clothes neatly folded, his shirt and jeans a stark contrast to the elegance of the surroundings. He dressed slowly, savoring the simplicity of these ordinary moments. He slid on his worn leather belt, adjusting his jeans, then pulled a simple dark T-shirt over his head. For a moment, he considered his jacket, but decided against it; the morning felt mild enough without it.

Turning toward the tall windows, Sean walked across the Persian rug, his bare feet sinking into its lush texture. He pushed aside the heavy velvet drapes and twisted the latch on the old-fashioned window, gently pushing it open. Cool, fresh morning air drifted into the room, carrying with it the gentle fragrance of dew-soaked grass and wildflowers. Outside, the expansive grounds stretched serenely, cloaked in a delicate mist that hovered just above the earth, catching and scattering the first golden rays of dawn. Birds chirped melodiously from the trees, their songs soft and calming, blending harmoniously with the gentle rustling of leaves stirred by a morning breeze.

Sean lingered at the window for another few moments, breathing deeply and savoring the rare tranquility. This place—far removed from the constant threat and urgency of his usual surroundings—felt unreal. Yet he knew the serenity was temporary. Soon enough, the pressures and dangers of their mission would push their way back into focus.

Closing the window carefully, he slipped into a comfortable pair of shoes he'd left near the bed and walked across the room to the door. As he pulled it open, the soft, inviting aroma of freshly brewed coffee drifted up from somewhere downstairs, greeting him warmly. His stomach rumbled gently at the promise of breakfast, and he felt a slight smile tug at his lips.

He stepped out into the hallway, pulling the door closed behind him, eager to join the others downstairs and begin piecing together the puzzle that awaited them.

Sean made his way down the hallway, stepping lightly across a soft carpet runner that muted his footsteps. The old wooden floor beneath creaked softly as he moved, the sound quietly comforting, a gentle reminder of the château's age and character. As he reached the grand staircase, he paused at the landing, glancing briefly out the tall windows that overlooked the sprawling grounds. The morning mist was slowly lifting, revealing the lush greenery beneath—a scene of timeless peace.

He descended the stairs, the smooth, polished wooden banister cool to his touch. He followed the subtle aroma of coffee and faint sounds of conversation drifting through the foyer, and turned down a wide hallway that opened into a spacious kitchen flooded with warm, natural light.

Antón stood near the stove, his back turned to the doorway as he stirred something in a skillet. The air was filled with a delightful blend of aromas—freshly toasted bread, eggs seasoned with herbs, the savory hint of potatoes crisping gently in olive oil. Near a marble countertop stood Jean-Marc, leaning casually against the cabinetry, sipping coffee from a white mug identical to the one Antón lifted in greeting.

"Good morning, Sean," Antón called warmly, glancing briefly over his shoulder with a bright smile. "You're up earlier than Jean-Marc expected."

Sean chuckled quietly, raising an eyebrow as he crossed the tiled floor toward the large central island topped with a smooth slab of polished marble. "Well, I'm not used to people waking up before me," he admitted, a faint smile playing on his lips as he slid onto a sturdy stool at the small bistro table nestled by a set of French windows.

Jean-Marc grinned, raising his mug toward Sean in a silent toast. "Old habits from the service. I don't know how to sleep past dawn."

Antón quickly poured coffee into another white ceramic mug and placed it carefully in front of Sean. "Coffee," he announced, his voice cheerful, "black, strong, the way Jean-Marc insists upon it."

Sean wrapped his fingers around the warm cup, inhaling the rich, comforting aroma. "Perfect," he said, nodding appreciatively as he took a sip, savoring the robust bitterness.

Antón wiped his hands clean with a linen towel and moved away from the stove, seating himself opposite Sean at the bistro table. The space felt cozy and intimate despite the kitchen's expansive size. Copper pans hung neatly from racks overhead, and shelves lined with cookbooks, jars of spices, and various kitchen utensils contributed to a sense of welcoming warmth.

Jean-Marc remained leaning against the counter, coffee in hand, enjoying the leisurely moment. He exchanged a brief glance with Antón, who gestured casually toward the stove. "Breakfast will be ready in ten minutes," Antón announced. "Scrambled eggs with chives, sautéed potatoes, toasted fresh bread, and fruit from the garden."

Sean raised his mug in quiet approval. "Sounds amazing."

Antón chuckled softly, genuinely pleased. "Good. No escargot this morning—I know Americans aren't typically keen on snails. And Jean-Marc mentioned you and Tommy avoid pork and shellfish, so we've kept it simple."

"Appreciate that," Sean said sincerely, relaxing a little more into his seat.

Antón leaned back comfortably, a thoughtful expression on his face. "And after breakfast, we can discuss what comes next. Jean-Marc mentioned you have some important decisions to make."

Sean nodded, sipping again from his mug, savoring the calm before the inevitable storm. "We do," he agreed quietly. "But first, coffee."

He blew across the surface of the steaming liquid then leaned over and took a long inhale, breathing in the rich smell of the coffee as he did so.

"How did you sleep last night?" Jean-Marc asked, raising his mug to his lips for a sip.

"Slept great," Sean said, still waiting for his coffee to cool off a few degrees. "That bed was really comfortable. I felt like royalty in that room."

Antón grinned. "Well, royalty used to live here, so that checks out."

"Should we go wake the others?" Jean-Marc wondered.

Sean glanced back through the entrance to the kitchen then shrugged. "Let 'em sleep a few more minutes. This whole thing has been exhausting."

He tipped the mug to his lips and pulled a swig of the hot coffee. It was perfect. The earthy, caramel flavor gave his senses a much-needed kick that preceded what the caffeine would do.

"This is excellent," Sean said, raising the mug to their host.

"Thank you. I only drink the good stuff." He set his cup down and crossed one leg over his knee. "So, what do you know about these men who were following you?"

"Nothing. And that's what's so troubling."

"What's so troubling?" Tommy's voice interrupted from the kitchen entrance.

Sean turned around and saw his friend standing there. His dark brown hair was disheveled, and dark circles hung under his eyes.

"Good morning, pumpkin," Sean said, teasing his friend.

"Yeah, yeah."

Antón stood and offered Tommy a seat at the table while he moved over to the coffee pot. "Please, sit," he said. "I'll pour you some coffee to shake off the drowsiness. Breakfast will be ready in a few minutes."

Tommy sat down as Antón poured him a cup of coffee. "How long you been up?" he asked Sean.

"Just a few minutes. I wonder if we should wake Evelyn."

A half second after the words left his mouth, they heard her voice. "Too late for that, I'm afraid. I've been up for an hour, boys."

They turned and watched her enter the kitchen and help herself to an empty seat at the table.

"Good morning," Sean said. The rest of the men echoed the same.

"How do you take your coffee?" Antón asked.

"Black, please," she said.

Sean grinned at the response.

"So, what have you lot been up to?"

"Nothing yet," Tommy answered. "We were waiting for you before we began discussing our next move."

Jean-Marc set the coffee down in front of her, then Tommy. He took the last empty seat at the table and picked up his mug again.

"Any thoughts?" she asked. "By the way, something smells good."

Antón smiled. "Food should be done in a few minutes. And as to your question, I have some ideas."

Antón leaned forward slightly, resting his forearms on the table, a thoughtful expression settling onto his face, Sean saw. "There are three locations in Poitiers that stand out historically, each connected deeply with Joan's legacy," he began, his voice calm yet serious, the cadence of a seasoned historian slipping naturally into his speech.

"The first, and perhaps the most famous, is the Palace of the Counts of Poitou, now known as the Palais de Justice. This site carries substantial historical weight because it's the precise place where Joan was examined by theologians and clerics to assess the truth of her divine calling. Imagine a young peasant girl, barely eighteen, standing before skeptical scholars and men who held immense religious and political power, calmly declaring her divine purpose. The palace itself is imposing, a fortress of heavy stone walls, vaulted ceilings, and vast rooms capable of echoing the whispers of centuries past. There are numerous hiding places within—secret compartments hidden behind thick oak panels, niches carved into stone walls, even hollowed beams overhead. Given Joan's dramatic moment there, it seems an ideal place to hide something as symbolically significant as the ring or, at the very least, a clue to its final resting place. Its historical relevance alone makes it a strong candidate."

Antón paused briefly, allowing his words to settle as Sean and the others listened intently. Evelyn watched him with a mixture of curiosity and respect, clearly impressed by the precision and passion in Antón's delivery.

"The second option," Antón continued smoothly, "is the Church of Saint-Hilaire-le-Grand. This church predates Joan significantly, its foundation laid long before her birth. It's one of Poitiers' oldest and most revered religious sites, renowned for its sacred crypt and the extensive collection of relics housed there. Joan herself was deeply religious, as we all know, and she was guided profoundly by visions of saints and heavenly messengers. It is entirely plausible she would have trusted such a significant artifact—or instructions regarding its hiding place—to a religious sanctuary, believing its holy aura would protect it from corruption or misuse. Imagine for a moment the crypt beneath Saint-Hilaire, lined with ancient stone, dimly lit and quiet, filled with tombs and relics of saints and church fathers long past. A small reliquary or an obscure alcove could have easily concealed

Joan's secret, preserved by faith and forgotten by time. It's a compelling possibility, deeply connected to Joan's spirituality."

Antón took a slow sip of coffee, the liquid soothing his throat before he continued. Jean-Marc sat quietly, absorbing the details, his eyes flickering briefly toward Sean, silently gauging his reaction. Tommy quickly tapped his phone, taking notes, clearly captivated by Antón's historical insights.

"The third site," Antón resumed while placing his cup down carefully, "is perhaps the most enigmatic—the Baptistère Saint-Jean. Unlike the palace or Saint-Hilaire, this location is unique in its ancient symbolism. The Baptistère Saint-Jean was built upon Roman foundations, making it one of Europe's oldest Christian monuments still standing. There are historical references, though subtle, to Joan receiving a blessing within this very baptistery before facing her interrogators. This place holds a profound symbolic meaning—an ancient site of rebirth, purification, and divine protection. Consider the hidden chambers beneath its stone floors, the foundations dating back to Roman times, the ancient fonts and ceremonial rooms once used for baptisms. Joan could easily have hidden something important here, either personally or through a trusted follower. Its depth of history and symbolism would have made it an ideal place for concealment, a location that could easily go unnoticed by historians focused solely on the more famous palace and church."

Antón leaned back slowly, allowing silence to fill the space momentarily. The ticking of a clock on the wall seemed suddenly loud, marking each passing second as they each considered his words carefully.

"Each location," Antón concluded thoughtfully, "has its merits, its historical validity, and a strong narrative connection to Joan's life. The palace represents authority and examination, Saint-Hilaire embodies spirituality and sanctity, and the baptistery stands as a symbol of rebirth and secret devotion. My own inclination would lean toward the palace first, primarily due to the documented significance of Joan's trial. The event at the palace was public, historically critical, and profoundly tied to Joan's own claim of divine authority. It seems a logical starting point, though the others certainly merit attention if the palace yields nothing."

Antón's words lingered in the quiet that followed as each of their minds spun with the information. Before anyone could respond, a faint beeping broke through the contemplative silence, startling Antón slightly. He glanced quickly at his watch, a warm smile replacing the seriousness on his face.

"Ah," he said, rising swiftly from the table. "Breakfast is ready. Perfect timing."

Pulling open the oven door, Antón leaned slightly away as a fresh wave of warmth spilled into the room, carrying with it the unmistakable aroma of freshly baked bread mingled with savory herbs and melted cheese. He carefully reached inside, first removing the quiche, a golden masterpiece baked in a porcelain dish, its edges crisp and perfectly browned, topped with just a sprinkle of freshly ground pepper and herbs. The tantalizing scent of eggs, cheese, and herbs filled the air, immediately causing everyone at the table to unconsciously shift forward slightly, eager to partake.

Antón placed the quiche carefully on the stovetop, where the heat-resistant porcelain clinked softly against the polished metal grates. Next, he reached back into the oven and withdrew a baking tray loaded with small baguettes, their golden-brown crusts dusted lightly with flour. Steam rose from them in delicate spirals, each loaf a perfectly formed tribute to traditional French baking. As Antón set the tray beside the quiche, the warm, yeasty fragrance filled the room completely, mingling harmoniously with the savory notes of the freshly baked quiche.

Jean-Marc inhaled appreciatively, and a satisfied smile curved across his lips. "You're spoiling us, Antón," he said warmly, leaning back into his chair. "If you're not careful, we'll never leave."

Antón chuckled softly, sliding the oven mitt off and setting it aside. He turned to a drawer beside the stove, withdrawing a gleaming knife that he tested briefly against his thumb. "Well, if good food is all it takes to keep you here, I'll make sure breakfast lasts forever," he joked while expertly slicing the quiche into precise, generous wedges, each movement practiced and smooth.

At the table, Evelyn tapped her fingers against her coffee mug, clearly still processing the earlier conversation from Antón's perspective. "You make a compelling case for all three locations," she admitted, addressing Antón but glancing briefly at Tommy and Sean. "Though I'm curious, Antón, if you have a personal inclination about where to start."

Antón nodded thoughtfully, his knife slicing through the quiche with practiced ease. He lifted each delicate slice carefully with a thin spatula, placing the steaming pieces onto pristine white plates, arranging them neatly. "I confess my bias," Antón admitted. "For historical and practical reasons, my instincts lean strongly toward the Palais de Justice."

Tommy nodded, taking quick notes as he always did. "It certainly fits," he agreed. "Joan's trial was one of the best-documented moments in her entire story, and the location offers a variety of hiding places—more than the others."

Antón turned to the baguettes, carefully lifting each one from the tray and placing them into a woven bread basket lined with a clean, white linen napkin. "Precisely," Antón agreed. "The palace has more significance and likely more practical places to search."

Sean watched carefully as Antón arranged the bread, considering the details they'd discussed. "But the other two locations have distinct merits as well," he reminded them gently. "The crypt beneath Saint-Hilaire has spiritual significance. It feels exactly like the kind of place Joan would trust to protect something valuable."

Antón nodded thoughtfully while carrying the basket of warm baguettes toward the table before placing it in the center within easy reach of everyone. "True," he admitted. "And the crypt's long history would make hiding something there both symbolic and secure. Not many would dare disturb a place so holy."

Jean-Marc took a baguette, breaking it gently apart and inhaling its fresh aroma. "Then again, the Baptistère Saint-Jean would also offer secrecy," he pointed out, a crease forming on his brow. "Its ancient Roman origins and symbolic importance would certainly make it ideal. Perhaps even more obscure, since fewer historians consider it directly tied to Joan."

Antón carried the plates, two in each hand, and began placing them carefully in front of his guests, the steam from the quiche curling gently upward. "Precisely the dilemma," he remarked while placing the first two plates in front of Sean and Evelyn. "Each location offers compelling historical logic. Each possesses unique possibilities."

The first bites were accompanied by a long, companionable silence, the clink of forks against ceramic the only sound in the kitchen for several minutes. The quiche was light and buttery, the crust perfectly crisp, while the warm egg filling carried a rich, savory blend of herbs and subtle cheese. Delicate hints of chives and rosemary lingered on the tongue, and the soft tang of goat cheese melted into the comforting warmth of each bite.

Sean took a moment to savor his second forkful, closing his eyes briefly as he leaned back in his chair. "You might be the most dangerous man in France," he said, finally breaking the silence. "If we weren't in the middle of a mystery involving a sacred relic, I could forget about the rest of the world and just eat."

Antón grinned, tearing off a piece of his baguette and using it to mop up a corner of his plate. "Don't tempt me to open a bistro. Jean-Marc's been trying to get me to settle down for years."

Evelyn smiled gently as she reached for another slice of bread. "If this is what retirement looks like, you've earned it." Her tone carried warmth, but her eyes still showed the undercurrent of weight they all shared. The ring. The mystery. The danger.

Jean-Marc chewed thoughtfully then nodded toward his plate. "You know, if your friend from the army had cooked like this, I might've stayed enlisted longer."

Antón let out a laugh—short, genuine—and waved a dismissive

hand as he reached for his coffee. "Nonsense. You never liked taking orders."

Tommy, meanwhile, barely spoke. He was too absorbed in the food, cleaning his plate with methodical precision. The only time he paused was to scribble a note on the corner of his napkin—perhaps about the flavor, or maybe just a stray idea related to the investigation.

The warm light of the kitchen filtered in through the wide windows, soft and golden as it spilled across the stone countertops and polished table. Outside, the birds had begun their late morning song, and a distant breeze whispered through the garden leaves. For a moment, the world outside—their hunt, their mission, and their fears—felt like a distant echo. For a moment, they were just people sharing a meal.

But the moment passed.

Antón leaned back in his chair and set down his mug. His gaze moved between them, serious once more. "As for where to begin," he said, voice low but certain, "I still believe the Palais de Justice is our strongest lead."

Evelyn glanced up from her plate. "Because of her trial?"

"More than just the trial," Antón said. "That place wasn't just symbolic. It was transformational. Joan went in as a peasant girl with a mission and emerged with the backing of people who had once doubted her. Her resolve was tested there. Her purpose reaffirmed. If she ever doubted her calling—or wanted to leave behind something sacred tied to her path—that's the place she would have chosen. Not just to protect it... but to honor it."

Sean nodded slowly, absorbing the logic. "And it's a building with countless corners," he added. "Places that might've been altered or concealed over time."

Jean-Marc leaned forward slightly, folding his hands on the table. "Security might be tighter. But that also means fewer people think something's hidden there. It's the last place anyone would expect us to look."

Tommy gave a firm nod. "Then that's our next stop."

Antón's gaze shifted to each face in turn. "We'll need to be careful," he said. "The palace isn't open to the public for full access, and there will be red tape. We'll need to approach it with more than just curiosity."

Sean tapped a finger against the side of his mug. "We've worked with less."

29

A sheen of gray light filtered through the cracks in the rotting wooden walls of the abandoned barn. The soft chirp of morning birdsong didn't reach Mercer's ears—he was too focused on the dull ache pulsing behind his eyes, a weight born of too little sleep stretched across too many days. He sat on an overturned crate near the barn's wide entrance, one boot propped up against the rung of an old wooden ladder, the other flat on the packed dirt floor. He hadn't moved in an hour.

The slope outside the barn dipped down into a shallow valley, where the two-lane road meandered toward the distant village and, more importantly, to the narrow lane that fed into the gate of Antón Durand's château.

Mercer had eyes on it.

Through a pair of compact field binoculars, he studied the front gate—the long drive stretching in a straight line toward the estate's façade, flanked by stone pillars and wrought iron fencing. The morning sun was only beginning to clear the line of trees beyond the house, casting long, soft shadows across the gravel. A faint mist still clung to the treetops, evaporating slowly in the growing warmth.

Nothing had moved through the night, or even in the early morning.

Behind him, one of the men stirred—coughing into a gloved hand and shifting against the support beam where he'd been dozing upright.

Mercer didn't look back. "They're stirring," he said aloud, mostly to himself.

They'd been watching the place all night, taking shifts. Two men on watch, two sleeping, one always listening to the scanners. They hadn't seen a vehicle leave the gate. No movement at the front. No lights on in the middle of the night. Not so much as a whisper from the gravel. Mercer had begun to wonder if Wyatt and his companions had even slept.

He knew the type. Had worked with men like him before.

Mercer stood, stretching the stiffness out of his legs, then walked to the far side of the barn, where a threadbare blanket covered another slumbering figure. He nudged the man's boot with his own. "Up," he said. "They're moving."

The man groaned and sat up slowly, blinking against the morning haze. "You sure?"

Mercer gave a small nod and turned to the others. "Nikolai. Santos. Let's go."

Santos emerged from a corner alcove behind an old workbench, his face still carrying the weight of sleep, but his eyes sharpened quickly as he reached for his coat and rifle. Nikolai said nothing, already on his feet, rolling up a weather-stained sleeping mat and tucking it under his arm. His movements were silent, practiced.

Mercer walked back to the crate and knelt beside a small pack before pulling out a protein bar. He tore it open with his teeth and chewed with mechanical indifference. It wasn't nourishment. It was fuel.

The others moved around the barn in quiet readiness, packing away the bare essentials and extinguishing the small camp stove in the corner. One of them yawned, and Mercer shot him a look—not out of irritation but a reminder. Tired wasn't an excuse. Tired got you killed.

He stepped back into the open air, scanning the landscape one more time. From this elevated position, they had a clear view of the château's gate and the winding drive that cut through the grove leading to the main house. He adjusted the binoculars again.

There it was. More movement.

The tall iron gates had begun to open, turning slowly on their ancient hinges. Through the thin gaps in the hedgerow lining the gravel lane, he saw the glint of a car's hood. The light caught it at just the right angle, a polished silver curve nosing forward like a wolf testing the air.

He raised a hand, signaling without speaking.

The others joined him at the opening of the barn, now fully awake and silent, every one of them alert and watching. Even with the chill still lingering in the air, sweat dotted one man's brow.

Mercer didn't blame them. They were exhausted. Even hardened veterans of a hundred dark operations had limits. Combat might carve steel into a man's bones, but it didn't stop the body from needing rest, food, or warmth. And they'd had little of any since the failed confrontation in Domrémy.

But this was the job.

He could see the backseat passenger now. From the side profile, there was no mistaking it. Sean Wyatt.

Mercer handed the binoculars to Nikolai, who grunted in confirmation. "That's them."

Wyatt's crew had loaded up, likely heading into town. Mercer watched the car's rear tires crunch against the gravel as they passed out of view beyond the tree line. The gates remained open for another ten seconds before beginning their slow closure.

That was all he needed.

He turned to his men. "Pack it up. Quiet. We move in two minutes."

They nodded. No one spoke. No questions. They knew the drill.

As the team moved with practiced efficiency, Mercer glanced back at the château. From the outside, it was idyllic—peaceful, even. But whatever lay inside those walls, whatever secrets Wyatt had uncovered, the time to act was slipping through Mercer's fingers.

He hated that.

Not just the loss of time but the reminder of how this operation had unraveled more than once. Two dead. Wyatt always a step ahead. It gnawed at him like rot beneath the surface of otherwise perfect skin.

But this wasn't over. Not by a long shot.

Mercer checked the clip in his weapon then slung it back beneath his coat. He pulled out his phone and checked for updates. Nothing from the two men left behind in Domrémy. No new intelligence from the satellite feed they'd managed to patch into for sporadic surveillance. Not yet, anyway.

He moved to the edge of the barn and stepped onto the dew-slick grass as his boots sank slightly into the soft earth. In the distance, the dust from Wyatt's departure still hung faintly in the morning light.

This time, they would stay close. Even with the tracking beacon on Wyatt's vehicle, Mercer wanted to be ready to pounce the second Wyatt discovered the ring, or whatever they were here to find.

He pulled a black ball cap down low over his brow and motioned to Nikolai, who had already started the vehicle and backed it slowly from the patch of brush where they'd hidden it. The gray Renault had been dust covered and discreet, blending well in the early morning shadows.

Mercer climbed in last, the door clicking shut behind him with a soft finality.

They pulled onto the gravel road moments later, slow at first, letting the others fall into their own rotation. No rush. No reckless tailing. He wanted this clean.

He watched the dust settle from the gates again, replaying the sight of Wyatt's car disappearing into the distance.

Wyatt was on the move again. And there was no way Mercer and his crew would lose him this time.

30

The Mercedes rolled smoothly along the narrow country road, the morning sun throwing long shadows across the rolling hills of Nouvelle-Aquitaine. Antón had offered the sedan to them earlier so they wouldn't have to drive the shot up vehicle that brought them here.

Fields unfurled on either side, the golds and greens of cultivated farmland broken only by clusters of trees and the occasional stone wall mottled with moss and age. Rows of grapevines sloped down shallow hills, trimmed and even, stretching like neat stanzas of poetry across the land. Every so often, a stone farmhouse punctuated the view—shuttered windows, slate roofs, gardens heavy with spring bloom.

Sean leaned an elbow on the door's edge, window down, the wind threading through his hair. The air out here smelled of turned soil and blooming lilac, of dew evaporating off warm stone. He could appreciate the beauty of it—might've even let himself relax—if not for the pit in his stomach that hadn't left since Domrémy. Every curve of the road brought them closer to Poitiers, and closer to the unknown.

Jean-Marc drove with steady hands, eyes scanning the road and mirrors. He didn't speak. He didn't need to.

Tommy sat in the passenger seat beside him while flipping through a leather-bound notebook. Sean had seen it before—Tommy's journal, where he kept track of details that weren't meant for digital records. Handwritten notes, symbols, connections that wouldn't make sense to anyone else. Now and then, he glanced out the window, toward a distant hillside or a passing village sign, noting landmarks or muttering a thought to himself.

In the back, Evelyn sat next to Sean, hair tied loosely at her neck, her eyes fixed on the view but clearly not seeing it. She held a folder in her lap, full of notes and copies of Henri's research. Sean could feel her tension in the way she sat—shoulders just a little too tight, breaths just a little too shallow.

The outskirts of Poitiers rose gradually ahead, its ancient silhouette emerging between the trees like a city only half awake. Red-tiled roofs angled toward the sun, clustered together in tight lanes and squares, while the spires of old churches pierced the sky like watchful sentinels. Low stone walls bordered the first homes, and soon the road curved gently into a more urban rhythm—shops and cafés, flower boxes in windows, wrought iron balconies holding up vines that reached for the light.

They passed an old bookstore on the right, its sun-faded awning hanging low, and just beyond it, a modest café with chairs still stacked from the early cleaning shift. A few people walked the narrow sidewalks, coats draped over arms, others with baskets hooked in their elbows, returning from the morning market. There was no rush to the movement of the town. It carried the elegance of old places—timeless and unhurried.

Tommy closed the notebook and turned in his seat to address the group. "Antón said the director's name is Laure Girard. He's worked with her before. Trusts her."

"What's her role?" Evelyn asked, eyes flicking to him.

"Chief director of the Palais de Justice. She's handled preservation, restoration, and historical archives there for over a decade.

Antón said she's passionate about the building's history—obsessed with the late medieval period."

Sean grunted. "Let's hope she's curious enough to help without asking too many questions."

"I don't think it will be a problem," Jean-Marc said from the driver's seat. "You three have enough credentials to walk into the Vatican and ask to see the vaults on a moment's notice."

Tommy laughed. "Not quite. Believe me. I've tried."

Sean turned and looked out the back window, and his eyes narrowed as a silver sedan passed them in the opposite direction. He watched the car until it disappeared into the curve of the road behind them.

"See anything unusual?" Tommy asked without looking.

Sean shook his head. "No. Not yet, but you know me. I can't let my guard down."

Jean-Marc guided them into the city center, where the narrow lanes branched into a web of older streets and courtyards. Stone buildings three and four stories high leaned in toward the roads, their upper levels jutting just enough to throw parts of the street into shade. The cobblestones glistened faintly, damp from the earlier fog. Here and there, pedestrians crossed in front of the car—an elderly man with a cane, two students arguing gently in French, a cyclist gliding past with a baguette under his arm.

Despite the peaceful veneer, a pall hung in the air, like sitting around a campfire in the woods knowing there are wolves in the darkness just beyond the reach of the firelight.

Sean counted the turns they'd taken since entering the city. Tommy casually checked the time twice in less than five minutes. Jean-Marc's right hand never drifted far from the pistol holstered beneath his coat.

The car slowed as Jean-Marc took a right turn at a small roundabout and continued along a narrow street lined with tall buildings. Sean spotted a sign ahead mounted to the wall just above an arched stone gate, but the letters were too distant to read yet.

Sean leaned slightly forward in his seat as Jean-Marc slowed the car, his eyes narrowing at the structure ahead. They'd emerged from the tight city streets onto a broader square flanked by buildings that whispered of centuries past, but it was the Palais de Justice that immediately commanded attention.

It wasn't ostentatious in the way of Versailles or some royal château. No sprawling gardens or dramatic fountains. The elegance here was quieter, worn into the ancient stone like an old warrior's scars—earned and enduring.

They passed through a narrow arch that looked more like a delivery entrance than something ceremonial, the car's tires crunching lightly over pale gravel. A modest black gate, fixed open against the stone wall, framed their entry. There was no guard station, no high-tech scanner, just an old brass plaque affixed beside the arch, etched with Palais de Justice de Poitiers in weathered serif letters.

Sean took in the exterior as Jean-Marc steered the vehicle into the small parking area off to the right, where a row of unassuming cars—mostly government-issue sedans and scooters—lined the narrow lot. The building before them rose in a patchwork of Gothic and Romanesque styles, its façade marked by pointed arches, fluted columns, and worn sculptures perched high in alcoves like silent watchmen. One of the gables bore the unmistakable markings of the medieval period, the stonework traced with soft shadows beneath the midmorning sun.

To the left of the entrance, two turrets flanked a central arched portal, where a pair of heavy wooden doors had been modernized with glass panels. Above that, narrow windows sat like slits in the wall, lending the place an austere presence. Time had streaked the limestone exterior with shades of gray and ocher, but the building stood solid, rooted in history.

A few people stood near the front steps—two in business attire conversing beneath the lintel, a third scrolling through a phone while leaning on a bicycle. No swarms of tourists here. Sean figured most wouldn't know—or care—that this building had once echoed with the footsteps of Joan of Arc herself.

He could almost feel it. That residual weight. The ghosts of judgment, of consequence. It was a feeling he'd experienced more times than he could count. He felt it every time he visited a historic place, from an old Civil War battlefield in Chattanooga to the Taj Mahal.

Jean-Marc pulled into a narrow spot at the far end of the lot and killed the engine. The hum of the city gave way to a softer quiet; the breeze brushing over the car, the distant ring of a bell from somewhere deeper in town, the faint shouts of schoolchildren echoing down a far alleyway.

Sean stepped out of the car, the soles of his shoes crunching lightly on gravel. The air smelled of old stone warmed by sunlight, mingled with a hint of something floral—wisteria maybe—trailing from a wall they'd passed moments before.

Tommy climbed out next and stretched his back with a quiet groan. Evelyn followed while adjusting the strap on her satchel. Jean-Marc scanned the surroundings in his usual fashion—subtle but thorough, his eyes pausing just a moment longer on every window, every shadow.

They stood together beside the car, all eyes drawn toward the structure ahead.

"So," Tommy asked, his voice low, "where exactly are we supposed to meet this director?"

"Is that her over there?" Evelyn asked.

Sean followed Evelyn's gaze toward the front steps of the palais. A woman stood just beneath the archway, speaking quietly with two staff members in matching navy blazers. She was dressed in tailored slacks and a cream blouse that moved subtly with the breeze. It was the kind of outfit someone wore to look professional, something Sean hadn't had to do in a long time. A lightweight gray jacket hung over her shoulders, draped more than worn. Her dark auburn hair was pinned back in a practical twist, though a few strands had slipped loose in the wind, softening the line of her profile.

She appeared focused but not tense, her tone even, her hands gesturing with precise, practiced ease—someone used to giving instructions and being obeyed. Then she noticed them.

She offered a small, confident smile—not overly rehearsed, not false—and raised a hand in greeting. Not a wave, exactly. More of an invitation.

"That her?" Sean asked.

"I believe so," Jean-Marc replied quietly.

As they approached, the two staffers peeled away, walking briskly toward the side entrance. The woman stepped forward to meet them.

"Bonjour," she said, her accent clipped and educated. "You must be the delegation from Monsieur Marchand." Her eyes flicked briefly between them with quick, appraising precision—not unfriendly but observant.

"That's right," Tommy said, stepping forward. "Although I'm not sure I'd call us a delegation. I'm Tommy Schultz. And this is Sean Wyatt, Evelyn Langley, and Jean-Marc."

"Laure Girard," she replied, offering a hand to each in turn. Her grip was firm but not forceful. "Welcome to the Palais."

"Thanks for making time for us," Sean said.

"Of course. Antón said your research might benefit from a closer look at our archives and spaces. I'm always glad to assist for the sake of history where I can. Do you know much about this place?"

"Not really. But hopefully we will after our visit."

"I hope we're not taking up too much of your time," Evelyn said. "I know you must always be busy managing all this."

Laure shrugged. "Yes, it can be quite the undertaking, but it's work I love." She looked at the building with admiration in her eyes. Sean could tell she was in the right career.

"So, is there anywhere you'd like to begin? I can show you a few key points of interest to get you started, but I'll need to break away in half an hour to handle some other things. I suppose I should ask what brings you here. I seem to have gotten ahead of myself. Antón said you were doing research on Joan of Arc, but he was vague on the details."

"We're trying to piece together bits of her history in hopes of filling a few gaps that remain," Evelyn said smoothly, to the surprise of the men. She wasn't lying, but she sounded confident in her answer that could have been riddled with nerves. "We think there may be much more to learn about Joan than the mainstream history books tell us."

Laure smiled at the answer. "Well, if you are able to shed light on anything new, it will surely be appreciated. After I show you around, you can move around and look at whatever you want. I trust you'll be okay on your own?"

"Yes, ma'am. We'll be fine," Sean said, relieved that they'd be able to roam freely. For how long he didn't know, but some time was better than none.

"Great," Laure said. She turned toward the entrance, her heels clicking lightly against the stone as she led them into the shadowed archway. "Right this way."

31

The great doors of the Palais de Justice eased open with a resonant groan, the sound of old wood and iron yielding to modern hinges. Inside, time itself seemed to exhale. The air was cooler, touched with the faint scent of limestone, polished wood, and something older still—like the faint trace of parchment and forgotten incense.

Sean stepped across the threshold and took it in. The vaulted ceiling soared overhead, ribbed in stone and held aloft by fluted columns that reached upward like the trunks of ancient trees. Light spilled in from arched windows along the upper walls, casting pale ribbons across the tiled floor and catching the dust motes in their drift. Every footstep echoed, even those softened by the centuries of wear in the stone underfoot.

"This way," Laure said, her voice low but clear.

She led them down a wide corridor, and the group moved through a sort of pervasive hush, as if entering sacred ground. Panels of aged oak framed the walls, bearing the patina of time and the faint impressions of countless fingertips. At intervals, plaques offered brief descriptions in French—dates, names, brief notations about trials and decrees, most of them dry to the modern eye. But the walls held deeper stories.

"The Palais was once the Palace of the Counts of Poitou," Laure said, pausing at the base of a stone staircase. "Later, it became the seat of the Duke of Aquitaine—and for a time, that meant it was the seat of power for Eleanor of Aquitaine herself."

She gestured upward.

"The Salle des Pas Perdus—the Hall of Lost Footsteps—is just above us. That's where Joan of Arc stood during her examination in 1429."

She began up the staircase, her heels barely making a sound from step to step. The others followed, moving more slowly now, their eyes drawn upward by the changing light and the play of shadow between the high-set lancet windows.

At the top of the stairs, they entered the hall. It stretched wide and long, the roof soaring in graceful wooden arcs—a medieval marvel of engineering. The timber vaulting was exposed, criss-crossing in a network of braced ribs, burnished now by the passage of time. One end of the hall held a raised dais beneath an ornately carved canopy, the place where judgments were once handed down. The chamber felt still, though not dead—more like a place waiting to speak if one only listened long enough.

"This room was once part of the great ceremonial hall," Laure said quietly. "It's seen countless legal proceedings and state declarations. But for many, it is remembered best as the place where Joan stood before scholars and priests, subjected to questions intended to break her, to disprove her divine claim."

She paused, letting the weight of the place speak for itself.

Sean let his eyes wander over the walls, over the rafters, and the way the windows scattered light in oblique shapes across the floor. He could picture it. A teenage girl in chain mail, her hair shorn, eyes wide but unflinching, standing before a tribunal of elder men wrapped in robes and dogma.

No shouting here. Just interrogation by candlelight. Words sharpened like blades. A hundred ways to call someone a liar without ever raising your voice.

Laure turned and moved again while beckoning them to follow.

They passed into a smaller chamber off the main hall. The ceiling lowered here, but the décor became richer. Tapestries hung on the walls, and one side opened into a series of high-set windows framed by carved stone. She gestured to a long table flanked by narrow-back chairs.

"This would have been a council chamber—used for more intimate proceedings. According to some accounts, Joan was questioned privately here on the nature of her visions."

She paused before a window then turned back to them. "Imagine being sixteen. A peasant. Illiterate. Standing in this space while some of the most powerful minds of France dissected your faith, your purpose, your sanity."

No one said a word.

From there, they continued to a small gallery where art and artifacts lined the walls. Framed letters, depictions of heraldry, even a few medieval relics on display behind glass. Laure stopped before one—a tattered fragment of a standard, mounted carefully on faded red silk. The weave barely held together, but the embroidered fleurs-de-lys were still visible, ghostlike.

"This is one of the only known flags linked to Joan's campaign. Its provenance is debated, but it remains a powerful symbol here."

Sean took in the piece: its edges browned by blood or battle or the ravages of the centuries, the thread nearly invisible in spots. It looked like it had been touched by fire and rain, then rescued at the last moment before fading into dust.

They moved slowly, past plaques and paintings, into another corridor that brought them toward a set of high doors, this time closed. Laure paused there.

"This section is normally closed to the public. It contains archived judicial records from the eighteenth century onward. We won't be entering today, I'm afraid."

Sean gave a small nod, his attention not on the doors but on the distant sounds echoing through the corridor; the creak of wood, the faint thud of footsteps above or below. The building spoke in subtle ways.

The tour continued through a final gallery space—smaller, with stone walls and iron sconces affixed high. The lighting here was lower, more ambient. A single bench rested against one wall.

"This room was once used for deliberation. It's since been converted into a small reflection space for visitors. Many locals come here to contemplate Joan's legacy."

Sean didn't sit. But he could see why someone might. The room held a different vibe, imparted a quieter, more private tone; less official, more contemplative. Less judgment. More memory. He appreciated the tour, as well as the need to permit it. Everything needed to look natural to Laure. Even so, he could still feel the pressure of those who may have followed them here.

After a beat, Laure checked the slim watch on her wrist.

She smiled at the group. "I really wish I could spend more time with you, but I'm afraid I have an appointment in five minutes. I trust you'll be okay on your own?"

"Yes," Tommy said. "And thank you so much for showing us around. You're so knowledgeable about all this, which is no surprise."

"Well, it is my job," she said in a businesslike tone. She reached into a pocket and produced a card. "Here is my number should you need anything else while you're here."

"Thanks again," Sean said as Tommy took the card.

"Of course. Enjoy your visit."

They watched Laure Girard retreat down the corridor, her heels tapping a steady rhythm along the worn stone floor. Her charcoal blazer caught the light as she passed beneath an arched window, then faded into the dimmer stretch ahead. A moment later, she rounded the corner and disappeared from view.

For a few heartbeats, the group stood in silence, the soft echo of her departure still lingering.

Sean adjusted the strap on his shoulder bag. "All right," he said quietly, "time to get to work."

Tommy pulled the folded pages from the inside pocket of his coat; the photocopied notes from Henri. He opened them, smoothing them out between his hands as they walked a few steps toward the edge of the hall.

"We know she was examined in the grand hall," Tommy murmured. "But Henri's phrasing was strange. 'Where her silence spoke louder than her words.' I can't tell if that's poetic… or specific."

"It could be both," Evelyn said, glancing around. Her eyes scanned the stonework, the high beams, the carved friezes near the ceiling. "This place is layered with symbolism."

Jean-Marc remained silent, trailing slightly behind, turning to watch the corridor behind them.

Sean led them back toward the raised dais at the far end of the Salle des Pas Perdus. "Let's start here. If she stood in judgment, it would've been at the front of the hall. Maybe something's hidden near the bench—or the steps leading up to it."

They moved with purpose, their shoes tapping softly across the polished stone floor. Tourists passed here and there, a few snapping photos of the vaulted ceiling, but no one paid much attention to the four travelers examining a centuries-old seat of judgment.

Tommy crouched down near the dais and ran his fingers along the bottom edge of the raised platform. "These stones are too smooth. They've been restored… maybe replaced."

Sean joined him and ran his hand along the side of the low steps. "Nothing here feels out of place. No chips, no gaps. If there was something hidden here, it's long gone."

Evelyn had moved to a tall, narrow window near the rear of the hall and was studying the stained glass. "Henri mentioned symbols. He wouldn't say 'echoes' and 'silence' without a reason. What if we're in the wrong spot?"

Tommy stood up and dusted his hands on his jeans. "Then we regroup. There are smaller rooms, galleries. Maybe it's not where she spoke—but where she was silent."

Sean turned from the dais and surveyed the space again. "Let's split up. Tommy, you and Jean-Marc team up, and I'll go with Evelyn.

Not far—just check the adjoining rooms. Look for anything unusual. An odd engraving. A mismatched stone. Something that doesn't belong."

He didn't say the obvious aloud: that whatever they were looking for had been deliberately hidden, camouflaged amid centuries of architecture and reverence.

They exchanged quick nods and moved out in different directions, the vastness of the Palais swallowing them one step at a time.

32

Mercer stepped out of the sleek, gray Renault, his tailored overcoat catching a breeze that drifted through the narrow street leading up to the Palais de Justice. The morning sun peeked through a thin layer of clouds, casting soft light on the limestone façade of the ancient building. Beside him, two men exited the car in sync—one tall and wiry, the other with the build of a rugby forward, both in dark suits and black sunglasses.

He adjusted his cufflinks as he approached the iron gate, the engraved placard catching his eye: Palais de Justice de Poitiers. Mercer offered a thin smile, rehearsed and perfectly in character. He carried himself with the cool composure of a man who belonged wherever he chose to be. Today, he wasn't a hunter. He was a benefactor.

Laure Girard stood just inside the courtyard, chatting with two staff members near the base of the steps. Mercer recognized her from the dossier.

As he entered the gate, she turned and offered a cordial smile.

"Monsieur Langford?" she asked, extending a hand.

"Indeed," Mercer replied, taking her hand briefly. "A pleasure, Dr.

Girard. Thank you for meeting on such short notice." He put on his best aristocratic smile to go with the smooth, confident tone of someone with tremendous wealth. It was a persona, like so many others in his closet, he could slip on as easily as a T-shirt.

"It's not every day a patron of cultural preservation expresses interest in our humble institution." She gestured toward the doors. "Shall we go inside?"

Mercer gave a slight nod. "Lead the way."

The two men trailing behind remained just outside the entry doors, posing as professional security detail. Laure glanced at them, unsure whether to be flattered or wary. But they didn't speak, and their posture was neutral—no different than the personal protection she'd seen accompanying visiting dignitaries or ambassadors.

Inside, the Palais seemed to shift in tone. The aged stone and thick air carried the weight of centuries, and Mercer's eyes lingered a second too long on the vaulted ceilings and arched entryways. He didn't care about the architecture. Not really. But appearances mattered.

"Dr. Girard," Mercer began as they entered a smaller corridor off the main hall, "I wanted to express my gratitude. Too often, sites like this fall prey to budget cuts and neglect. I've seen it myself—history swallowed by disinterest."

Laure glanced at him, intrigued. "And you want to help prevent that?"

"I do. I represent a consortium of donors, all very interested in maintaining the heritage of key historical locations across Europe. Your work here has not gone unnoticed." He glanced around the corridor, then added, "Especially given this place's ties to one of France's most iconic figures."

"Joan of Arc," she said softly. "Of course."

Mercer offered a calculated smile. "Precisely. I've been fascinated by her since university."

Laure slowed, her arms folding gently in front of her as she turned to face him fully. "Forgive my curiosity, Monsieur Langford...

but why now? This court has been standing since the fifteenth century. What's prompted this sudden interest?"

Mercer didn't blink. "Some of our partners are funding a documentary series—on historical figures whose stories still shape national identity. Naturally, Joan is near the top of the list."

Laure's skepticism softened. "That makes sense. And yes, this site was the setting for her theological examination in 1429. An important moment—when the Church had to decide if she was a heretic or a chosen warrior of God."

"And your role," Mercer said, shifting the conversation gently, "must give you unique access to archives the public never sees."

Laure tilted her head, a cautious smile on her lips. "Some things are protected, yes. But history isn't meant to be hidden, monsieur. We are only its stewards."

Mercer chuckled. "That's what I admire."

She motioned toward a doorway farther down the corridor. "This way. I'd be happy to show you some of the lesser-known spaces."

As she led him deeper into the building, Mercer's thoughts narrowed. He didn't know what Sean Wyatt and his crew had found here, or what they were looking for—but now he had a foot inside the same house. And while his enemies crawled through the shadows, he could smile in the light, shake hands, and see everything.

Laure led Mercer down another vaulted corridor, her voice carrying lightly in the stillness. "The deeper we go, the older it gets. Many of these wings haven't been updated in centuries. You can still see the original beams in some places."

Mercer kept pace beside her, his hands tucked into the pockets of his charcoal coat. He gave a small nod, his eyes scanning every doorway they passed, noting the curvature of each arch, the density of the stone, the position of surveillance cameras—none in this hall.

"Impressive," he murmured, his tone neutral, but there was calculation behind his gaze. His mind was mapping every corridor, every possible entry and exit.

Laure paused beside a heavy oaken door; the wood gnarled with age and bearing the scars of time. "This room was once used for private hearings. It's off limits to the public now. Structural safety reasons."

She pulled out a ring of keys from her coat pocket, then paused. "I probably shouldn't..." she said, half laughing.

Mercer leaned slightly forward, voice soft. "Please. Just a glance. I'd like to understand the scope of what you're preserving." Something in his tone—respectful, restrained, just curious enough—made her relent. She slid the iron key into the lock and opened the door with a slow creak.

The chamber inside was dark, lit only by a tall window that filtered in a wash of pale morning light. Dust drifted in the still air. A long wooden bench ran along the far wall. Stone slabs paved the floor in uneven rows.

Mercer stepped inside slowly. The door clicked softly behind them. Laure followed him in and gestured toward the ceiling. "Note the timberwork. Original from the early fifteenth century. We believe this was where minor theological inquiries were held. Not heresy trials, per se, but vetting."

He studied the beams but said nothing. His focus had shifted. He wasn't interested in the architecture. His instincts—honed through years of work in places where silence and steel spoke louder than law—were picking up something.

A faint echo in the stone. The feel of space behind the walls. He could almost sense it.

He turned back to Laure. "Remarkable."

She nodded. "You know," she said with a thoughtful tilt of her head, "most people think Joan of Arc's trial happened here. But that was in Rouen. This... this is where her journey was legitimized."

He offered another smile. "Validation before the world watched."

"Exactly."

A soft knock on the oak door interrupted them. One of Mercer's men peeked in—Klein, the lean one with the sharp nose and colder eyes.

"Forgive me," Mercer said, stepping to the door. He leaned toward Klein and whispered something. The other man nodded and disappeared again.

Laure looked puzzled. "Everything all right?"

"Just my associate checking on our schedule," Mercer replied smoothly. "We have another appointment in Limoges this afternoon. A restoration site."

"Busy day," she said with a smile.

Mercer walked slowly around the chamber once more, pretending to admire the worn inscriptions etched into the stone window casings. "Places like this… they remind me that history is never really buried. Just forgotten. Until someone cares enough to dig."

Laure regarded him curiously, uncertain whether to be flattered or wary.

"You're very poetic, Monsieur Langford."

Mercer turned toward her with an unreadable expression. "I'm just a man who understands the importance of legacy."

A few heartbeats passed in silence.

Laure glanced down at her watch. "Well, I suppose I should return to my office. I have another appointment shortly, but if you'd like to schedule something formal for your foundation—"

"Oh, yes," Mercer interrupted gently. "That would be ideal. I'll have my assistant reach out to coordinate specifics."

They walked back into the corridor, the sound of their footsteps tapping faintly against the stone floor. Just before they reached the main atrium, Mercer slowed.

"Dr. Girard," he said softly.

She turned.

"If I may make a suggestion…" He held her gaze just a moment longer than necessary. "Be careful who you share the past with. Sometimes, what we protect can be the very thing that attracts danger."

Her brow furrowed slightly, unsure if it was advice or a warning. "Is that a threat, monsieur?"

"Not at all," he said with a faint smile. "Just a thought. History doesn't only belong to those who study it."

With that, he nodded courteously and rejoined his men waiting by the entrance.

Laure stood in place for a moment, watching him go, unsettled in a way she couldn't quite describe.

33

Tommy Schultz moved slowly beneath the vaulted ceiling of the eastern wing, his footsteps muffled by the ancient stone floor and the occasional creak of aged timber above. The Palais de Justice, with its layers of history baked into every wall and beam, exuded the weight of centuries. Paintings hung in quiet reverence along the corridor—portraits of monarchs, bishops, and magistrates long dead. Each one watched with indifferent eyes as Tommy passed, their expressions stoic, their oil-preserved gazes stuck in time.

Jean-Marc trailed a few steps behind, his movements cautious but deliberate. His eyes scanned more than just the artwork or the display cases—they flicked toward doors, corners, shadows. The soldier in him remained on edge, even in a place of culture and legacy. Especially in a place like this, where secrets liked to hide behind reverence.

Tommy stopped before a set of double doors. A plaque beside them marked the chamber beyond as Salle des Pas Perdus—the Hall of Lost Footsteps. He smirked. "Sounds promising."

Jean-Marc gave a quiet grunt of approval and reached forward, pushing the heavy doors open with ease. The space within felt cavernous, though it wasn't particularly large. Echoes lingered long after each step, the acoustics bouncing sound in odd patterns.

"Used to be a waiting room for court," Tommy whispered, almost reverently. "It's said Joan of Arc might've passed through here when she was brought in for questioning."

The light in the room was dim, filtered through narrow Gothic windows high along the walls. Shafts of sunlight slanted down, cutting through dust motes that danced in the air like tiny ghosts. The stone walls carried the faint scent of age and lichen. Cold seeped in from the floor, making the air dense with stillness.

They split up to cover more ground—Tommy weaving along the left wall, eyes scanning for carvings or hidden recesses. Jean-Marc took the right, pausing occasionally to examine decorative insets and inspect the mortar between stones.

"It's got to be somewhere," Tommy muttered. "Henri was too specific."

Jean-Marc didn't reply, though Tommy could hear him moving—a shuffle here, a creak there. Every once in a while, a tap echoed off the wall as he knocked gently with his knuckles, listening for changes in sound.

The far end of the room held a raised platform, once used by court officers. Tommy stepped onto it, studying the floor beneath the thick wooden paneling. He crouched down, brushing his fingers along a seam that looked less uniform than the rest.

He paused and leaned closer. A scratch. Not a tool mark, but recent. Human. Like someone had tried to pry it open.

"Jean," he called.

Jean-Marc joined him, crouching beside the platform.

Tommy pointed. "There. See the mark?"

Jean-Marc nodded. He reached into the inside of his jacket and produced a compact flashlight, clicked it on, and angled it to illuminate the floor.

The scratch glinted. It wasn't deep, but the wood around it looked slightly darker than the rest. Worn. Disturbed.

Jean-Marc ran his fingers along the edge, probing gently. "Could be a storage compartment," he said. "Might be nothing."

"Might not," Tommy said, already pulling out his multi-tool.

A minute of gentle coaxing proved the panel wasn't ready to give up its secrets. Whatever hinges or catches it once had were long corroded—or gone altogether.

"No good," Tommy said, straightening with a sigh. "If there's something down there, it's sealed up tight."

"Maybe that's the point," Jean-Marc offered. "Not everything's left open to find."

Tommy gave a half smile. "You'd think if someone went to the trouble of hiding something, they'd leave a key behind."

"Or a riddle."

They exchanged a look. Then Jean-Marc tilted his head, listening. "Footsteps," he said.

They both went quiet. A distant sound echoed from somewhere down the corridor. Not the practiced tread of a tourist. No, these steps were deliberate. Heavy. Muffled by rubber soles, not the heel-click of a casual visitor. Jean-Marc stood slowly and motioned toward the door with a small nod.

They left the chamber silently, blending into the corridor like two shadows slipping between columns.

Fifteen minutes had passed since they split from Tommy and Jean-Marc, but to Sean it might as well have been an hour. He and Evelyn had explored room after room in the east wing—once courtrooms, now exhibit spaces and archival chambers—finding nothing beyond elaborate architecture and the occasional historic placard.

They entered another gallery space, this one darker, the windows high and narrow. Framed documents and wooden display cases lined the walls. Sean paused near a window and took a breath. "We've got to be close," he murmured.

Evelyn ran a hand across a carved molding. "Maybe the 'voice' in the stone doesn't mean something we hear. Maybe it means something we have to see."

Sean followed her gaze to a raised dais at the end of the room, once used for trials. Behind it was a massive wooden panel—dark, undecorated, and out of place. He stepped forward.

"This wasn't always here."

Evelyn joined him. "You think it's covering something?"

Sean examined the edges. Near shoulder height, he found a faint engraving: a circle within a circle, and within that, a fleur-de-lis. He pressed it.

A soft click answered him, and a seam appeared as the panel split down the center. Dust swirled. A hidden stone alcove emerged, narrow and tall.

Inside, resting on a pedestal, sat a single wooden box, no larger than a shoebox. It was dark with age, bound with tarnished iron bands, and featured no keyhole—only four brass discs etched with Latin letters and faint symbols.

Sean stepped in. "This has to be what Henri was leading us to."

Evelyn joined him, eyes fixed on the box. "How do we open it?"

Sean pulled out Henri's notes. One passage stood out: "To those who swear loyalty in the shadow of truth, may your honor unlock what is hidden."

"It's not a riddle to open another door," Evelyn said. "It's a riddle for the box itself."

Sean nodded. "Exactly."

He knelt beside the pedestal to examine it more closely, and just as he reached forward to inspect the surface of the box—

A voice, low and calm, echoed from behind.

"That's far enough," it said, crisp with an unmistakable English accent.

34

Sean froze. The hair on his neck lifted as he slowly straightened. Tommy didn't move at all, though Sean could feel the tension rolling off him in waves.

They, along with Evelyn, turned as one.

In the archway stood a man in a slate-gray suit, tailored with the kind of precision that screamed money and danger. His expression was relaxed, almost polite. But his eyes—cold, flat, predatory—told a different story. Behind him stood two other figures, one broader, dressed in dark clothes, one holding Dr. Girard. He squeezed her throat with his forearm while pressing a Glock to her temple. The other man and the speaker both held similar weapons pointed at Sean and Tommy.

The man's gaze locked with Sean's.

Sean also noticed the striking absence of Jean-Marc. He had no idea where the Frenchman had gone, and hadn't even noticed him slip away.

"Step away from the box," the Englishman said. "Slowly."

The pistol concealed under Sean's windbreaker beckoned to his right hand, but he was in no position to make a play for it. Any twitch of a wrong move, and those guys would start shooting.

Sean withdrew from the alcove, retreating deliberately with every inch so as not to unleash the interlopers' desire to shoot. The firearms were equipped with suppressors, so there would be no sounds to hear in other parts of the building. No one would know until their bodies were found.

"What do you want with that box?" Sean asked while carefully raising his hands to shoulder level.

"You're not the only ones looking for the ring of Joan of Arc," the man said. Sean noticed a tattoo on his arm as he spoke. It was a symbol he recognized, though at first he thought it was Catholic. The second he saw the letters, however, he realized who they were dealing with. And it defied belief.

For the moment, Sean kept that to himself.

"I do appreciate you bringing us to it," the leader said. "I thought we could find it on our own, but following you made things so much easier."

"Happy to help, Mister...."

"My name isn't relevant. Now, please step aside."

Sean did as he was ordered and only then saw the shadow lengthen on the floor around the corner behind one of the henchmen.

"We don't even know if the ring is in there," Tommy cut in. "Or if it's even real."

"Yes, well, Mr. Schultz, I can understand why you would be halfway around the world looking in a previously hidden alcove for something that you don't believe is real."

"That was a little thick," Tommy grumbled.

"Santos, if you don't mind," he said with a flick of his wrist toward the bigger man with dark hair and bronze skin.

He stepped forward and into the alcove, only pausing for a moment to inspect the interior. He grasped the box and lifted it gently, as if worried there might be some kind of trap. Sean watched the man's foot, planted firmly on the off-color tile directly in front of the dais.

The moment Santos lifted the box, a low grinding sound echoed from above—a heavy, ancient rumble like stone against stone. Sean's eyes darted upward.

Suddenly, a massive slab dropped from the ceiling with terrifying speed.

The impact was instant and brutal.

The enormous stone slammed into the top of Santos' head with the force of a battering ram, driving his skull down through his spine. Bone shattered. His neck snapped like a twig. Blood burst outward in a violent spray, painting the alcove's walls and streaking across the floor into the corridor. Laure let out a sharp, terrified scream and staggered backward, hand over her mouth.

The stone slab struck with such force that it bounced once, then came to rest with a dull thud—resting flush atop the stone dais that had once held the box. Only that narrow platform had stopped it from slamming all the way to the floor.

The box tumbled from Santos' lifeless hands, clattering to the edge of the alcove, just outside the slab's crushing path.

The Englishman stood frozen, face blank as he stared down at the bloodied mess where his man had stood seconds before. His jaw clenched, fists tight at his sides.

Sean's mind clicked through what he'd just seen, the geometry of the trap—its cold design.

"You were supposed to kneel," he said quietly, half to himself. "Whoever took the box... had to kneel."

"Yep," Jean-Marc said, appearing around the corner. "And now you can kneel right there. Hands up where I can see them."

He pointed his pistol at the Englishman, whose weapon was now aimed at no one, only generally in Sean's direction.

"I was wondering where you went," Sean said, his voice perking up.

"Sorry, I slipped away. I thought I heard something suspicious, so I snuck off while you three were focused on that."

"This is all well and good," the Englishman quipped, "but I don't think you're in any position to negotiate. We still have Dr. Girard. So, if you want her to live, put your weapon down."

Jean-Marc grinned fiendishly. The expression betrayed something deeper—a familiarity.

"Interesting to bump into you here, Mercer," he said. "I thought you'd be off babysitting for some billionaire by now."

"That kind of work is boring. Second only to a desk job."

"Yes. Well, I still have a round with your name on it, so tell your man to put down the gun, or I end you right now like I should have years ago."

Sean had no idea what the connection between these two might be, but it didn't sound like they'd parted amicably.

"Not going to happen, old friend. You kill me, you know he'll kill Dr. Girard. You and the others might get out without a scratch. Or maybe he clips one or two of you before you take him out. But she still dies. Can you live with that? You want to add that to the roster of ghosts from your past mistakes?"

Jean-Marc hesitated. It was easy for everyone to see Mercer had hit a nerve.

"Then what do you suggest, old friend," he said the last part with contempt.

"Step aside. I take the box. You take Dr. Girard. A fair trade, I would say."

"You know we won't let you out of the building, much less off the premises."

"That's my problem to handle."

"How can I know we can trust you?"

"You don't," Mercer said with a sour grin. "But I can't trust you either, now can I? So, it looks like we're going to have to take a little leap of faith together, huh? Appropriate for this little quest."

Mercer crouched slowly, his expression unreadable as he reached for the box. His eyes remained fixed on Sean. Blood still glistened on the floor from Santos' brutal end, but Mercer paid it no mind. He slid a hand under the artifact and lifted it with unsettling calm, treating it more like a found curiosity than the object of a deadly chase.

The box looked strangely ordinary in his grip—small, unimposing—but it carried the weight of centuries, and the death it had just caused hung in the air like static. Mercer didn't react. His face was a study in focus, a man accustomed to seeing death and walking through its wake without missing a step.

The other mercenary still held Laure by the arm, guiding her carefully past the remnants of the trap. Her eyes were wide with terror, but she didn't struggle. Not yet.

Sean's hands curled into fists at his sides. He wanted to charge, to do something, anything, but one wrong move, and Laure might be gone in a flash of gunfire.

Evelyn took a small step forward before stopping herself. Tommy's hand shot out instinctively to hold her back.

The two gunmen began to retreat.

Jean-Marc stood at the end of the corridor, a shadow with steel in his hands. His pistol remained fixed on Mercer's chest, unwavering. His breath was low and slow; controlled. The way he held the weapon said it all—he would shoot to kill and do it without hesitation.

Mercer met his eyes as he advanced, steps slow, careful, deliberate. The corridor's shadows draped around them like curtains.

They reached the corner; the exit just beyond.

"Let her go," Sean demanded.

"Of course," Mercer said. "I am, after all, a man of my word."

He nodded at the man holding Dr. Girard, who shoved her forward. As she took a step away from them, Mercer turned his pistol and fired a shot into her lower back.

"No!" Sean shouted a second before her legs crumpled and she fell to the floor.

Jean-Marc's pistol discharged. The weapon was obscenely loud in the building, and would have been heard all the way at the other end, and probably outside.

The round struck the corner, missing the target and exploding in dust and debris.

The Frenchman stepped to the right, trying to open the angle of attack again, but this time Mercer fired at him and forced him back for cover.

Sean drew his weapon and surged ahead to join his French friend. Tommy pulled his pistol as well but turned and told Evelyn to stay there before hurrying down the other direction of the corridor and disappearing around the next corner to attempt to flank the enemy.

Sean waited for a moment, then he and Jean-Marc moved as one, each communicating with the other silently as if they'd done this sort of thing a million times together.

They led with their pistols, leaning to the right, both aware that they could catch a bullet in the face if Mercer was waiting for them.

Their movements were quick, a short test of dipping out from behind their position and back again. But when they looked, Mercer and his henchman were gone.

Sean rushed toward Laure, who lay on the ground, blood oozing from her lower back and her abdomen.

Jean-Marc joined him by his side, kneeling down to inspect the damage.

"Call an ambulance," Sean ordered.

Jean-Marc was already taking his phone out of his pocket.

Evelyn scurried across to them. She looked down, horrified at Laure, her bloody clothes and the pained, terrified look on her face. Tears streamed from her eyes.

"It's going to be okay," Sean said, taking her hand.

Jean-Marc stood and stepped away, speaking rapidly in French to the dispatcher on the other end of the line.

"I'm... so cold," Laure said.

Her skin felt clammy in Sean's hand. He knew she was going into shock.

He let her hand go for a moment and took off his jacket, then tore a piece of his T-shirt from the bottom, wadded it up, and pressed the fabric against the bloody wound. The sticky red liquid covered his fingers as he worked. Then he tore another piece off his shirt and lifted her carefully, tipping her over so he could patch the wound in the gut.

Laure's face was ghostly white.

"Any sign of them?" Sean asked, looking up at Tommy as he lowered Laure back to the floor.

"No. They're gone," Tommy said.

Jean-Marc finished his conversation on the phone and moved back to where Sean knelt next to Dr. Girard.

"The police and an ambulance are on their way," he said.

"I just hope they can get here in time," Sean replied. "She's losing a lot of blood."

"Sean, give me your gun. You too, Tommy," the Frenchman added. "We don't want to be caught with these when the police arrive."

Sean nodded, wiped his fingers on the tattered remains of his shirt, then handed the pistol to his friend. Tommy did the same.

"I'm going to see if I can find them," Jean-Marc said. "And while I'm out there, I'll take care of these. You three stay here." He removed his jacket and wrapped the firearms in the folds, wadding it up so it looked as if there were nothing in it. He turned and trotted around the corner and disappeared, leaving nothing but the repetitive sounds of his footfalls echoing through the cavernous silence.

Sean took Laure's hand again, keeping eye contact with her as he spoke.

"It's going to be okay. Help is on the way."

He just hoped she could make it long enough.

35

The car hummed along the country road, engine low and steady. Gray light from the overcast morning flickered through rows of trees that lined the narrow ribbon of asphalt, like guards watching the passage of something profane—or dangerous. Mercer's fingers drumming against the smooth lid of the sealed box resting on his lap.

The wax seals remained untouched. Unbroken. They were worn, yellowed with age, but still intact—one bearing a faint etching that might've been a fleur-de-lys. It was hard to tell under the layers of time and grime. But he knew what this box was. Or rather, what it might be. Enough that people had bled for it.

Mercer tapped his earpiece.

The line rang once before a voice answered. "I hope you have good news for me," Victoria said demurely.

"It's done," Mercer said. "We have the box."

A beat passed. Victoria's voice returned, even, neutral. "You're sure?"

"I'm looking at it."

"And the others?" she asked.

"They were there," Mercer said. "Wyatt, Schultz, Langley. Jean-Marc too."

"The director?"

"She was there as well. It got messy."

Another pause.

"Messy how?"

"We lost Santos."

There was a long silence on the other end. A crow launched from a nearby fence and glided across the road ahead of them. Nikolai, silent at the wheel, adjusted their speed ever so slightly as the trees thinned and the road curved gently toward a rolling expanse of vineyard.

"Explain," Victoria said.

"Pressure plate inside the chamber. Triggered some kind of stone trap—slab from the ceiling came down like a hammer. There wasn't time to stop it."

Victoria exhaled, almost imperceptibly. "That's unfortunate." Her condolence felt hollow.

"Gruesome," Mercer replied, his voice flat. "He was dead before the box hit the floor."

She let that sink in. "And Dr. Girard?"

Mercer watched a narrow road split off to the left. A white hatchback pulled out from behind a tree-lined driveway and passed them slowly. "Shot her," he said. "Mid-back. She went down hard."

"Is she a liability?"

"No. She doesn't know who we are. Of course, she may be dead already."

There was the sound of movement on her end—a creak of furniture, maybe a shift in her chair.

"Fine," she said, blowing off the possible death of an innocent person as if she were a gnat. "Did anyone follow?"

"No one tailed us," Mercer said. "We exited clean. Jean-Marc was closest, but we had the angle and speed. Plus, we're not exactly flying through the countryside. We're ghosting it."

"Good."

The Renault moved past a crumbling stone chapel at the crest of a hill, its steeple crooked like a drunk leaning on a lamppost. Mercer didn't turn to look. He'd seen too many of those in Eastern Europe during missions no one was allowed to talk about.

"I'm assuming it hasn't been opened," Victoria said.

"Not yet."

"I'd prefer it stayed that way."

Mercer's jaw tightened slightly. "You don't want confirmation?"

"We'll confirm when it's in my hands."

He looked down at the box. "It's authentic. I'd bet my life on it."

"You nearly did."

"I want to be clear about something," he said. "I've lost three men. My name's going to start echoing in the wrong rooms soon if we run into much more trouble. This op wasn't a simple smash-and-grab job. We did the whole tattoo thing like you asked as part of your little initiation. But what I really need to know is if I'm getting what you promised."

"You will," Victoria said, her tone sharp but controlled. "Exactly what we discussed. No less."

"I want what was due my dead men split between the rest of us who are left. And we'll need long-term insulation."

"Of course."

Mercer let that settle. He didn't enjoy pressing her, but after what happened to Santos, the margin for uncertainty had closed significantly.

Ahead, the road dipped between two groves of trees. Somewhere in the distance, a tractor grumbled through a field.

"If this is what you think it is," Mercer added, "you're about to make history. Again."

"That's the idea."

A pause. The wind whispered through the slightly cracked window. Nikolai adjusted his grip on the wheel.

Victoria's voice returned, cooler now. "Well done."

Mercer didn't reply.

Mercer waited for Victoria to finish her pause on the other end of the line. The soft hum of the vehicle's tires on the narrow country road filled the silence in the Renault. Finally, her voice came through again, this time laced with precision.

"You'll bring it to me directly. The estate. This evening."

Mercer nodded, though she couldn't see him. "We'll be there in a few hours."

"Good. I'll alert security to expect you."

Mercer looked out the windshield as a spire of an old countryside church appeared in the distance, its stone face catching the slant of the sun. He made a note of the time and direction. "Understood. We'll be there."

There was a pause, then Victoria added, "Well done, Mercer. Well done."

The line went dead.

Mercer lowered the phone from his ear and slid it into the pocket of his jacket. The quiet inside the vehicle settled again, save for the occasional chirping of birds outside and the steady drone of the engine.

He turned his gaze toward Nikolai, who drove with the patience of a man used to both violence and silence. The road curved ahead, bordered by thick hedgerows and fields dotted with grazing sheep. The spire of the old church slowly disappeared behind a row of trees.

"We'll need to meet up with the others before we get close to the estate," Mercer said.

Nikolai gave a subtle nod. "There's a market town a few kilometers ahead. We can park near the canal. Less traffic that way. Meet them there."

"Good. Klein, call Soren and Moreau, let them know where to meet us."

Klein sat silently in the back, checking his weapon. The smell of gun oil clung faintly to the air. Putting down his gun, he picked up his phone to make the call.

Mercer leaned back in his seat, running one hand across his jaw. The box sat between his feet, unassuming in its appearance yet pulsing with the weight of centuries. They didn't know exactly what was inside. But Victoria believed it to be the key to something far greater than wealth.

He wasn't sure he believed in relics with power. But he believed in leverage. And Victoria Sterling was a woman who paid handsomely for leverage.

The countryside stretched around them in waves of green and gold, the sky above having cleared some. Despite the calm beauty, Mercer felt the tension behind his ribs coil tighter. Something about this mission felt different. Not just the stakes but the sense that for the first time in a long while, he was chasing something that wasn't running from him—but something waiting to be found.

The road narrowed as they descended into a shallow valley, the trees pressing close. Mercer rolled down the window, letting in the cool country air. The scent of loam and pine filtered in, mingling with the sharper scent of steel and sweat.

He glanced down at the box.

"Whatever you are," he murmured, "you'd better be worth the blood we've spilled."

36

Sean sat on the bench with his face buried in his palms. The smell of soap and hand sanitizer couldn't wash away the guilt cutting through his chest.

Tommy and Jean-Marc stood close by, identical emotions painted on their faces.

Evelyn sobbed while speaking to a police officer from the backseat of the cop's squad car.

The courtyard outside the Palais had transformed into a controlled frenzy. Blue lights strobed from the tops of four police cruisers parked at varying angles around the entrance. Their doors stood open, radios crackling with clipped French dispatches. Two ambulances idled nearby, their engines humming while paramedics leaned against the rear, solemn and waiting. One of the stretcher teams had already completed their grim duty—Laure's body was now sealed behind the cold, zipped curtain of a black bag.

Around the courtyard, crime scene tape fluttered in the rising breeze, cordoning off a perimeter that included the grand wooden doors of the Palais and the stone walkway leading up to them. A small cluster of onlookers had gathered behind the tape; their hushed murmurs cut by the sharp commands of uniformed officers holding the line.

The sky had dulled to a pewter gray, the early afternoon sun buried behind a thick shroud of clouds. Distant thunder rolled, low and sullen, like the growl of something ancient and angry stirring just beyond the horizon. A humid heaviness hung in the air, pressing against the skin like a damp wool blanket, thick with the scent of stone, dust, and something metallic beneath it all—blood.

Two police officers stood near the entrance. They wore stern expressions on their faces as a silent warning to any who might dare enter the crime scene without authorization. Another officer walked briskly across the scene holding a clipboard, nodding silently to each team as he passed.

A plainclothes detective, identifiable only by the badge clipped to his belt, stood off to one side making notes and talking on a cell phone. His face was blank, but his eyes darted from Sean and his group to the surrounding chaos with quick, analytical sweeps. Everyone here had seen death before. But this one felt different. More personal.

And overhead, the clouds kept coming, darker now, closing in. None of the men said a thing.

Sean ran his fingers, his mind still seeing the pained expression on Dr. Girard's face before she died.

The vision sent another dagger through his heart. He tried to swallow, but a lump filled his throat, and it took some effort to choke it down.

Tommy wiped tears from his eyes and took a deep breath. He shook his head and looked as if he were about to speak but couldn't form the words.

What do you want to do?" Tommy asked pointedly.

Sean watched as the coroner loaded the stretcher with the body atop it into the back of an ambulance.

He and the others had already spoken to the police. They'd explained they were there to investigate part of the museum, how they'd discovered the secret panel and the alcove behind it.

Sean had given a few references the cops couldn't ignore, as had Jean-Marc, and the questioning had ended quickly. Both he and his friend had dropped the names of high-ranking government officials, and suddenly they were no longer suspects in the murder.

Emily Starks, Sean knew, had played a small part in that. As director of the redacted agency known as Axis, her reach extended around the world, and carried the authority of the president of the United States.

Sean considered Jean-Marc's question and shook his head. It wasn't often he didn't know what to do in a given situation. But the death of Laure Girard had hit him hard, like a wrecking ball dipped in shards of broken glass.

"I... don't know," he confessed. "I really... It's my fault she's dead."

Tommy shook his head and placed his palm on Sean's shoulder. "No, man. This isn't your fault. We all had a hand in this."

"I should have been more careful. More alert." On top of that, the fact that he didn't take the shot when he had the chance ripped his insides apart like a rusty chainsaw. He almost never doubted himself in situations like that. For some reason, in the moment, he didn't believe that Mercer would do what he did. Sean made a mistake. And it cost an innocent woman her life. Of all the deaths that hung around his neck like a chain, that link was the heaviest.

"We all make mistakes," Jean-Marc consoled. "If I had just taken the shot when I had it...."

"It was too dangerous," Sean countered.

"I could have done it. I could have eliminated that gunman. Then it would have just been us and Mercer. It would all be over." Pain rippled through his voice.

"I know you're good. But you did the right thing."

Jean-Marc merely shook his head in derision.

"Look," Tommy said, "I know this sucks—"

"Sucks?" Sean interrupted. "An innocent woman just died because of us. This goes way beyond sucks, buddy."

"She died because this Mercer guy shot her. Now, we can't just let him get away with this. Who knows what he'll do next. Especially if he finds the ring."

"Unless he already has it. We don't know what's in that box. It might be the ring."

"All the more reason for us to get off our tails and figure out where he is."

Sean's shoulders shuddered as he chuckled grimly. "And how do you propose we do that?"

Tommy looked back over his shoulder, buying himself a second to think. "We know what they're driving."

"Then we find the car, and figure it out from there, unless we come up with something better." Sean was despondent. Normally, he could compartmentalize things, even extreme stuff like this. But now, all he could see was Laure's dying face in the front of his mind. Her fear, the tears streaking down her cheeks. He could still feel the blood on his hands, blood that no amount of soap and water could ever wash away.

"I can check with my connections," Jean-Marc offered. "And Antón may be able to help us as well. I'm with Tommy. We can find these guys, and make them pay." He glanced over his shoulder to make sure no one was listening.

"Did you see the tattoo?" Sean asked. The question must have seemed like it came out of nowhere to the other two.

"What tattoo?" Tommy replied.

"Your old buddy, Mercer you said? He has a tattoo on his wrist."

"What about it?"

"I never noticed it before, but I saw it today," Jean-Marc said. "I didn't get a close look at it."

"Yeah, well, those guys are not working for themselves. They're not treasure hunters or collectors. They're working for someone else."

"How do you know that from a tattoo?" Tommy pressed.

"It's a symbol of an organization. A logo, if you will. It hasn't been around in a long time. They faded off the map in the 1800s. The tattoo," he said, drawing out imaginary lines on his wrist, "is three crosses joined at the base in a triangle. With the letters *E*, *I*, and *C* between them. And we know how much these groups love esoteric ciphers."

Jean-Marc didn't recognize the description, but it hit Tommy within two seconds. "No," he said. "That can't be right."

"I know what I saw."

"What?" the Frenchman insisted. "What is it?"

Tommy turned to him to answer. "It's the logo for the East India Company."

"What is that?"

"Back a few hundred years ago," Tommy explained, "they were a dominant force. Their military was bigger than most nations, including Great Britain's."

"What does that have to do with any of this? Why would that organization be involved with hunting for Joan of Arc's ring?"

Sean pulled himself out of the dark pit of his mind and looked up at the other two. "The EIC was put to bed a long time ago. Their licenses were revoked; their land and titles were ceded to the British government. It was one of the biggest acquisitions of all time. The company was enormous. We're talking ships, guns, manpower, huge swaths of land, entire colonies. Their power reached all the way to the Americas and beyond."

"This was the company from that pirate movie, yes?" Jean-Marc clarified.

Tommy cracked a smile. "Yes. That one."

"And everyone around the world just sort of accepted that the company was done. Some of the men in charge were given positions within the British government. But some, as I recall, were left out in the cold. They lost everything. Those guys went from being some of the wealthiest non-royals in the world... to nobodies."

"How did that happen?" Jean-Marc wondered. "If they were so powerful, it's surprising they allowed the British government to take it all away."

"There was a rebellion in India," Tommy answered. "The EIC put it down, but they were brutal, and it demonstrated to the British government that perhaps their grip was loosening. They weren't going to fight their own either. All of the men in their service were British. Their first allegiance was to the Crown and their fellow countrymen. The company's leadership understood this, and most of them wouldn't have wanted a war either. So they relinquished their power and faded into obscurity."

The Frenchman thought for a few seconds, obviously trying to fit the pieces together. "Okay, but I still don't understand what this has to do with the ring. If the company is no longer around, why do these men have tattoos representing it?"

"There are really only two options," Sean said, a grim tone hovering in his voice like the dark clouds looming in the sky. "One, they're just trying to be cool with some obscure historical fandom."

"And two?"

Sean met his friend's gaze with his piercing blue eyes. "Or the company never really went away, and these guys are some of their enforcers."

37

The statement took Jean-Marc by surprise at first, and Sean could see the man was skeptical.

"But how? They had everything taken away."

"Yes," Tommy agreed. "They lost every charter, their military, land, titles, all of it. But Sean's right. What if they never really stopped operating? What if they simply retreated to the shadows, still running things from behind a veil? People in positions of power don't give that up lightly."

Sean's mind spun.

The death of Laure Girard still hung heavy around his neck; like a thousand-pound chain. But now his analytical mind was running, fueled by an old feeling he usually tried to keep at bay—a thirst for vengeance.

Revenge was a powerful motivator that often disguised itself as justice. It was a delicate line to toe, and Sean knew it. He wanted to make this Mercer, and anyone else associated with him, pay; including whoever was above him giving the orders.

He folded his hands together, clenching them until his knuckles whitened. "If we really are dealing with the EIC, we need to find the head of the snake."

"And how do you propose we do that? If they're real, they've been hiding, as you said, for a long time. They won't be easy to find."

"No. They won't."

"Where do you suggest we start?" Tommy asked as Evelyn approached.

"Start with what?" she asked, stopping next to Tommy. Dark circles hung under her eyes, both from fatigue and from the horrific events that had unfolded earlier. To her credit, she looked as though she'd spent every emotion possible and was ready to move forward.

"The men who were following us, who did this," Tommy explained. "We think they work for the East India Company."

Evelyn's expression changed. For a second it looked as if she thought Tommy was joking. When she saw he wasn't, she scoffed at the notion.

"That company has been defunct for well over a hundred years. What on Earth would make you think that?"

"The men had tattoos of the EIC logo on their forearms," Sean said. "It's possible that the company never went away. They could have consolidated what little they had left and continued operating under the table, away from the watchful eye of the British government."

Evelyn still wasn't sold on the notion. "Even if that were true, and your hypothesis is correct, we would never be able to catch those men. And what would the EIC want with the ring? Are they collectors?"

"Usually, in our experience," Tommy interjected, "collectors don't go to these kinds of extremes. It happens now and then, but most of the time they have another motive."

"Such as?"

"If Joan's ring really does have some kind of power, it could be that whoever is in charge now wants it. Maybe they believe it will return them to their former glory."

"But like she said," Jean-Marc cut in, "we don't know where those guys went. And Mercer is a ghost. Finding him would be like finding a drinkable merlot—nearly impossible."

Sean chuckled at the statement, and for a moment the ice that had formed around him cracked a little.

Then an epiphany hit him. "We don't need to find Mercer," he said. "We need to find the person calling the shots."

"What do you mean?" Evelyn asked. "Like the head of the company?"

"That would be just as hard if not harder than tracking down Mercer," Jean-Marc added.

"Maybe not." Sean looked at Tommy. "Can you access Malcom from here?"

"Anywhere there's a cell signal or Wi-Fi."

"Who is Malcom?" Evelyn asked.

"Not who. What. It's an AI we built. It helps us with research most of the time, particularly research that isn't readily available to the public with a quick Google search."

"Why did you name it Malcom?"

Tommy shrugged as he took out his phone and tapped on the screen. "I don't know. We had to name it something. Alex and Tara came up with it."

He looked at the screen, tapped on the private app marked with a black M over a white background, and then spoke. "Malcom. I need your help with something."

"Good afternoon, Tommy. How are things going in France?"

Evelyn and Jean-Marc both looked shocked.

"I notice you gave it an English accent," Evelyn said.

Tommy smirked then answered the AI's question. "Not great." He glanced around at the chaotic scene. "But I have an unusual request."

"Tommy, we both know almost none of your requests are normal or usual. It's one of the reasons you built me."

"True," Tommy said with a snort. "You're aware of the East India Company, yeah?"

"Of course. That organization hasn't been around for over a century. Why do you ask?"

"I'm wondering if you can find information on who the top leaders were from the EIC at the time it was disbanded."

"Certainly. One moment."

The group waited while the AI conducted the search. Based on their expressions, Evelyn and Jean-Marc could barely believe the interaction was happening.

"I have the list," Malcom said. "Would you like me to send it to you?"

"Maybe," Tommy said. "But first, I want to know if there are any known descendants of the men who were in charge. Did they have children? Grandchildren? We need to know if there are any still around."

"Interesting. You were correct. This isn't a usual sort of request. I'll check."

Again, everyone watched Tommy in silence as the AI worked its magic.

"I have located one surviving descendant," Malcom said after thirty seconds.

Sean stood up, suddenly more interested in the answer.

"Go ahead," Tommy said.

"Victoria Sterling is her name. She is the descendant of Robert Martin. Accessing archival profile... Robert Martin – East India Company Executive Tier.

"Martin served as a pivotal yet shadowy figure within the upper echelons of the East India Company during the latter half of the eighteenth century. Unlike the high-profile governors and military commanders, Martin operated behind the scenes, primarily as a financier, strategist, and covert facilitator of the company's more discreet dealings.

"His influence stemmed not from battlefield conquests but from his ability to manipulate economic leverage. Martin specialized in orchestrating backdoor trades, off-ledger agreements, and the acquisition of rare assets—including religious artifacts, cultural heirlooms, and even manuscripts deemed too dangerous for public knowledge."

The group listened intently as Malcom continued.

"Records suggest he oversaw the establishment of a network of private vaults and safekeeping chambers, rumored to span from

Lisbon to Goa. He also maintained direct relationships with secretive banking houses and monastic orders willing to house sensitive items in exchange for protection and bribes.

"Internally, Martin chaired a small, unofficial committee known as the Council of Nine, composed of silent partners whose names never appeared in formal documents. Their role: to secure the long-term survival of the company through clandestine operations—both during and after the company's decline.

"Notably, Martin's bloodline continues to surface in modern financial power structures. Victoria Sterling is believed to be his direct descendant, inheriting not only his wealth but access to confidential archives, though sources on this last part are possibly based on rumor."

Sean appreciated the history lesson, but if this Victoria woman was the only living descendant of Martin, she had to be the one behind all this. It was a jump, but not a leap.

"Malcom," Sean said, "what can you tell us about Victoria Sterling?"

"One moment, please. Compiling data."

"Victoria Sterling is a British-born financier with dual citizenship in France and the United Kingdom. Educated at St. Paul's Girls' School, followed by Oxford University, where she studied international economics and early colonial trade systems. From a young age, Sterling was immersed in the legacy of her ancestry—most notably, Robert Martin. Unlike other descendants who distanced themselves from the colonial past, Sterling embraced it—viewing her lineage not as a stain, but as a blueprint.

"After graduating top of her class, she entered the world of global finance, quickly ascending the ranks at Castellan & Ward, a private banking firm with known connections to offshore holdings and discreet asset movement. Within six years, she broke away to form her own holding company—Sterling Meridian Group—which now functions as a shadow bank, facilitating "quiet" transactions for the ultra-elite.

"Sounds like she was groomed to take over the EIC," Tommy noted.

"Yes, it does," Sean agreed.

"Would you like me to continue?" Malcom asked.

"Please. By all means."

"In recent years, Victoria's profile grew more opaque. Public appearances dwindled. Interviews ceased. Around the same time, her name began surfacing in dark web forums, cryptocurrency intelligence briefings, and blacklist files from multiple intelligence agencies—most notably MI6 and DGSE. Not for criminal charges—yet—but for patterns that aligned with high-risk asset recovery, cultural trafficking, and clandestine acquisitions of historical importance. What's peculiar is that it appears many records were later destroyed. Odd for government agencies to cover something up of that import."

Sean cast Tommy a knowing glance.

"Yeah, at some point we're going to have to have a conversation," Tommy said.

"A conversation?"

"Yes, but for now just focus on Sterling."

"Intelligence indicates she operates a private network of recovery specialists, ex-intelligence operatives, and contracted mercenaries—organized via encrypted dark-web channels. Surveillance reports suggest she uses these assets to locate and acquire items of significance tied to power, prophecy, and legacy. Her current interests include medieval European relics, religious artifacts, and items rumored to hold metaphysical value.

"Behavioral analysis indicates she possesses high narcissistic traits, exceptional long-game strategic thinking."

"Fascinating," Sean said. "Someone like that could easily develop an obsession with reclaiming the prominence she believes her bloodline is owed."

"That's why she wants the ring," Tommy realized. "She's going to use it to raise the East India Company from the grave, or wherever it's been. Who knows what after that?"

"Her finances remain secure through untraceable shell companies across Lichtenstein, the Cayman Islands, and the Seychelles," Malcom said. "She maintains at least three residences—one in Mayfair, London, another in the French countryside near Dijon, and a third, more elusive property in the Alps—location redacted from open databases."

"Can you isolate those home locations?" Jean-Marc asked.

"Malcom, did you get that?" Tommy said.

"I'm an AI, Tommy. I'm not deaf."

Sean giggled at the response.

"And yes, sir, I can locate two of the three. The one in the Alps is off grid. I could access more information, but it would take time."

"No," Sean said, shaking his head. "Don't worry about that for now. I think we can rule out the place in England. At least for now. If she's hunting for Joan's ring and has a property here, then she'd want to be as close as possible."

"Well, that was easier than looking for a car! So, Dijon then?" Evelyn asked.

"Sounds like it. But you're not coming with us."

"What do you mean? I have to see this through. You can't just leave me here."

"I already got someone killed this week, Evelyn. I don't want to have more blood on my hands. Not yours, anyway. It's going to be too dangerous."

She stood up straighter, posturing as if she had some kind of power over him. "These people are going to try to kill me. Do you understand? There is nowhere I'll be safe, especially if you don't make it back. They will hunt me down and erase me. I'm a loose end."

For an archaeology professor, she certainly had a firm grasp of how those sorts of people operated. She wasn't wrong. If Mercer and his men, and Sterling, prevailed, they would come after Evelyn next.

Sean knew there were measures he could take to hide her, at least for a while, but long term she would be found, one way or another. In some ways, being with him and Tommy might keep her safer than if they entrusted her to someone they didn't know. Then again, he considered the possibility of leaving her with Antón. He seemed to be a good guy, and Jean-Marc trusted him. He had decent security at his château. That option seemed to check all the boxes.

The problem was, would she go quietly and stay there, or would Evelyn do something stupid and try to follow them to Dijon? As hell-bent as she seemed to be over the issue, Sean figured the latter. Plus, would Antón want his peace disturbed by a target hunted by some very violent people?

"Okay," he surrendered. "But you have to do as I say. Understood?"

"Fine," she said. "I can do that."

He doubted that would be true when the chips were on the table, but what else could he do? She had a mind of her own, and free will to use it.

Sean could see the concern on Tommy's and Jean-Marc's faces. He knew they were having the same thoughts, but they also weren't going to vocalize them, at least not in front of Evelyn.

"I guess we're going to Dijon," Sean said. "Tommy, get the address from Malcom if you don't mind."

"On it."

Then Sean looked to Jean-Marc. "I suppose we'll need some new…tools," he said, looking around calmly at the police in the area.

"Not a problem. I still have the tools from before. They're in a safe place."

That was a relief. Going up against Mercer and his goons would be difficult enough with firearms. Without would be virtual suicide.

Either way, he knew Victoria Sterling would stop at nothing to find the ring. And he and his companions were the only thing standing in her way.

38

The French countryside unfolded in a serene, uninterrupted stretch of color and subtle motion. Pale green fields stitched with low stone walls were awash in an ocean of bright yellow mustard blooms, which were now approaching their peak flowering for the year, and everything undulated gently in the early afternoon light, broken here and there by clusters of trees with leaves just beginning to shift from spring's bright energy into summer's deeper hues. The air had that unmistakable clarity that followed a morning shower, crisp and clean, with the faintest scent of mustard blooms and damp grass drifting through the cracked windows of the Renault.

Mercer sat in the front passenger seat, legs still stretched out, showing no sign of the tension from the earlier escape, his right elbow resting against the door as his fingers tapped rhythmically against the armrest. The cigarette he'd crushed out an hour ago still lingered on his fingertips, mingling with the ever-present musk of gunpowder and sweat that clung to the interior of the car. He hadn't spoken in several minutes—not since they'd left the edge of Poitiers behind—and neither had the others.

The only sounds inside the vehicle were the occasional gravel crunch beneath the tires and the low groan of the engine as Nikolai navigated the narrow, winding roads with the same methodical precision that marked all of his movements. Behind them, the road stretched back toward the village, narrowing to a ribbon as it disappeared into the gentle hills. Ahead, the terrain rose slightly and shifted to old-growth forest interspersed with vineyard plots and solitary barns, their slate roofs glinting dully in the cloud-covered sun.

Mercer watched with a soldier's eye how the landscape changed, noting the stone markers, the hidden driveways, the ancient wooden signs at intersections so weathered they seemed to exist only by memory. He'd operated in dozens of countries under just as many covers, but rural France had always carried with it a deceptive quiet. It lulled you if you weren't careful.

In the back seat, the others remained silent. They'd said little since the group had reunited on the outskirts of town, the men absorbed in their own thoughts. Even trained killers needed mental rest, Mercer knew. Exhaustion was setting in like rot in wet boots. He could see it in the slump of their shoulders, the long blinks, the way Moreau's fingers curled tightly around the stock of his weapon despite the safety of their current drive. They needed a break. All of them.

Mercer turned his head as they passed a weathered chapel on a hilltop, its stone steeple crooked from centuries of standing alone against the wind. A half-collapsed wooden fence encircled a small cemetery, the gravestones worn smooth by time. The sight lingered with him. Not because it meant anything but because it reminded him of how fast time buried everything—including men like Santos.

He hadn't said the name out loud yet. He wasn't sure if he would.

They crested a hill, and there it was. The wrought iron gate emerged from behind a line of sycamore trees, its twin pillars flanked by ornamental lanterns atop moss-veined stone. The gate itself was black, heavy, and intricately designed—old-world craftsmanship that spoke of money, power, and an obsessive attention to detail. It bore no family crest, no lettering—just strength.

Nikolai slowed the vehicle and rolled to a stop before it. Beyond the gate, a long, tree-lined lane disappeared into the heart of the estate. Sunlight filtered through the boughs above, casting dappled shadows across the cobblestone drive. The branches rustled faintly in a breeze that carried the earthy scent of damp leaves and lavender from deeper in the forest.

Mercer leaned forward slightly and narrowed his eyes at the gate.

With a soft mechanical hum, the wrought iron gate creaked open, swinging inward in a graceful arc as if inviting them onto sacred ground. Nikolai eased the Renault forward, the tires crunching gently over the beginning of the cobblestone drive. The gate shut behind them with a heavy clang that echoed faintly between the trees.

The road ahead wound through a thicket of forest, the trees dense on either side—mostly oaks and beeches—their branches tangled high above in a leafy archway that cast mottled shadows across the stone path. The last remnants of daylight poked through the gaps in the canopy like golden threads, flickering over the windshield as if scanning them with every yard they progressed.

None of it put Mercer at ease.

The drive curved slowly, following the natural contours of the land before straightening out at the forest's edge. The trees fell away, replaced by a grand avenue flanked by two rows of evenly spaced plane trees—tall and elegant, their pale trunks smooth and speckled like marble. They stood as a living corridor, guiding the vehicle toward the estate that finally came into full view ahead.

Victoria Sterling's manor dominated the early evening landscape like a queen presiding over her kingdom. The building was palatial—three stories tall and sprawling in both width and stature. The stone façade was pale ivory; the surface etched with subtle flourishes and ornamentation carved centuries ago. Shutters, painted a deep forest green, framed tall windows. Some were open to the afternoon breeze, gauzy curtains fluttering from within like whispers.

In front of the manor, a circular driveway branched out to encompass a roundabout with a central stone fountain. The water trickled quietly from the mouth of a sculpted lion, the droplets glinting in the dappled light. Surrounding the drive were beds of immaculately tended roses, lavender, and boxwood shrubs trimmed into perfect domes. Tulips flared in bursts of color along the edges, their vibrant petals dancing in the wind.

The lawn was impossibly green, the kind of manicured perfection that only came from daily care by unseen hands. No weeds, no stray leaves, just nature sculpted into order.

Statues dotted the grounds: figures in motion, warriors and muses carved in white marble, some partially obscured by the hedgerows. One stood near the fountain: a woman holding a sword aloft in one hand and a shield in the other. Her face was stoic; her eyes fixed toward the horizon. Joan of Arc, Mercer realized.

The front steps leading to the main entrance were wide and shallow, built from pale stone that had been polished to a fine sheen over time. Two tall columns flanked the grand doors: double-width, blackened oak reinforced with bronze hinges and rivets, the handles shaped like serpents devouring their own tails.

The Renault came to a stop at the base of the steps. Nikolai killed the engine.

Mercer glanced toward the entrance. No one was there to greet them.

He stepped out of the car, and his boots tapped softly on the cobblestone. He raised his arms up over his head and then bent down to stretch out his legs for a few seconds. His muscles thanked him with relief after sitting in the car for so long.

Soren and Moreau joined him, their eyes scanning the façade, the windows, the perimeter. The place was beautiful. Regal. But that only made it more unnerving.

Mercer adjusted the collar of his coat and ascended the steps, his footsteps heavy with travel, tension, and unanswered questions. At the door, he paused, gave a final look over his shoulder, then reached out and rang the bronze bell mounted beside the doorway.

They waited.

The door opened a moment later, revealing a tall man in a black suit—trim, late fifties, with a cleanly shaved head and dark eyes that gave nothing away. The butler's expression was impassive, his posture perfect, hands clasped in front of him.

"Mr. Mercer. Welcome back," the butler said in his native French accent.

"Thank you," Mercer said. "Is she in?"

"Of course. She's been waiting for you. Follow me. She is in the study."

Mercer thought it odd she wasn't here to greet him herself, but he knew she had a flare for the dramatic, and this was one more little layer to that flamboyant persona.

The butler stepped aside, allowing Mercer and his men to ascend the stone steps. The heavy double doors shut behind them with a muted thud, leaving the countryside hush behind.

Inside, the air was cooler—tempered, fragrant with polished wood, aged paper, and the faintest note of violet. The foyer was expansive, paneled in rich walnut wainscoting beneath walls of pale ivory. The ceiling stretched high overhead, adorned with hand-painted plasterwork depicting a constellation of stars in muted golds and silvers. A massive chandelier hung at the center, not ostentatious but elegant—its tiers of crystal catching and scattering soft glints of light. The floor beneath was Italian marble, its veins of charcoal gray threading through a sea of white.

A long oriental rug, its reds and deep blues dulled with age, guided them forward.

The butler walked with silent precision, his gloved hands clasped behind his back. "This way, gentlemen."

They passed beneath a wide arch framed by Corinthian columns, their fluting carved with meticulous detail. The interior was a museum of old money and inherited power—sculptures in alcoves, antique furniture spaced with perfect restraint, and oil paintings of unknown aristocrats staring out with ghostly calm.

A staircase swept upward to the second level, curving at the halfway point beneath a dome skylight. The balustrade was wrought iron, shaped into ivy and thorned roses. The steps themselves were polished oak, their centers covered by a runner of deep burgundy velvet that muffled their footfalls.

Halfway up, Mercer glanced over his shoulder at Nikolai, who met his eyes without speaking. The others,—Klein, Soren, and Moreau—moved in silence, tense with the kind of alertness bred from long exposure to violence. None of them liked being this deep in someone else's stronghold.

At the landing, the hallway stretched out before them like a gallery. Tall windows to the right let in the gray afternoon light, filtered through sheer linen drapes. Between the windows, the walls were decorated with classic French paneling interrupted by large gilt-framed paintings—landscapes of Normandy, darkened portraits of long-dead Sterling ancestors, and scenes of imperial grandeur.

Gas-style sconces had been fitted with electric bulbs, each one casting a steady amber glow that gave the hall a timeless, candlelit warmth. On polished mahogany credenzas, priceless artifacts rested beneath glass cloches: a flintlock pistol with engraved metalwork, a Roman oil lamp, a fragment of embroidered tapestry with threads of gold.

The butler stopped at the final door on the left; a broad one with dark oaken panels and iron hinges. The doorknob was brass, dulled by time but clean and polished.

"She's in there," the man said, his voice formal, but not unkind. He turned, gesturing for them to enter.

Mercer gave a brief nod then stepped forward. From the threshold, he saw her.

Victoria Sterling stood by the tall windows at the far end of the study, her back to them, the pale evening light silhouetting her sharp profile. She wore a cream blouse with flared sleeves and high-waisted trousers, a glass of red wine held in her right hand. Her other hand rested on her hip as she looked out over the manicured grounds and distant tree line, posture straight and still as a marble figure.

She didn't turn around as she spoke. "Beautiful, isn't it?" she asked. It almost sounded rhetorical.

Mercer made a motion to his men to stay there in the corridor then stepped inside.

"It's a lovely place you have here." It wasn't his first visit to her French estate, but he appreciated the views every time he came.

She stood there for a moment, as if making him wait for her response. "Yes. It's quite lovely."

Victoria turned slowly, the light from the tall window catching the subtle gold undertones of her hair as she pivoted to face them. Her gaze settled on the object in Mercer's hands—the box that had cost the lives of four of his men.

Her eyes widened slightly, a flicker of fascination lighting behind them. "Is that it?"

Mercer nodded once. "Recovered at the Palais."

Victoria's eyes glinted. "Bring it here."

Mercer crossed the study, his boots silent on the Persian rug beneath his feet. He approached the desk—an enormous piece of antique craftsmanship carved from one solid piece of dark walnut. Its surface was smooth, reflecting the ambient light, save for a few shallow scratches that hinted at the desk's age and use. Ornate brass inlays decorated the corners, and lion-claw feet anchored it in place atop the rug.

He placed the box down on the center of the desk with careful precision, as if unsure whether even the desk was worthy of holding something so old.

Victoria moved around behind the desk, her hand brushing lightly across its edge as she eased into a high-back leather chair. It groaned softly under her weight, but she didn't notice—her attention was fixed entirely on the box.

She set her wineglass down on the blotter to her right, the red liquid catching the window's light like a garnet in glass. Then she leaned forward.

The box was roughly the length of her forearm and no more than six inches high. The wood had darkened with age and preservation— no doubt lacquered and sealed centuries ago. A faint sheen still clung to its surface, a testament to the resin that had protected it from decay through years spent hidden in stone.

Her fingers hovered just above it at first, reverent.

She traced the edges with her manicured nails, absorbing every nuance of its surface, the subtle rise and fall of the grain, the hand-carved detailing along the border, the faint grooves of a long-eroded emblem near the latch.

A thin seal of wax—once crimson, now faded to a dull russet—spanned the seam where the lid met the base. It wasn't a lock that held it shut, but a preservation seal, its purpose not to protect from thieves, but to protect what lay within.

Victoria reached toward a silver letter opener that lay beside an inkwell on the desk. She angled the blade delicately and slid it under the wax seal. It cracked, dry and brittle, flaking like old bark as it separated. The sound was nearly imperceptible—a soft crinkle of crumbling history.

She set the blade aside then lifted the lid with a slow, deliberate motion.

It creaked faintly as the centuries gave way.

Inside, cushioned in folds of aged blue velvet, was not a relic of gold or gem-studded opulence. There was no ring.

Instead, resting in the hollow of the box, lay a single piece of parchment—rolled tight, bound with a faded ribbon that had once been red. The color had leeched away with time, leaving behind something closer to rust than crimson. The scroll looked impossibly fragile, the parchment browned and speckled, its edges curled inward.

Victoria's face remained neutral, but something behind her eyes shifted. Surprise. Then calculation.

"No ring," she murmured, more to herself than to Mercer. "But this... this might be even better."

She reached in and lifted the scroll carefully, as if it might crumble to dust in her hands. It was light—far lighter than it should have been—but solid enough to hold.

She turned it over, inspecting the ribbon. Her fingertips trembled slightly as she adjusted the scroll, not out of fear but anticipation. She had waited so long for this. Spent millions chasing a myth—scouring archives, bribing curators, bankrolling mercenaries.

This scroll was the first physical proof that the myth was real.

Her thumb caressed the ribbon as she stared down at it, lost in thought, the edges of her lips twitching at the possibilities it held.

Mercer remained silent, watching.

Victoria's fingers trembled with another rare flicker of reverence as she slipped the white gloves over her hands. The scroll—aged to a deep parchment yellow and bound by a faded red ribbon—sat on her desk like a relic drawn from the breath of myth. She touched it as though she might wake it, some sleeping entity that pulsed with forgotten knowledge.

With great care, she slid the ribbon off and unrolled the fragile scroll, its creases resisting at first, as though the document itself guarded its secrets.

Her eyes moved across the faded ink.

At first, it was a sprawl of medieval French, difficult even for her well-practiced mind to decipher in full. But as her gaze adjusted to the old script, she noticed a rhythm—a stanza. A riddle embedded in verse.

"Where shadows fell on sacred halls,
And popes once walked behind high walls,
Beneath the rose where silence clings,
The breath of saints shall stir lost kings."

Victoria's brow creased. She whispered the lines to herself, tasting the weight of each word. This first riddle—it pointed to a place, hidden beneath the symbolism of churchly power and cloistered secrets.

But another passage followed—just beneath the first. Smaller, tighter script, as if whoever penned it meant for only the worthy to find it.

"The path lies not in steps,
But in the kneeling of the bone.
Before the light, the veil shall fall—

When humbled hearts unlock the door."

She read it again, slower. This wasn't just a location—it was an instruction. A test. The first stanza named the destination in metaphor, but this second riddle hinted at what must be done once one arrived.

Her thoughts churned. The "kneeling of the bone"? Was it literal? Ceremonial? Some hidden mechanism?

And "before the light"... Could it refer to sunlight? A particular time of day? Or something more symbolic?

She leaned back in her chair, hands resting atop the parchment, and stared across the room in silence. Somewhere, the ring waited. Hidden for centuries by those who believed in Joan's cause, protected by faith and misdirection.

And now, it had slipped just within her grasp—only to tighten into smoke.

She closed her eyes for a moment, the weight of anticipation thrumming in her chest like a distant drumbeat.

"What does it mean?" she whispered, the question rising into the quiet hush of the study.

39

DIJON

Sean couldn't remember the last time silence had felt so loud.
The city of Dijon unfolded before them like a centuries-old painting, rich in color and heavy with history, but Sean hardly noticed. The Mercedes moved along the winding roads like a ghost slipping through the living world. Tires murmured against the asphalt, the low hum of the engine the only sound inside the cabin. Every bump in the road seemed to rattle the hollow space left behind by Laure Girard.

No one had said much since leaving Poitiers. Conversation, at this point, seemed like an offense to the tragedy they'd witnessed.

Sean sat in the front passenger seat, elbows resting on his thighs, fingers knitted together beneath his chin. His eyes wandered out the window, not seeing much. Fields of golden wheat swayed in the afternoon breeze, interrupted occasionally by rows of vineyards climbing low hills like green veins on the earth's surface. Patches of oak and fir clustered in the valleys, and far in the distance, an old stone watchtower stood sentinel on a rise, half swallowed by ivy. Fields of wild mustard were in bloom for at least the next few weeks, but Sean barely noticed.

Jean-Marc drove with both hands on the wheel, his focus absolute. His expression had settled into a hardened mask; the same one Sean had seen him wear back at the Palais when things went from bad to worse.

Evelyn sat behind Sean, her shoulder pressed against the window, gaze distant. Her hands had been clenched tightly in her lap for most of the ride. Tommy was next to her, arms folded across his chest, one boot rhythmically tapping the floorboard. He hadn't said a word since they'd gotten on the road.

Even the countryside seemed subdued, as if the land itself carried the same solemn mood. Dijon approached in stages. The wide openness of the hills began to narrow into quaint stone villages, red-tiled roofs and weatherworn shutters watching from behind walled gardens. Sean spotted a flock of sheep penned in a pasture, the shepherd resting in the shadow of a gnarled tree. A tractor stirred dust in the distance.

Then came the outskirts; clusters of newer homes, modest stores, cafés with tables facing the narrow roads. The familiar architecture of Dijon crept into view: steep gables, half-timbered façades, wrought iron balconies draped in ivy. The towers of Cathédrale Saint-Bénigne loomed above the skyline, wrapped in a gray overcast haze. Pigeons scattered as the Mercedes turned onto Rue des Forges and passed beneath hanging flower baskets and streetlamps that flickered against the growing dim.

A hush had settled over the team like fog. The loss of Laure hung between them—undiscussed yet omnipresent. It weighed on their movements, their thoughts, their posture. The last few hours played on a loop in Sean's mind: the flash of gunfire, the sound of Laure's gasp, the sight of her collapsing to the floor. And then her blood, bright against the ancient stone.

He clenched his jaw. They should have seen it coming. Should have been prepared. But guilt was useless now. Action was all that remained.

Jean-Marc slowed the car as they neared the historic center of the city. Narrow streets opened up to a small square with a fountain in its center. The Mercedes came to a stop at the corner of a quiet side street, away from the foot traffic.

"It isn't far from here," he said, speaking for the first time in nearly ten minutes, "but I'll need to get some fuel."

Jean-Marc eased the Mercedes away from the quiet square and merged onto a side street, the soft clatter of cobblestones shifting beneath the tires.

Jean-Marc's voice was gravelly. "There's a station up ahead. We'll stop there."

No one objected. The silence was heavy, but the rhythm of the road filled it well enough.

A few minutes later, they turned into a small gas station on the edge of a roundabout. The place looked like it had been there since the '70s—simple, no frills. A single row of pumps stood beneath a rusted metal awning, and the small convenience shop attached to the side bore a faded sign with chipped lettering.

Jean-Marc stepped out of the car, giving his shoulders a slow roll as he turned toward the gas pump. The cool air carried the scent of diesel and motor oil, which mingled with the faint sweetness of freshly baked bread wafting from somewhere nearby—an unwelcome mélange of France's two national fragrances. He unscrewed the fuel cap and picked up the nozzle.

Sean stretched his legs and walked around to Jean-Marc's side. The Frenchman glanced at him and nodded toward the small convenience shop.

"Would you grab me a coffee?" he asked. "And something flaky if they've got it. Doesn't matter what."

Sean nodded and turned toward the little shop's entrance, holding the door open for Evelyn and Tommy as they followed him inside. A soft chime sounded overhead. The warmth hit them first and washed over their skin, which had been chilled by the breeze outside. Inside, the scent of dark roast coffee mingled with buttery pastries and something faintly peppery—perhaps sausage or seasoned eggs.

Sean stepped up to the counter and scanned the items in the pastry dome. He pointed at a savory croissant folded around melted gruyère and thin-sliced roast beef. "Two of those," he said in French, "and two coffees to go."

The woman behind the counter—older, with her hair tied up in a bun and deep lines around her eyes—nodded. "Pain au fromage, peut-être?" she asked. Her eyes lingered on Sean for a moment, and he noticed them flick up and down, inspecting his physique. He resisted the smile that threatened to come with the unspoken compliment, and simply answered, "Parfait," he said the French word for perfect. He turned and waved toward Evelyn and Tommy. "Put whatever they want on the same ticket."

Tommy wandered over to the cold case, eyes landing on a small paper-wrapped package labeled *fromage et fruits assortis*. "I'll take this," he said, lifting it out. "And one of those egg tarts," he added, nodding toward the warm pastries behind the glass.

"I'll have the same," Evelyn said, choosing a similar fruit-and-cheese pack and a savory tart with tomato and goat cheese. She lingered a moment at the espresso menu above the machine before asking for a cappuccino in carefully practiced French.

The woman moved with a kind of unhurried rhythm, used to the morning shuffle. She boxed the tarts, bagged the pastries, then turned to the espresso machine, which hissed softly as she pulled two shots of coffee.

Sean took his wallet out and handed her a few bills. She returned the change in exact coinage, tapping it into his palm with the faintest smile. "Bonne journée," she said with a flirty look that matched her tone.

"Merci," Sean replied.

They stepped out into the parking lot together, and the crisp air sharpened the aroma of the warm food in their hands. Sean handed Jean-Marc the pastry bag and coffee. The Frenchman accepted them with a grateful nod and immediately took a long sip, and his eyes narrowed with appreciation.

"Thank you," he said.

"We all gotta eat. Who knows the next time we can."

"Shame it had to be gas station food," Tommy said. He peeled back the wax paper on his tart and took a bite. The look of satisfaction washed over his face. "Even so, the pastries here put anything back home to shame. And we don't have stuff like this at the gas stations back home."

Evelyn was already breaking her tart into neat pieces, nibbling each with quiet focus.

Sean, still holding his croissant in one hand and his coffee in the other, scanned the road again. Nothing unusual. Still, a feeling clawed at the edges of his mind.

They needed to keep moving.

He climbed back into the car, and the others followed suit. They made quick work of their humble meals and disposed of the trash in a bin next to the fuel pump.

Jean-Marc finished the last bite of his pastry, brushed the flakes off his lap, and turned the key in the ignition. He took a sip of his coffee, then placed it in the cup holder before shifting the vehicle into drive.

Jean-Marc checked the map on his phone. "The directions say we're fifteen minutes away from her estate."

"All right, then," Sean said. "Let's see if we can find a way in."

The car rolled through the narrow streets of Dijon, tires whispering over ancient cobblestones slick from a recent rinse of rain. Storefronts with wrought iron balconies and faded wooden shutters flanked both sides, their windows catching glints of the soft afternoon light. A few pedestrians lingered near cafés, sipping espresso under striped awnings, unaware of the storm of secrets brewing just beyond their quiet lives.

Sean glanced at the stone façades, the weathered charm of the old town masking the tension simmering in the vehicle. Every alley they passed seemed to watch them with knowing eyes. Jean-Marc navigated confidently, easing the Mercedes through tight turns and under arched walkways until the streets widened and the town began to thin.

The transition from urban charm to rural sprawl happened gradually—row houses became stone fences, then open fields framed by slender trees swaying in the wind. Soon, the heartbeat of the city faded behind them.

The road wound through the lush outskirts of Dijon, narrowing as the city slowly gave way to the countryside. Dark trees flanked the two-lane road, reaching across from either side as if trying to clasp hands overhead. Their leaves flickered in the wind.

Jean-Marc kept the Mercedes tucked behind a slow-moving delivery van for a stretch, not eager to draw attention or push too fast. The hum of the engine was steady, barely rising above a whisper inside the cabin. Sean sat in the front seat, his elbow resting against the window, watching as the scenery passed in a blur of wildflowers, vineyards, and ivy-draped stone walls. The gentle rhythm of the drive contrasted with the heaviness in his chest.

The backseat remained quiet. Evelyn had leaned her head against the glass, her arms folded loosely across her stomach, lost in thought. Tommy scrolled through notes on his phone, cross-referencing everything they'd learned in Poitiers with possible leads on Victoria Sterling.

The silence wasn't awkward—it was respectful, pensive. The kind that lingered when the weight of grief still sat freshly on everyone's shoulders. There were no forced conversations or idle banter. Just the sound of tires rolling across smooth pavement and the occasional whistle of wind rushing through the frame.

As they moved deeper into the countryside, civilization thinned. Rows of lavender, not as common in this part of the country, stretched out in neat lines in one direction. In the other, rows of grapevines curled across rolling hills like emerald braids. Occasionally, a rustic farmhouse or old cottage would appear beyond a break in the trees, their stone exteriors stained with time and lichen.

Jean-Marc slowed as a sharp turn crested a low hill, then shifted down as they approached a gravel side road. A discreet wooden sign near the turn-off bore a name carved into it—barely noticeable to anyone not looking for it. He followed the lane, the tires crunching softly over the loose gravel.

The land opened again and revealed a wide meadow that led to a dense patch of woodland. A small creek paralleled the road for a few meters, twisting between gnarled tree roots before vanishing into the woods. The road curved again—one final bend—and then the estate appeared.

Sean leaned forward as the tree line parted.

The front gate stood like a bastion of wealth and secrecy. Tall wrought iron bars with curled finials glinted in the sun. Beyond it, a long cobblestone drive stretched ahead beneath a canopy of plane trees. At the end of the drive, the tip of Victoria's manor peeked through the trees—graceful, palatial, and unmistakably fortified. It was the kind of house that didn't just belong to money, it belonged to power.

Jean-Marc pulled off to the right and eased the car into the shadows of a thicket across the street. From there, they had a clear view of the estate gate.

Sean scanned the gate and its surroundings. A pair of discreet surveillance cameras pivoted on either side of the iron archway. The intercom panel was clean and modern, tucked into the stone wall next to a bronze plaque bearing the name of the estate. No guardhouse. No visible security personnel.

But he knew better.

"She'll have cameras at the gate, and probably in other areas around the property," Jean-Marc said.

He opened his door slowly and stepped out, followed by the others. The air was still warm, but a light breeze carried the faint scent of tilled earth and distant flowers. Jean-Marc stood beside the hood, peering across the road, fingers curled on the edge of the car door.

"Going in that way's not an option," Sean said, eyes locked on the gate.

Jean-Marc nodded once. "Agreed. Cameras would have us pinned before we even reached the entrance."

Tommy stepped up beside them. "Then we'll need to find another way in."

Sean's gaze shifted toward the side of the property, following the tree line. His mind was already searching for possibilities.

The breeze picked up again, rustling through the leaves and the vines on the estate's outer walls.

40

Victoria sat with her elbows planted on the desk, hands steepled beneath her chin, eyes locked on the piece of parchment stretched out in front of her like a map to a kingdom she couldn't see. The ancient script shimmered faintly beneath the amber glow of a nearby lamp, the delicate ink strokes preserved through some forgotten alchemy of time and care. She had read the riddle aloud twice. Then silently. Then aloud again. It hadn't helped. The words still danced with veiled intent, taunting her with their elegance and elusiveness.

She leaned back in her chair, and the old leather groaned faintly beneath her. Across the study, Mercer stood like a statue, arms crossed, jaw tight, gaze drifting idly across the room—waiting. Always waiting.

She didn't bother looking at him this time. Mercer wouldn't be of any use. Combat, logistics, guns; those were his domain. Riddles and relics were not.

"I don't suppose you've had a sudden revelation," she said without shifting her eyes from the scroll.

Mercer shook his head. "No. That isn't really my forte."

Exactly, she thought.

"It sounds like there are going to be more tricks, though." His voice carried a hint of concern. After what he'd said happened to Santos, Victoria wasn't surprised. Mercer would be in no hurry to sacrifice more of his men, much less himself.

With a sharp sigh, Victoria pushed back from the desk and stood. She stepped away from the parchment, as if distance might grant her new perspective. The heels of her shoes clicked softly against the hardwood floor as she paced between the desk and the long window overlooking the garden. Sunlight glinted off the glass, casting reflections that shimmered across the floor like water.

She crossed her arms and began to mutter the lines of the riddle again.

"Within the halls where secrets keep,

Below the cross where shadows sleep,

One must not knock, nor call, nor plead,

But walk in silence on broken knees."

It was poetic—too poetic. And frustrating. The reference to a cross could mean any number of things. A church. A cathedral. Even a forgotten tomb. But it wasn't just about the cross. It was about what lay beneath it. Something hidden. A chamber? A crypt?

She turned back to the parchment and studied the final stanza, the one that had unsettled her the most:

"The path lies not in steps,

But in the kneeling of the bone.

Before the light, the veil shall fall—

When humbled hearts unlock the door."

Victoria narrowed her eyes.

That had to mean something. A hidden door. Perhaps even a false wall.

She bit the corner of her lip and folded her arms tighter. She had been in hundreds of old churches, cathedrals, and palaces over the years. So many of them had strange alcoves and walled-off corridors. But which one was this pointing to? France had no shortage of stone sanctuaries. And if this was linked to Joan of Arc's final resting secret, it would be somewhere deeply symbolic—yet hidden in plain sight.

She stopped pacing and turned toward the desk once more.

There had to be a clue within the clue.

She crossed back to the desk, sat down with a quiet huff, and reached for the mouse. Victoria clicked the mouse and opened a browser window. She copied the first part of the riddle from the parchment and pasted it into the search bar.

Poetry blogs. A collection of religious lyrics attributed to anonymous eighteenth-century monks. A reference to a Gothic-themed tabletop game. Even a Reddit thread about haunted monasteries in Eastern Europe. She scrolled slowly at first while scanning for key phrases, proper nouns, anything remotely connected to Joan or the past.

Nothing useful.

She clicked a few of the links anyway, holding on to hope. One brought her to a crumbling archive site in French, but the content was off topic. Another redirected to a travel agency pitching "sacred journeys."

She leaned back, lips tight. She had expected as much. Even the most powerful search engine in the world was only as good as what people knew. And she was dealing with secrets purposely hidden for over five centuries.

Still, she wasn't one to give up after a single attempt.

She copied the second part of the riddle and pasted it into the bar. Another tap of the Enter key.

This time, the results were even more disappointing. A gothic novel excerpt from an amateur writing site. An old tourist blog about ruins near Avignon—useful, perhaps, but not definitive. A YouTube video of a self-proclaimed clairvoyant talking about sacred geometry beneath churches. She grimaced.

Victoria resisted the urge to bang her fists on the desk. Instead, she tapped her fingers on the surface. The sound echoed softly through the study.

In her world, answers were either purchased or extracted. They didn't arrive neatly packaged on a Google results page. But this scroll, this clue—it was different. It was like speaking in a dead dialect, trying to decipher symbols that had changed meaning over centuries.

She stood up abruptly and crossed to the wide window once more. The vineyards rolled out below, bathed in the early afternoon sun, their lines clean and endless. Somewhere out there, Wyatt was still chasing this same mystery. And he had a head start. He had context she didn't. She had the scroll, yes, but he had experience and instincts sharpened by years of work in the field, and Victoria found herself wishing she could use them to figure out the solution to this puzzle. But that wasn't an option.

She'd hoped Mercer was bringing her the actual ring, not another clue. Even so, opening the box hadn't disappointed her. It had heightened her resolve. But she hadn't expected to face this level of challenge.

Victoria folded her arms; her gaze locked on the parchment like it had personally insulted her.

History had been her passion long before it became her weapon. As a teenager, she devoured books on ancient empires and medieval power struggles while her peers were busy memorizing fashion trends or pop songs. Where others saw the past as a dead thing, she saw it as the blueprint of control—each victory and betrayal a lesson, every fallen kingdom a warning.

She'd studied at Oxford and later under private tutors in Vienna and Prague, immersing herself in the obscure and arcane. Her interests had always leaned toward the hidden truths behind accepted narrative: secret alliances, forgotten relics, veiled power structures. It wasn't just curiosity that drove her. It was hunger. Understanding history gave her an edge in the present. Most people were driven by the moment. Victoria was driven by the long game. And with her wealth and power, even at that young age, she'd known she had to learn all the rules of that game before she could control it.

That was why this riddle gnawed at her pride.

It wasn't merely a matter of decoding a poetic phrase or interpreting old metaphors. It was the implication that Joan of Arc, a peasant girl with no formal education, had left behind a trail too clever for Victoria Sterling, heir to centuries of wealth and education, to follow.

She clenched her jaw and turned away from the window. She paced across the floor, turned, and went back to the window again. Mercer simply stood there and watched, awaiting his next order.

There had to be something she was missing. Something not digitized, not referenced, not searchable. She needed knowledge that lived in the shadows of academia—between the lines of old books, in the memories of curators, or in the dust-covered archives of forgotten abbeys.

She returned to the desk, staring down at the scroll. The parchment looked no different than it had thirty minutes ago—fragile, delicate, deceptively simple. The ribbon lay folded beside it, a ghost of whatever hands had once tied it.

The riddle was right in front of her. But until she could understand its language, it might as well be written in smoke.

Victoria remained at the desk, staring at the scroll, the words no less mysterious despite her careful scrutiny. The parchment's surface shimmered faintly in the light seeping through the nearby window, as though it might reveal more if only she stared harder. Her gloved fingers hovered near it again, not to touch but to trace the invisible threads of meaning she had yet to uncover.

The quiet in the room was broken by the soft creak of the study door opening.

Nikolai stepped in, his posture rigid but respectful. His voice, low and composed, carried a quiet urgency. "Apologies, Miss Sterling." He turned to Mercer. "Sir, may I have a moment?"

She looked up, brow raised slightly. Her instinct bristled—Nikolai wasn't one to interrupt unless something required attention. She gave a brief nod to Mercer.

He followed Nikolai out and closed the heavy door behind them with a quiet thump. Even with the door closed, she could hear the muted sounds of their voices from the hallway, though picking out distinct words proved impossible.

Victoria remained alone, surrounded by books and antiques that had long lost their ability to surprise her. The study was a room she usually found comfort in, a space curated for control. Rich walnut bookshelves lined the walls, filled with centuries of knowledge, treaties, memoirs, philosophical works, and even a few first editions. The hearth at the far end of the room held the smoldering remains of a morning fire, casting faint lines of heat against the stone. Her wine glass sat untouched beside the scroll.

She rose and wandered to the nearby shelf and ran her hand along the spines of books she'd read dozens of times. Her mind still clung to the riddle, playing with phrases, trying to reframe them. She paused before an old bronze globe that rested in a cradle of polished oak. Spinning it slowly with one finger, she watched the continents blur.

Victoria didn't like being in the dark. She hated when things were kept from her. Some would say she was a control freak, and they would be right. *Why leave important things to those who were beneath her?*

The door creaked again, and Mercer returned alone.

He didn't need to speak for her to know something had changed. There was a subtle shift in his posture, his cool demeanor now tempered with something tighter beneath the surface.

"Well?" she asked, returning to her seat.

He stepped closer, his voice even. "We may have found an answer to your problem."

She tilted her head, curious. "What kind of answer?"

"Your security detail spotted something of interest on the cameras at the front gate. They just informed Nikolai."

"Ugh," she groaned. "Out with it, Mercer. I don't like to be kept waiting."

Mercer gave a slow smile that didn't reach his eyes. "Sean Wyatt is here."

41

Sean and the others had moved away from the gate's view and parked the Mercedes off a narrow country road where wild hedgerows grew tall and thick, hiding the vehicle from passing eyes. They moved on foot now, boots crunching over the uneven ground of a long-abandoned access path that led toward a wide, open field bordering the forest edge of Victoria Sterling's estate.

Tall grasses brushed against their thighs and swayed in the afternoon breeze. Yellow wildflowers dotted the field in scattered bursts, their heads nodding gently beneath a sky partially veiled by thin, drifting clouds. The sun, though filtered, still cast a muted heat over their shoulders.

Sean led the way, his posture low, eyes scanning the horizon and the tree line ahead. He paused occasionally, not just to reassess their surroundings but to listen; ears tuned to the wind, the call of birds, and anything unnatural that might give away the presence of someone else nearby.

Behind him, Evelyn adjusted her jacket and brushed back a strand of hair the breeze kept tossing into her eyes. Jean-Marc followed a few paces behind, his eyes sweeping the tree line to the left, alert to movement. Tommy brought up the rear, his gaze lingering more often on the estate in the distance, which was partially obscured by the gently sloping hill and the woods beyond.

They crested a shallow rise in the terrain and found themselves at the edge of a perimeter fence—an old wrought iron barrier coated in a fresh layer of matte black paint. Rust hadn't had the chance to creep in yet. Along the fence, fixed at intervals, were metal signs with bold red letters spelling out the warning in both French and English:

PRIVATE PROPERTY. TRESPASSERS WILL BE PROSECUTED.

Sean humored a brief thought about the laws here and how they might differ from the ones back home.

Beyond the fence, the forest rose thick and dark, the trees pressing in tight as if guarding secrets. The grass on the other side was trimmed shorter, and Sean noticed faint lines that might have once marked a path now overtaken by weeds.

He knelt beside one of the metal posts and inspected the base where the iron met concrete. "Reinforced," he muttered. "This isn't just to keep the locals out."

Tommy peered down the fence line. "She's got sensors on it?"

"Probably motion detectors. Maybe low-level pressure triggers," Sean said. "But nothing obvious. It's too clean. Too deliberately minimalist. She doesn't want people to know how well guarded this place is."

Jean-Marc stepped up and tugged off a glove to press his palm against the metal. "No current running through it. No hum. Not electrified, at least not here."

"Still doesn't mean it's safe," Sean said, rising again. "We'll need to find a blind spot. Somewhere the coverage thins."

Tommy stood still, watching the estate's distant rooftop peek over the tree line. "This entire setup feels military grade," he said softly. "Not the kind of thing you'd expect for a wealthy recluse with an art collection."

"She's not a recluse," Sean replied. "She's a predator. She's hiding something."

The four of them began to move again, following the fence line through the field, the grass swishing around their legs. Flies buzzed lazily in the warmth. A hawk circled high above, wings stretched wide as it cast a flickering shadow over the slope behind them. The birdsong had quieted as they'd drawn closer to the trees—a silence Sean didn't like.

After a few minutes, they came across a shallow dip in the terrain. Here, a cluster of taller bushes had grown close to the fence, offering some measure of concealment. Sean motioned for everyone to crouch.

"Here might be our best shot. The ground drops a little, and the brush could help cover us if we move fast."

Jean-Marc nodded. "We'd need to check for pressure plates or tripwires. Normally, I wouldn't think that might be an issue, but based on this setup, she might well have thrown down more money for that kind of system."

Sean crouched, pulled a compact scope from his jacket, and scanned the immediate area beyond the fence. "I don't see any buried nodes or cabling. But that doesn't mean they're not there."

Evelyn turned slightly, glancing back toward the road. "I don't like this. If we get caught…"

"We won't," Sean assured her. "But we're not climbing over anything until we're sure. Let's keep moving. Circle the edge until we find a way in that won't get us lit up like a Christmas tree."

They moved again, slowly, crouched in the tall grass as the field stretched on around them, open and exposed, with the manor's secrets waiting just beyond the trees.

Sean moved slowly along the inside edge of the field, eyes scanning the ground where patches of dry, trodden grass suggested the presence of deer or perhaps wild boar. The sun had crested past noon, spilling a dull gold light over the distant hills, but here in the narrow depression just outside Victoria Sterling's property, the air felt oddly stagnant. Even the birds had gone silent.

He brushed his hand across the tall grass, fingertips grazing the brittle stalks. To the left, Evelyn kept pace beside him, her eyes narrowed on the perimeter fence that ran just beyond the slight ridge. Jean-Marc walked point up ahead, near the tree line, while

Tommy trailed close behind, double-checking the terrain for cameras or buried sensors.

The fence loomed up through the grass like a serpent's spine, capped in barbed wire and spaced with crisp white signs warning Propriété Privée – Passage Interdit. Sean had seen enough restricted zones to know this wasn't a bluff. These warnings against trespassing weren't to be taken lightly.

Then it hit him. A chill—not from the wind but from the sudden absence of it. It was one of those moments where things were too quiet, too peaceful. He stopped, glanced back.

Something shifted in the grass behind them.

He saw it—not a shape, not clearly, but a ripple in the fabric of the landscape, like a heat mirage that didn't belong. His heart thudded once, hard. He opened his mouth.

A voice snapped through the stillness. Calm. Clipped. British. "Hands where I can see them."

Sean's blood ran cold. He recognized the voice from back in Poitiers. Mercer.

He raised his hands slowly, instinct overriding thought. Evelyn followed suit beside him, then Tommy. Up ahead, Jean-Marc froze after his back straightened. He lifted his arms too, careful and slow.

More movement followed. Four men emerged from the grass like ghosts, weapons drawn, black-gloved hands steady. Mercer's crew.

Footsteps squished softly against damp soil as the men fanned out, surrounding them with surgical precision. One brushed past Sean's shoulder and began patting him down—arms, ribs, waistband. The holstered pistol Sean had concealed under his jacket vanished in an instant. Another man moved to Tommy, stripping him of his weapon with equal ease. Evelyn, unarmed, stood rigid, eyes burning with alarm.

Jean-Marc's jaw clenched as the muzzle of a sidearm tapped his spine.

Mercer himself stepped into view then—just far enough back to stay in control, close enough to make sure they saw him. His face was unreadable. Detached. Professional.

Sean met his gaze briefly. No posturing. No clever quips. Only the simmering stare of a man who realized he'd made two incredibly huge mistakes on the same day. One had cost a woman her life, and now this could have the same consequence.

The confiscated weapons were collected quickly. No one said a word. The men worked with the silence of experience—this wasn't the first time they'd run a clean extraction in open country.

"How nice of you to come see me again, old friend," Mercer said to Jean-Marc.

"Glad you're happy about it," the Frenchman countered. "I would have preferred the opposite."

"What do you want?" Sean asked. "If you were going to kill us, you'd have already done it. Quiet. Clean. No witnesses." He made a show of the empty countryside around them.

"Good assessment, Sean. You are correct. We're not going to kill you. Yet. My employer has a bit of a problem, you see. Seems she needs someone to help her figure out something to do with what was in that box."

"Sounds like maybe she's in the wrong business," Tommy snapped. "A little in over her head?"

"I personally don't care," Mercer snarled back. "I just want to get paid. Cash out. And disappear."

"None of that is surprising," Jean-Marc said with contempt. "You're all about the money."

Mercer ignored the barb and glanced at his watch, then nodded to his left.

"Take them back to the manor. I don't want to keep our employer waiting."

42

The double doors groaned open, and Sean stepped through first, flanked by two of Mercer's men. The grand foyer of Victoria Sterling's manor swallowed them in polished opulence. Sean's boots echoed on the glossy marble floor, and his eyes instinctively scanned the vaulted ceilings and carved woodwork. A massive crystal chandelier dangled overhead like a jeweled sword waiting to fall.

He took it all in—arched entryways, oil paintings in gilded frames, the faint scent of some expensive, floral diffuser. The kind of place that dripped wealth in quiet, deliberate ways.

"Place has a real I-wish-I-was-royalty vibe," he muttered to Tommy without turning his head.

Mercer either didn't hear the comment or chose to ignore it. He gave Sean a rough nudge between the shoulder blades to keep him moving.

They climbed the staircase in silence, footsteps absorbed by the rich runner carpeting the steps. Ornate sconces glowed warmly along the walls, casting soft shadows that danced across decorative molding. The tension among Sean's group was thick as the lacquered doors of the study loomed ahead.

Mercer strode past them, his stride sure, confident. He rapped twice on the door with the edge of his knuckle then opened it without waiting for a response.

Inside, Victoria Sterling sat behind her imposing mahogany desk, a half-full glass of deep red wine positioned near her elbow. She didn't rise. Didn't greet them with fake pleasantries. Her attention remained on the parchment stretched out before her; brow furrowed in faint irritation.

But then she looked up.

Her expression shifted into something cooler, amused even. Her dark eyes gleamed with satisfaction.

"Come in," she said, her voice smooth as ever. "I'm so glad you could join us."

"That makes one of us," Sean replied.

He didn't move. Not until Mercer stepped behind him and shoved him across the threshold. The others were prodded forward, one by one, until they stood in a row, facing the woman who had orchestrated the entire pursuit.

Sean took a moment to study her, the room, the parchment on the desk.

Whatever she was searching for, she hadn't found it yet.

"You seem to be a difficult man to catch," Victoria said, her voice demur, with a hint of curiosity. It was a tone that she might have used while observing an exotic animal out of its domain.

"Not difficult enough," he said. Then he cut straight to the point. "I hear you're having some trouble with that." Sean gave a nod to the box and the parchment.

Her eyes flicked toward the object then met his again. "Yes. I thought, perhaps hopefully, that my men had brought me the ring itself. But upon opening it, I realized it was another clue to the ring's location."

"What do you want with it?" Evelyn demanded.

Sean sensed her urge to rush forward, the need for revenge that fueled her. Two innocent people had died as a result of Victoria's quest, one of whom had been a friend.

"Justice, of course," she answered, as if it should have been obvious.

"Justice?" Tommy wondered. "For what?"

She cocked her head to the side and sighed. "A wrong that was done a long time ago, by a great many people in powerful positions."

"You're the last heir to the East India Company," Sean said. "We already figured that much out. You're carrying a 140-year-old grudge against people that are long dead, and you think finding this ring will return you, and your organization, to power. We get that. What he means is, how?"

She studied him for a minute, curious how it wasn't clear to him. "Joan's ring is more than a symbol of power, Sean. Whoever wears it commands the forces of the universe. Joan had only just begun to understand this when she was taken. It frightened her to bear it, to carry such a burden of great responsibility. In the end, it was that humility that cost her everything. Had she accepted it, and continued along her path, she would have been unstoppable. She could have ruled the entire world."

"So, global domination through a mystical, enchanted ring," Tommy summarized. "You could have just said that."

"Hmm. I prefer to think of it as a tool to right a wrong, a wrong that brought my family's fortune to the ground, something they'd built for centuries."

"That's exactly what a sociopath would say," Sean quipped, leaning on the psych degree he'd earned so many years ago. "And you know, Victoria"—he whistled as he turned and gazed around the room before locking on to her gaze again—"I wouldn't exactly call what you're living in, poverty."

"Sticks and stones, Sean," Victoria said. "And while my house might not be on Skid Row, as you Yanks call it, this *austere* lifestyle that's been forced upon me is as close to poverty as I ever intend to get." She tapped her nails on a desk that had cost more than Sean's first car, or even his third car.

"But back to the issue at hand, dear boy. This bit of parchment has thrown me for a loop. I've studied it, but I can't seem to figure out the answer."

"Sounds like a personal problem," Jean-Marc said, speaking for the first time since entering the room.

"Indeed." The jab didn't seem to faze her. "Now, I'm sure you all know how this works. I have my men threaten to kill one of you if you don't come up with the answer. If you don't, then they either execute someone, or worse, shoot them in the top of the foot, the kneecap, the top of the hand, the shoulder. Or we could use knives, but I've found that when you shatter bones, that seems to be the most effective. And while bullets can do a nice job of that, a good hammer is so much more painful."

She pulled back the top drawer of her desk and produced a hammer with a wooden handle.

"You just keep random tools all over your house?" Tommy asked. "Everything should have a place."

"I'll start with you, Mr. Schultz. Thank you for volunteering."

"I didn't realize that was the request."

Two of the men behind Tommy grabbed him by the arms and shooed him forward. He struggled, momentarily freeing himself before one of the men rammed an elbow into his middle back.

He dropped to his knees, gasping for air.

"Jeez," he spat.

"Do you have any idea how many times he's been punched in the kidneys?" Sean cut in. "Hope he doesn't have long-term problems because of it. If so, you'll be hearing from his lawyer."

She nodded to Mercer, who instantly punched Sean in the face, which snapped his head sideways.

The blow stunned Sean. His jaw throbbed, and for a second, everything was in a daze. He didn't fall, though his balance wavered. Then he regained his composure and stood tall again.

One of the other men grabbed the hammer from Victoria and stepped back over to where Tommy knelt on the floor.

"So, would you like me to begin with a foot? A hand? Knee? I hear shins are one of the worst. I have to say, that's the most painful when I bang mine against something."

The man with the hammer stood next to Tommy while the other flipped him over onto his back then dropped his knee down onto Tommy's throat so he couldn't move.

"Isn't there a component of this where you want me to analyze the parchment?" Sean asked, his voice dark, composed, full of malice.

"That's the spirit," Victoria said with a smile. "Please. Have a look." She stepped aside to keep her distance.

Sean reluctantly moved around the desk and leaned over the parchment.

Sean's eyes scanned the aged parchment lying across the desk. The texture of the paper crackled slightly beneath his fingertips as he leaned in, careful not to smudge the ink or draw Mercer's ire too soon.

He cleared his throat and read aloud the first line, his voice low but steady:

"The path lies not in steps,

But in the kneeling of the bone."

On the floor in front of him, Tommy grunted as the man pressing down on his neck shifted his weight. Sean kept his eyes on the parchment, refusing to look up.

"Seek the crown that no king wore, beneath the altar none dared bless."

The words settled like dust across the room. Even Victoria was silent now, her arms crossed tightly as she listened. Sean could feel her eyes boring into the side of his face, like she was measuring each syllable for hidden intent.

Then he read the second part.

"Before the light, the veil shall fall—

When humbled hearts unlock the hall."

Sean blinked and read it again, slower this time. The weight of it hung there. He knew this wasn't just poetry. It was instruction. A layered code written by someone who understood misdirection and secrecy.

"The humble shall find the door. But speak, and it stays closed."

His eyes narrowed slightly. The implication of the second riddle hit him like a whisper from the past. A test. Just like Joan had endured herself.

He looked up, slowly, at Victoria.

"What makes you think we can figure this out?" he said, not as a challenge but as a fact.

"Because you're the best at this sort of thing," she answered. "So I've heard. But if you can't help me, I suppose I don't need to keep any of you around."

Sean had anticipated that response and chose to ignore it. "Tommy will be a lot more helpful if your guy takes his knee off his throat."

Tommy groaned from the floor. The man holding the hammer tensed, ready.

But Sean didn't flinch.

"Let him up," Victoria ordered, albeit with reluctance.

The man pinning Tommy to the ground stood up and pulled Tommy by the armpit.

He gasped for air for a few seconds while rubbing his throat. Then he turned to the man. "Not sure if you noticed. But your knee was on my neck."

The goon merely stared at him with vapid eyes.

"What does it mean?" Victoria asked pointedly.

Tommy joined Sean behind the desk, and his eyes immediately scanned the parchment. He leaned closer, hands resting on the polished edge of the desk, careful not to touch the fragile scroll itself. Sean took a half step back to give him room, but his own gaze stayed locked on the script.

Sean remained perfectly still, his arms crossed tightly over his chest, blue eyes narrowing as he reread the riddle. "Only the silent path shall open the way," he murmured under his breath, repeating the line to himself like a mantra. "Where voices cease, and feet must kneel…"

"It's poetic," Tommy said, "but that doesn't help us much. The symbolism is layered. Religious, obviously. But it could also be literal."

Sean pointed to the last line. "This part—'But speak, and it stays closed'—implies more than reverence. It's an instruction. A warning, even."

Tommy nodded slowly. "Right. And this bit—'seek the crown that no king wore'—has to refer to papal authority. Not royalty."

"That narrows the location," Evelyn added, shifting her weight from one foot to the other. "There are only a few places with that kind of connection. The Palais des Papes was practically a fortress for the Church at one point."

Sean tapped a finger next to the parchment. "And 'beneath the altar none dared bless.' That's got to be a specific spot inside the palace. An altar left untouched, or one that's been sealed off."

Tommy frowned. "But we were at the Palais. The local one. We didn't see an altar like that. And we weren't in Avignon."

"Maybe the scroll's pointing there next," Evelyn said. "This could be the bridge between locations. A clue meant to send us onward."

Sean leaned forward, elbows now on the desk and his eyes narrowing as he focused on the upper line again. "'Where fire and water meet the veil…' Fire and water, flesh and soul. It's metaphysical. Could be a description of baptism, or purification rituals."

"Or confession," Tommy offered. "The old kind. The kind where you went into a dark room, got on your knees, and whispered secrets to a man hidden behind a screen."

Evelyn's brow furrowed. "Do you think it's meant to be metaphorical, then? Or are we supposed to take this literally?"

Sean straightened up. "Maybe both. It could be describing a specific room or feature of a location that also carries symbolic weight. It's not uncommon in ancient religious architecture for symbolism and function to blend."

They all became quiet for a moment.

Tommy rubbed a hand over his jaw, glancing at Victoria, who stood silently across the desk, arms folded, her gaze sharp and impatient. "The problem," he said finally, "is that this doesn't tell us where the next location is. It only tells us how to act once we get there."

Sean sighed, reaching down to gently shift the edge of the parchment. "Which means there could be more clues we haven't uncovered yet. Something to narrow it down. A landmark, a name, anything."

Evelyn stepped back while glancing toward the window. "Then we're running out of time."

Tommy nodded grimly. "And we're doing it under the roof of the person who'll take whatever we find and use it to destroy everything we're trying to protect."

Sean didn't respond. He just kept staring at the parchment, as if willing the ink to rearrange itself into a clear answer.

But it didn't.

Frustration mounted, and Sean could tell by the look on Victoria's face she was about to start making more threats.

But she didn't. The woman remained silent as she watched.

Sean's eyes flicked back to the parchment. His heart pounded so loudly it threatened to drown out his thoughts. He didn't need to glance at the pistol pointed at Evelyn's head to know it was still there. The room felt heavier with every passing second. The ornate study, with its gleaming shelves and carved crown molding, might as well have been a tomb.

Tommy leaned closer. "We're missing something," he muttered.

Sean traced the lines again, reading them silently for what felt like the twentieth time.

"Where fire and water meet the veil,
Only the silent path shall open the way.
Where voices cease and feet must kneel,
Seek the crown no king has worn."

"It's metaphor stacked on metaphor," Tommy said. "This isn't literal. It's symbolism wrapped in historical context."

Sean nodded absently, eyes darting across the lines. He could feel the seconds slipping away. "The veil—what is that? A literal veil? Or something symbolic?"

"Could be death," Tommy said. "A place of transition. A barrier between the living and the divine."

Sean's mind spun. The imagery—kneeling, silence, fire, and water—it all pointed toward something sacred. Something buried.

Tommy scratched his jaw. "Not a church. Too broad."

Sean looked up at the towering bookshelves and then back at the scroll. "Could be a chapel. A hidden one."

"Where?"

"I don't know yet," Sean admitted.

The room buzzed with quiet tension. Victoria remained behind the desk, arms crossed. She studied them like a cat watching cornered prey. Evelyn knelt motionless, jaw tight, expression unreadable. Jean-Marc stood with his fists clenched at his sides. The guards didn't blink.

Still, no one moved.

Tommy snapped his fingers. "A monastery?"

"No. The crown line—'Seek the crown no king has worn'—that's not a king's crown. That's something else."

"A relic? Something symbolic?"

Sean shook his head. "A papal crown. The tiara."

Tommy's eyes widened. "The Avignon papacy."

"Exactly. But if it's not the Palais itself..."

That's when Victoria's patience cracked. She let out a slow, deliberate breath and stood up from behind the desk.

"That's enough," she said sharply. "You've had your chance. Time's up."

She gestured to the guard. The man moved like a machine, grabbed a fistful of Evelyn's hair. The click of the pistol hammer drew every eye.

Sean's stomach dropped. The air drained from the room. Tommy took a half step forward before another guard shoved him back.

"No!" Sean barked. "Wait!"

Victoria raised a single eyebrow. "I'll give you three more minutes," she said. "That's generous. Make them count."

"Three minutes?" Sean asked. "This could take years to solve."

"You have three minutes," she reiterated. "Well, two-forty-five now."

Sean wanted to throw her through the window, but he had to focus. He swallowed hard and turned back to the parchment. Tommy stared at it as well.

Sean exhaled slowly, trying to steady his thoughts. "Fire and water... veil..."

"It's a metaphor," Tommy whispered again. "Fire and water—maybe opposing forces. Could be candlelight and baptismal fonts. Or incense and holy water."

"Or symbolic of purification. A rite."

Sean scanned the last line again. "'Seek the crown no king has worn.' That's the key."

"Papal," Tommy said. "Definitely papal."

Tommy stood beside Sean, staring down at the parchment with narrowed eyes. He crossed his arms, then uncrossed them and rubbed his chin. "Okay," he muttered, mostly to himself, "if it's definitely papal, that narrows it to something ecclesiastical."

Sean nodded, eyes locked on the final stanza of the riddle. His mind ran in loops, grasping at clues that danced just out of reach. There were layers here—layers of allegory and history, faith and secrecy. "And it mentions a fall," he said quietly, tapping his finger on the scroll. "A fall from grace? Or maybe a literal fall. A descent?"

Behind them, Victoria leaned forward slightly in her chair. "You have two minutes," she said, her voice silk over steel.

Tommy shot a glance at her but turned his attention back to the parchment. "'The shadow of grace where the holy fell'... could be a site of exile," he whispered. "A place of disgrace. Or where someone hid after losing favor?"

Sean frowned. "No, no... not exile. The phrasing—it doesn't sound like judgment. It sounds reverent, almost sacred. The holy fell, but the shadow remains. That could mean the holiness is gone, but the echo of it lingers."

Tommy looked up at him. "A crypt?"

Sean's lips parted as if to respond, but nothing came. He turned back to the parchment, rereading the lines again. The final verse twisted through his mind like a fog refusing to lift. His gaze flicked down the lines once more. His jaw clenched.

"One minute," Victoria said, louder this time. "You may want to speed things up, gentlemen."

Across the room, Evelyn remained on her knees. The man behind her kept the pistol steady, and Sean felt the back of his neck grow hot. His fists curled at his sides. He could feel the weight of Laure Girard's death all over again, a fresh wound ripped wide open. Not again.

His voice came low and sharp. "Not helping."

"Less than one," she said flatly.

Tommy pressed his fingers into his temple. "'Sanctuary beneath the broken shepherd's mark...' That has to mean something."

Sean's gaze sharpened. "A shepherd's mark. What if it's a symbol? Something left behind. A broken one. A defaced carving? A destroyed statue? Something that's part of the building..."

"Thirty seconds," Victoria called out.

Tommy looked up from the parchment, his brow drenched in sweat. "Sean, think! What would symbolize a fallen shepherd?"

Sean felt the final gears lock into place.

His eyes snapped back to the parchment. "The shepherd's mark... it's not metaphor. It's literal. A statue. Of a pope. Or a bishop. Something broken."

Tommy's voice trembled. "Do we know a place where there's a destroyed monument? In a papal structure?"

Sean's mind flew back through their research. "There's a ruined papal chapel beneath the Palais des Papes. Part of it was destroyed during the Wars of Religion. There's a collapsed effigy in the crypt. A bishop, or maybe even one of the Avignon popes. It's cracked. Locals call it the 'Fallen Shepherd.'"

Tommy stared at him, then nodded slowly, a spark catching in his eyes. "Then that's it. That's where the ring is."

Victoria looked at her watch. A sly grin crept across her face. "With seventeen seconds to spare."

"Unless they're just telling you what you want to hear," Mercer chirped.

Victoria arched an eyebrow as she assessed the grim, slightly relieved expressions on Sean's and Tommy's faces.

"You wouldn't do that, now would you?" she asked.

"Of course we would," Sean answered. "But we aren't. Avignon is where it has to be. And if we're wrong, you're just going to kill us anyway."

"True. But I'm going to keep you around just in case we run into any other little snags."

Victoria turned to face Mercer. "Get the cars ready. We leave for Avignon right away."

"You're going to encounter a ton of security at the Palais de Papes," Tommy cautioned. "That place will be locked down tight. I'm talking guards, cameras, alarm systems. The works."

Victoria only hesitated for a breath before she answered. "Then I suppose you and Sean will need to be careful when you break in to take it."

43

AVIGNON, FRANCE

Even though the penthouse suite offered a lavish, spacious interior, it seemed to press in around Sean.
Ornate gold leaf designs swirled across the high ceiling. Floor-to-ceiling windows offered an unobstructed view of the Rhône, glittering in the afternoon sun. It felt like a cage with soft walls and a hard edge.

The suite sat perched atop one of the grandest hotels in Avignon, nestled in the heart of the old city, mere minutes from the Palais des Papes. The drive from Dijon had taken several hours, and most of it had passed in tense silence, save for the occasional directive from Victoria or a murmured update from Mercer. When they'd finally arrived, a valet had swept the cars away without a word, and the entourage was ushered into the building through a private entrance at the rear.

The penthouse itself spanned the entire top floor of the hotel—opulent, vast, and meticulously curated. Polished marble floors gleamed beneath their feet, reflecting the soft light from a collection of hanging crystal fixtures overhead. Intricately framed oil paintings lined the walls—landscapes of Provence, portraits of forgotten, stoic aristocrats—and lush rugs muted the sound of their footsteps.

At the center of the suite was the main salon—an open-concept space with a sweeping view of the medieval skyline. A long leather sectional wrapped around a glass coffee table adorned with crystal decanters, all filled with amber-toned liquors that no one had touched. Nearby, an antique writing desk had been converted into a makeshift command station. A laptop sat open beside a tablet, flanked by a scattering of printed schematics and maps of the Palais des Papes, its towers and chambers traced in red and black ink.

To the right of the salon, an arched corridor led to a series of rooms that had been repurposed. Evelyn and Jean-Marc sat on a plush, beige couch in the center of the room. They weren't tied up—but they might as well have been. They were watched, shadowed, and confined to silence unless called upon. Victoria had ordered their safety for now, but everyone knew that was a fragile promise. One misstep and the rules would change.

Sean looked out the window and stared out at the city. Avignon's honey-colored stone buildings clustered tightly together like a fortress against time. The turrets and buttresses of the Palais rose above it all—a relic of power and a symbol of secrets too ancient for the world to remember. Somewhere in that maze of history, buried beneath layers of stone and shadow, the ring waited.

Sean wished he could appreciate it all. He loved places like this. While he was proud to be an American, the United States didn't have much in the way of towns like Avignon, or so many others around Europe. These places were steeped in a history his country could only read about. The architecture back home could mimic that from various nations in Europe, but here it was real, authentic, original.

He turned and looked back at the dining table that Mercer and his men had converted to a command center. Multiple laptops sat open on the surface. The one named Soren sat at two of the laptops, his fingers tapping furiously across the keyboard.

Sean glanced over at his friend, who sat with his arms crossed in an armchair, a gunman standing behind him with his pistol pointed at the back of Tommy's head.

To his credit, Tommy didn't seem concerned at all. They'd lost count of how many times the two of them had been held at gunpoint. It wasn't a comfortable part of the job, but it seemed to be something they encountered with concerning regularity.

There was always another person or organization out there looking to seize power for themselves.

"Beautiful, isn't it?" Victoria asked, cutting through Sean's thoughts like a straight razor.

Sean nodded absently. "I was just thinking something like that."

She looked over at him, studying him for a few seconds. "I find it remarkable that you seem so calm even under the threat of death, to the point that you can still appreciate the simple beauty around you."

"I love history and cultures. And my life has been threatened before. You get used to it."

He wasn't lying. Over time, he had grown almost numb to this sort of situation, except for the problem that Evelyn was here this time. He didn't want any more innocent blood shed. The guilt from Laure's death still kept a knot in his gut that wouldn't ease.

"It's a shame we're on opposite sides," Victoria drawled. "You could have been a useful ally."

Sean kept his stare out the window. "I don't work with people like you. But thanks for the compliment."

"I'm in," Soren said from the table, interrupting the conversation.

Both Sean and Victoria turned and looked over at him. Mercer was standing behind Soren and looked up with a nod to confirm he'd accessed the security system.

"Excellent," Victoria said with a grin.

The monitor lit up with glowing wire-frame schematics of the Palais des Papes.

Sean moved over and stood in front of the far end of the suite's couch, crossing his arms as he studied the computer monitors.

Mercer kept a keen eye on him, making sure he didn't try anything.

Mercer motioned to the guard watching Tommy. "Let him up."

The man stepped forward, weapon low but ready, and jerked his chin at Tommy. "On your feet."

Tommy rose slowly while casting a brief glance at Evelyn and Jean-Marc. They looked calm, but he could feel the tension buzzing off them. He toyed with the idea of making a move—sweeping the guard's legs, going for the weapon. But Evelyn sat between him and Jean-Marc. Too many angles. Too many chances for something to go wrong. If it turned into a firefight, Evelyn and Jean-Marc might not survive it.

He joined Sean at the desk and stood there staring down at the schematics.

Sean stood a few feet back from the monitor, studying the layout. He wasn't close enough to touch anything, Mercer had made sure of that.

Tommy stopped beside him, three paces from the desk, just inside the glow of the screen.

"There," Soren said while zooming in on a narrow corridor at the northern edge of the palace. "Maintenance tunnel. Not used for public access. Internal only. I've confirmed no camera coverage and no motion sensors along this path."

"Where does it lead?" Tommy asked, squinting.

"Down to the sublevels. This stairwell," Soren pointed, "takes you into the original foundation. The crypts. From there, you'll be within thirty meters of the chamber you're looking for—if it exists."

Victoria, seated off to the side, cradled her glass of wine and watched the screen as though it was some great chessboard.

Sean stepped a little closer, instinctively, but the guard behind him cleared his throat and stepped forward. Mercer didn't need to speak. The message was clear.

"Everything else is too well guarded for any of the main routes," Soren continued. "But this tunnel here?" He dragged a finger along the schematic. "It's your only option. One entrance point. One exit. In and out."

"Any chance the crypt is sealed?" Tommy asked.

"Possibly," Soren said. "But from what I'm seeing, there's no steel or reinforcement that would've been added recently. If it's locked, it'll be mechanical. Old school."

"Any cameras inside the crypt area?" Sean asked.

"No. Nothing in that zone. Once you're down there, you're invisible."

"And backup?" Tommy asked. "In case something goes sideways?"

"I'll be monitoring patrols in real-time," Soren replied. "You'll have an earpiece. I'll be in your ear the whole time."

It felt dirty to be working with these guys, especially with what had rapidly turned into a heist, but Sean didn't have a choice. For now, this was how he'd have to play it.

Victoria swirled the last of her wine and set the glass down gently. "And because we have your friends, we know you won't try to get away, call the police, any of that nonsense."

Sean didn't bother arguing. They all understood the terms.

He stared at the screen, tracing the path with his eyes, committing it to memory. The entrance. The tunnel. The stairs. The crypt. A tight, linear plan. No detours. No help from the outside. And a tight window of time before security rotated again and eyes swept back over those halls.

Sean gave Tommy a look, and his friend nodded once.

"So," Sean said, exhaling slowly, "let's say we've found our way in. What about the guards?"

"I have control of the camera feed," Soren said. "If anyone is coming toward you, I'll know it."

Sean had to admit these guys were good, particularly the one called Soren. Maybe the museum didn't have the best security in place, but to be able to hack into their systems so quickly, regardless of the level of tech, was an impressive feat.

"They're on a rotating schedule," Mercer added. "They make a round every fifteen minutes, then take a break for fifteen minutes."

"That's good work if you can find it," Tommy joked.

Mercer glanced at Nikolai, then turned to Sean and Tommy. "You'll need these."

Nikolai approached, holding out two black backpacks. Neither man moved right away, their eyes fixed on Mercer, waiting to see what the catch was. When Mercer gave a curt nod, Tommy reached out, took the pack, and slowly slung it over his shoulder. Sean did the same.

"No weapons," Mercer said plainly. "You'll only carry what you need to get in and out clean."

He raised a hand and counted off with his fingers. "Lockpicking tools. A compact pry bar. Radios—synced to channel nine. And headlamps. You'll need them once you're inside. The crypts don't have power, and you'll want to keep your presence as quiet as possible."

Sean unzipped his bag and peered inside. He pulled out the radio, examined the dial, then checked the earpiece tucked beside it. "How long is the range?"

"Long enough," Mercer replied.

Sean didn't bother inspecting the gear. He'd used kits like this before. Spartan. Efficient. Stripped down to what mattered.

"We'll drop you off at the access point," Mercer went on. "Keep in mind that if you try anything such as calling the police, we won't hesitate to execute your friends here." He motioned to Jean-Marc and Evelyn, both of whom wore loathsome expressions.

The Frenchman looked particularly irked. Sean could understand why. It was like corralling a wild stallion. He could take out any of the men in this room if he were freed, something that Mercer must have been keenly aware of.

"Okay," Sean said, slipping on the backpack, "let's go break into a museum."

Tommy chuffed. "There are two words I thought I'd never hear you say."

44

The SUV rolled through the narrow, winding streets of Avignon with a silence that spoke volumes. The tires whispered across ancient cobblestones, passing shuttered storefronts and sleeping homes tucked beneath the overcast night. A heavy stillness pressed against the windows, as though the city itself were holding its breath.

Sean sat in the middle row of the vehicle, jaw tight, hands resting in his lap. Beside him, Tommy shifted slightly, eyes trained on the window, scanning the world beyond for something—anything—that might shift the odds in their favor.

In the third row, Mercer leaned forward just enough to rest the muzzle of his pistol against Sean's ribs. The pressure was gentle, almost casual, but it spoke of intent. Mercer didn't need to say a word. The cold steel said everything.

The interior of the SUV smelled faintly of leather and oil, with an undertone of stale coffee from an old cup in one of the front holders. Nikolai drove in silence, hands steady on the wheel, eyes fixed on the road ahead. Not a glance into the mirror. Not a word.

Streetlamps passed in intervals, washing the interior in rhythmic pulses of dull amber. Shadows darted across the contours of Mercer's face and glinted faintly off the weapon in his hand. Sean could feel the tension in Tommy's posture—tight, ready—but they both knew there was no room for heroics. Not yet.

They passed the Palais des Papes without comment, its towering silhouette a jagged cutout against the night sky. Sean glanced up at it through the window, absorbing its looming presence. Somewhere inside those walls, buried beneath centuries of dust and secrecy, was the ring. The object Victoria Sterling believed would change the world.

He couldn't let her have it.

The SUV turned sharply down a narrow alley, tires crunching over gravel. The buildings grew fewer here, replaced by tall iron fences and patches of sloping grass that led toward the quieter sections of the city's ancient architecture. Ahead, beyond a line of dormant hedgerows, Sean saw the faint shape of the service entrance they'd studied on the screens back at the hotel. A delivery access point—unguarded, overlooked, and just vulnerable enough.

Nikolai eased the vehicle to a stop and killed the headlights. The SUV idled for a moment, the low hum of the engine the only sound.

"This is it," he said quietly, eyes fixed ahead.

Mercer didn't move for a beat. Then, slowly, he withdrew the pistol from Sean's side and leaned back.

"Good luck," he said, the words dry, stripped of sincerity.

Sean didn't reply. He opened the door and stepped out into the chilled night air as his boots landed on gravel that shifted beneath his weight. Tommy followed while slipping the rucksack over his shoulder and quietly closing the door behind him.

The SUV lingered for a moment longer, then turned back the way it came and melted into the shadows between streetlamps without a sound.

Sean watched it vanish, then looked at Tommy. No words were needed. They both knew: This was it. No backup. No margin for error. Just the two of them, a satchel of gear, and the weight of the world.

They turned toward the building and stared for a second.

The maintenance entrance to the Palais des Papes loomed ahead in the darkness, tucked beneath a moss-streaked archway that had likely seen a thousand years pass in silence. A rusted service door stood embedded in the ancient stone wall, unassuming, unnoticed by most tourists who passed within a hundred feet of it during the day. Now, it was their way in.

Sean crouched in the shadow of an overgrown hedge, his rucksack pulled tight against his back. Beside him, Tommy adjusted the strap of his own bag as his eyes scanned the narrow alleyway behind them. The city had gone quiet, save for the distant hum of a scooter and the occasional clink of glass from a nearby café as it prepared to close for the night.

Sean exhaled slowly and looked at the building. "We move on go."

Tommy nodded once.

Sean waited a second, then said, "Go."

They darted across the open space, their footsteps muffled on the uneven cobblestones. Sean reached the door first, dropped to one knee, and retrieved the lockpicking tool from his pack. The lock was old but not crude; a reinforced tumbler installed within the last decade, likely to keep curious maintenance workers or trespassers out.

Tommy knelt beside him, headlamp already strapped to his forehead but switched off for now. The darkness worked in their favor.

Sean inserted the pick, working the tumblers gently. One... two... He paused, feeling resistance on the third. Sweat rolled down his temple. The fourth tumbler clicked. Then silence.

"What's wrong?" Tommy whispered.

Sean shook his head. "False set. Give me a second."

A car passed at the end of the alley, headlights sweeping across the stone wall but not reaching their position.

Sean adjusted the pick's angle and applied more pressure. Click. The last tumbler slipped into place.

"Got it."

He pushed the door inward. It creaked faintly, the sound far too loud in the oppressive silence.

They slipped inside and closed the door gently behind them.

"We're inside," Sean said into the radio.

"That was fast," Mercer answered back.

"Yeah, well, we wouldn't want to keep your owner waiting."

No reply.

Inside, the air was dense with mildew and dust. A set of ancient stone steps led downward, lit only by the ambient glow of Sean's dimmed headlamp. Water dripped somewhere in the distance, echoing through the corridor like a slow metronome.

They descended slowly, boots soft against the damp stone. Pipes ran along the ceiling—modern intrusions against medieval bones. At the landing, they found a door; this one heavier, with a steel plate welded over the lock.

Tommy reached into his bag and pulled out the pry tool.

The pry bar groaned against the seam as he worked it under the steel plate. A sharp pop echoed when the cover came free, clattering to the ground.

Sean tensed. "Subtle, Schultzie," he whispered.

Tommy grimaced at the sound, hoping the mistake hadn't just stopped the entire operation before it began.

They waited in silence. No footsteps. No alarms. Only the slow, steady drip in the distance.

Sean turned the handle. It opened. They slipped through into another corridor, this one branching in two directions.

Sean glanced back. "Left or right?"

Tommy pointed right. "The map showed the crypt entrances are west of this hallway. That should be it."

Sean nodded, and they moved on, deeper into the belly of the fortress.

The dim service lights overhead gave the place an eerie, clinical glow, reflecting off the pale walls and casting long, ghostlike shadows. Sean moved in step with Tommy, both of them crouched low as they approached a metal junction in the hallway; a fork with one corridor veering left, the other right.

Sean paused and pressed the button on the side of his radio. "We're at the fork. Which way?"

Static answered first, then Soren's voice, hushed and urgent. "Hold your position. You've got movement to your left. Guard just came out of the west corridor. He's on a patrol."

Both Sean and Tommy froze. Sean slid behind a support beam and tucked himself into the shadow. Tommy flattened against the wall beside a fire extinguisher box.

They could hear the footsteps now. Slow, steady... boots tapping against the tile. The sound grew louder, closing in with each step. Sean's breath slowed. He tightened his jaw and steadied his posture, trying to become part of the wall.

A moment passed. Then two. The footsteps stopped.

Tommy risked a glance. The guard stood about ten feet away, peering down the adjacent hallway, his back to them. He lingered there for what felt like an hour.

Then he turned.

Sean gripped the strap of his rucksack. He really didn't want to take out a guard who was just doing his job. The last thing that guy expected was to be knocked out by a couple of intruders on what would normally be an easy, uneventful shift.

To his relief, the guard walked off, back the way he'd come.

Soren's voice crackled through. "All clear. Take the right. You've got a short window before he circles back."

Sean exhaled silently and glanced at Tommy. They exchanged a look then crept forward. The hallway narrowed slightly, and the air changed—less circulated, heavier with the scent of stone and old moisture.

"This is older construction," Tommy whispered, just loud enough for Sean to hear. "We're close."

Sean nodded but didn't answer. "We're through the turn."

Soren responded, "You've got one more hallway to go through.

Straight for thirty meters, then down a staircase. Crypt level. Mercer says it should be deserted."

They moved quickly, their steps padded by thick rubber soles. A faded sign pointed the way toward maintenance access and an older substructure.

As they reached the top of the stairwell, Sean clicked the mic again. "Beginning descent."

The stairs creaked under their weight, metal groaning from age and neglect. Sean worried every little sound would alert the guard, but he kept moving. At the bottom was a locked door, a rusted latch padlocked tight.

Sean pulled out the compact lockpicking tool. "Cover me."

Tommy stood watch while Sean worked, the tiny instruments whispering against metal. Within moments, the lock popped with a soft click. He eased it open and slid the latch back.

The door swung inward and revealed a narrow stone hallway that descended gently into the earth.

Sean kept his head on a swivel, eyes flicking to the corners of the crypt, as he ensured every footfall was carefully placed to avoid alerting anyone. The faint yet steady beam of his headlamp illuminated a series of faded engravings on the limestone walls, worn almost smooth by time and touch. Tommy walked beside him, silent, absorbed in the ancient markings and the stillness that surrounded them.

They had left the better-lit areas of the Palais behind them, descending a narrow stairwell tucked behind a tapestry that depicted the coronation of a long-dead pope. At the bottom of the stairs, they entered a section of the crypt not marked on the digital floor plans Soren had provided. A place that felt untouched by the modern world.

Tommy stopped abruptly. "There," he whispered and pointed to a section of the wall ahead. The stone looked different—less worn, more precise in its construction. A rectangular panel stood out from the surrounding stones, slightly recessed, almost imperceptible if not for the symmetry.

Sean moved closer, and his headlamp traced the edges of the panel. "This wasn't built at the same time as the rest," he said. "Whoever made this came after."

They examined it carefully, hands brushing along the stone, searching for clues. Carved faintly into the surface, they found a series of intersecting lines and symbols—a crude compass rose, a cross, and the letters *PSC* barely visible beneath the dust of centuries.

"Could be initials," Tommy muttered while studying the markings. "Or something else. Maybe Latin."

Sean knelt down to inspect the floor in front of the panel. He tapped lightly against the flagstones. One of them gave a different sound—a hollow thunk instead of a solid thud. He brushed the dust aside, which revealed a small metal ring embedded in the center of the stone.

"Found something." He looked up at Tommy. "Give me a hand."

Together they gripped the ring and pulled. The stone lifted with a scrape and a puff of stale, earthy air. Beneath it, a narrow shaft plunged into darkness, just wide enough for a man to descend.

Sean leaned over the edge. The smell of age and decay wafted up from below. He flicked on his radio. "Soren, we've found a shaft. Could be a hidden passage. Going down to check it out."

There was a pause before Soren's voice crackled back. "Copy that. No movement near your sector. Proceed, but stay sharp. Mercer wants status updates every five minutes."

Sean glanced at Tommy. "You first or me?"

Tommy raised an eyebrow. "I'll flip you for it."

Sean grinned faintly, then adjusted the straps on his rucksack. "Let me. If there's a trap, better I trip it."

He lowered himself into the shaft slowly, boots scraping the inner walls, heart hammering in his chest. The stone was cold and damp against his palms. He counted each breath, each foot of descent, until the shaft widened into a narrow corridor.

The passage ahead had a low ceiling, was built of rough-hewn stone, and sloped slightly downward. Tommy dropped down behind him, landing lightly, headlamp already scanning their surroundings.

They moved forward cautiously, deeper into the passage. Ahead, the corridor widened into a small chamber. At its center stood a slab of stone carved with intricate grooves.

"Another puzzle," Sean said, approaching. The grooves formed a complex pattern—a series of concentric circles interspersed with symbols and short Latin inscriptions.

Tommy stepped beside him. "Looks like a mechanism. A combination lock, maybe."

Sean crouched, and his eyes narrowed. "Soren, we found a secondary chamber. There's some sort of locking mechanism. Any chance you've got eyes on this?"

"Negative," Soren replied. "You're off the grid in that section. You'll have to figure it out."

Sean sighed, wiped sweat from his brow, and looked at Tommy. "Let's get to work."

The stone slab bore the inscription: *Fide et Labore.*

"By faith and work," Tommy translated. "Sounds like something a Templar would say."

Sean placed his fingers on one of the outer rings and turned it. It moved smoothly, clicking softly into place. Each ring bore letters and symbols, but the center held a slot—just the right size for a key or another object.

"This might be it," Sean said. "The final safeguard."

Tommy frowned. "Then what does it unlock?"

Sean pointed to the wall behind the pedestal. Carved in low relief, another panel showed a woman in armor standing before a set of stairs descending into the earth. At her feet: a ring held by a pair of doves.

Tommy stepped back. "That's Joan. Has to be."

They worked through the rings methodically, aligning the Latin phrases until a soft click echoed through the chamber. The floor beneath the pedestal trembled, and the wall panel cracked open with a hiss of released pressure.

Behind it, a narrow stair descended farther into the dark.

Sean exhaled. "You ever wonder how many of these secret passages we've explored?"

Tommy chuckled. "I lost count a long time ago, buddy."

"Me too."

"I do wonder how many more are out there, though."

"Same." Sean shone his light down into the stairwell. "I guess we're adding one more to our tally. If we didn't hate publicity, I'd say we should call the folks at Guinness and claim our world record."

45

The moment Sean set foot on the fourth step, the wall suddenly sealed behind them, swallowing the last trace of light from the chamber above. A hush fell over the ancient stairwell, broken only by the soft scrape of his boots on stone.

They both looked back at the closed passage.

"I guess we're not going out the way we came in," Tommy complained.

The light cut a narrow cone through the darkness, illuminating centuries of dust drifting like fog through the cramped shaft.

Sean glanced at Tommy behind him. "You good?"

Tommy adjusted the strap of his rucksack. "Sure. Just taking a moonlight stroll through medieval death tunnels. It's my happy place." He grinned in the glow of their lights, his sarcasm echoing off the walls.

Sean allowed a dry chuckle, but the weight in the air pressed heavier the deeper they went. The steps were uneven, worn to curves by time or passage—maybe both. The walls were slick with condensation and laced with dark moss. Whatever they'd just uncovered wasn't on any map. Not even Henri's notes had hinted at something this far below the Palais.

And yet what they'd found matched one of Henri's sketches perfectly. It had been dismissed as decorative. But the mechanism behind it had opened to reveal this staircase. Another clue Henri had pieced together with obsessive detail now came into focus.

A low groan echoed up from below, or maybe it was just the stones settling. Sean slowed, holding his light higher. The stairwell curved and abruptly ended at a heavy oaken door bound in rusted iron. A crossbar sat diagonally across it, splintered from age but intact.

Sean pushed it open.

The hinges gave a sharp protest before yielding, revealing a tunnel that stretched into the black. The floor was stone, the walls slightly arched and reinforced with centuries-old masonry. It was cooler here—damp and earthy, but with something else underneath.

Decay.

Tommy stepped inside and swept his light across the ceiling. "This wasn't just a passage. Look at the architecture—vaulted supports, recessed niches along the walls. This was built to last."

Sean moved forward, keeping his footsteps soft. "Or to be forgotten."

They passed a rotting wooden cart, its wheels collapsed, its contents reduced to dust. The tunnel widened and then narrowed again, as if the builders hadn't followed a strict plan but rather adapted the path around something—obstacles, terrain, maybe even tombs.

That's when Sean's light fell on the first set of bones.

Half buried beneath the rubble of a collapsed alcove, the skeletal remains of a man in tattered robes reached toward the wall. One bony hand clutched what might've once been a scroll, now fused into crumbling leather. The other hand was curled into a fist, as if defiant even in death.

Tommy knelt beside it. "Priestly garb. Fifteenth century by the cut and fabric. This guy wasn't just hiding—he died down here."

Sean nodded grimly while stepping past. The tunnel curved

again and began sloping downward. The smell grew stronger—old death and wet limestone, and something faintly metallic.

Ten paces later, they entered a chamber—not large but rounded like a crypt. Recesses lined the circular walls, with each holding a sarcophagus marked with faded crests. The floor had been swept clean long ago and then left to gather dust again.

Sean stood in the center, slowly spinning with his light.

"Joan's contemporaries," Tommy murmured. "This has to be them. Look at the armor detail. That one—he's got the De Rais insignia."

Sean turned toward the stone coffin with a rusted sword crossed over it. "That name showed up in Henri's journal."

"It did," Tommy confirmed. "De Rais wasn't just a knight. He was her commander. This crypt... This isn't just a hiding place. It's a vault of guardians."

Sean stepped forward and let his fingers brush over a strange indentation in the floor—a geometric pattern like a maze etched into stone. "Something tells me we're getting close."

Tommy scanned the walls again, and his light caught a faded mural half hidden behind centuries of grime. The painted scene showed a woman—tall, armored, crowned in flames—holding a ring aloft over a stone altar.

Sean's breath caught. "That's her."

Tommy stepped up beside him. "Then that's where we go next."

Sean moved closer to the mural and brushed a gloved hand along the painted surface. Flakes of old pigment drifted to the floor like ashes. "She's holding the ring above a stone just like this one," he murmured. "But look here—behind her. That spiral pattern. It's the same symbol carved into the floor."

Tommy was already crouching over it, tracing the maze-like design with his flashlight. "It's not just decoration. Look, there's a path. A very specific one."

Sean pulled a small notebook from his pocket and flipped to a page with Henri's sketch of the same pattern. The historian had labeled it *La Clef de Feu*—The Key of Fire. A symbol that, according to Henri's notes, had been used by a secretive brotherhood of knights who swore allegiance to Joan after her capture. They believed her mission was unfinished—and that something powerful had been entrusted to them.

Tommy glanced up. "So this floor is the key."

"Or part of it," Sean said.

As if on cue, a faint click echoed from behind the wall. Both men froze.

Tommy turned his head toward the sound. "Tell me that was Soren."

Sean brought his radio up. "Soren, we heard a noise. Are you picking up movement down here?"

A pause, then Soren's voice crackled through, hushed and tense. "Negative. Still nothing above you. But... you're very deep. Signal's starting to degrade. Be careful. Something's interfering."

"Almost sounds like you actually care for our well-being," Sean joked.

No response came from the other end, as expected.

Sean lowered the radio and looked at Tommy. "Interfering like electromagnetic fields? Or interfering like we just woke something up?"

Tommy didn't answer. Instead, he shone his light back to the floor and frowned. "Wait... these lines in the stone—they're not just grooves. They're channels."

Sean knelt beside him and studied the spiral. "Channels for what?"

Tommy's lips thinned. "Maybe liquid? Oil?"

Sean's stomach dropped. "Or fire."

He stood and scanned the room again. Near the far wall, something glinted faintly in the dust. He crossed the chamber and found a metal bowl was fused to the stone, with blackened residue inside.

"A brazier," he said. "They lit this thing."

Tommy joined him. "To illuminate the pattern on the floor?"

"Or to activate something."

They both turned back to the mural. Beneath Joan's outstretched arm, tiny red dots were painted along the spiral—five of them, each placed at a different point in the maze. Sean flipped through Henri's notes again. One of the final passages read, "Only the faithful will follow the fire's path. One wrong step, and the guardians wake."

Tommy frowned. "What guardians?"

Sean's light caught something above one of the sarcophagi—a stone carving of a helmeted face, mouth slightly open, as if caught in a silent warning.

"That's comforting," Sean muttered.

Tommy exhaled through his nose. "This is a trap. It has to be. A ritual and a trap. Start the fire, follow the path, and if you screw it up..."

Sean nodded. "It burns you alive. Or worse."

"What would be worse?"

"You survive."

"Fair point."

They stood in silence, listening to the steady drip of moisture somewhere in the distance. The tension in the air was a coiled wire.

Sean stepped toward the brazier, then froze and patted down his rucksack.

"Crap. I don't have anything flammable."

Tommy turned, brows furrowed. "You sure? No alcohol? No emergency fuel tabs?"

Sean shook his head.

Tommy muttered a curse under his breath and scanned the chamber. "There has to be something down here. They built this for a ritual. They would've stored supplies."

Sean's light swept across the alcoves, the sarcophagi, and then landed on an ancient wooden crate near the wall, mostly rotted but still intact in the corners. He moved toward it and carefully pried it open with the flat end of his pry tool.

Inside were crumbling rags, a sealed clay pot, and what looked like dried herbs or incense sticks long fossilized by time.

He popped the lid off the clay pot, recoiling at the sharp, sweet sting of pitch and myrrh.

Tommy stepped beside him, grinning. "That'll burn."

Sean grabbed a few of the brittle incense sticks and dipped the tips into the resinous tar. "Let's hope this stuff still lights."

Tommy held the flint and steel with both hands, struck hard, and caught a spark on one of the resin-soaked sticks. The flame caught slowly—then blossomed into a crackling blue-orange tongue.

Sean lit the brazier. It flared to life, heat licking the damp air.

Tommy nodded. "Now we follow the spiral."

Sean dipped the end of another stick and touched it to the first groove. The fire snaked forward, tracing the ancient path in the stone.

The trial had begun.

Sean dipped the second incense stick into the thick resin again, letting the blackened tip soak for a few seconds before lighting it in the brazier's flame. The heat flared and pulsed, casting their shadows large and twisted on the crypt walls.

"Here goes," he said while crossing back to the etched spiral in the floor.

Tommy crouched beside him, notebook in hand, holding it flat with one palm while angling the headlamp for a better view. "Five marks. Just like the mural. The first branch starts… here."

Sean nodded. He touched the flame to the channel, and it caught with surprising speed—a flickering line of fire curling into the pattern like a living ribbon of light. It hissed faintly but otherwise inched forward in complete silence.

The fire reached the first mark—the red dot near the spiral's outer edge—and hovered there, as if considering its next move.

Tommy held his breath.

The flame jumped to the next path segment and continued forward, hugging the ancient grooves perfectly. Sean stepped back, resisting the urge to move too fast or speak.

Then the sound came—a deep metallic thump from somewhere below the floor. It rumbled through their boots.

Tommy's voice was low. "That sounded like a lock disengaging."

Sean gave a tight nod; eyes fixed on the fire as it traveled toward the second red dot.

The moment it passed it, another sound followed—a long, groaning shift in the stone. Dust trickled from above. One of the sarcophagi gave a slight lurch forward, just enough to nudge its carved helmet loose. It fell with a soft clatter.

They froze.

Tommy swallowed. "Was that... supposed to happen?"

"I don't think anything here is just for show," Sean said while stepping lightly toward the sarcophagus. "This is the real deal. They built this as a test—and maybe as a warning."

As if in response, the flame reached the third mark and paused.

Then another sound—a mechanical groan, lower and deeper than the others. On the far side of the chamber, a vertical seam appeared in the wall, and the stone began to slide. It ground downward, slow and deliberate, revealing an alcove they hadn't noticed before. Inside stood a relief carving of the same armored woman from the mural—crowned in flames, arm raised.

Sean and Tommy moved closer, scanning the relief. The ring was missing from the woman's hand, but beneath her feet, a faint indentation marked its top, shaped like a disc or socket.

Before they could speak, the fire traced the fourth red mark. A sudden wind kicked through the crypt—not natural, but drawn from deep within the walls. The brazier behind them flared as though breathing in.

Then, all at once, the flames extinguished—snuffed out in perfect unison with a sharp hiss.

Darkness.

Sean clicked his headlamp back on, casting beams across the chamber. "It stopped," he whispered.

Tommy tilted the notebook. "All five points were reached. That was the right sequence."

Sean turned toward the wall. "Then something just opened."

Sure enough, the relief slid aside, revealing a tight corridor carved with ancient precision. The air that spilled from within was colder, drier. It smelled faintly of dusted incense and long-extinguished oil lamps.

Tommy stared. "They weren't hiding the ring. They were protecting it. Like it was holy."

Sean stepped into the passage. "Not just protecting. They were preserving a truth no one else could be trusted with."

The tunnel narrowed and also sloped downward like those before it. Tiny etched crosses lined the walls, hundreds of them, each no larger than a coin. Sean ran his fingers along them as he walked. Pilgrim's marks. A ritual passage.

Then, they reached the end.

The tunnel opened into a circular chamber, perfectly preserved. At its center sat a white marble altar, and on it, a stone box, unadorned except for a rusted iron band.

Sean felt it. The sense that this was meant to remain undisturbed.

Tommy stepped beside him. "This is it. This is what they died to protect."

Sean nodded slowly.

Sean circled the pedestal slowly, examining every detail of the stone box. The surface was smooth, but time had worked its fingers into the edges—hairline cracks, faint chisel scars. The rusted iron band that sealed the lid was fixed at four corners by small clasps, each one etched with a different symbol.

"A lion," Tommy murmured, pointing to the first. "Strength."

He moved to the next. "A flame. That one's obvious."

Sean leaned in at the third. "A crown. Royalty or divine right?"

Tommy nodded. "Or authority."

They both studied the final symbol: a skull wrapped in thorns.

Tommy stepped back. "That's not just death. That's judgment."

Sean frowned. "Four symbols. Four virtues or trials?"

"Maybe," Tommy said. "But they're in a specific order. Like a riddle."

He flipped Henri's notebook to the final pages. Sean watched as he traced a passage with his finger.

"Here—listen to this: 'To break the seal and face the flame, four doors must open without pride or shame. Strength bows first, then fire tames light. Only with death may the crown shine bright.'"

Sean absorbed the words in silence, then looked back at the clasps.

"We need to release them in order," he said. "Or this whole thing could collapse on us."

Tommy nodded. "Or worse."

Sean knelt beside the pedestal and placed his hand over the lion clasp. "Strength bows first."

With a steady breath, he depressed the catch. It clicked open with a muffled snap. Nothing moved. No stone crumbled. No hidden spears emerged from the walls.

Tommy pointed. "Then fire. It tames light."

Sean found the flame clasp and opened it with care.

Another clean click. Still nothing.

He moved to the skull, hesitating. "Death before the crown."

Tommy looked grim. "They were trying to teach something. Humility. Surrender. The idea that only through sacrifice does one earn authority."

Sean opened the skull clasp. A deeper click echoed beneath the pedestal.

Then, the moment his fingers touched the crown clasp, the box pulsed. Just once. Faint and cold.

Sean pulled his hand back and watched the box.

The light from their headlamps shimmered against the stone as though it were breathing. Across the inside of the chamber walls, a series of glowing words began to emerge, inscribed in Latin.

Tommy stepped toward them and read aloud.

"*Caveat qui coronam tangit... nisi pura cor eius.*"

Sean looked at him while translating silently in his mind.

Tommy's throat cleared. "'Let him beware who touches the crown... unless his heart is pure.'"

Sean returned his gaze to the box. "The final warning."

"Not just symbolic," Tommy said. "A real danger. They left it to scare off anyone who came here with the wrong motives."

Sean looked at the crown clasp again. "Do we qualify?"

Tommy nodded once. "I hope so."

Sean opened the final clasp.

The iron band fell away with a dull clatter, and the lid of the stone box shivered once... then slid back on its own.

Inside, nestled in a bed of weathered, black velvet, lay the ring.

It shimmered with a strange, almost inner light—a simple band of polished gold but glowing faintly from within, as though lit by a flame. At its center sat a tiny red stone—not a ruby but something older, less perfect. Alive.

The light flickered.

Tommy whispered, "That's not just a relic. That's something else entirely."

Sean stared at it, feeling an unease crawl up the back of his neck. "I have to say, Schultzie, we always find the best stuff."

"And the most dangerous."

"True."

Then they saw it—carved into the inside of the lid, nearly invisible unless the light hit it just right—a final inscription, written not in Latin but in Old French.

They both leaned closer.

"The fire does not choose," Sean translated. "It reveals."

His gaze met Tommy's. "Let's not touch it just yet."

Sean stood over the ring, still not reaching for it. The glow from the red stone pulsed faintly, a rhythm not unlike a heartbeat. For a moment, he could almost imagine it watching them—judging, just as the inscription warned.

Tommy broke the silence. "We're not walking out of here without it."

Sean nodded, though he felt the weight of the decision more than ever now. Slowly, he reached into his rucksack and pulled out a soft cloth—folded linen from an old preservation kit. He wrapped it around his hand.

"I'm not touching it with bare skin. Just in case I don't fit the criteria."

Tommy agreed. "Smart."

Sean reached down carefully, and the moment the linen wrapped around the band, the glow flickered. He lifted the ring from the velvet cradle. It was light—too light. Almost as if it resisted being held, as if it wanted to remain.

Then the pedestal beneath it sank.

A soft click. Followed by a deep rumble.

The chamber trembled. Sean looked at Tommy. "Move."

A section of the floor near the far wall cracked, stone grinding against stone. Dust plumed upward in violent bursts. From behind the wall of glowing Latin inscriptions, a section of stone burst inward, revealing a steep downward chute—a tunnel slick with moisture and lined with ancient bones wedged into the walls like a warning.

"Is that... an escape tunnel?" Tommy shouted over the growing roar.

"Or a death trap." The entire room was shuddering now. The pedestal split clean in two, collapsing inward. The walls around the chamber began shedding slabs of stone, one chunk nearly crushing the sarcophagus nearest the exit.

Tommy grabbed his arm. "I don't think we have another option."

The headlamps flickered. A low hissing sound emerged from somewhere behind them—a rush of pressurized air, or something worse.

Sean glanced back at the original corridor. "Agreed."

Tommy looked down into the chute. "That's insane. We don't even know where it leads."

Sean stared into the darkness, still gripping the ring inside the linen cloth.

"No time to figure that out, Schultzie."

Behind them, a blast of hot air surged into the room, followed by a flickering orange glow. Fire. Not from the brazier. From the walls themselves. The ignition channels that had lit the spiral earlier were reactivating in reverse, crawling back toward the chamber.

"They rigged the whole crypt," Tommy realized. "This entire place is designed to destroy itself."

A loud crack split the ceiling. A section of stone collapsed just behind them, smashing into the ground with thunderous force.

"Gotta go," Sean said. He clutched the ring tighter, turned toward the chute, and jumped.

Tommy shouted something and followed an instant later.

They plunged into darkness.

The walls of the chute were slick and cold. The bones embedded in the sides flew past as they slid by. The tunnel curved sharply, tossing them from side to side as the sound of the collapsing chamber thundered behind them. Sean held his arms tight to his chest, protecting the ring as the world became a blur of stone and shadow.

Their hearts pounded as they sped through the chute. Then, suddenly, the tunnel shot them out into a narrow, arched corridor, and they tumbled across the damp floor before skidding to a halt against a pile of loose stones.

Both men groaned and slowly rolled over.

Tommy looked back at the chute, now silent and dark.

"You okay?" Sean asked.

Tommy nodded, breathless. "Yeah. Yeah, I'm good. But where are we?"

Sean unwrapped the cloth just enough to peek at the ring. The red stone pulsed once, dimly.

"I don't know, but we still have the ring."

Behind them, a faint wind moved through the passage.

Sean rose, steadying himself. "Let's find our way out of this place before it decides to finish the job."

Sean swept his headlamp around the space. The corridor was narrow, maybe four feet across. The walls were carved stone, water-streaked and weathered, lined with occasional iron brackets for torches long turned to rust. The floor sloped slightly downward yet again, suggesting it may have once been part of a forgotten drainage system or a secret passage built for emergencies.

The air felt stale, untouched by time.

"Some kind of escape route," Sean said. "Old. Real old. Pre-papal construction maybe. Could've been part of the original fortress before it became a palace."

Tommy climbed to his feet and brushed off his jacket. "So now we just follow the spooky tunnel and hope it lets out somewhere that isn't under the Rhône River?"

Sean offered a tired grin. "That's the spirit." He turned and started walking while carefully cradling the linen-wrapped ring in one hand, his light sweeping steadily ahead. The stone beneath his feet was smoother now, almost polished in places. Signs of use—regular traffic, though long forgotten.

"What do you think this place was meant for?" Tommy asked as he glanced at the inset grooves in the wall.

Sean ran his fingers over one as he passed. "Maybe an escape route. Maybe something worse."

The silence pressed around them, broken only by the slap of boots against stone and the occasional drip of unseen water. The deeper they went, the more the air seemed to thicken, heavy with moisture and memory.

Then, ahead, the tunnel branched.

Sean slowed. Two passages diverged—one veering slightly upward, the other descending into a deeper dark.

He held the light toward the upward path. Faint markings scratched into the wall. A symbol—a circled cross, marked with a short line beneath it.

Tommy peered over his shoulder. "Seen that before."

Sean nodded. "Pilgrim sign. Marking the path to light."

"We go up, then."

Sean took the lead again, following the new path as it began a slow curve to the left. The incline was subtle but steady, and the texture of the air began to shift—still musty, but with a hint of movement. A breeze.

Tommy noticed it, too. "Airflow."

Sean nodded. "There's an exit up ahead. Has to be."

He glanced at the cloth in his hand. The ring pulsed again, faint but steady, like it sensed something.

Or someone.

They kept moving.

The air grew fresher with each step. It wasn't clean—still tinged with the heavy scent of limestone and mildew—but it carried the unmistakable taste of freedom. Sean pressed forward, one hand on the wall to steady himself as the incline steepened.

Behind him, Tommy muttered, "If we pop out into the middle of a tourist square, I'm pretending I'm lost."

Sean gave a soft chuckle but kept his pace steady. Their headlamps flickered across the stone, illuminating small alcoves carved into the sides of the passage—storage nooks, maybe, or hiding spots for guards long forgotten by time.

Finally, after another bend, the tunnel flattened, and a patch of rougher stonework caught Sean's attention ahead. A wall, but different— newer construction compared to the ancient passage behind them.

Tommy came up beside him. "Looks like someone tried to seal this off at some point."

Sean ran his hand over the masonry. Crude patchwork. Bricks shoved into place and mortared hastily, probably centuries ago when the palace had been expanded. Someone had wanted this passage hidden—buried.

Tommy tapped his boot against the lower corner. A hollow echo responded.

Sean gave a nod. "Weak spot."

Together, they dug out the pry tools from their rucksacks and set to work. It wasn't quiet—each crack and scrape echoed like cannon fire in the tight corridor—but urgency outweighed caution. After several minutes of straining and chipping, a narrow gap opened up, letting a sharp gust of cool night air blast into the tunnel.

Sean widened the opening enough to squeeze through.

"Ready?" he whispered.

Tommy nodded. "I don't think we should hang around here," he joked.

Sean pushed through first, wriggling out of the tunnel and into the open.

The night hit him like a wave—cold and damp, heavy with the scent of rain that hadn't yet fallen. He rolled to his knees and clicked off his headlamp, then blinked against the dim streetlights far in the distance.

They were in a narrow alleyway, the high walls of ancient stone pressing in on either side. Cracked cobblestones glistened faintly under the weak glow of a few scattered lamps. Beyond the mouth of the alley, wider streets sprawled out toward the heart of Avignon.

Tommy slipped through behind him, breathing hard. Both men crouched low while scanning their surroundings. It was late, the city had fallen into the deep hush of the early morning hours. No cars moved. No pedestrians wandered.

Sean pulled the radio from his belt and thumbed the mic.

"Mercer, come in. We're clear."

Static crackled. Then Mercer's voice came through, calm and clipped. "Status?"

Sean glanced at Tommy then down at the cloth in his hand. "We have the package. Rendezvous point?"

There was a slight pause on the other end, then Mercer answered. "Northeast side. Rue de la République. We'll pick you up."

Sean gave a short reply then stuffed the radio back onto his belt.

Tommy stood slowly and flexed his shoulders. "Not to jinx it, but that went smoother than I expected."

Sean gave him a look. "We're not out yet."

He tucked the linen-wrapped ring deeper into the folds of his jacket and started toward the mouth of the alley, every sense on high alert. The city might have been asleep, but the ring still pulsed against his chest like a second heartbeat.

They kept to the shadows as they moved, slipping from the alleyway into the quieter veins of the old city. The Palais des Papes loomed somewhere behind them, a silent giant brooding over the stone labyrinth of Avignon.

Sean tucked the wrapped ring closer against his chest and

adjusted his pace, keeping his head low. Even in the dead of night, he didn't trust the quiet. Especially not after what they had just disturbed.

Tommy jogged a few steps to catch up. "Feels too easy."

Sean nodded without breaking stride. "That's because it is."

The narrow streets around them were a warren of ancient stone buildings, their walls leaning slightly inward as if conspiring against anyone who dared pass. In the distance, a clock tower struck a soft, hollow chime—three notes—marking the hour past midnight.

They turned onto Rue des Teinturiers, following the thread of a small, dry canal that glinted faintly under the dim streetlamps. A few windows flickered with soft golden light from late-night readers or insomniacs. But otherwise, the city was a hushed, waiting thing.

As they approached a wider intersection, Sean held up a hand and froze.

Across the square, two figures loitered beneath a crumbling archway.

Not tourists. Not locals out for a midnight stroll.

Both were dressed in dark clothing, posture stiff, heads sweeping in slow arcs—watching. Waiting.

Tommy leaned in. "You think Mercer's people?"

Sean studied them a moment longer. "No."

The figures shifted, one tapping an earpiece.

"They're looking for someone," Sean said. "Probably us."

Tommy swallowed. "Did we set off an alarm or something?"

"No idea. Maybe Soren isn't as good as he thinks."

Sean's mind raced. They couldn't risk a confrontation—not carrying what they were carrying. They needed to reach Mercer and disappear into the night before anyone realized what had been taken. He scanned the square and spotted a side passage—a narrow, crumbling corridor half hidden by shadows.

He jerked his chin toward it. "There."

Without another word, they slipped down the side passage, boots silent against the uneven stones. The alley tightened, barely wide enough for them to pass single file. The scent of damp earth and ancient mortar filled their nostrils.

Behind them, faintly, the sound of rapid footsteps echoed against the walls.

Sean didn't look back. He focused on the path ahead, calculating, measuring every turn and option. They had maybe thirty seconds before their pursuers closed the gap.

The alley fed into another street—wider, better lit. A few late-night cafés still had their shutters half raised, and the scent of bread and coffee drifted faintly on the breeze.

Tommy spotted it first—the black van idling near the curb, hazard lights blinking softly.

Sean saw the silhouette behind the wheel. Nicholai.

Relief threatened to uncoil his muscles, but he shoved it down. Not yet. Not until they were inside.

"Move," Sean hissed.

They sprinted the last stretch across the street. The SUV's back door flung open with a metallic clatter, and Tommy dove inside. Sean followed and pulled the door shut just as the first of their pursuers rounded the corner, shouting in a harsh, clipped voice.

The SUV peeled away from the curb with a squeal of tires, accelerating down the empty avenue.

Sean leaned back against the cold metal wall, chest heaving, heart pounding against the cloth-wrapped ring hidden beneath his jacket.

For a brief moment, the city fell away—the chase, the danger, the narrow escape—all drowned out by the heavy, rhythmic beat of something ancient and powerful now resting in his hands.

"Is that it?" Mercer asked, looking at the object. His eyes brimmed with mistrust and curiosity.

Sean answered between deep breaths. "Yeah. This is it."

"You're sure?"

"Of course we're sure," Tommy fired back. "You know what we just went through to get that thing? Jeez, man. We did what you said. Just take us back to the suite so we can give your handler her prize."

Sean glanced over at his friend. He saw what Tommy was doing, and for a few seconds he thought it might actually work.

"Handler?" Mercer said. "Is that what you think she is? My handler? No one controls me." His voice turned cold, dark. "She pays me well, and that's fine by me. We all take orders from someone. Some of us just get paid more for it than others."

"How very noble."

"I don't think you're in any position to judge. As soon as Victoria has her little artifact, you two and your friends are done."

46

The ride back to the suite was quiet, save for the low hum of the SUV's tires rolling over the cobbled streets of Avignon. Sean sat in the back, one hand resting protectively over the linen-wrapped ring hidden beneath his jacket. Across from him, Mercer sat rigid, arms crossed over his chest, eyes like ice.

Tommy slumped beside Sean, exhaustion written into the lines of his face, but his hand never drifted far from the radio clipped at his belt. Neither man spoke. Words felt dangerous in this space, where Nicholai glanced at them through the rearview mirror with a wary, assessing stare.

Sean's mind spun the whole way back. Options, he thought. There had to be an option.

They couldn't give Victoria the ring. But at the same time, trying to fight their way out would be suicide. Mercer had them boxed in from the moment they stepped back into the city. Every escape scenario Sean conjured—darting down an alley, leaping from the moving SUV, turning the tables inside the suite—collapsed under the same truth: too many guns, too little time.

Even if they somehow overpowered Mercer and his men, what

about Evelyn? Jean-Marc? If they were hurt—or worse—it would be on his hands.

No. Reckless wasn't the answer. They needed something smarter. A pressure point. A crack in the wall.

But every avenue Sean considered was blocked. Mercer was too disciplined, Victoria too calculating. They weren't amateurs, they knew what they were holding, and they knew exactly how dangerous Sean and Tommy could be if given the slightest opening.

The SUV turned off the main avenue and began threading through a quieter district. Elegant old buildings loomed overhead; dark windows like watching eyes. The suite wasn't far now.

Sean caught Tommy's eye briefly. No words passed between them, but the look was enough. Stay alert. Look for anything.

Minutes later, the SUV pulled into an underground parking level beneath a boutique hotel. Concrete walls, fluorescent lights buzzing overhead, the stink of oil and old water puddled in the cracks. Two guards were already waiting near the elevator, dressed in dark suits, the subtle bulges under their jackets making their threats clear.

Sean and Tommy were ushered from the van without ceremony, their rucksacks taken immediately. No weapons to even pretend they had a chance.

The elevator ride up was suffocating. Sean watched the numbers tick by, every second dragging like an hour. Finally, the doors slid open onto the penthouse floor.

Soft lighting. Plush carpet. The quiet, sterile air of wealth.

Sean stepped out first, Tommy close behind, and Mercer's men last but then moving up to flank them. They crossed the hall and stopped at a wide, ornate door already cracked open.

Inside, there she stood. Victoria Sterling.

Poised near the bar, a glass of something golden in hand, a smile playing at the corners of her mouth. She was beautiful. Sean had to give her that. But he didn't go in for the regal, holier-than-thou, murdering sociopath type. He found himself wishing his wife, Adriana, was here to knock her down a peg. She was always so good in situations like this, better than him in many ways.

"Oh look," she said, her voice syrupy and amused. "You made it."

"Did you think we wouldn't?" Sean asked, his tone full of venom. He glanced over at Jean-Marc and Evelyn. For what it was worth, they looked like they hadn't been harmed while he was gone. It was a small consolation, but he'd take it for now.

"I had reservations. There were several unknowns. But... you're here now." Her eyes fixed on Sean's hands and the cloth he held within the cage of his fingers. "That hardly seems a fitting way to carry such an important, priceless artifact."

"I didn't want to scratch it," he lied.

She looked at Mercer and nodded.

The man immediately reached out and took the cloth from Sean.

"Careful with that," Sean warned.

Mercer ignored him, though he seemed to adjust his grip on the cloth as if concerned about dropping it.

He walked over to where Victoria stood with both hands out and placed the folded cloth into her palms.

She gently unwrapped the folds like a child opening a Christmas present. When her eyes fell on the ring, she stopped moving, stopped breathing. Victoria cradled the ring in her open palm, her fingers curling slightly around it but not closing. She didn't speak. She didn't move. She simply stared, as if the little golden band had spoken to her in a voice none of the others could hear.

The room around them seemed to hold its breath.

Sean shifted his weight subtly, never letting his gaze leave her. Every instinct screamed that this moment was critical, that whatever happened next could shift the balance they so desperately needed.

The ring pulsed faintly in Victoria's hand, the tiny red stone at its center glowing with a heartbeat all its own. Not bright, not blinding —but alive.

A few of her henchmen edged closer, their stances no longer rigid professionalism but something more hesitant, almost entranced. Even Mercer, whose stoicism rarely cracked, was watching intently now, but with a shadow of caution in his eyes.

Tommy leaned slightly toward Sean. Not enough to draw attention, just enough that they caught the same thought flashing between them—the warning.

The words carved inside the lid of the box whispered through Sean's mind.

The fire does not choose. It reveals.

Maybe—just maybe—Victoria had already sealed her fate.

Hope stirred in Sean's chest; sharp and dangerous.

But he crushed it down before it could take root. Hope was not a plan. Hope was a rope you grabbed when the ground was already giving way beneath you.

He knew better. Only action saved you when the world turned sideways. And when the moment came, it would come fast.

Across the room, Victoria's fingers tightened slightly around the ring. She inhaled slowly, as if drawing the power of the object into her lungs. The corners of her mouth twitched—not quite a smile but something close to satisfaction.

Then, with the same slow, reverent movements, she raised the ring higher, bringing it up to eye level to inspect it more closely. The pulsing glow illuminated her face, throwing strange, almost inhuman shadows up across her cheekbones and eyes.

The ring's light flickered brighter for an instant, like a living thing straining toward its master—or its executioner.

Sean's muscles tensed. Whatever Victoria thought she was about to gain... she had no idea what she was holding. Or maybe she did. Maybe she'd researched this more than he thought.

Victoria tossed aside the cloth and held the ring aloft for a moment, as if about to don a crown in front of thousands of adoring fans. Then, with all eyes watching, she slipped the ring onto her finger.

For a beat, nothing happened.

Then the air changed.

A deep, almost imperceptible vibration ran through the suite. The lights flickered, as if the very molecules of the room were rearranging themselves to accommodate what had just been awakened.

A soft golden glow emanated from Victoria's skin, subtle at first, then blooming outward in gentle waves. It wasn't just the ring anymore—it was her. The light wrapped around her like a mantle, a living aura that shimmered and danced with each small movement she made.

Her head tilted slightly as if she were listening to something only she could hear. She smiled. It was a wicked, satisfied expression.

"I can feel it," she whispered, her voice low and awed. "I can feel the power running through me."

The guards exchanged wary glances. Even Mercer, who had held steady through every twist of the operation, shifted his weight unconsciously as one hand brushed closer to the inside of his jacket.

Sean watched it all, every muscle in his body coiled tight. The guards didn't even realize it, but they had instinctively taken a step back, putting a few precious inches between themselves and Victoria.

In that brief lapse of rigid formation, Sean moved. It was nothing overt. A simple adjustment of stance. A slight pivot of the hips. Barely noticeable, unless you were looking for it. But it brought him within reach of the gun holstered under the jacket of the man to his left—a tall guard whose attention was now divided between the wonder unfolding before him and the fear gnawing at the edge of his instincts. Sean didn't move farther. Not yet. Not until it was time.

Across the room, Tommy took the same cue and shifted his weight as well, but kept his hands loose at his sides, ready.

Victoria lifted her hand higher, admiring the ring as if it were the crown jewel of the world. The golden glow thickened around her, casting strange, stretched shadows across the walls and floor.

Her expression had changed from awe to something closer to rapture. Her pupils dilated; her breathing slowed.

"This…" she murmured. "This is what they feared. This is what they tried to bury. They wanted to keep this power hidden. But now, now it is mine to command."

Her voice rose slightly, taking on the lilt of a queen issuing commands to unseen legions. "No more hiding," she said. "No more limits. The world will kneel to me. And I will reclaim what is rightfully mine."

She closed her eyes and tilted her head back, the golden aura surrounding her now almost a living flame. Her arms opened slightly at her sides, as if inviting the power fully into herself.

The guards held still, frozen in place between awe and confusion. Sean's fingertips brushed the inside of his left sleeve, inching closer to action.

Then Victoria's eyes snapped open. Wide. Unblinking. In an instant, the expression on her face twisted into something far more primal.

Fear.

Something was wrong. Everyone in the room could see it, but they had no idea what it was.

Victoria's breath hitched.

For one suspended second, the world seemed frozen around her, the golden aura still flaring bright against the walls, the guards rigid with shock, Mercer staring with a frown just beginning to form. Then her body jerked violently.

Her skin flushed a deep, angry red, as if blood were rushing to the surface in a sudden, furious wave. Beads of sweat broke out along her forehead and temples, glistening in the eerie golden light. Her fingers twitched uncontrollably at her sides, and the muscles in her arms spasmed.

Sean watched the horrific display with fascination but didn't let it distract from his plan—catch the nearest gunman off guard.

Victoria stumbled, gasping for air, and staggered toward the large window overlooking the dark city. She grabbed blindly at the heavy curtains to steady herself, her knuckles whitening around the thick fabric.

"Help me," she rasped, her voice hoarse and panicked. "Help—"

No one moved.

The guards, Mercer included, instinctively retreated a step, fear overtaking discipline. Even men who had faced down bullets and knives recoiled at the raw, unnatural wrongness radiating from her.

Victoria clawed at her hand, digging her nails around the ring, desperate to pull it off. But it wouldn't budge.

The golden glow began to darken, shifting from light to something meaner—an ugly, searing heat that shimmered in the air around her.

Everyone watched, hearts pounding, as thin trails of smoke began to rise from Victoria's skin. Her beautiful designer gown, immaculate moments before, clung to her like a second, suffocating skin, already starting to discolor at the seams.

Victoria screamed. It was a raw, bloodcurdling sound that tore through the suite and froze the blood in every vein. It was a sound of pure agony.

She stumbled backward through the open balcony doors, her hands flailing, batting uselessly at the smoke now pouring off her body. Her hair, once perfectly coiffed, sizzled at the edges, the delicate strands curling and blackening.

The air filled with the acrid stink of burning flesh.

The sprinkler system triggered with a sharp mechanical pop, and jets of cold water sprayed down from the ceiling, soaking the furniture, the carpet, and the stunned occupants.

The fire alarm began blaring overhead, a shrill, pounding wail that seemed almost distant compared to the horror playing out in front of them.

Victoria shrieked again, but her voice cracked and broke mid-scream.

Flames burst from her back and shoulders, leaping higher in a sudden, violent surge. Her arms flailed, her body staggering against the balcony railing, droplets of burning liquid flinging outward in every direction like sparks.

She looked one last time toward the room—face contorted in terror and betrayal, mouth open in a final, silent plea.

And then the fire consumed her.

With a sharp thud of bone on metal, Victoria collapsed against the railing. The iron bent beneath her weight, and she toppled over the edge. A second later, she exploded into a swarm of glowing embers—a cloud of ash and soot blasted high by the wind, scattering out into the night sky like the remains of some fallen star.

The ring dropped to the balcony with a weak clank, rolled for a second, and then settled where Victoria had stood only a moment before.

Sean sprang into action.

The nearest gunman hadn't fully processed what was happening. His gaze was still fixed on the empty balcony where Victoria had burned and fallen—his instincts dulled by the impossible horror he'd just witnessed.

Sean moved fast. He caught the man by the arm, wrenching the weapon away in one brutal motion. The guard stumbled and slipped on the drenched floor, and Sean shoved him down hard. Before the man could recover, Sean drove the barrel of the stolen pistol against the side of his head and pulled the trigger.

The suppressed shot gave only a soft puff. The guard's body went limp, crumpling to the floor in a growing pool of water that was now turning a pinkish hue under the man's skull.

Across the suite, Tommy was already engaging the next target.

Tommy's opponent was faster—already drawing his sidearm when Tommy reached him. The two collided shoulder to shoulder in a tangle of soaked clothing and flailing limbs. The guard swung wildly, landing a glancing blow against Tommy's ribs, but Tommy absorbed it, grabbed the man's wrist, and twisted sharply.

The pistol dropped to the floor with a metallic clatter.

Tommy drove his knee up into the man's midsection, which forced the air from his lungs, then he slammed the man against the nearest wall. The guard tried to rally by shoving Tommy back, but Tommy spun, grabbed the falling weapon, and in a smooth motion brought it up under the man's chin.

Another muffled pop.

The second guard collapsed into a heap.

Meanwhile, near the edge of the suite, another gunman raised his weapon, his sights locked onto Tommy's exposed back.

Jean-Marc moved without hesitation.

He crossed the space in a blur, diving low and slamming into the man's midsection. The impact knocked the would-be shooter clean off his feet. They hit the ground hard and slid across the puddled floor in a tangled mess of arms and legs.

Jean-Marc fought with quiet brutality, his movements efficient and merciless. The guard tried to punch free, but Jean-Marc shifted his weight, wrapped one arm around the man's throat, and locked in the choke hold.

The man thrashed, boots kicking against the drenched carpet, but Jean-Marc squeezed tighter while adjusting his grip until the struggling slowed... then stopped altogether.

Jean-Marc shoved the unconscious body aside and rose, soaked and breathing hard.

A movement near the fallen pistol caught Sean's eye.

Evelyn.

She scrambled from where she'd been crouched against the wall and snatched up the weapon the last guard had dropped. Without hesitation, she turned, bracing the gun in both hands, and aimed toward the far side of the room.

Sean whipped around to see what she was aiming at.

Mercer.

He and Nikolai were sprinting toward the suite's door, cutting through the chaos with single-minded precision. Their escape was almost clean—almost.

Evelyn fired.

The shot clicked sharply despite the round slamming into the wall just beside the doorframe. A spray of plaster dust exploded outward.

Mercer didn't flinch. He shoved the door open, disappearing into the hallway beyond. Nikolai was right behind him, vanishing into the shadows of the penthouse corridor.

Sean turned back to Evelyn, who stood frozen, the gun still aimed at the now-empty doorway, her breathing ragged.

"Stay here!" Sean barked.

Jean-Marc was already stepping toward him, his face set and grim.

"Schultzie, stay with Evelyn."

Tommy nodded while wiping water from his face with his sleeve and steadying the pistol as he joined Evelyn by her side.

Sean turned toward Jean-Marc.

Sean's mind locked on to a single, burning focus as they chased after Mercer and Nikolai. "Time to end this," Sean muttered.

47

Chaos spilled into the hallway outside the suite as panicked hotel patrons rushed out of their rooms.

Sean hid his weapon so he didn't freak people out further while scanning through the disarray. The fire alarms blared in his ears, an endless, wailing klaxon, and the sprinklers overhead poured water in shimmering sheets. The elegant penthouse corridor had turned into a river, carpet and marble alike slick with puddles. Guests stumbled and shoved one another, some shouting for family members, others gripping suitcases or shoes or nothing at all, their faces blank with fear.

Beside him, Jean-Marc waited, weapon tucked behind him, eyes sharp and focused beneath the streams of water running down his face.

Sean stared through the mayhem, and then he spotted them—two shapes moving with grim determination, not panic. Mercer and Nikolai.

They were maybe thirty yards ahead, slicing through the confusion with brutal efficiency. Mercer shouldered a disoriented man aside without slowing. Nikolai shoved a housekeeper and her rolling cart into the wall, sending towels and toiletries sprawling across the wet floor.

They were headed for the stairwell.

Sean didn't hesitate. He surged forward into the stampede with Jean-Marc right behind.

The two of them moved like blades through fabric, weaving between the terrified guests, careful not to draw fire or spook anyone into sudden movements. A woman shrieked as Sean brushed past her, but he ignored it, his entire focus locked on Mercer and Nikolai retreating toward the heavy stairwell door.

The corridor tilted, warping with motion and noise, the alarms, the running footsteps, the hiss of water splashing underfoot. Sean kept low, balancing speed and caution, every step measured but urgent.

The stairwell door swung wildly on its hinges where Mercer and Nikolai had slammed through it. Beyond, a yawning concrete shaft stretched both up and down into shadow and chaos.

Sean and Jean-Marc burst through together.

They stopped just inside the landing, weapons raised, sweeping both directions in quick, sharp movements.

People rushed by them, bumping into them as they hurried down the stairs toward safety. The stairwell echoed with the metallic rattle of shifting pipes and the far-off roar of the storm outside. Lightning flashed somewhere beyond the walls, throwing stark bursts of white into the tight, gray space.

Sean's instincts kicked hard. He dropped his gaze downward first, scanning the stairs below.

Nothing. Only the hotel patrons fleeing the top floor on the spiral of concrete steps descending into deeper darkness.

He snapped his head upward. At first, nothing but the twisting staircase winding toward the upper floors. Then—a flicker of movement. A hand, gripping the railing one flight up. Just for a second. Then it disappeared.

Sean's heart kicked against his ribs.

"They're going up," he said, voice taut.

Jean-Marc didn't reply. He was already moving.

Sean took off after him, boots hammering on the wet steps, the whole stairwell shuddering under their chase. The concrete was slick with sprinkler runoff and the humid press of stormy air leaking through hairline cracks in the walls. Every step up brought them deeper into the tightening coil of the building, closer to the inevitable clash waiting above.

Sean's mind raced even faster than his feet.

Mercer wasn't running without a plan. He wasn't the type to flee blindly. The roof would offer no escape, unless they had a helicopter up there that Sean wasn't aware of. Nevertheless, Sean understood the move. Police and firemen would be arriving downstairs. If Mercer could get to the roof, he and his partner could possibly wait it out until the coast was clear.

Sean's boots splashed through puddles gathering on the landings as they rose higher. Around them, the stairwell grew narrower, tighter, the walls closer. The moaning of the storm outside grew louder, rain hammering against the building like thrown stones.

They reached the next landing between the top floor and the roof. Sean pointed his weapon upward, but there was no one at the upper level.

Sean clenched his jaw and drove upward, mind locked on to one single, ironclad focus: This was the endgame. And he wasn't letting Mercer or Nikolai slip away this time.

Sean and Jean-Marc reached the final landing.

The heavy metal door leading to the rooftop stood before them, its frame rattling slightly from the gusts of wind that howled down the stairwell. The storm was close now. Thunder cracked overhead, vibrating the very walls.

Sean edged forward, weapon raised, and pushed the door open slowly with his foot.

Rain-laced wind lashed his face immediately, carrying the sharp tang of ozone and wet concrete. Through the narrow gap, he caught the flash of movement. Nikolai.

The rooftop stretched out before them, sprawling and cluttered.

Massive ventilation ducts snaked across the concrete, pooling water already gathering around their bases. Rusted stair platforms climbed to small maintenance hatches. Huge, boxy air conditioners squatted in rows like silent sentinels. Electrical boxes, piping, scaffolding—all offering countless places to hide, to ambush.

The rooftop door shuddered against the gusting wind, rainwater already trickling underneath. Lightning flashed beyond the glass panel set high in the frame and threw brief, fractured shadows across the stairwell walls.

Sean gave a quick nod. Together, they moved.

Sean eased the door the rest of the way open with the barrel of his pistol, clearing the corner with his shoulder as he pushed through and into the storm.

Sean barely had time to register the scene before movement again caught his eye.

Nikolai stepped briefly into view beyond a row of ductwork, pistol raised, teeth bared in a grimace.

Sean reacted instinctively and fired twice before the man could even steady his aim.

The bullets clipped Nikolai, sending him staggering backward behind a cluster of steel air conditioners. His weapon skidded across the slick rooftop, lost in the growing puddles and darkness.

Sean moved to the edge of a ventilation shaft and scanned the rooftop's chaotic terrain.

No sign of Mercer—yet.

Thunder cracked overhead, loud enough to rattle his bones.

The rain was coming harder now, driving in sheets across the open expanse, masking sounds and blurring motion into shadow.

Beside him, Jean-Marc scanned the rooftop with sharp, deliberate precision. Without turning, Jean-Marc spoke low and certain. "Mercer is mine."

Sean nodded once, no argument necessary. He knew the Frenchman had unfinished business.

In a split second, they separated.

Jean-Marc peeled off toward the right side of the rooftop and disappeared into the maze of machinery and scaffolding. His silhouette blended almost immediately with the rooftop shadows, moving with the smooth efficiency of a man who knew how to stalk dangerous prey.

Sean veered left, moving toward the place where Nikolai had vanished.

The Russian was wounded but not finished—not yet.

Sean tightened his grip on his weapon and pressed forward into the storm.

Rain battered the concrete in relentless sheets, filling the air with a constant hiss. Lightning tore the sky again and cast the rooftop momentarily in stark whiteness before plunging it back into a deeper, heavier dark.

Sean moved carefully between the hulking air conditioning units, pistol raised, senses stretched to their limit. His heart pounded in his ears, but he forced each breath to stay slow, controlled. Nikolai was wounded, but that didn't make him any less dangerous. A cornered animal was often the most lethal.

He edged around a bank of ventilation ducts, and his boots slipped slightly on the wet surface.

The rooftop felt endless; every massive pipe, every rusted scaffold a potential hiding place. Another flash of lightning—and for a fraction of a second, a shadow moved to his left.

Sean spun, weapon tracking—but too late.

Nikolai sprang from the darkness with a guttural roar, a gleaming knife flashing in his fist.

Sean fired once, but Nikolai barreled into him with brutal force and slammed Sean's shooting arm aside. The shot went wild into the storm, and the pistol spun out of Sean's grasp, skidding across the flooded rooftop into the darkness.

Sean staggered, trying to regain his balance, but Nikolai didn't give him a second.

The knife came in fast. Sean twisted, feeling the blade slice across the outside of his forearm as he barely redirected the killing thrust. Pain burned hot and immediate, but he didn't have time to feel it.

Nikolai drove into him again, forcing Sean back against a thick steel wall of an industrial exhaust vent. The metal was slick and freezing against his soaked jacket.

Sean gritted his teeth, both hands clamping around Nikolai's wrist, struggling to keep the knife away from his throat.

The Russian's face was twisted in rage, rain streaking his skin, teeth bared like a feral dog.

The blade hovered inches from Sean's neck, trembling as Sean strained with everything he had left to keep it at bay.

Muscles burned. His wounded arm screamed in protest.

Nikolai pushed harder, using his weight and his fury, grinding the blade closer with brutal, relentless force.

Sean's boots slipped against the water-slicked rooftop. With his back pinned, the knife edged closer with every heartbeat.

One wrong move now, and it would be over.

JEAN-MARC MOVED like a shadow through the storm.

The rain blurred everything: the skyline, the rooftop, even his own breathing. Every step was calculated, boots gliding over slick concrete, weapon steady.

Mercer was up here somewhere. Waiting. Watching.

Jean-Marc knew him well. Professional. Ruthless. He didn't run without a plan. He didn't panic. Mercer wasn't trying to escape; he was trying to set the terms of the final fight.

Jean-Marc welcomed it.

Lightning exploded overhead, and the sudden brightness split the rooftop into harsh whites and deep blacks. In that flash, Jean-Marc caught movement—a dark figure sprinting across the far side, slipping behind a row of towering ducts.

Mercer.

Jean-Marc shifted instantly, raised his pistol, and fired two sharp shots through the storm. The suppressed rounds hissed into the night, but Mercer was already diving for cover. One shot pinged off a ventilation unit, the other disappearing into the mist.

Return fire snapped back immediately with tight, controlled bursts. Jean-Marc ducked behind the broad side of an air handler as two rounds sparked off the metal inches from his head.

He didn't retreat. He counted the shots—listened.

Mercer fired three rounds. Paused. Fired two more.

Jean-Marc leaned out during the gap and fired again, this time forcing Mercer to withdraw deeper into the maze of rooftop machinery.

No words were exchanged.

No threats.

No bravado.

Jean-Marc slid from cover to cover, each move sharp and deliberate, trying to flank Mercer before the man could disappear again. But Mercer was good. Very good.

Another flash of lightning—and Mercer was gone, swallowed by the shifting angles of the rooftop, somewhere deeper in the labyrinth.

Jean-Marc's pulse remained steady, even as tension coiled tighter around his spine. He scanned the rooftop quickly, piecing together Mercer's likely movements, calculating where a man like him would reposition for a kill shot.

The rain intensified, rattling against the machinery, distorting sounds, masking movements. Jean-Marc crouched lower, his pistol up, his finger steady on the trigger.

The next move would come fast. It had to.

THE KNIFE HOVERED an inch from Sean's throat, the steel glinting each time lightning flashed above them.

Rain dripped from his hair, his jacket, the burning slice across his forearm. His muscles trembled from the strain, from exhaustion, but Sean locked his mind down, refusing to yield.

It wasn't about strength now. It was about will.

Nikolai's face twisted with effort, his entire body leaning into the knife, forcing it closer. The Russian grunted, breath hot and ragged, trying to overpower him.

Sean drew a slow, steady breath through his nose.

Then he made his move.

In a sudden burst of motion, Sean leaned into the blade—not away—and pressed forward just enough to create a crucial sliver of space between the back of his head and the slick wall behind him. The knife nicked his skin shallowly as he shifted, a warm trickle of blood mixing with the rain.

Before Nikolai could react, Sean dropped his weight and shoved the man's knife hand down and to the right, stepping forward at the same time. His left hand came up under Nikolai's wrist while lifting and twisting the weapon hand violently upward.

The move threw off Nikolai's balance.

Sean didn't stop. He planted his right foot behind Nikolai's knee and drove forward, walking the Russian back into an awkward, off-center stumble. The pressure on the arm grew unbearable for his opponent—then Sean shifted again, changing the angle in one brutal, fluid motion.

Nikolai hit the ground with a sharp splash of water, roaring in pain.

Sean didn't hesitate. He yanked hard on Nikolai's wrist, planted his knee squarely against the man's elbow, and wrenched backward. A sickening crack tore through the storm.

Nikolai screamed, the sound raw and animalistic, echoing across the rooftop. His knife clattered to the ground, forgotten.

Sean started to rise, but Nikolai, fueled by fury and desperation, lashed out with a wild, low kick. His boot caught Sean's ankles, knocking his legs out from under him.

Sean slipped as the rain-slicked concrete spun beneath him.

For a breathless second, he tumbled toward the edge of the rooftop. He slammed to a stop just short of the ledge, his arms still pinwheeling, his gut still twisting.

The street below gaped like a mouth, dizzyingly far away, red and blue lights swirling from the emergency vehicles now clustering around the base of the hotel.

Sean's stomach lurched. His Achilles' heel, an acute fear of heights, grabbed at his mind and filled it with nightmares in an instant.

Then movement drew his focus away from the phobia.

Nikolai, wounded but not beaten, was charging straight at him in a final, reckless burst of rage. The plan was obvious: Take the enemy with him. Sean quickly got off the ground, and sidestepped, pivoting with practiced precision, and planted both hands against Nikolai's back as he passed.

The momentum carried the Russian forward. There was a split second where their eyes met—Sean's steady and cold, Nikolai's wide with the realization of what was about to happen.

Then Nikolai was airborne. He fell with a howl, arms flailing, body twisting before he struck the ground.

Sean watched the body hit the ground then turned and surveyed the area, looking for Jean-Marc. The heavy, wet thud rose faintly over sirens far below.

He staggered back from the edge, chest heaving, every nerve on fire, then hurried away from the ledge to find his friend.

48

Jean-Marc moved through the labyrinth of machinery, every sense tuned razor-sharp.

The rain battered down around him and pooled in the dips of the rooftop, slicking every surface until it gleamed under the intermittent flashes of lightning. The storm thickened the air, distorted sound, its echoes bouncing strangely off the massive ventilation ducts and industrial piping.

Somewhere in the chaos, Mercer was waiting.

Jean-Marc kept his steps deliberate, controlled. He moved deliberately, always low, always sweeping his sectors with a soldier's patience. Mercer wouldn't make the mistake of panicking. He was the kind of man who thrived in moments like this.

The kind who killed without hesitation.

A flash of movement caught the edge of Jean-Marc's vision. He pivoted instinctively and raised his pistol just in time as a bullet tore past him—so close he heard it crack the air just above his shoulder.

Jean-Marc dropped into a crouch behind a massive duct and scanned the rooftop frantically.

Another flash of lightning lit the world in stark black and white—and he spotted him.

Mercer stood half exposed behind a maintenance stairwell, pistol raised, face cold and cruel. Jean-Marc ducked back into cover as another shot ripped into the metal structure he crouched behind, sending shards of rusted debris flying.

Then Mercer's voice drifted through the storm, calm and cutting. "You were always second best, Jean-Marc."

Jean-Marc didn't answer.

He shifted low around the duct, circling wide, staying in the shadows.

Mercer continued, his voice taunting, baiting. "Always good enough to follow orders. Good enough to do the clean work. Never the dirty jobs. Never the decisions that mattered."

Jean-Marc felt the words trying to dig under his skin, but he let them pass through him. Mercer wanted him angry. Reckless. He gave the man nothing.

Instead, he moved silently, weaving between the machinery, watching for the faintest trace—footsteps splashing in water, a shadow moving wrongly, the brief flash of metal. He caught another glimpse—Mercer's shoulder disappearing around a far corner.

Jean-Marc advanced slowly, weapon raised, breath steady. Lightning cracked overhead and blinded him for an instant. Jean-Marc reached the edge of the large duct and swung around it, pistol ready.

Empty.

A cold realization prickled at the back of his neck a split second too late.

Then, click.

The press of a gun muzzle settled against the back of Jean-Marc's skull.

Mercer's voice was close now, practically in his ear. "Drop it."

Jean-Marc hesitated. The rooftop was silent but for the storm, the sirens below, and the thundering beat of his own heart. He tightened his grip on his pistol for a fraction of a second, measuring, calculating the odds.

Could he spin? Could he risk it?

No. Not a chance.

With a slow, controlled breath, he opened his fingers and let the pistol fall. It clattered against the wet concrete and spun once before settling in a puddle at his feet. Jean-Marc raised his hands, palms outward, fingers spread. He felt Mercer's chuckle more than he heard it.

"Good boy."

SEAN MOVED CAREFULLY through the downpour, slipping between the rusted scaffolding and soaked machinery. His heart hammered a brutal rhythm against his ribs, every step a study in control.

The rooftop had become a battlefield, a maze of steel and concrete, rain and lightning.

Ahead, through a slant of falling water, he caught sight of movement.

He froze behind a bank of air conditioners, peering through the shifting curtains of rain.

Jean-Marc. Hands raised, standing still.

And behind him—Mercer.

The enforcer held a pistol pressed tight against the back of Jean-Marc's head, his body low and balanced, his stance perfect.

Waiting. Watching.

Sean's gut clenched.

He had the drop on Mercer—but it wasn't clean.

The angle was bad—too much distance, too much risk of hitting Jean-Marc even with the best shot he could take.

Sean slowly raised his own pistol and sighted down the barrel while weighing it.

One chance. Maybe.

But maybe wasn't good enough.

Sean took a slow breath and called out through the storm.

"Drop it, Mercer!"

Mercer didn't startle. Instead, he turned his head slightly, just enough to show the glint of his eyes in the strobing lightning. "Sean

Wyatt," he said, almost laughing under his breath. "Didn't think you'd make it up here."

Sean kept the sights lined up, though he knew the angle still wasn't clean.

Mercer's tone turned sharper. "You and I both know you don't have the shot."

Sean stayed silent.

Mercer shifted his stance slightly and dragged Jean-Marc a half step to the left, using him as a living shield. "Come on, Sean," he said, voice low and taunting. "You're good. Better than most. But not that good."

The words hung in the air between them, thick and heavy with the rain.

Sean's fingers tightened against the grip. Every instinct screamed to act, to move. But he forced himself to think. This wasn't a moment for reckless bravery. This was a moment for survival.

He lowered the pistol slowly.

"Okay, Mercer," Sean said, his voice calm over the storm. "I'm dropping it." Deliberately, he eased his weapon down and let it dangle from two fingers before tossing it into a puddle with a soft splash.

Mercer's mouth twisted into a smirk. "That's more like it."

Sean raised his hands slowly, palms open.

Across from him, Jean-Marc's jaw clenched, the Frenchman's muscles coiled tight under the surface. Waiting. Watching.

Mercer pressed the gun harder against Jean-Marc's skull. "You always were predictable, Wyatt. Brave, sure. Skilled, no doubt. But predictable."

Sean said nothing. He let Mercer talk. Let him feed his own arrogance.

"So, what now?" Sean asked finally, voice steady. "You kill us both and fly off into the night?" He jerked his chin toward the chaos below —the swirling lights, the mass of emergency vehicles flooding the streets around the hotel. "There are a hundred cops down there. You'll never get out of here."

Mercer chuckled, a deep, humorless sound. "Why not?" he asked, almost lightly. "I'm just another innocent customer trying to evacuate a burning building. No gun on me. No witnesses. You two? You're just two more bodies they find when they finally clear the mess."

Lightning cracked overhead again and illuminated the rooftop in ghostly brilliance for a fraction of a second.

Mercer smiled grimly. "All I have to do," he said, "is walk away."

Sean felt the moment stretching taut—an invisible thread straining between them, ready to snap. He kept his breathing even, his hands high, waiting for the next move.

The storm howled around them.

"Where you going to go, Mercer?" Sean asked, trying to keep him talking as long as he could, buying seconds. "The EIC is done. Victoria is dead."

Mercer shook his head. "Oh, no. It isn't done. I have access to everything. Call it a little failsafe in case something happened. I have to admit, I didn't expect her to spontaneously combust, but hey, it did the job."

"So, it will just be business as usual then."

"Pretty much. I'll have to figure out what to do with that ring, but I'll manage. Maybe sell it to the highest bidder."

Sean shook his head. "You still have the little problem of my friend Tommy Schultz being out there. You can kill me, and you can kill Jean-Marc, but Tommy will hunt you down. You have no idea how deep his resources go. There is nowhere you can hide, Mercer."

Mercer shook his head. "Nice bluff, Sean. But I have resources too." With Sean unarmed, he forced Jean-Marc's head over the edge of the rooftop, pressing the muzzle to the base of the Frenchman's skull.

Sean remained perfectly still, even though the instinct inside him was to rush to his friend's aid.

"Don't worry, though, Sean," Mercer said. "After I kill you and my old friend here, I'll find your pal Tommy. He shouldn't be too hard to find. Doesn't exactly keep a low profile."

Mercer raised the weapon and turned to take aim at Sean. "I think I'll do you first, Sean."

"We all know that's what she said," Sean blurted.

"A joke is a fitting end for your life."

A muted pop whispered across the rooftop against the sounds of the storm.

Mercer remained still for a second. Then his arm fell to his side, the gun loosening in his grip before it fell to the ground. A black hole above his nose began to ooze blood. Then he fell to his knees and over onto his face.

Tommy stood twenty feet away on the other side, a pistol extended away from his body.

Jean-Marc looked around and then stood. He glanced down at Mercer then back over at Tommy.

"I was wondering if you were going to help out," the Frenchman said with a smirk.

Tommy lowered the sidearm and walked over to join the others.

"Is Evelyn okay?" Sean asked.

Tommy chuckled. "She seems like it, considering everything that's happened. Better than expected, honestly."

"I hoped that would be the case."

"What happened to the other one?" Tommy asked.

"He's down on the street," Sean said in a callous, almost joking tone.

Tommy took a second to put the meaning together, then smiled. "Understood." He shook his head. "I can't believe you did the 'that's what she said' bit as he was about to kill you."

Sean shrugged. "When death smiles at you, all you can do is smile back, I guess."

Tommy shook his head and started to turn around. *"Gladiator* reference."

He started back toward the access door to the stairs. Jean-Marc looked at Sean, confused. "What is he talking about, *Gladiator* reference?"

Sean slapped the Frenchman on the back. "I'll tell you later."

49

By late afternoon the next day, the city of Avignon had mostly returned to itself.

The square was alive again—tourists drifting between shops and cafés, children chasing pigeons near the old stone fountain, the hum of normal life slowly smoothing over the violence that had erupted less than twenty-four hours earlier.

Sean stood across the street from the hotel entrance, hands in the pockets of his jacket, watching the ebb and flow of the crowd. He spotted Tommy first, who was leaning against the corner of a small bakery, munching absentmindedly on a baguette. His hair was still a mess from the night before, and a fresh bruise had started to bloom along his jaw, but he wore a crooked, tired grin when he saw Sean.

Sean crossed the street and joined him.

Tommy offered him a torn piece of bread, which Sean waved off with a smirk.

"Still standing," Tommy said around a mouthful of food. "Always a good sign."

"More or less," Sean said.

A few minutes later, Evelyn arrived pulling a small, wheeled suitcase behind her. She looked clean, rested, dressed down in jeans and a light jacket. Her face was composed, but there was an ease in her shoulders that hadn't been there yesterday.

Jean-Marc came last, stepping out from a side alley, a canvas bag slung casually over one shoulder. He wore fresh clothes and carried the faint smell of strong black coffee with him, as if he'd already planned to disappear into the countryside the moment the dust fully settled.

They gathered naturally, like gravity drawing them back into orbit one last time. For a long moment, no one spoke. The bells from a nearby cathedral chimed out the hour—four o'clock—and the square vibrated gently with the noise.

Finally, Jean-Marc broke the silence. "So... the ring?"

"The official answer is that it's being held for 'study and security assessment,'" Tommy said. "The French government hasn't decided yet whether they'll allow the IAA to take it back to Atlanta for research. I did submit the request, so that's all I can do for now."

"Well, I hope you get to study it further," Jean-Marc said.

Evelyn adjusted the strap of her bag. "At least it's not in the wrong hands anymore."

Sean nodded. "For now, it stays here. Under more guards than the Crown Jewels."

They stood quietly for a moment, each absorbed in their own thoughts. A cooling breeze moved across the plaza, carrying the scent of fresh bread and damp stone.

"What about you guys?" Sean asked, glancing around the group.

Evelyn offered a small smile. "I'm heading back to Cambridge. Catching a late flight tonight. I've got lectures piling up and students who probably think I vanished off the face of the earth."

"You'll enjoy the normal chaos," Tommy said.

She chuckled. "Chaos sounds positively relaxing after this."

Tommy finished off his baguette and dusted crumbs from his jacket. "I'm flying back to the States tomorrow. Got about two months of reports to catch up on. Not exactly glamorous, but someone's got to keep the paper-pushers happy."

"And you?" Sean asked, turning to Jean-Marc.

Jean-Marc gave a rare, brief smile. "A visit to Antón. Then perhaps a week of quiet somewhere with more wine than responsibility."

Tommy barked a short laugh. "First time for everything."

Jean-Marc shrugged. "Even wolves must rest."

Sean glanced toward the south, toward the horizon where the golden afternoon was already beginning to deepen toward evening.

"I'm catching a flight to Florence tomorrow morning," he said. "My wife's waiting for me just outside the city. We planned this trip a long time ago. Feels right not to put it off."

Evelyn touched his arm lightly. "She'll be glad to have you back."

Sean smiled, warmth rising through the fatigue still clinging to him.

He was glad too.

The conversation drifted easily, the tension of the past day finally loosening its grip.

They talked about little things at first—Evelyn's favorite cafés in Cambridge, Tommy's grumbling about the mountain of paperwork waiting back at the IAA, Jean-Marc's half-serious plan to disappear into a vineyard and not be heard from for weeks.

It felt good to talk about normal things again. Real things.

For a few minutes, the world outside the square—the danger, the conspiracies, the ancient ring still locked away somewhere in a government vault—faded into the background.

A sleek black sedan pulled up to the curb a few yards away, its windows tinted against the late afternoon sun.

Evelyn checked her watch and gave a small sigh.

"That's me," she said, hoisting her bag onto her shoulder.

Sean stood as she approached him, and they shook hands firmly.

"Take care of yourself, Evelyn," he said.

She smiled. "You too, Sean. And thank you... for trusting me."

Tommy grinned and pulled her into a quick, one-armed hug. "Don't get too comfortable with those dusty old maps. You're a field agent now, whether you like it or not."

Evelyn laughed, the sound light but genuine. "One trip to hell and back doesn't make me a veteran."

"It's a start," Tommy said.

Jean-Marc offered her a small, respectful nod. "Until we meet again, Dr. Langford."

"Hopefully under better circumstances," she said, her eyes glinting with humor.

She stepped back, gave them all a last wave, and climbed into the waiting car. The driver shut the door behind her, and within moments, the sedan pulled away, weaving into the soft hum of late afternoon traffic.

Sean watched until the car disappeared around the corner.

The group seemed a little smaller without her.

Jean-Marc adjusted the strap on his satchel. "Any new cases coming up soon?"

Tommy shrugged and rubbed the back of his neck. "Just the normal transportation and security stuff. Artifact moves, museum transfers. Nothing flashy."

He smiled faintly, adding, "But you never know."

Printed in Dunstable, United Kingdom